Lilacs in the Snow

A Novel

by

A. K. Henderson

CCB Publishing
British Columbia, Canada

Lilacs in the Snow: A Novel

Copyright ©2011 by A. K. Henderson
ISBN-13   978-1-926918-70-9
First Edition

Library and Archives Canada Cataloguing in Publication
Henderson, A. K., 1940-
Lilacs in the snow : a novel / by A. K. Henderson.
ISBN 978-1-926918-70-9
Also available in electronic format.
I. Title.
PS3608.E5253L55 2011   813'.6   C2011-905092-7

Cover art provided courtesy of the Gottesman Libraries at Teachers College, Columbia University.

Publisher: CCB Publishing
             British Columbia, Canada
             www.ccbpublishing.com

LILACS IN THE SNOW

Immortal? I feel it and know it,
Who doubts it of such as she?
But that is the pang's very secret-
Immortal away from me.

James Russell Lowell

Author's Note to Her Readers

My book *Lilacs in the Snow* is dedicated to my husband Jim who obliged me by listening to each chapter read aloud with infinite patience and a trained ear to discern the perfect phrasing. He also used his trusty red pen to correct my punctuation errors and strike out excesses. His effusive praise of the lyrical qualities of my writing propelled me ever forward. I dedicate the book as well to my dear daughters Alisa and Alana whose indisputable love sustained me through the harrowing years of my ordeal. They never let me falter and continued to believe I would be here to complete my writing. I owe a debt of gratitude to author Murray Kalis and Professor W.F. Smith who took the time not only to read my book but also to write their glowing reviews. The book cover art is a photograph of a mood painting created by me circa 1955, a figure projection of self expressing sadness. Lastly, I am grateful to have found Paul Rabinovitch, Publisher, CCB Publishing, who worked personally with me to take my completed manuscript off the secluded shelf and into the light of day.

My need to write this riveting story about fortitude evolved in dark nights fraught with the pain and terror of illness. Sleepless, I sought the comfort of my laptop computer, a bedside lamp, and an imaginary heroine Caasi. At the outset, Caasi seems to be made of paper, as if the slightest breeze might blow her away. She proves to be brave, resolute, and plucky affirming the quiet kind of courage that grows out of the improbable without design or contrivance.

Lilacs in the Snow, as it unfolded on the pages, emboldened me, and I wanted to be rewritten in the book of life. Inexplicably, I seem to have been granted time to complete what I began and to look ahead to the promise of more. My wish is to reach the hearts and minds of all my readers, to foster hope, inspiration, and endurance, and to believe all is possible.

The titling of the chapters is unique. I have used quotes from varied sources, such as T.S. Elliot, Lord Tennyson, Shakespeare, Milton, Donne, Chaucer, and William Cullen Bryant. It may seem to the reader that words are improperly spelled. Quoted exactly, the spelling is consistent with the English language of the time. Some dialogue is written in Yiddish, French, and Hebrew. The meaning is made clear within the context of the sentences so that there was no need to single out the words and provide translation. I have chosen to spell the words, other than English, as they appear in nonscholarly texts in the manner of parochial school and home teaching.

The years I spent as a physician in my general practice, subspecialty in adolescent medicine and consultant at an inpatient facility for emotionally disturbed teenagers, introduced me to children, young adults, and families with intriguing problems and disparate interactions. Providing care, observing, engaging, learning, and ultimately recalling complex and precise details guided me in the construction of this fictional narrative. As an adjunct, my life in Montréal as a child proved to be an invaluable source for my book.

The style of writing may remind you at times of the closely-webbed, intricate human elements of Malamud and the impudent witticism of Richler woven into a textured and singularly troubled fabric. The short chapters are linked like cultured pearls on a necklace; the result is a shimmering, circular piece. I trust you will find yourself drawn into the story, challenged, stormily tossed about, momentarily subdued and ultimately quietly reflective. By closing the distance you can immerse yourself in the resonance of life's profound pain and pure joy.

A.K. Henderson

Contents

Part III 1948-1952

Part IV 1953-1957

Part V 1957-1958

Part VI 2002-2003

Part I
1996

The eye-it cannot choose but see;

It seemed I could hardly walk the streets of Centre-ville Montréal without a glimpse of a woman, oddly familiar, turning a corner, gazing in a shop window, or entering a portico to a garden. Was she a mere shadow, an illusion to mislead me? So strange a vision, I was baffled as she moved gently, scarcely rippling the sodden air, yet producing all the emotions which a face to face encounter would excite. Stealthily I watched her as a cat does a mouse, wary that the click of my heels on the pavement might be heard. The woman continued to elude me; only a fleeting backward glance erased doubt to certainty. Then she paused as if savoring the slivers of sunlight darting between buildings. I was too distracted to value the slight favor of warmth. The moment was tread under foot, snuffed out by grim skies and sudden stormy blasts of cold. My eyes watered and tears ran down my windblown cheeks. I saw her through a hazy film as I mopped my wet face with a wadded up *Kleenex* I found in my pocket.

She was wearing a russet wool tam, a faded *Harris Tweed* coat, kidskin boots, sadly stained, and a scarf of fine sea blue silk about her neck draped with a hint of style. The chilling wind caused her to flinch and nestle securely into her upturned collar. Her features were finely molded contrasting with a firm jaw, slightly squared. Strands of dark brown hair, though primly pinned back, slipped out from the ornamental barrette and guilelessly flicked across her pallid cheeks. She carried a worn leather purse, clenched tightly by the handle, pulling it close to her body as if it were holding her life together.

I called to her. She did not seem to hear or notice. Wanting desperately to overtake her, my steps sped after her in a whirl of haste, risking failure for the sake of the one small but only chance of success. The wind rose rushing up my jacket sleeves and whipping my skirt hem around my knees making pursuit tricky. The woman imprudently hurried, acting without delay as though having little time. I chased her into the crush of downtown Rue Ste. Catherine. Masses of people, compressed to anonymity, doggedly rushed past blocking my view as the mysterious woman deftly wove her way between the throng. Pushing through the loud and raucous crowds, I caught sight of her once more as she boarded a passing streetcar and stood swaying, hanging on to the strap, oblivious of the other travelers. Obscured in part by the sooty film on the windows, I thought I discerned a silent nod of recognition and minutest alteration of her hand like a mother's gentle caress or a reluctant wave in a sad goodbye. I felt her touch glide across my head smoothing my hair to corn silk. Rooted to the corner of Rue De la Montagne, I watched the trolley vanish out of sight, darkly seen against a cold slate sky. The intervening long years had condensed to chance when I might have reached her and wrapped my arms about her and prevented her from leaving once more...*When had she left me before?* ... All again was lost and in an instant gone. Floating on the surface of my mind, the vision of her blurred, dwindled, and passed away, clouds of dust left in its wake.

A bus smudged by copious black fumes pulled up to the curb. A fat man got out of a taxi fumbling in the pocket of his bulky overcoat, while behind the taxi, traffic blared furious horns. He shoved past me with a grunt and a barely audible, "Excusez," as I clumsily searched the faces filing by in relentless procession. Hope dimmed and fear seized me. I squinted against the reflected sunbeams from the shiny windows of the cars and buses. The clamor of the crowd, the distant peeling of the bells of Cathédrale Marie-Reine-Du-Monde, and the screeching of brakes and skidding of tires; none of this seemed real.

My past mingled with the present like a wave, broken and spent, ebbing back, crossing and interfering with the new wave flowing in, an imperfect fusion of various places, then and now, woven in mixed colors of sadness and regrets. *Why had the streetcar and its tracks, connector cables, and overhead sparking wires vanished... and what color were her eyes? ...*

Immortal? I feel it and know it,
Who doubts it of such as she?

... Indecisive, yet calmed, I returned from my brief lapse into the intangible past. The cold air made it difficult for me to breathe. I bent my head into the wind, seeming to lose ground with each forward step. There was no real reason to prowl the streets any longer. In that instant, the wind dropped off and the sun reemerged and I opted, in the least, to see some of the downtown changes. Shaking off the unsettling images, I walked the cross streets between Rue Ste. Catherine and Rue Sherbrooke. Up and down Bishop, Crescent, Drummond, and Stanley, the ethnic restaurants and fashionable art galleries intruded between glitzy towers of reflective glass and partially rebuilt brick buildings, still pitted and crumbling. Once grim alleyways were now quaint cobblestone lanes flanked by bookstores, charming cafes, and boutiques with colorful awnings. Shoppers dressed in leisure and affluence chattered earnestly of trifles as they paused to admire the window displays. These were the only sounds that intruded on the silence of my memory of abysmal bleakness and despair. An electric crispness and chic elegance dissipated the inner city austerity. I sensed my presence unwelcome.

Sixteen years of my childhood were strangely missing. Little was familiar. Like shadows falling obliquely on a surface, the modern city was a troubling and sad distortion. The sights seemed to be heavy with meaning and in this hour, heavy with possible sorrow. The deception heaped up stones of emptiness. Lost in the conflict of new and old Montréal, the visible changes opened untimely depths of doubt.

I headed back to the car where I had left it parked on Rue Peel and following the rental agency directions drove north on Av Du Parc taking an unplanned detour over to Rue St. Urbain to see my high school where I had spent four years of my life. This part of the city appeared to have separated itself from the rest. It was an island of concrete and plainness, all so commonplace, and nothing to distinguish itself from other old streets in other Canadian cities. I found the same uneven sidewalks with patches of moss, the gutters cluttered with paper scraps, cigarette butts, and pieces of glass. Only fluttering breezes and a rare passerby disturbed the still streets. Wobbly wooden stairs leaned against ramshackle houses with peeling boards and eroding brick; the washed-out midday sunshine crept in through the curtainless windows. Clotheslines with empty pegs stretched between balconies. Chipped clay flowerpots on window ledges trailed leafless stems.

The passage of time had transformed the high school building, once proud and stately. Decay reduced it to an affecting sight. I would have preferred an empty lot or an abandoned warehouse with windows jaggedly cracked and boarded up. I remembered it as it was in 1953 arriving in my freshman year, a timid yet excited graduate of elementary school. The three story solid structure resembled a strong impregnable castle, the entrance marked by double wooden doors with impressive looking polished brass handles. Each school day I draggled up the stone steps sliding my hand along the smoothly rounded concrete balustrade as I headed to the landing. Massive and hard to open, the right door slammed with a resounding thud after each incomer. Only when a herd of students charged through in cavalry fashion was the weight passed from hand to hand. Whenever I arrived tardy, I was unable to sneak in because, try as I might, the door swung shut with a firm reverberant sound. Alerted by this, the school principal Mr. Alexander stalking the corridors invariably trapped me at the lockers. Catching hold of my sleeve he grumbled, "Caasi, what, late again?" Nodding yes, I hung my head in disgrace and stammered some pitiful excuse. "Be off then." The words followed me to class as I sprinted up the stairs to face my homeroom teacher who was far less lenient.

Unnerved by the deterioration of my old school and unable to invoke the folly and clatter of playful students or the faces of my youthful friends, I grimly left the region. I traveled streets with familiar names, Boulevard St. Laurent, Av Van Horne, Jean-Talon, now displaying unrecognizable billboards and road signs. It seemed to take forever to arrive at my destination of Rue Beaumont and Rue Birnam, a distance of only six or seven miles from Centre-ville Montréal.

I felt shaky and disoriented almost like rousing from a faint, all memory lost and peering into uncertainty. In my mind I kept returning to my brush with the enigmatic woman on Av Du Musée and follow-ing her to Rue Ste. Catherine, a meeting so brief and accidental, unno-ticed in the dissonant furor or by the man who brusquely pushed past me. Her likeness, flimsy and elusive traveled with me now as it had over the many years. The portrait of her was but a remnant, a piece of a phrase, a sound that shaped me; ageless fragments bonded with priceless amethyst.

Tumbling and jumping through a hoop...
and dancing upon the tight~rope

Inevitably, I spotted the address and parked the car across the road from a dingy flat-roofed tenement building and slid out closing the door gently so as not to make a sound. Low in the sky, the sickly sun barely pared the chill. The brisk air nipped at my back. Distraught, I was tempted to get back into the car and to simply drive away. My hands were both icy and sweaty tucked inside my leather gloves. Unhinged, I tottered as if walking on a narrow ledge; a single misstep could tumble me into the street. I felt shakier than during my interview for admission to graduate school years ago. The kindly dean had calmed me with a funny comment. "I believe you can manage the curriculum. But what of the hapless young men who will be in your classes... can they contend with you?" The twinkle in his eyes led me to believe that he was only teasing. Appeased, I answered the posed questions. Now, there was little lightness of heart and nothing to smile about. Random notes of childhood discord played in my head, unclear thoughts not keeping time.

Cautiously, I went down a short flight of stairs to the lower level and knocked on his front door. There was no answer. Lacy curtains veiled the view into his basement apartment. I tried to peek through the grainy glass panels. Knocking again, I waited. Minutes elapsed, an eternity, so it seemed, until I heard some shuffling sounds, the unlatching of the lock and the door opening. The entry was dim. A delicate beam of sunlight eased the gloom. Quietly immobile, a slight, stoop-shouldered, unshaven old man dressed in a frayed maroon colored cardigan, navy blue trousers and loose, sloppily-fitting slippers stood in the cubicle. As I stepped in, we stared at each other. No words or embrace were exchanged in greeting. His eyes dominated his haggard face as he intently studied me. We were like two marble sculptures related in some faulty way. It occurred to me that through all our years I had never gazed directly into his eyes. When small I would warily peek up at him, and when older I still was not tall or bold enough to confront him. The passage of time had made an inconsistent reversal. I was almost his height as he was now bowed by crushing burdens laid on his back.

Finally satisfied with what he saw, he motioned for me to sit in a chair from which he removed the clutter. Appreciatively, I sank in. I scarcely took note of the small rooms adjoining the entrance as I settled in the leather seat arranging the pleats of my skirt to drape below my trembling knees. It was unpleasantly cold inside. He gingerly sat down on a metal folding chair that teetered precariously at the edge where worn carpet overlapped the concrete flooring. The way the chair was angled, he did not quite face me, and it proved harder to gauge his responses. After a moment or two of rocking, the chair found its stability while I still searched for mine.

"How are you, Dad?"

The words dispersed into hollow air. My throat was parched and my voice seemed unnatural.

"So, Professor, you're here," he announced, as if I were a rude discovery, an unqualified entry into his life. "I wrote you not to come."

It was clear that my father still said expressly what he thought. This day promised to be no different. His greeting was not entirely unexpected. After I received my PhD in Art and Art History and started teaching at Illinois State University, his letters to me began with the salutation, *Dear Professor.* I ascribed little significance to this, finding it humorous and somewhat inexplicable to be addressed by my faculty title instead of Caasi, my name. What better strategy to tip the balance, to keep me from being real to him, and to blot out unresolved questions and chaos from our past.

As calmly as possible I said, "I ignored your suggestion. It seemed unreasonable."

"Unreasonable to you but it made sense to me."

His sharp retort was a stinging reminder. As always, his words bewildered me.

"I owed you a visit."

The air was suddenly heavy with reserve gathering like the frost on the ceiling pipes. Was it reckless saying that? He never intimated that I owed him anything, just the reverse.

In a voice moderated by remorse, my father said, "It's been too long."

Not returning to Montréal was his idea. Years ago, after departing the city, I received a letter in which he wrote, "If and when you become self-sufficient, forget about me. Birds do not correspond." I disregarded his request and did write to him; surprisingly he answered my letter. His reply was more disturbing. "I have problems writing to you. 'Tis a sad commentary to make at this stage of the game of life, but you don't know me, you never knew me, and you will never get to know me."

I painfully embraced his convictions, incapable of untangling truth from fiction. I avoided traveling to visit him. There was always tomorrow or next month, stretching into years. Now that I was here, he thought it overdue. I could not buy back the lost time. How to initiate a conversation with him under the circumstances was an ordeal. *Why was it so difficult to reason with the man?* The question was pointless. We rarely could discuss ideas in friendly terms or cordially chat. If we could simply manage to talk amicably, the trip would take on untold value.

Unendingly on trial, I was outwitted by my father. In the many letters we exchanged, he held nothing back. His reproof began with the stamped envelope. By some process, I always misjudged the postage to Canada. Not writing on both sides of the page irritated him as evidence of wasting paper. The mere slip-up of writing his name in full, in lieu of his initials E.W., displeased him. The censure then increased and his nettle was plain.

Whatever I wrote, he examined carefully for inaccuracies. Defensively, I replied to his letters, but in his next letter he criticized my last one. I was always one step behind, a chess game of words, and one I was destined to lose. Unable to be an architect of a single solid phrase, my remarks never escaped being torn to shreds.

In the room sitting with him, I dared not begin.

I smiled at him and he smiled back, a sort of crooked smile, unrehearsed and unfamiliar. This simple gesture made him less scary. It seemed to indicate that he could be non-judgmental, and I might venture to speak with less restraint. I chose to gamble with present-day matters. Opening doors to the past with my father was as risky as colliding with a nest of hornets.

"I was eager to see a display of paintings at Musée d'art contemporain de Montréal."

"And why?" he asked, curious.

"The artist Jairo Prado from Columbia paints not unlike a Mexican painter Rufino Tamayo, whose work I greatly admire."

"So, there's more…"

"Tamayo's art is of Mexican figures infused with very earthy colors, burnt sienna, yellow ochre, and magenta, as if they are part of the soil."

Not intending to sound as if I were lecturing to my students, I paused at this point uncertain if my father was engrossed. He feigned inattentiveness, but his eyes betrayed him.

"Prado's technique is similar. His work is also folk-art and his canvases have an emotional intensity."

"Was it worth the trip?"

I inhaled deeply and chose my next words.

"The exhibit enticed me back to Montréal."

"So you decided to stop by after all."

"Naturally, I wanted to see you. What did you expect?"

Over the years, rarely had I glimpsed a definitive overture to soften our connection. We had come to terms but not to trust.

"I never expect, I construe," he replied.

Another complex montage of his making, a pitfall I was able to bypass.

"Now that I'm here, Dad, at least say you're okay with it."

"Okay is fine, happy no."

He was ever capable of providing an invincible reason and an infallible argument. I guessed that there was no way to sidestep his remarks.

"I'll settle for okay," I answered with a rueful smile.

"I admit I have the same problems as people over sixty get, lapses and forgetfulness. But something sticks in my mind from 1978. I was walking back from my broker's office when I passed *Galerie de le Place Royal.* It's on Rue Saint-Paul Ouest, but that's unimportant."

As my father spoke, he sorted through the mess of papers on the nearby tray table. Finding what he was looking for, he showed me a folio from the gallery.

"That abstract was done by a Montréal born artist, Michel Dupont," he explained. "It is la sérigraphie. He uses the colors you seem to like plus elements of surprise and suspense, love and hate. Look him up."

Now I was the one caught off guard. His interest in art was sincere. I had forgotten without the excuse of aging memory gaps that he had studied art at Montreal High School.

"Remember, Dad, I once sent you a postcard of Andy Warhol's *200 Campbell's Soup Cans* as a sample of Pop Art. In your next letter you commented, "I have them in my pantry." I stole your line and used it in one of my lectures dealing with Post-Modern art. My students laughed uproariously.

His eyes showed wariness but no misgivings. He stood up and I noticed how unsteady and lame he had become; the grimace on his face suggested that his arthritis had worsened making it difficult for him to walk.

"I've lost much too much weight. On top of everything I'm saddled with the same aches and pains."

"I was sorry to hear about your fall in the Montréal Métro station."

"It was a bad omen. I was on my way to execute a trade at RBC Dominion Securities. At Place D'Armes, I slipped on an oil slick. I never made it there. My silver stock took a big hit that day."

"The fractured ribs must have been painful."

"I used *Bayer Aspirin*, that's all."

"Have your ribs healed?"

"I get around."

"Dad, I wish you had gone to the hospital emergency room."

My father looked at me queerly.

"I'm still suffering from the last 'civilized' Chinese torture I went through in the hospital. It's still touch and go."

The habitual and firmly compressed mouth reflected his implacability. Instantly I remembered his dislike for anything medical: hospitals, doctors, antibiotics, diagnostic tests, even mandatory surgical procedures. Against medical advice, he had once checked out of the Montreal General Hospital as his surgeon was scheduling him for removal of gallstones. Such was his obduracy and mulishness.

"Please don't ignore a problem. You need to find out what's causing your weight to drop," I discreetly suggested.

Unconcerned with my comments, he fumbled through a stack of books arranged on the floor adjacent to the kitchen entry extracting a worn leather-bound volume of an antique text of medicine from the early 1900's. Opening it with care, he alertly handled it turning the pages with an uncommon show of tenderness. I could see that he cherished this find and had read the vellum pages, now worn and yellowed with age. When he found the searched for passages on diagnostic methods, he placed the book in my hands.

"That's when medical doctors used their seichl; you know what that Yiddish word means, acumen and good sense. I have no reverence for today's trained products. They are impersonators, no better than old women, dimmed in the darkness of their so-called astuteness. I can't get any decent answers from them."

I was silenced by my naïveté of the medical profession. Shifting uncomfortably in my seat, I knew I could not win this man's heart by confuting him.

"That's why I stay clear of doctors," he said in response to my silence.

Quickly changing subjects, I commented, "I stopped by Baron Byng High School."

"You shouldn't have bothered," he said pointedly. "It's not a school anymore. The whole area is kaput. Like academic downfall."

His description on two levels reminded me of his clever mix. He was able to move back and forth between simply annoying and inviting controversy in every possible way. He used his words as testy barbs or for meaningful gain.

"The old building...it saddened me. I felt a sense of loss."

"You lose... I lose... I'm in an ugly mood for 101 different reasons. No matter where we look we'll find casualties."

This was the father revealed to me over the decades of our separation, an angry, defiant and inflexible man. Even now he was not unlike the father of my childhood. That father was one I once wished away. I would have willingly traded him for Gerard, the father living in the building next door. Gerard would sit on the stoop in his cheap tattersall pajamas buttoned close around his throat and drink whiskey from a bottle. Under his breath he would mutter profanities while his family was at Sunday church service. When I chanced to meet him in the street, he would leer away and cross over to the other side, as one mortified of what he had done. My own father seemed to be never sorry, never discomfited, and never ashamed.

Watchfully he made his way to the kitchen.

"Would you like tea? Maybe something to eat..."

"Just tea, please...."

"I could make you a plate of sardines with sliced tomatoes and onions."

"No thanks, Dad. I stopped to have lunch at *Le Cafe Fleurion* in the *Hyatt Regency* near the Place des Arts. I ate a small tuna salad and some grapes."

While my father puttered around arranging teacups on matching saucers, I took a moment to look about noticing what I had only sensed when I walked in. His surroundings captivated my imagination. The room was out of a Charles Dickens novel, a *Miss Havisham's* parlor of muddled and dusty disarray. Books, newspapers in tatters, posters and magazines, old coins, a *Felix the Cat* wall clock, rusted bicycle parts, and oil paintings dominated the small space. An ancient refrigerator, like a store display model, sat unplugged and nonoperational. His television set mounted on a tower of books was turned to a news channel but muted. The kitchen beyond was a stark contrast. A rack with washed dishes neatly adjoined the sink and the *Formica* counter tops were spotless.

My father carried over a plate of dried Turkish figs and sliced apples and set it down on the arm of the leather chair.

"Thank you. I love these," I said as I nibbled on a fig.

"Well, professor, what made you study art?"

'It was what I always wanted to do."

"What you just said is ambiguous. The classes you chose were all in the sciences and math."

"To please you, I studied chemistry, biology, physics, and calculus, but in my spare time, what little there was, I found myself at museums and reading books on art. Even in physics class, I saw the diagrams of force and motion as symbols, lines, and shapes as if made by bold brushstrokes."

"It's no wonder you needed a tutor to get a passing grade."

My father genuinely smiled at his own comment. He remembered my endeavors to grasp the concepts of defining matter and energy in vectors and equations.

"Didn't I write to you about my shift to the arts?"

I wondered, had he truly forgotten or was this some ploy to chip away at my credibility? His letter to me when I lived in Evanston studying in the Art History Department at Northwestern jolted me with this insertion: "Also, I don't comprehend what you write. I find you are repeating yourself. When children leave home, they become total unknown strangers. If you did write, it was your usual gobbledygook."

I knew then the specific letter he was referring to. I had tried to put into words the idea of unrevealed images moving across canvasses in deepening shadows or in the brilliance of light, deceptively simple or convoluted patterns and forms, pure and engaging, with all the possibilities of astonishing. It was my attempt to describe why studying art had become my reality.

"After I got my undergrad degree, I happened by a gallery in Vancouver. A lithograph in the window demanded that I stop. I walked into the shop and bought it."

Scoffing and laughing his derisive laugh, he asked, "Is there any logic to this?"

His almost toothless grin was hard to ignore. Looking at him with vague edginess, I shook my head thinking maybe no.

"The litho was *The Flautist* by the Chilean artist, Roberto Matta. I was entranced by his fanciful figures, so like the drawings I used to do as a kid and paste on the walls of the bedroom."

"Matta…it sounds like you wasted money on a shmate, you know a rag."

I had to laugh. The lithograph was prominently displayed. When I returned home, I would surely chuckle whenever passing it.

13

"Seriously, Dad, it confirmed my love for all forms of art, architecture, and sculpture: the geometric regularity of ancient Egyptian art, the rich deeply layered paintings of Rembrandt, the bronze emotional figures of Rodin, and the delicate capturing of light on the canvases of Monet. It was then I applied to Yale, Northwestern, and University of Pennsylvania graduate programs."

"And now you're teaching. Is that enough?"

"That's an odd question, Dad. I was offered a position as museum curator but turned it down."

"You once wanted to be a renowned artist. What happened with that pipe dream?"

I paused before saying, "It was a lofty ambition but being a teacher is far more rewarding."

"I wonder..."

My father left his spoken thought unfinished like one of my paintings that charmed but lacked the impact of poetry. I had never regretted what I was doing. My rejoinder would have been swift and tenable if he could have discerned how intrigued my students were by the infinite forms of artistic expression. Many former students who were modest, quiet, and shy later developed into artists who made a significant impact on the art scene.

I looked down at my folded hands as I was musing. My own watercolors, although without commercial success, were delicate and whimsical filled with Kandinsky-like abstractions. My fingers were slender and nimble. Suddenly they seemed plain as if in one swift turn they had become inelegant, callused by the rarest of blunders made in childhood. As my father confounded me, I was filled with doubt. I needed common ground, something I was doing that he would not go after.

"Did I tell you I write a weekly column for children? My recent article dealt with creativity, children expressing themselves with crayons, markers and paints. Their imaginative world expands. For some, it's also a safe haven. I think that was why I was always drawing and painting as a child."

My father slowly turned his face to peruse me, looking squarely at me and not through me or around me as he had been doing to this

14

point. As he absorbed what I said, his approval consisted of a nod. Writing was important to him. We shared in common the love of the written word. As a child he insisted I read the dictionary at bedtime. I would fall into a sound sleep cradling in my arms a tattered edition of *Webster's* expecting the words to somehow sear into my brain.

He hobbled back to warily lower himself into his armchair. We faced each other so that I could clearly see and absorb how the cumber of the years had broken and stooped my once powerful father. His eyes, still an intense shade of blue as if an artist had splashed in a stroke of brilliant azure, startled me in their clarity and authority.

"Lately I haven't been feeling too well. I've only traveled the Métro twice in the past three months," he said.

Retreating from his disclosure, which seemed to make him all the more uncomfortable, he turned to politics, the stock market, Israel's problems, history, and lastly family. He shifted skillfully from subject to subject like an ice dancer sharply changing direction. He was articulate and informed. I felt ill-equipped for what was to follow, as if I were sitting for final examinations without ever having studied the courses. He would eventually drag out every detail; it was precisely this that made for the apprehension. He wanted an explanation as to why I had decided to leave Montréal when I was just seventeen.

The suddenness of the question confused me as if I had entered a time warp. Heedlessly, my father had turned the clock back to what he considered an ill-fated judgment on my part. Had he forgotten the primary and dominant role he had played? Searching remote memories, I floundered in my reply. The simplest was the one that eluded me. Dad, I believed I was doing right.

"You miscalculated. I could've warned you had you asked."

I nodded my head giving him the validity he wanted. I had heard that refrain often. It was a pointed reference to the time before I ran away from home. By reshuffling the tragic human actions in my childhood, he held himself blameless. I lived with my assumed guilt, the guilt he had transposed to me to bear. How was he able to ignore his culpability? I chafed at his arrogance, his confidence of being free from fault.

"I don't want to enlarge on it because this will shake you up. Your choices haven't been wise." He spat out these words trying me.

The opportune moment was here. I desperately wanted to diffuse his harsh and untruthful words. Fleeing my home saved me. My rebuttal took the form of an attack.

"What of your mistakes?" My voice was minimally audible.

He regarded me with an austere look.

"Only watches can be fixed. Mistakes can't."

We had reached another standoff. This obduracy of father and daughter was something I had to contend with alone.

His shoulders shot forward to a rigid pose. It signaled the end of the review.

"Is your daughter well?"

I noted that he did not refer to her as his granddaughter. The formality he had shown to me still included her. As I pulled out photographs from my wallet and handed them to him for inspection, his eyes lit up.

"Thank you," he said as he returned the pictures, "she has grown into an elegant young lady since the last photos you sent to me. Votre fille est jolie."

He nimbly switched from English to fluid French in his compliment of my daughter. Did it escape him that she was a part of his family as well?

The meager sunlight faded. Time had no measure that afternoon. My father, instead of tiring, became more animated. He seemed to want to capture the missing years in one sitting. Once he completed the portrait, silences began to settle in. We talked of many things and lapsed at times into silence. We could not alter the past and my brief stay would comprise a lifetime. Old sins, like spiteful elves cluttered the walls and dusty shelves. I recalled that beneath my father's surface frailty persevered an unyieldingly tough and inscrutable iron will. It would eventually reappear.

When the falsehood ceased to be credible

A disquieted look crossed my father's face, his composure disrupted. Searching deep into his past, this old man was doing all he could to unearth roots of fond recollections. These were intertwined with trivial and common themes.

"Did you know I was once accepted to McGill University on a scholarship?" he asked. The pride in his voice was restrained by regret.

"You told me a long time ago."

"I never told you the whole story. In 1927 just after my father died, my mother, l'hasholem, may she rest in peace, your grandmother Ada and my sisters and I emigrated from Russia to Canada. We lived in an apartment building on Rue St. Joseph, a three room flat on the top floor. I climbed 240 stairs to reach my door because there was no elevator."

The recital was familiar and one that he had often chosen in the past to relate. Out of respect to my grandmother and my requisite need to please him, I remained attentive.

"My mother worked night and day. She was supporting me and Mildred and Cora. Her small grocery store was quality, only the freshest ingredients."

The whistling kettle interrupted the story. He paused to make the tea, moving about the small kitchen in slow motion, each step painfully cruel.

"I worked in my mother's store before school, after school, doing what needed to be done. The groceries had to be delivered, boxes unloaded, shelves restocked with canned goods. When customers wanted herrings or cucumbers, I rolled up my sleeves and plunge my arms into the barrels of brine. It was no picnic but we got by..."

I watched him examine the lemon he had selected for our tea. He washed it thoroughly, rubbed it dry, and cut it into precisely matched wedges.

"A supermarket moved in to the neighborhood just next door. My

17

mother's business was ruined. I had to take a job there from 4:00 PM till midnight, so we wouldn't starve. Twenty-five cents an hour..."

He handed me my cup of tea. A teaspoon, a wedge of lemon and a cube of sugar rested on the saucer.

"That's what I earned. We were poor, always struggling to make ends meet. Money was important in its scarcity."

The guarded expression on my face caused my father to hesitate. I was listening, interested in what he was relating. It evoked for me long buried relics.

"Dad, do you remember Larry Schulman?"

My father looked at me, puzzled, searching his own stored memories.

"The grandson of the owner of that supermarket... the wealthy but nondescript guy I dated after high school."

His secluded remembrances nourished by the moment unfolded in free flowing words.

"Larry, aha, what a little pipik! You really did a number on him," he said.

My father laughed, pleased with this little scrap of mischief. I joined him in the hilarity thinking he meant pipsqueak and then recalling it was the Yiddish word for belly button. He slapped his thigh with a resounding thwack while I giggled like a school girl. The thrill and the laughs were short-lived; unswerving, he would finish his narrating of his troubled past. He rubbed his chin between his thumb and forefinger, a staid contemplative tendency of his as he set his thoughts in order.

"My prized possessions were my books and a radio. We never owned a car or had fancy clothes. My hours were long and demanding, but I graduated from Montreal High with all A's. I gave up hope of McGill. I educated myself. I have my doctorate in sociology."

My father smiled at his own joke.

"Seriously, do you know I can judge a person in one minute?"

Laughing weirdly, he pointed his finger at me.

"Jordy, that kid who drove up to our apartment on Chambord in his flashy car, the one from your school... He thought he was such a hotshot. I saw him flick his ash from his cigarette out the window. I went right up to his face and said, "Get the hell out of here."

I saw the scene as if it were projected on a theater screen, gradually curling and melting away, the warped movie reel senselessly spinning the torn film.

"He was dangerous. I saved you from trouble. I don't know why you cried."

The irony of his words provoked me. What had happened was offensive to a shy thirteen year old girl just starting to make friends. Compared to the unendurable torture of my earlier years, it should not have even ranked. During the long hours of conversation, he had never once referred to that part of my life with him. At any time I could easily have turned on him and said, Dad, you committed the most profound errors and our lives were forever changed. Instead, I found myself on the defensive, dragged backwards, a child again at his mercy.

"I guess I was a cry baby. I didn't know any better."

The tone of my voice was unreasonable; I was uncertain as to why I blurted that out. It sounded trite, like a line from a soap opera or something I might have said only to irritate. There were other raw and pointed assertions which would have better served to contest his reality.

What was it I wanted from him? Admission, owning up to, was that it? Acceptance of the consequences would not alter what had taken place. The obvious was hard to swallow. I was simply grasping for some display of approval and still desperate for a show of love.

"After that, my days at school were hellish. Everyone heard about what happened. No one talked to me. Jordy was being a jerk but your reaction was excessive. You were hateful. Just living with you was hard to take. You drove me away..."

"You're talking nonsense," he said. "I saw to it that you had everything you needed. It was your decision to get on that CN railcar and leave Montréal."

My father had shrewdly sidelined my comments. He truly believed he had fulfilled his obligation to me and I in turn had failed him. Now his composure was rattled and the wild-eyed look with the thin, tightly stretched lips appeared. This unyielding face made my words uncontainable. The mounting ordeal caused me to lash out and disclose my truth, the painful truth I had carried with me from the past.

"You broke my heart and crushed my spirit. My childhood was a prolonged nightmare from which there was no reprieve or escape."

The words hovered expectantly in the air, contentions wafting then negligently falling to cloak my father in grief. I believed that he had heard the worst in my carefully nuanced words: the loss of a life and the breakup of life.

Abruptly, I rose to go; it was getting late in the day and too late for reprehension. My dad followed close behind. I turned around and hugged him, my arms holding vestiges of an enduring impression, scarce any trace remaining. His short, unshaven bristles coarsely grazed my cheek. The smell of his skin was musty like that of old library books. A trace of wetness filled the hollows between our touch. My hand strayed to the back of his neck. His hair there was in need of a trim, unkempt and wispy. A pathetic shudder convulsed his chest.

We held hands as he accompanied me to the door. It was impossible for me to be unkind. Our parting was an awkward and poignant moment. I lamented what had been and what could never be. Aware of his discomfort, I withdrew from his grasp. My composure was contrived. In the same way I had set forth long ago, the 'goodbye' word was not said. Inside I writhed with discontent and dark doubts agitated me. I had an urge to demand once and for all, "Why didn't you love me? I loved you."

I struggled to forgive my father; he too was hurting from the pain of long ago. There remained a deep and wide chasm between us percolating with desperate rage. The intricate knot of my stony-hearted father and my gentle, good-hearted mother could not be untied. I would never say what was in my thoughts. Dad, you bent her and broke her and when she was gone, you then failed to create a genial life for the two of us. You drove me away even if you believe that I chose to go. With great effort I prevailed over the heartbreak; you are alone with the solace of disdain. It fills the crevices of this basement hovel and pollutes the air.

As I stepped into the deserted street, I heard the door to my father's flat softly close, just a little click of the latch making it final. The wind roused raking up the dust around the rental car and snatching the key from my hand. I knelt down to retrieve it sifting through bits of litter and shriveled leaves. My hands were shaking and my legs buckled under me. A baffling odor of dried rain fouled the air, a nauseating effluvium of steel, and I felt the sharpness of anger in my chest. Unlocking the door was a challenge, and I let myself fall in a rumpled, shapeless heap onto the front seat.

Haunted by vivid memories of her, still missing her so, ever mourning her loss, I sat in the car. As I gripped the steering wheel to steady the upheaval and portentous rumblings in my head, one by one the windows to the past opened. Without starting the engine, I embarked on a rough road, replete with dangerous twists and turns, furrows and steep embankments. I wept as I journeyed back to where it all began...

Part II
1945-1958

Affectation, a curious desire of a thing
which nature has not given,

...A faint sensation from the past grasped my hand and tugged me along. I was five years old. My mother Emma urged, "Hurry, we'll be late."

"I don't want to go."

"Don't be ridiculous," she said. "Of course you do."

The afternoon was bitterly cold. Puffs of wind sent my jacket sleeves flapping, and my legs felt the pinprick of coarse street debris flying about. My mother's wool tam, tweed coat and kidskin boots offered her little protection from the clinching chill. As she tried to keep her tam in place with one hand, she extended the other to pull me along. She got a firm grip of my mittened hand, but I was too fast and jerked free leaving her dangling a woolly thumb.

I stopped short and stamped my feet on the sidewalk, and then started walking in the reverse direction, darting ill-mannered glances of defiance back over my shoulder. My mother caught up with me and held me fast as I squirmed mightily and wriggled to no avail.

"Stop this nonsense this minute."

Foolishly crinkling my eyes, I assumed a sassy pose, a faint grin tickling the corners of my mouth. My fingers were turning to little sticks of ice.

"I need my mitten...please?"

"My mother handed it to me without reproof. With designed nonchalance, I put on my mitten and a look of regret.

"Do I still have to?"

"Caasi, don't be a little twit," she reprimanded. "You wanted art lessons." Her voice was patient, mildly chiding and at the same time perturbed.

"Just watercolor painting…"

"The Musée des Beaux-arts has a new program. You'll enjoy the classes."

"No I won't!"

My mother's reassurance failed to mollify me. I was carried away with an immodest affectation, a notion that I was uniquely talented. The disconnected dabbling and drawings that filled my sketchpads made me want the impossible: a private teacher, my own ceramic palette, expensive sable brushes and tubes of cerulean blue, burnt umber, cobalt violet, cadmium red and other colors. My father could ill-afford these luxuries.

We had arrived at the museum on Rue Sherbrooke Ouest, a noble, elegant structure with its white marble façade, dignified colonnades and monumental staircase- a most solemn and pompous building. My uncivil behavior and concerns made me falter, my sulkiness dispersed by winds of regret.

"Don't make me go in," I whined.

Troubling me was something I could not confess. Unused to other girls my age, having few playmates except for cousins who did not count, I was wary of girls dressed in fancy frocks with sashes, their hair in elaborate ringlets or neatly woven, ribbon tied braids. I felt bumbling around them from the very moment when I was wholly conscious of being a misfit. Now timorous, expecting the worst, I heard my mother say the words that silenced me and put a tiny crack in my pretense.

"I already paid for your lesson."

Remembering how my mother had begged my father for the five dollar fee, I let her half-guide, half-push me into the children's studio and seat me in a small chair at a long worktable. Young children of a similar age were chattering like magpies. Dozens of boxes were brimful with a formidable array of crafts: glittering stars, ornamental felts, bands of lace, satin, velvet and chiffon, string, feathers, tiles and buttons, construction paper, photographs, glass fragments, wood chips, dried flowers and leaves.

"See, what fun," said my well-meaning mother. She removed my jacket, folded it over the back of the chair and patted my head encouragingly.

"Is that man the teacher?" My words dejectedly trailed off.

"You must address him as Monsieur Léger, and do stop staring."

"He's forgotten to shave," I said, turning away.

24

"He's an artist." My mother answered as if to excuse him.

Monsieur Léger stepped forward extending his hand in greeting. I hopped from my chair and rounded the table to stand in front of him. Pettishly, I switched from foot to foot.

"Bonjour," he smiled.

There was a whiff of cigarette smoke and turpentine in his clothes, not at all unpleasant as I shook his hand politely.

"Hello," I said blushing with a slight droop of my chin so my eyes looked at his feet. He was wearing sandals without socks. How wacky, I thought.

My mother set out to view the exhibits but hastily returned to place a comforting hand on my shoulder. Speaking softly, she entreated, "Good behavior."

"Don't leave me," I implored as she disappeared through the doorway. Contrite and unassertive, I now wanted my mother close by. I was too shy to talk with the girls in matching sweater sets, pleated tartan skirts and knee- high stockings with folded cuffs and buttoned patent shoes. Every pucker and seam was smoothed down, not a rumple in sight. Knowing that my white smocked muslin blouse had lost its freshness and my coarse blue linen jumper was dingy and wretched from wear, I sat apart. Without pleats and folds, I begrudged them, my simple heart clothed in envy.

Urging myself forward with thoughts like *I'm big now, I'll be in first grade soon and who cares anyway about these pampered rich girls*, I searched for paints and brushes. Finding none, I followed the teacher's instructions to create an abstract form of art. Léger explained that there was beauty to be found in common objects, which he described as everyday poetic images. His words did not make a whole lot of sense to me.

"Use your imagination and be daring," he said.

I bobby-pinned loose hair out of my eyes and cuffed my sleeves. Dutifully, I started pasting together a collage. A tad of my earlier hesitation lingered, but the thought of disappointing my mother and also Monsieur Léger goaded me on. Using a photograph of a llama, I pasted on pieces of paper, beads, string, wool tufts and sequins. My palms became sticky with curlicues and streamers of newspaper cut-

25

tings and I glued several fingers together. At times I paused and merely glanced about, not knowing what I was trying to create. The result of my endeavor was a creature with bulging eyes and feathered claws dressed flamboyantly for a monster's ball.

My mother returned, gratified and excited from her ambitious tour of the canvasses. Monsieur Léger was at my side inspecting my work, satisfied with the artistic flair and sense of the absurd.

"Bonjour, Monsieur Léger. I am Caasi's mother, Emma Lichman. How was it for her?"

"Pas mal," he answered. "She's focused. Mais elle préfére...to be aloof, à distance. Les autres filles conversent mais Caasi fait attention elsewhere... à rien, seemingly at nothing in particular. She did not interact with the other girls."

"That's one of my fears," my mother answered. "She spends her time toujours alone. Often she seems distracted. À maison, she's très, très docile."

"C'est mauvais. That is bad. Cependant... she'll perhaps be a great artist one day. Artists tend to be insular."

With a kindly wave, Léger turned to speak to the other waiting mothers.

"Mama, what was Monsieur Léger telling you?" I had struggled to follow their English/French conversation.

"He told me that you have talent and should paint, just as you said you wanted."

She examined my project and exuberantly declared. "It's just what Picasso or Braque would do. They are famous artists who use dynamic colors and odd forms."

I was not entirely won over by 'Picasso and Braque' but my mother's return to claim me was comfort enough.

"Where did you go?"

"To the gallery of 'Revolutionary Artists'. I saw *Still Life with Fruits* by Paul-Emile Borduas- deep purple, greens and red. And John Lyman's *Card Players*, two women playing cards by lamplight and, oh my, *Purple Lilacs*. Beautiful..."

I knew nothing of the persons and canvasses that fascinated my mother. No matter... Her words seemed sincere. I clutched her hand bringing it to my lips to kiss her fingers. The creamy softness of the skin and a subtle scent of *White Lilac* banished my sadness. I jumped from my chair and hugged her. So unforeseen...I looked up in my embrace and heard the vague sighing of the wind and felt hot raindrops fall from my mother's eyes to my own cheeks.

From the imposter the entries pass to other hands

Declining to promote me to the first grade, my kindergarten teacher Mrs. Edelstein and the school principal Mr. Glick, confronted my father and me in a conference at my school. I rarely had contact with the principal before. In deportment, he was meticulous. He smartly walked about the school with short hasty steps occasionally stopping by our class to say, "Good morning kinder." If there was a ruckus in the class and one of the children was outspokenly silly, he chided the offender with his favorite expression, "You are speaking narishkeit." He was unable to put up with nonsense. Above all, disorder riled him. One recess after a windstorm, I saw him in the courtyard. He was deftly picking up scattered leaves and rumpled sheets of foolscap paper whirling about in the remaining gusts. As he fussily moved about and bent over, I noticed that his head was bald and shiny; above his shirt collar, unruly tufts of hair sprouted upwards as far as his ears. That seemed to be the only detail at odds with his precision

"Caasi interacts poorly with the other children, is uncooperative, detached, surly and uncommunicative."

Only Mrs. Edelstein spoke. Retreating to the safety of his corner desk, Mr. Glick disclosed his unrest by twisting and pinching the ends of his pencil thin mustache. With a reproving sigh, he polished his metal rimmed spectacles to a glossy finish. He removed a starched handkerchief from his vest pocket and mopped his head. Now both his glasses and head were nicely shined. Spellbound, I watched Mr. Glick, only just aware of the teacher's awful words.

Mrs. Edelstein's impolite evaluation was not entirely unfair or unwarranted. I had started school at the tender age of four, a bashful, solitary mixture of awkwardness and chubbiness. My mother tried her best to confirm that I was a pretty child finding virtue in my dimples and button nose. Refusing to believe her, I acted disgracefully. In my discomfiture, I shunned my classmates and was remote and obstinate. I resisted looking directly at my teacher and held my head tilted to one side as if expecting a smack in the face. To protect my vulnerability, I wore a permanent scowl. The consequence of my anti-social behavior was exposure to the greater penalty of being the kindergarten outlaw, totally alone and friendless.

My father was incensed by the school's insistence, knowing full well that I was adroit, and more than capable of doing the work. Pulling me aside, he asked me an important question.

"Caasi, do you want me to protest this farce and demand that the school promote you?"

"No, it doesn't matter," I said, "I don't mind repeating kindergarten."

I answered without giving much thought to what I said. Just being in the principal's office with the teacher was punishment enough. Mrs. Edelstein was tall and homely with hard lines to her face, dark hawk eyes without a trace of warmth, a sharp nose, and a pensive mouth. She infrequently smiled unless a parent arrived to pick up one of the kindergartners, and then it was a forced smile showing large gapped teeth. Soldier straight with hands on her hips, she watched as my father and I discussed the consequences.

"Mr. Lichman, we're waiting for your answer," she called out.

My father looked at her with total disregard.

"Our decision has been made." Mrs. Edelstein affirmed the outcome.

"My daughter alone accepts your ruling."

My father's reply placed the blame of lack of common sense solely on me. I shrugged my shoulders and turned away so I could make a silly face. I was trapped in a clash between giggles and tears.

My father strode from the office. I followed in his outraged steps feeling the heat of his displeasure. On the way to the kindergarten classroom, he berated me for being foolish.

"That was a stupid choice, one you'll soon regret."

"Probably," I said.

Leery of change and nuisance, preferring the existing state of affairs, I was also pleasurably influenced by the toys and arts and crafts in plain view. I smiled meekly at my father wanting his defense of my weighty decision, but he merely shook his head in frustrated incredulity.

"I think you've lost your marbles."

Those were his final words on the subject.

The second session in kindergarten played out as a monotonous redo of the first and I rejoiced in its completion. In the fall of the next year, I entered grade one. The first day of class, I was in a state of ecstasy and abject fear. Waking long before breakfast, I scrupulously attended to my appearance. My short, wispy, biscuit-colored hair was a trial. Above my ears on each side, I adjusted the uncooperative filaments with bobby pins and scrubbed my face until my cheeks glowed ruddy. I wore a gaudy purple, nubby, woolen sweater, a half-decent green and black checkered skirt, ankle socks with little cuffs, and my polished, worn brown shoes shiny like mahogany moons. In my school bag, I carried an exercise book, a pencil box with sharpened colored pencils, a ruler, a gum eraser and a box of *Chiclets*.

My desk assignment was in row four, seat three on the far side of the room. Irving sat behind me and Faigie sat in front of me. Before the bell sounded, the incessant chattering, the pushing and shoving, the hoots and hollers, the horseplay, and derisive comments made me twitchy. It was simpler for me to keep my distance, avert the eyes of the other children, and sit staring at my desk tracing the carved initials, squiggles, and hearts etched by previous first graders.

Mrs. Landry was now our teacher. Her age was hard to determine. In manner of dress, her nature and her movements were at odds. Thin as an old willow by the river, her face was narrow and droopy and her back plaintively bent in concession. At her desk, the surface painstakingly organized with blotter, pencils, chalk, paper clips and notebooks, she sat with her shoulders resignedly slumped. She tended to wear wool jersey shirtwaist dresses with demure bowed collars or dresses of a meticulously woven check or herringbone pattern in pastel heather or mauve colors. From the neckline, a single row of buttons darted primly to her belted waist. The fabric then flowed conscientiously to mid-calf level. Below the hem, her prudishly crossed ankles validated her years of self-denial and application to teaching. Although she rose hesitantly from her chair, she fluttered breezily about in the noise of the classroom, a modest butterfly in a garden of mayhem. She seemed in search of a hardier voice; the one she had was merely above a murmur, an effete intonation accompanied by delicate hand waving.

"Quiet please."

The class paid no heed and went on with their prattling and drivel.

"Girls and boys, I said quiet please."

Mrs. Landry found her voice. Her sharp eyes regarded us with fevered intensity and her mouth conceded a lukewarm smile.

To ease the transition from the random meandering of kindergarten to the more ordered first grade classroom with rules, clocks, and compliance, she suggested we play a word game. She explained to the class that the objective of the game was to solve the puzzling comparisons by carefully examining the words and not the subject matter. Only those particulars were made known. At the first grade level, the game was not a simple one. Mrs. Landry had high hopes for her first graders.

She wrote on the board," Butter and eggs are right, milk is wrong."

We stared at the sentence.

"Does anyone know why?"

Malka raised her hand.

"We all love bread, spread with butter and jam, but we hate to drink milk."

Libby chimed in.

"Soft scrambled eggs are yummy."

"No, that's not it, let's try another."

"Umbrellas and boots are right, but galoshes are wrong."

Moishe raised his hand.

"Umbrellas are opened above our heads but galoshes go on our feet... and they're horrid."

"Boots also can be worn," said the teacher. "The puzzle is still unsolved."

Freda sitting behind Moishe pinched him. He let out a yelp. The class snickered.

With alarming emphasis, Mrs. Landry stated, "I will not permit any childishness in my classroom. You are not now in kindergarten."

Trying again, Mrs. Landry wrote, "Soccer and football is right, badminton is wrong. Look carefully at the spelling of the words."

Irving raised his hand.

31

"That's easy," he said. "Soccer is for guys and badminton is for wimpy girls."

The boys guffawed and the girls booed.

"Class, behave yourself," Mrs. Landry said. "You're all still missing the idea."

Slowly I raised my hand.

"Yes, dear...."

The two words were encouraging yet her voice was numb with fatigue. With foreboding and shaky knees, I walked to the front of the class. Using the formal spelling of my birth name and the informal spelling I now and again used, I wrote on the chalkboard in neat bold print, "**Caasi is right**, but **Casi is wrong**."

Mrs. Landry applauded with delight.

"Very astute, you are absolutely correct."

Astonished, the girls and boys sat in silence. They still did not make the connection. Their faces were blank with puzzlement.

"Don't you see?" Mrs. Landry asked. "Only words containing double consonants or double vowels are right."

Awareness had not yet registered. Mrs. Landry went to the board. Her chalk smudged fingers underlined all the double consonants and vowels. The markings screeched across the board.

The class turned on me, accusatory eyes burning with resentment and spite. They mocked my name in squealing tones, stuttering it out Caa... caa... si...si... changing it to Caca, calling me smelly egghead, jerk, teacher's pet, tweedle-dee tweedle-dumb. Irving was the most vehement. In a high-pitched squeak he vocalized the letters, "D u m **b** not d u m **m**!" Mrs. Landry was obliged to rap sharply on her desk in an effort to bring the class to silence. They refused to quiet. I stood before them- an exposed, bruised, teary- eyed object to make fun of.

My snuffling incited more scorn.

"Cry baby, cry baby, piss in bed, five cents a cabbage head."

I moved slowly toward the open door escaping into the hallway. I heard Mrs. Landry shrilling, her thin voice razor sharp, "Oh no you don't. Get back in here." Mockery chased me down the corridor, disapproval rang in my ears, and contempt hacked me into pieces.

I had deceived myself into believing I could be accepted among my peers and then swindled myself of the possibility by showing off and showing them up. I hated the real Caasi and the imposter Casi, both in the wrong.

There is a Fault, which, tho' common, wants a Name

After supper, my father, immersed in grumpiness, settled into the washed-out lumpy armchair, his feet propped up on the faded tapestry footstool. Distractedly he rubbed his stubbled chin and then picked up his newspaper. Disturbed by rumors at his job, to which he had alluded during the meal, and a raspy cough, he was particularly bad humored. His packet of *Export A* cigarettes lay untouched on the side table, the ashtray unused. The fizz in his glass of bicarbonate of soda sputtered out. One lamp behind the chair cast a meager yellow light on his shoulders resting there like a murky cloak. The opened pages of the *Montreal Star* obscured his face. Though hidden by the paper, his demeanor was suspect. What I dimly understood only frightened me. I knew it had something to do with money. The lack of it was always in the air. Behind closed doors, he and my mother unceasingly discussed it. In plain view it simply hovered and flapped like an ailing crippled bird, the one that once hit our front room window and flopped to the sidewalk trembling and writhing until it lay still.

Close to the worn soles of my father's shoes, I was kneeling on a little pillow. Spread out in front of me littering the carpet were loose pages, pencils and erasers, a metal ruler and tiny sharpener, my *Dick and Jane* primer, and my homework lesson. I had completed several chapters in *We Look and See*. Finding 'see Spot run' no longer amusing, I practiced cursive beneath the printed words in my writing workbook, a task that was not yet required. Hoping for praise, I was always moving forward wrestling with my demons. My skirmishes at school made it hard for me to ease up. The derision followed me home and waited for me on my return.

I idled while my father scrupulously folded back the section of paper he was reading into a neat one-quarter crease and then turned to skim the next columns. Avidly, I checked to see if he was still miffed. His face was severe, the forehead lines enhanced in deliberation and his lips pursed and tight. I debated with myself about bothering him. An hour expended in the parlor twilight suited his thoughtful mind, yet the gloom around him seemed implacable. When I could not stand the suspense, I decided to talk aloud whether it was safe or not.

"The kids made fun of me in class today."

That simple statement caught his attention. He peered around the edge of the paper, and I could see his face darken with a sullen shadow and a warning scowl furrowed his brow.

"Why?" he asked. His tone was curious yet guarded.

"Because of my name..."

My father cleared his throat with a grating, coarse fit of coughing. When the spasm relented, the jumbled springs in the old chair made him shift and twist about uncomfortably.

"What's wrong with your name?"

"It's weird."

"So?"

"Every other girl has a normal name."

He exhaled a laugh that sounded more like a snort.

"You have an honored name." His voice rose in exasperation.

"I don't like it."

Pushing aside the footstool, my father half-rose from the chair and then sat back, deciding to explain rather than punish. Trembling now for having been outspokenly blatant, I earnestly chewed on my pencil putting little bite marks into it.

"Before you were born, I was certain you would be a boy."

"What made you think that?

"Don't interrupt me. An esteemed name was chosen adhering to Jewish tradition of passing on the name of a family member not with us anymore... my father, Isaac."

"But, I wasn't a boy."

"Yes, that's apparent."

"Is that why you don't love me?"

The impulsive words slipped out of my mouth and could not be recanted. The color in my cheeks heightened. Jumping up, I began to noiselessly back out of the parlor, cowering under my father's ghastly stare. He judged me with a terrible frown. The question of love would not be answered.

"Come back, I'm not mad at you. Try to understand this. Expecting a son, I believed I was cheated. It was a setback. Not you, Caasi, but the mistake of presuming too much."

Unable to come to terms with what he said but relieved that I was not about to be punished, I asked him, "Why did you name me Caasi?"

"We considered the name Chayka, naming you after my great grandmother. The name didn't sit well on my tongue. I named you after my father Isaac to keep his memory alive. I reversed the letters of Isaac and ended up with Caasi.

"I like the name Lilli better."

Remembering the word game in class, I wished I was a 'Lilli" or a 'Lilly' or anything but a 'Caasi'.

My father ended the distraction and resumed reading his newspaper.

"Go get ready for bed," he commanded.

This rebuke shut me up. It was clear that he was done with me and took no pleasure in the reflection of what might have been otherwise.

I tried to focus on the lined sheet of paper. The words of the quote I had been abstractedly writing in cursive popped out: *Better is a good name, than many riches.'*

Supposedly a good name is better than riches. I was required to accept this theory and go to school with it as if it were a shield. It did not protect me. My shoulders slumped with the yoke of our poverty. The snooty girls at school wearing their pert frocks and their disdain made me even more conscious of the plainness of my mended old clothes. Distressed and disheartened, I often cried at night falling into a sleep of release from sadness.

Stubbornly, I rejected the whole idea of my name. Nor did I feel worthy to be named after my grandfather Isaac of whom I had no prior knowledge and could not make a connection. I was stained by my name and stuck with it and my father's disdain. Whatever inconvenience and misfortune followed, this was not the first of many burdens for my father, or the last of my many deterrents.

I am too absent-spirited to count;

"At the least, wear your rubber boots," were the final words of my mother's warning as I bounded to the door.

Steadfastedly, I spurned her advice and distanced myself from the distress in her eyes. Her concern disconcerted me. I was impatient to be on my way, and this small request made me feel generally cross and irritably resentful.

"I don't want to, Mama."

"You'll catch pneumonia," she said.

Being a good or bad little girl, I knew there would be trouble in store for me when I returned home.

"What do I care?"

My mother sighed and stared away to some inaccessible place. She seemed to sink deeper within her flannel robe, the front closures tightly buttoned. A vapid melancholic look ensnared her, removing her. Unaware of my mother's desperate need for something to hold on to, someone to talk with, my flippancy was still reprehensible.

The month of November in Montréal was drab and cold, an inauspicious prelude to winter. Partly concealed by charred layers of clouds, the early afternoon sun sulked and slipped away. A few insipid beams snipped the overcast, a fleeting display choked by the ominous spread. As I pranced along, drops of rain began to pour urgently turning into a waterfall. Buckets of rain gushed from the leaden skies. The wind howled, churning up the storm. Caught in the deluge, my tatty wool coat unbuttoned at the neck, and skimpy cotton scarf offered little protection. Messy and wet, my hair dripped water off the end of my nose. My teeth chattered. In my sodden shoes, my feet were now soaked and numb. Shivering with wetness, I was too stubborn to return to my warm and dry home where I could change my clothes and change my sullen words.

Avoiding the gaps in the sidewalk, I walked in random patterns, humming to myself, *step on a crack, and break your mother's back.* Though the cold gnawed impassively at my bones, I hopped on one leg across fallen branches picking up acorns and withered maple leaves, scattering them to flail in wind flurries or toss about in the muddy streams. Overhead, dark birds streaked across the dark sky unassailed by the squall.

Heedless of the squishy noises leaking from my soggy shoes, I sloshed in the troughs, some ankle deep. In the desolate streets, murky puddles swallowed the reflections of tall, wet telephone poles starkly naked, lifeless. I crossed Rue Napoleon struggling against the current of surging water overflowing the drains. The only sound heard was the rat-a-tat of the incessant storm. Solitude rained dismally on my back drenching me in sorrow. The ground was as saturated as the bed of a lake. It was difficult to walk without drowning.

To thwart the loneliness I sang aloud.

"I was walking around the corner, not doing any harm/ when along came a policeman and took me by the arm..."

The relentless rainstorm quickened my steps. A small, dark form skittered by, probably a rat, and slipped through a brick crevice, a secret passage to the basement of a dilapidated dwelling. Trembling, cold cleaving to my bones, I wished for the cap and sweater left behind in the dresser drawer. My mother's cautionary voice replayed in my mind. *It will probably rain and your head will get soaked. At the least, take the hat. Don't be stubborn, dear. And for God's sake, wear a sweater under that coat. You'll freeze. You know how you tend to get sick in this miserable weather. You're so prone to ear infections. At the least, wear your rubber boots.*

On Av Duluth, just around the corner from my street, Av Coloniale, an austere red brick building sat dismally in the rain. A wrought iron fence surrounded the school's courtyard locking out the squalor of the streets. No grass dared to grow in the footpath by the fence. It was a place to find bottle caps, cigarette ends, rusty hairpins and *Double Bubble* wrappers, the ones with the little comic strips. I shuffled through the gritty bits and sodden matchboxes hoping to come upon by chance lost marbles or perhaps a penny, but the rain had turned the dirt to sludge burying any discoveries. Convinced of the futility, I picked up the lyrics of my little tune.

"Six o'clock in the morning, I looked upon the wall/ the bedbugs and the cooties were playing a game of ball..."

This part of the song made me laugh. My face brightened, deflecting the gloom of the day. I did a little spin turn and spotted Irving following at a safe distance. He was plodding along in the pelting rain hunched and deliberate like an old English bulldog. Waiting for him to catch up, I continued to whirl faster and faster singing my little ditty, and madly spraying water. I knew Irving was watching, awestruck by my antics. He was rapping a stick along the railings of the fence clanging out the beat of my song.

"The score was six to nothing, the cooties were ahead/ the bedbugs hit a homerun and knocked me out of bed..."

"It's raining hard, Irving, where's your hat?"

The rain spattered on his head and shoulders and spotted his eyeglasses. His pimpled face flushed into a grin. It was unusual for me to talk nicely to him or show the least assurance.

"I don't need a hat," he said with bravado. "I'm not made of sugar. I won't dissolve."

I tugged away the sopping wet paisley-patterned scarf that was trailing from my neck. In one abrupt motion, I folded it in a triangle to make a kerchief and put it on Irving's head tying it under his chin.

Irving was mortified. He stood with his stick, unmusical, his eyes bulging through his lenses. I laughed pitilessly and curtsied.

"Nah, nah, nah, Irving is a girl."

I ducked into the courtyard to join a group of newcomers leaving Irving with my kerchief and his dismay.

39

Laughter and grief join hands. Always the heart

On Sunday, to amuse and entertain the children, my elementary school showed motion pictures in the gymnasium. As the students sauntered in, the appointed monitor rolled down the white fabric screen from a fixture on the wall behind the basketball hoop. Mr. Kaminski, a teacher of the upper grades, operated the projector and changed the reels of film. In grainy black and white, Hopalong Cassidy, The Lone Ranger or Roy Rogers galloped across the screen. It was inevitable that I would love cinema. The images on the screen, the fantasy and enchantments, became my world of reality.

I was awed by the mysterious masked Lone Ranger. Excitedly I had listened on the previous Sunday to the announcer saying, *A fiery horse with the speed of light, a cloud of dust and a hearty Hi-ho Silver... the Lone Ranger rides again.* As much as I revered the cowboy, my much loved films were from the Tarzan series. On this day, *Tarzan's New York Adventure* was the feature and a warm gush of pleasure streamed through my sodden body. Mesmerized, I followed the plot of Tarzan and Jane on their way to the United States to rescue their adopted son Boy from an evil circus promoter who had lured him away. Tarzan was handsome and tenderly portrayed as a man of valor, great physical strength and agility.

"Jane need clothes," he said. "Tarzan better without clothes."

Sitting cross-legged on the solid hardwood floor between the red and blue lines, I inhaled the steamy smells oozing from the damp clothing of the other kids and drank in the celluloid flickers through strobes of light. I booed the projector when the film strip tore and earnestly desired to trade places with Jane.

"Me Jane, you Tarzan," I imitated the dialogue.

I wanted to live in Tarzan's tree house in the West African jungle. I traveled there in my imagination to swing on vines, play with Cheetah, watch my hero wrestle man-eating lions to the ground and command mighty herds of elephants. I was transported far away from the storm pounding the roof of the school and the storm of turbulence in my mind. The movie provided a safe refuge from uncertainty. At home, doubt was my constant ally, loyally showing up on my doorstep each morning and contorting my pillow in the night.

The next movie began. My friend Sylvaine, nicknamed Vinnie, was leaning against me. She was a shy, singularly diffident girl, graced with a head of burnt-orange curls, wisplike eyelashes, and a mist of freckles splashed across an upturned nose. We laughed together at the antics of the Three Stooges, Larry, Moe and Curly. I pretended to bop her on the nose and she popped me on the head with a candy bar.

"Vinnie, Vinnie, you're a little pick a ninny."

I made up the lyrics and the refrain, repeating it, unaware of the implication of the words, not comprehending their impropriety, never having been told that it was an offensive term for a small black child. There was much I did not know or had not learned.

Vinnie tired of me. Normally, the teasing provoked merriment, but today she struck back.

"Aw fatso, go home," she said to deflect the taunt.

Vinnie had touched a sensitive chord. I pulled away and turned my attention back to the screen. The word 'fatso' made my ears burn and my eyes smart. I sucked in my cheeks, clamping my teeth on the soft folds in my mouth trying to indent my face. Holding my breath, I tugged at Vinnie's sleeve, pointing desperately to my newly scooped out shape until in one swoosh, my air escaped and the roundness returned. Vinnie and I giggled and made snuffling sounds until the nearby kids collectively spat out, "Shudup." We stifled our tittering by burrowing our faces in our coats until our silliness at last subsided.

Irving, sitting alone several rows behind us, strained to hear what the laughter had been about, but the racket from the speakers excluded him from our banter. I turned to see if he was still annoyed with me, and he crossed his eyes and stuck out his tongue, which made me happy knowing he was not ignoring me. *Why was I so mean to him when we had met outside the school before the movies? I wondered about my behavior, not comprehending the rashness and disdain.* Uneasy, I stared about the gym gazing at the vertical ropes released from the ceiling beams, the pole vaults, the stacked mats, the climbing racks, and the stored volleyballs. There were no answers to be found in the paraphernalia. I shrugged off the feeling and surrendered myself once more to the film.

My headaches always came after watching two movies and a short. The unruly exodus from the gymnasium shoved me outside, my eyes blinking in the stark brightness. Depleted of rain, the wretched clouds had receded revealing a lusterless sky, and a grating wind made me cringe with cold.

"Vinnie, Vinnie, you're still a ninny!" I called out to my friend as a parting jeer.

"Goodbye, fatso!"

Vinnie turned and fled, her little chin thrust ahead of her and her soft hair carelessly blowing.

Let the world's sharpness like a clasping knife

Alone, I walked in the road gutters clogged with sodden leaves and horse shit, kicking at the rubbish with my brown Oxford shoes, agilely sidestepping the fractured asphalt concrete and large potholes. I was in no hurry to get home. The pain in my temples settled behind my eyes in a drone-like throb. It was less of a concern than the dreaded reprimands waiting for me at home. In the wake of the rainstorm, the wind continued its petulant whine. I favored the whirr and the filth of the streets. The outside ugliness began to ease the pervasive ache. I passed a vacant lot strewn with crumpled, partly singed newspapers. Heaps of ashes clustered around a crumbling chimney, the sweepings of a house now gone save for an imperishable hearth choked with grubby cinders. Brick tenement houses stretched block after block in uninterrupted sloppy rows linked by sagging clotheslines and shared staircases. Draped or shuttered windows permitted only an edge of light to creep out into the early approach of dusk. A rare fenced-in yard littered with trash and castoffs disrupted the bleak pattern. I spied an old sofa with popping springs, a rusted, warped bed frame, a broom handle and shards of Coke bottles, all forsaken items guarded by two scruffy, yapping dogs. The mongrels, thin as skeletons, their long tongues hanging out, tentatively approached my offered hand. Patches of unshed hair clung to their sides and tails.

"Here, doggies," I called amenably.

The frowzy terriers quit their howling for a brief spell, sniffed my fingers hoping for morsels of food, and then resumed their frustrated barking. Backing away, I passed an exposed cellar where the building had been razed; mortar, chipped brick and rubble lay in piles of disarray. Mangled pipes and tangled wires were entwined resembling seaweed and coral branches deep in the bottom of the ocean. The wreck of twisted coils and knots seemed not unlike the snarl of my own world. As I stood quietly staring at the disorder, my thoughts turned to my family. Hammering about in my head were muddled inklings of my father. I was convinced that he was unable or unwilling to love me.

My efforts to win him over fell short and I fearfully thought that he would simply cease to care. Day to day my timorous mother lived in heavy defeat and uncertainty, incapable of protecting me or defending herself. This jumble of beliefs could not be unraveled let alone defined. Morosely I moved on walking with downcast eyes.

Some clatter and scuffling noises forewarned me. A vigilant glance over my shoulder picked out a few of the neighborhood French kids following me. It was not unusual for them to trail along behind me miming me or calling out abuses. Raised by Catholic families that fostered hatred of Jews, they relished the chance to inflict harm. Today, they stuck their tongues out at me, contorted their faces into sinister grimaces, and made pig noises. I was not terrorized of them even when they congregated in groups. I recited in my head, *Sticks and stones can break your bones, but names can never harm you.*

I heard, "Juive cochonne", words in French that translated into an insult. Their maliciousness swirled around me. Once the previous winter, they had pelted me with snowballs, the glazed, rock hard ones stored in their snow forts. The ice chopped at my legs. I had run home dodging the attack, frantically climbing the front steps, slipping on the doorsill, staggering and stumbling into a flow of safe, warm air in the entry. My father was home rigidly standing in my path. I had not expected him. His eyes were sharper and icier than the French kids' snowballs.

"You're late...you need discipline...army discipline."

"No, please, no..."

Recalling that late arrival, I instinctively picked up my pace and hurried on home. I watched as my father entered the house having just returned from his trip to *Schwarz's Delicatessen*. He was lugging two bulging sacks. I lagged behind until tempted by a piquant aroma; it wafted from the house through the open door. I sniffed expectantly suddenly appreciating how hungry I was.

"Mama, I'm here".

I announced my arrival hoping to ward off the inevitable. Walking guardedly down the long passageway to the kitchen past the living room, single bedroom and entrance to the cellar, I traced my fingers along the wall. The lighting in the corridor was dim, except for a small alcove where my mother's old *Singer* sewing machine and basket sat. Pausing, I inspected the contents: spools of colorful thread, buttons, assorted pins, zippers, hemming tape, fasteners and small satin rosettes. My mother was making flowered clips to fix my hair into tight neat braids instead of letting it droop in a sorry state. I knelt down to work the foot pedal with my hands. The needle bafflingly bobbed up and down.

"Did you wash your hands?"

My mother's question sent me darting to the bathroom. First, I removed my shoes that were waterlogged and caked in filth. I began to rinse them under the tap in the tub. The water splashed off the shoes coating the sides of the tub making a splotched mess. Hastily, I tried to wash away the soiled evidence, but the stains, like cocoa in a porcelain cup, could not be blunted without scrubbing with *Bon Ami*. I had no time to accomplish the task before lunch, so I hid the shoes in a niche behind the toilet.

"Please, God," I silently prayed, "keep him from finding my shoes."

As I washed my hands at the sink, I dubiously checked my face in the cracked mirror above the basin; my reflection was split into parts fitting together like errant puzzle pieces. Sections of fine limp hair still damp from the rain were plastered to my head, and little pearls of water clustered on my pasty skin like beading on my grandmother's shawl. Fear and senseless images stared at me from the mirror, eyes brimming with uncertain tears.

"I'm all ready, Mama...coming."

Tiptoeing into the kitchen in my socks, I deposited wet imprints on the dappled beige linoleum squares, the gap between each step becoming progressively shorter as indecision slowed my feet.

The table was set with bright orange platters, cheap imports made in Japan, but festive. Each was hand- painted with delicate yellow and lavender dew-flecked flowers outlined in gold. Starched linen napkins and silver-plated utensils were set out next to the plates. My mother had already made the sandwiches; slices of Jewish rye bread thickly coated with *French's* mustard were piled high with spicy, smoked meat, warm, steamy, and irresistible. There were tempting side dishes of herring in sour cream and onion sauce, stuffed kishke, pickled green tomatoes, and chopped chicken liver. I slipped into my chair, craftily withdrawing so that only the top of my head was visible. My father, sipping seltzer water, was preoccupied; bundles of bills were painstakingly arranged around his lunch plate according to his system of what he could pay and what would have to wait. The charges for my mother's visits to the doctor made him grimace as he critically examined and methodically added them to the expenses. A red glow appeared to radiate from the envelopes and sheets of paper; I imagined they had caught fire from my father's marginally contained fury. A single utterance issued forth, a word spoken in rancorous tones, "Useless."

My mother served and cleared in a silent, subdued manner without any display, pausing briefly as she rounded the table to place a firm hand on my head. I ate in spite of my dread. The beef intestine casing packed with savory sausage filled my starving stomach and then hardened into a stony consistency. I dragged out the time at the enamel tabletop playing with the breadcrumbs, lining them up in battle formation to fend off the ever-encircling wolves with sharp teeth and nails. I memorized the table with its nicks in the white enamel and haphazard flecks of black on painted green legs, sturdy and functional.

I could feel the dissonance coming, the biting words, the out of control curses and the final blows. My father snarled at my mother. The snarls turned to rage, cold rage, hot rage, wicked rage. The violence erupted in volcanic fury. A stream of molten rock gushed from the crater of my father's irrational anger. We were swallowed up. He stormed and menaced. My mother retreated slowly into the corner of the room by the water heater, her eyes moist, bewildered, no words of her own to buttress her, no hand raised to deflect the noise and blows. The cruelty shocked me into passivity. Traveling what seemed like miles to reach across the kitchen, puny words trickled from my throat issuing as a shuddery cry.

"Daddy...don't...don't hit my mama."

Heh, heh, heh,
Who knows what evil lurks in the hearts of men?

I loathed the narrow hallway that ran the length of the house. There was nowhere to hide. It was always damp. On washday, laundry hung to dry on a clothesline strung from hooks between hallway doors, one to the cellar and one to the bathroom. Wooden pegs dangled school gym shorts, my mother's aprons and girdles and my father's old army socks. I would duck between the sodden garments slapping at them until they flapped unrestrainedly. Once when walking in my sleep, I wandered into the long continuous tunnel heading for the front door. Lisle stockings and wet teddy blouses witnessed my near escape. My mother tenderly led me by the hands back to bed, careful not to startle me to wakefulness. I never reached the door.

In the morning, I tumbled out of bed rubbing the sleep from my eyes. Eager for breakfast and some time alone with my mother, I hastily changed into my school clothes she had put out for me the evening before. To reach the kitchen, I had to brave the hall, dim and creepy in the morning gloom. The hall blended into the kitchen. Lacking a pantry, we had in its place a tall but very plain oak hutch. It came with varied size pull out drawers for storage of rice, flour, noodles, onions, potatoes and sugar, and shelves on which to stack our dishes. Just beyond, a scratched up door led to a small storeroom which housed a wooden icebox originally painted in white. Over the years, the paint had flaked off exposing raw rough spots. Propped up on old tired legs, the icebox always seemed to be at a slight tilt. The metal hardware and latches were corroded. Inside, near the top, was a large, slowly melting block of ice on a tray, and below was space for butter, cheese, and bottled milk. Fruit, eggs, vegetables, fats for cooking and leftovers were arranged on the side. A drip pan under the box had to be emptied at least daily. The shed was an ungainly cold place and a haven for rats. At the rear, a door opened to the alley riddled with assorted plate scrapings and rotting garbage deposited by neighboring apartment dwellers. Foraging dogs and cats scattered the rubbish about so that I never dared venture there.

"Please, Caasi, go get the milk for your cereal."

My mother was busy lighting our stove. I sat at the table eating *Rice Krispies* out of the box with the cartoon characters *Snap, Crackle,* and *Pop.* Pretending not to hear, I disregarded her simple request.

"Also, please pour out the water from the drip pan into the pail at the back door."

In slow motion, I set down the box and anxiously made my way knowing that monsters lurked in the shed. My dissension mounted with the added task. Hoping to scare off the rats, I stomped my feet on the unsteady, wood plank stairs.

I shouted out, "Stupid rats stay away!"

Slit eyes shone in the dark and slick bodies with long tails scurried back to their hiding places. The stowed cardboard boxes and discards cast irregular shadows in the meager light from the single dangling overhead bulb. Furtively, the knotted cord swung back and forth. I had a sudden onrush of terror. The rats slithered out of sight and never touched me. At times they haunted my dreams but I was less fearful of them than my father's punishing hand.

The house was a haven for dust. It seeped like mildew into the walls and old furniture. In the parlor it settled on the claret colored cotton drapes until they listlessly drooped. The upholstered sofa had worn down uneven patches alternating with clusters of burgundy velvet/mohair fabric. A discolored leather wingchair with matted padding served as a reminder of some former refinement, now wanting. The burnished walnut side tables had lost their veneer and a fine silvery powder hid their former elegance. Flower patterned lamps wore tasseled, pale yellow shades slanted at odd angles to provide the maximum light in the living room. Sunbeams speckled with dust funneled into the room through the front double paned window. The carpet, a lackluster pattern of multicolored wool tufts, trailed a border of fringes across the mahogany floor. When it was newly bought, I rolled around on the mossy surface gently stroking the finish as if it were a living thing. Now it was just another collector of grime.

The *Philco* console radio box jammed into the corner suffered from neglect. I toyed with the plastic dials and pushbuttons controlling the stations and the volume but never turned on the radio without permission. I inspected the back of the box, marveling at the glass tubes and maze of circuitry. On Monday at 8:30 PM, *The Fat Man*, tilting the scales at 270 pounds, confirmed his skillful crime fighting techniques on ABC radio. My father permitted me to listen to the one half-hour detective show each week even though it was past my usual bedtime.

Scattered newspapers, books, pencils and crayons littered the occasional table where I did my homework under the watchful scrutiny of my father seated on the sofa or in his armchair. At the outset, he was patient and never raised his voice when I asked him for help in arithmetic. To diminish the complexity, he transformed the problems to apples and oranges; numbers took on identifiable forms and assumed dimensions. I noted the orderly and logical structure of each calculation and it seemed reasonable. The deduction of the more difficult questions evaded me for a time. When it dawned on me, it came tardily. His composure lapsed when he noted my reticence.

"You're not paying attention," he said, his voice tight with reproof.

"I'm trying," I stammered.

"If you divide an orange into quarter sections, then cut each quarter section in half, you now have eight sections. Each section is 1/8 of the orange. $1/4 \times 1/2 = 1/8$. So far, so good, right?

"Yeah...I guess so"

"Then you do the same to the eight sections. How many pieces are on the plate and what fraction of the orange is each piece? That's the math: $1/4 \times 1/2 \times 1/2$."

"I'm not sure..."

I knew he would grab me by the arms, pressing his thumbs into my flesh, and shake me until the correct answers somehow emerged, wrenched from my brain, rattling like jacks tossed on the hardwood floor.

"I'm sorry, Daddy."

The calculation of sixteen pieces and 1/16 sputtered out between the jolts. The hold on my arms slackened and I was set free.

Ignoring me and retreating into his past, my father intoned, "When I attended school, not only did I study Latin, English, French, history, science and mathematics, but I worked to support my family. No one helped me with my homework. Uncompromising, I read and studied late into the night."

Speedily, I completed the assignment and neatly stacked the books. My father glared at me, his eyes emblazoned, his jaw clamped, his lips thinned to a jagged wire.

"Go to your room and read the dictionary until I tell you to come out."

Even if it is a hard struggle

As the Sunday closest to November 11th drew near, in commemoration of those killed in the World Wars, my father became increasingly agitated and morose. He randomly spoke and only in short unplanned outbursts. His daily newspapers went unread. Struggling with his demons, he stomped about the house inspecting the damaged walls, the splintered baseboards, and the ceiling water marks. I caught up with him in the dim vestibule brushing the dried mud from his rubber overshoes, lining up my sadly smeared little kid-boots and my mother's plastic shoe covers and rigorously going at the small space with a broom. It was unusual for me to ask him a question, always playing it safer in silence. I found the tension agonizing.

"Daddy, is something the matter?" I asked.

He had that look on his face, the same defined grimace as when he grated horseradish, its pungent odor turning his eyes bitter and creasing the corners of his mouth in tight grooves.

"What's the matter can't be put right," he said.

He leaned the broom, handle down, in the corner and walked to the bedroom. I followed him and watched as he retrieved a shoebox from the top shelf in the closet. He removed the lid blowing the dust from it and took out loose, black pages folded and tied with a piece of string. It was an old photo album with the pictures individually mounted, each of the corners tucked into little, black, gummed-on triangles. Sorting through, he located the picture he wanted and wordlessly handed it to me. It was a photograph of my father dressed in military uniform and standing in front of an army tent, a bayonet- rifle, barrel down, supported in his right hand.

I gaped in astonishment.

"I was in the Black Watch Infantry Division of the Canadian Armed Forces," he stated, as if he were reporting for duty.

I studied the photo noting all the details. Jauntily moored on his head was a distinguished tam with a small pompom. His long overcoat extended mid-calf level and was anchored above the waist by a belt with a silver buckle. Below the coat, his wide britches flared to the ankles with tapered buttoned leggings just covering the tops of his boots. A large canvas bag was attached to the front of his chest just below his chin.

Pointing to the picture, I said, "You never told me you were in the army."

"I was stationed in Halifax in 1942."

"You mean when I was just two years old?"

"That's right. It was late summer."

"Sometime around my birthday, August 10th?"

"Exactly nine days after your birthday, my troop joined British Commandos and American Rangers for a frontal attack on the French Port of Dieppe. We were to go in at gaps in the cliffs at Puys, two-and-one-half miles to the west. German mortar and machine-gun fire pinned down the troops. Most of the men were killed."

I did not understand the language of the attack plan, but the last words my father said frightened me. Men were killed, never to come home again. I could not quite grasp why he was frustrated and unhappy to be safe at home.

"But you made it, Dad? Pourquois avez-vous l'air fache?"

"I'm enraged, don't you understand, because I never went!"

He savagely spat out the words.

"Would you believe, me, never sick a day in my life, and I came down with pneumonia just before the men in my division shipped out. I was hospitalized for three months. I lost twenty-five pounds and then was discharged home to finish my recovery."

"If you hadn't gotten sick, you might have been shot," I reasoned.

"That's not the point. Don't you get it? Cela ne fait rien, je t'assure. I should have been there."

His voice trailed away. The circumstances of chance and his feelings of shattered expectations angered him. For my father, the fiends were always lurking like a pack of mad and hungry dogs, fate playing its trickery and denying him his triumphs.

He made a move to snatch the picture from me, but fearing he might rip it to shreds, I pocketed it. His muscles in his face tensed.

"En somme tout est fini. Tu as compri?"

My father believed everything was finished for him. He did not suspect that the hardest battle was yet to follow and we would be the ones to fail.

From goblins that deceive you, I'm unable to relieve you

The tumbledown dreariness of my home increased my timidity. The rooms wore unsightly faces blushing in disgrace and ignominy. Paint peeled off the walls in strips of poverty and failure; there was no money for repairs or reason to replace the threadbare furnishings. My mother's focus was on feeding the family decent meals, saving pennies by frugal shopping for the limited groceries, stoking the wood stove to keep it lit, and using the plunger on the clogged drainage pipes. Relatives, in their infrequent visits, bore gifts of fleischik chickens, cheese blintzes, and apple strudel, ever watchful for my father's sudden appearance, a gust of indefensible cold with piercing scowl and frosty glare. We grappled with scarcity, but much like the hare caught in a net, the more we flailed the faster we were ensnared.

Trivial vanities lacking, I refrained from asking anyone from school to spend the afternoon for play or to sleep over. Only on one occasion, overpowering the need to conceal, I dared to invite Kathy, a classmate, to my home. She hesitated at first, disguising her own secrets until hunger prodded her to accept. At lunchtime, we walked arm in arm, swinging our books and gaily chattering. When we entered my house, the sordidness set in as discomfiting as cemetery silence. My mother had prepared sandwiches of sliced salmon with lettuce on buttered *Wonder Bread*, wedges of fresh, juicy D'Anjou pears for dessert and for our beverage she had set out cold tomato juice in cute jam jar glasses. We ate the tasty sandwiches terrified of the soundlessness and skulking evil of scarcity, choking down the fish as if it were still alive. Then we gathered up our books and raced back to school looking over our shoulders pursued by ghosts and goblins hooded in must and dust.

Indebted for the lunch, Kathy implored me to come to her house to help her with *Mischievous Kittens*, a picture puzzle she had received as a birthday gift. After my homework was diligently completed, I walked the short distance to Rue Roy, rounding the corner to where she lived in a two- room flat on Rue St. Dominique, a street uglier than Av Coloniale. At the start of the school year, I had stopped by to lend her my notebooks when she missed attending class as a result of being sick. The apartment was chilly, no warmth issuing from the steam radiators, the cylindrical array of metal tubes steely cold to the touch.

The front door was ajar. Unnoticed, I simply walked inside without knocking. Kathy's father was hunched over the kitchen sink. He was wearing a tattered, sweat stained undershirt tucked into his work trousers, the suspenders loosened to his knees. A damask dish towel edged with blue posies was flippantly draped across his shoulders. On the shelf above the sink sat a round glass jar filled with bits and scraps and leftover strips of soap. I watched as he reached up, grabbed a handful, and began working the soaps into his wet hair until it became sudsy. Unchecked, the foamy lather streamed down his face. Dabbing at his eyes with the towel, he cried out, "Le savon a brûlé mes yeux!" and without delay stuck his head under the tap letting the water rinse away the copious suds and soot and ease the stinging pain in his eyes. Shivering profusely, he folded the skimpy towel around his head cursing the icy cold water. I snuck past him to find Kathy in the bedroom arranging the puzzle pieces on the floor. Her face red with humiliation, she confessed that they could not afford the price of coal for the furnace.

There was no toilet paper in Kathy's home. I discovered the lack of it when I had to use the bathroom. The pipes made weird rumbling and gurgling noises, and I balanced on tiptoe to reach the handle to flush the toilet. The water-closet box was latched and bolted, but a little leak dripped water on my head, pitter-patter, pitter-patter, the sound of rain on leaves. Shakily standing waiting to crash, the lopsided sink was on only one of the two supporting metal legs. The other had snapped near the base. Having been instructed by my mother to wash my hands after using the toilet, I twisted and turned the moldy faucet until cold, rusty water spurted out splashing me. No scented *Ivory Soap* was to be found in the small ceramic dish, just a gel-like residue left from whatever was used before. In the narrow, compact space, there was also no tub. Kathy's family was even poorer than mine. I wondered how she managed to keep herself clean and tidy. Her hair was a vibrant strawberry red, always shiny and healthy looking. I guessed that she washed her hair at the kitchen sink just like her father.

I searched for a napkin or washcloth with which to dry my hands. Small squares of newspaper were neatly stacked in the corner under the pull chain. Draped over the chipped porcelain bowl, a mottled square of cheesecloth served as a hand wipe. I interpreted the absence of real toilet paper, soap and fresh cloth towels as petty impediments but was unable to brush away the subtle cobwebs of vulgar destitution.

And he said, "Do not raise your hand against the boy, or do anything to him."

The school I attended was a parochial school, established and maintained by respected and enlightened Jewish and Christian teachers. Mr. Solkovitch and Mrs. Landry taught English, French, history, geography and mathematics to the younger students in the morning. After lunch, my second grade class studied Hebrew with Mr. Stern and read Yiddish stories with Mrs. Bessner. Learning the Holy Scriptures, the Tanakh in Hebrew, was difficult, but the tales appealed to me.

"In the beginning God created the heaven and the earth... And HaShem God planted a garden eastward, in Eden; and there He put the man, Adam..." I viewed with serious agitation the serpent's temptation and Adam and Eve's forced expulsion from the Garden of Eden. Jacob's impersonation of his brother, depriving Esau of his birthright, saddened me, especially when Isaac said, "Thy brother came with guile, and hath taken away thy blessing." I had dramatic and unsettling dreams about Joseph and his coat of many colors cast into a desolate pit without water. My favorite tale was that of baby Moses in his basket fashioned from reeds set adrift among the bulrushes on the River Nile. It inspired me to draw and color pictures which I carted home to attach to the bedroom wall. All the Torah stories were real to me in their depiction of greed, envy, duplicity, love, trust, and faith. I tried to identify with and make sense out of God's unpredictable plans for His people.

We were in the midst of reviewing Abraham's relationship with God to underscore God's power and the need to trust in Him even when put to the test. Mr. Stern read the Torah section in Hebrew and then translated to English. "And they came to the place which God had told him of; and Abraham built the altar there, and laid the wood in order, and bound Isaac his son, and laid him on the altar, upon the wood. And Abraham stretched forth his hand, and took the knife to slay his son..."

I raised my hand interrupting the narrative. Resenting the intrusion, Mr. Stern squinted at me above his wire-rimmed glasses, his gentle face gathering a look of rebuke.

"Yes?"

"Mr. Stern, why would Abraham slay his own son?" I asked.

"He was instructed by God," he answered.

"But it's a wicked act."

"God in His wisdom makes certain determinations."

"Why is my father unkind?"

"You must ask him that question."

"He's not God, is he?"

"No, he's your father."

"So he shouldn't be mean."

Normally a tolerant man with an excellent nature, Mr. Stern showed his displeasure; his face turned beet- red and his voice trembled with irritation. The other children started to snicker and poke fun at me.

"Sha," he said, "zei schtil, keep quiet. This has gone too far. You are trying my patience, disrupting the class, and causing bedlam."

I put my head down on the sacred Torah book wondering if I could get in touch with God to answer my questions and help me understand why my father wanted to sacrifice me on his altar of anger.

"And then an angel of the HaShem called unto Abraham from heaven...Do not raise your hand against..."

Mr. Stern's voice droned on, lightly passing over me.

The merest flaw that dents the horizon's edge

At recess, I played in the schoolyard. More often than not, I busily entertained myself without company, frolicking merrily, oblivious to my seclusion and isolation. Hopscotch was a favorite and with persistent practice, I could leap from square to square, eyes shut, balancing on one foot, scooping up the flat rock, and landing on 'safe'. When I tired of skipping about, I boisterously bounced a black lacrosse ball made of hard rubber as I recited verse with singsong uniformity. Each of the sentences had to contain, in alphabetical order, a word beginning with the letter A, then B, the next, C, and so on to the end of the alphabet. If I slipped up, I started again from the beginning.

"My name is Annie and I come from Boston and I eat cherries and I have a daddy but I don't celebrate Easter and I want to fly..." Each recitation varied from the previous so that it was always a test. "My name is Abigail and I come from Babylon and I like the circus and I hate December and I ride on an elephant and I have no father..."

Ever the lonely outsider, humiliated by my clothing, unable to divulge the sordid details of my life at home, I did not make friends easily. Distrust, jealousy, and chagrin locked me in my barren world. If we played a game with two opposing teams, all the girls lined up for 'choosing sides'; as name after name was called, the team captains always left Vinnie, Clara and me to the end. Vinnie disliked games and Clara stuttered, but why I was unacceptable appalled and disparaged me.

When the children lined up for entry into the classrooms, I faked enthusiasm and joined in the coy joke telling of silly, confounding or forbidden words, made up book titles, and other nonsense so as to be accepted by the group. We prodded one another, laughed outlandishly or uttered rebukes and threats.

Sasha, "Your epidermis is showing!"

"So what!"

Evelyn, have you read "The Open Kimono by Seymour Hare?"

"That's dumb. I'm going to tell on you!"

"The Yellow River by I.P. Daily," sang Melvin aloud, dissolving into uncontrollable mirth.

Pushing and shoving, the line of kids moved into the school, each student off to a classroom. Sometimes I accompanied the popular girls, fetchingly dressed in starched linen blouses and rustling skirts, into the confines of the bathroom cubbies to reverently watch them pee. Yet I never felt as if I fit in with the choice crowd. The privileged girls formed an impenetrable clique with limited access making my days at school unhappy and cheerless. I chose to stay at home or to read books in the library on Rue Clark instead of dealing with the day to day hurdles.

My skirts and sweaters were natty, selected from boxes of used clothing, defective cast-offs in cartons like the spoilt oranges in the dented crates at the Rue Rachel market stalls. Each day I tried to concoct a suitable outfit. One morning as I rummaged through the miscellaneous items, I chose a pair of cotton panties embroidered with daisies, a slip, and a pleated linen dress with puff sleeves and daintily stitched collar. The dress had suffered through repeated washings, and the tired fabric emitted a chalky odor. I could not bear to look at the smudged trimmings, drably beige instead of snowy white, and the unraveling hem. At school the elastic waistband of the throwaway underwear suddenly started to give way. I grabbed my side, hanging on with one hand, as I continued to work on the mural painting stretched out on the classroom floor. When the panties began to precariously slip, I knelt down rocking back on my heels twisting and wriggling. Mrs. Landry noted the hassle.

"Stop squirming!" she ordered and lifted me to my feet. "No more painting for you."

The punishment was unnecessary. I was standing in a cotton shroud of shame.

Though I am young, and cannot tell

In the classroom, Irving, sitting directly behind me, stacked his desk with texts and notebooks. He sneaked a peek at me from behind his barricade hoping I would notice him. I countered his daft antics with cruel, intractable gibes. Occasionally, I sneaked a peak at his test paper as he slid it over the edge of his desk tempting me to copy his answers. I never dared. He always had a supply of *Blackjack* chewing gum, which he generously shared and then chided me for sticking the chewed blob of gum to the underside of my bench seat.

"The teacher will kill you if she finds the gum."

"I don't care," was my tart reply.

Irving liked me, a minor triumph for me, but I pretended to hate him. A chance smile elicited dimples in my cheeks and a subtle sweetness in my vivid green eyes, at once heartening and breaking Irving's heart. It mystified him why I seemed upset, at times quiet and contemplative, then abruptly callous and scornful. My acerbity and snide jabs induced him close to tears. The lenses of his thick glasses bridged his wide squat nose and magnified his eyes into smoky marbles. His face, dense and lumpy, looked like a relief map made out of paste and salt. Tousled clumps of frizzy black hair recoiled from his greasy forehead as if he had shocked himself by placing his finger in an electric socket.

Trying to impress me, he leaned forward to ask me a riddle.

"What is black and white and red all over?"

I stared at him as if he were indistinguishable to me. Abstracted and lost, I avoided replying or affirming his effort to make me laugh. In a hurry for my reaction, he blurted out, "A newspaper- you know **r e a d** like **r e d**."

He spelled out the letters of the identically pronounced words thinking that I did not catch the humor. His laugh spurted raucously and then sputtered to a vapid snort as I turned away, repelled and cross. Often and frequently offended, what saved him from infinite ridicule was his persistence in trying to break down the barriers I set up, never giving up hope I would respond.

In secret, I did covet respect and approval not only from the elitist girls who plainly slighted me, but I also wanted Marty to notice me. He was the charmer in my grade. He had wavy light brown hair, a pleasing face, long eyelashes that sheltered cat-like aqua blue eyes, and a cherubic smile. In his collared shirts, beige cashmere V-neck sweater, and pleated wool slacks, he was strikingly good-looking, an opinion he unabashedly shared. Not one of the brighter students, the distinction between broad layers of stratus clouds and rounded cumulus ones evaded him, but he dribbled the basketball with finesse.

Marty had a crush on Flora. A head taller than Marty, she towered over him, and when he purposely backed her into a corner of the room to talk, his eyes were riveted on the milky white skin of her neck. She lisped affectedly, simpered by plan, and in her conceit, endlessly primped her silky-smooth, honeyed hair. Blinded by my infatuation and without personal airs, I had no awareness as to why Marty was enamored with the girl. My jealousy was intense and consuming.

One day in the corridor outside the classroom, Marty sidled up to me. He rested his chin on my shoulder and placed his hand on the small of my back. I remember feeling excited and breathless at his impertinent familiarity.

"Hi, Marty," I said, flushing demurely.

He slyly encircled my waist and then reached up and pinched one of my nipples between his thumb and forefinger hurting me and then walked away with a carefree shrug.

Stunned into meekness, I entered the classroom and quietly slid into my seat. Irving chose that very moment to dip the ends of my braided hair into his inkwell. I attacked him with rampant venom. He slunk into a silent glob like a slug.

The siege will take a heavy toll,
and few who live to the end of it will survive

When invited, I visited with Vinnie in her apartment on the top floor of an ancient stone building on nearby Av Laval. Streaky gray marble stairs worn smooth from years of footsteps led to the upstairs hallway. On each floor, cooking odors mired with decay inundated me making me gag. I climbed vigilantly clutching the wrought iron railing so as not to trip and fall and withheld leaning over for a fleeting look down the spiral of steps.

Vinnie lived with her family in a small one bedroom interior unit, windowless and dark. There was a tiny kitchen cramped and over-heated, often reeking with the overpowering smell of cabbage soup simmering on the stove. Ruffled curtains, stiffly starched and bordered with crocheted lace, hung on the walls as decoration. On the ledge above the sink, were framed photographs of unidentified family members. Their indistinct and creased faces guardedly inspected me. Permanently set up next to the washtub, an ironing board served as a place to do homework. The round kitchen table was covered with a fruit and berry print cotton cloth. The decorative pattern of yellow pears, red apples, and clustered cherries was the one bright spot in the room. Vinnie warned me not to set my books down on the tablecloth, always freshly ironed and tidily arranged.

Vinnie's older brother Roland was only five feet tall at age sixteen. Roland was dominating and spiteful. His short stature made his head seem too large for his squat turnip- shaped body. Enormous eyes appearing to be unlidded consumed his smallish face. Imperious and arrogant, he regarded us with direct owl-like looks whenever we disrupted his studies. I avoided Roland's incessant queries about my own family and never approached him for help with an assignment. Surrounded by French and English books and manuscripts, Roland read voraciously, dedicated to a distant and ideal world of literature.

Vinnie's mother Martine had not yet returned home from her job. My mother once told me that Martine was employed as a seamstress in a garment factory on Boulevard St. Laurent and was overwrought from needing to work each day, morning to late evening. Martine took a dim view of me believing that I distracted Vinnie from her homework and her chores and interfered overall with the orderly and efficient habits of the family. At home she seldom spoke except when necessary and then conversed briskly in French with Vinnie and Roland. No words were ever said about the father of the family.

I was dimly aware of a number tattooed on Vinnie's left forearm in ineffaceable black ink, undetected under long-sleeved blouses or sweaters. Only this day was I forward enough to question her. She was at the kitchen sink, sleeves neatly folded to her elbows, scouring a scorched pan.

"Vinnie, why are there numbers on your arm?"

Distressed, Vinnie let fall the bundle of steel wool and reached for the towel to dry her soapy hands. She put a finger to her lips to signify not to say more, and we walked to the bedroom so that Roland could not hear us converse even if he strained his ears. Vinnie's eyes moistened. Grabbing my hands in hers, she swore me never to tell. The story emerged in hushed tones.

"In December 1944, one night we were taken from our home in the village of Saint-Brice."

"Where's that?" I asked.

"In the north-central region of France," she answered knowledgeably.

"Why did they take you?"

"The French police worked with the Gestapo to round up French Jews. Orders were shouted in German. We were dragged out in our night clothes. I was very young and afraid. What happened next is a blur. A Nazi officer in the police station did this. Much later, my mother explained that the tattoo was to be my prison camp number."

She traced her fingers lightly along the inky numbers.

"By some miracle, I was released, and in the cover of darkness, a courageous neighbor brought me to a Catholic convent and left me there. The nuns were kind and cared for me. Sometimes I was forced to hide in a tiny closet."

"Oh no," I cried out.

As tears dripped unheeded, Vinnie's nose turned red. She buried her face in the pillow on her bed. Her voice was muffled as she talked on.

"My mother was deported to Ravensbrück, a concentration camp north of Berlin. Her beautiful hair was shaved off."

With concern, I patted her back. She sat up holding her little pillow. The cotton muslin case with embroidered lavender flowers was now crushed and damp with tears.

"My mother told me how she was first forced to do hard labor. But she was expert in sewing so she was put in a barracks with other women to repair and re-tailor the Nazi army uniforms. She was starved, tortured, and abused."

"I'm so sorry, Vinnie."

"She became...what is the word... pensive...always lost in thought...much like she is now."

We lingered in the recounting of bygone events, eyes fixedly and unwaveringly sad.

"My mother stayed alive, thin, and sickly until the camp was set free. During this time Roland was in a French hospital. I think he had a gland problem and so he didn't grow very tall. When the war ended in 1945, my mother returned for me and Roland, and later on we managed to come by ship to Canada."

I did not know what else to say in comfort. We had become fast friends at school even though she was two years older than I and was in the third grade. The other girls shunned her as she spoke English with a French accent. I found her inflections charming, lending her an air of culture, and she stoically tolerated the insensitivity of our schoolmates without striking back. Before hearing Vinnie's harrowing story, I was less affected by the real problems of others. I was struggling to survive in my own hell. In school, when we studied world history, Mrs. Landry had explained to us about the mass murder of the Jews from 1939-1945 and the few thousands who had managed to escape. At the mention of Hitler's name, my father told me to spit on the sidewalk three times. The calamity of the Shoah seemed far removed from my life... until Vinnie. I was jolted into accepting how tough it was for us to be Jewish and I sorrowed for my friend. She consoled me.

"Caasi, we were the lucky ones. We lived."

Glistening through her tear-filled eyes was a spark of stubbornness and will. The taunting of the French kids on my street was minor compared to what Vinnie and her family had suffered. I felt sorry about teasing her at school and vowed never to offend her again.

Between the time used up on school assignments and discussing the peculiarities of classmates, we two friends dialed telephone numbers at random asking farcical questions and when answered would say nonsense and then abruptly hang up.

"Do you have Prince Albert in a can?"

"You do?"

"Well, you'd better let him out!"

We laughed at our own silliness as Roland stared at us, his face contorted in reproach.

"Deux enfants sont conduisent sottement. You make me sick, you two imbeciles."

It was apparent that he meant this only for me and not for his sister. He considered me selfish and incapable of empathy because I had not suffered through the war. For this he appeared to despise me.

When Martine arrived home from work, she glumly trudged in, a tired middle-aged woman, overweary, drained of energy, and her face bitter with dark suspicion. Shoulders hunched in fatigue and defeat, she glared suspiciously at Vinnie and me. No greeting at all, not even for her son and daughter. Removing her shopworn coat and scarf, she hung them with care on the coat rack in the kitchen near the stove. She emptied the contents of her purse thriftily counting the few paper dollars and coins and tucked them away into a flat, pink tin box labeled *Dessert Digestif*, a biscuit container. Always eager to snack, I was about to ask if I might have a cookie when Vinnie signaled me to leave, thrusting my coat and mittens into my arms. Nodding agreeably, I sensibly stole away, a sense of relief overtaking me. As I walked home, I still thought it was better there than at my house.

I would think until I found

There were friendless Sundays. I skulked around the house in meaningless restraint, confined to loneliness. In the parlor, the protruding sill of the double-hung windows seemed to provide a superb refuge from solitude. Noting the random spiky splinters that protruded from the weather softened wood, I borrowed the flimsy cotton spread from my bed and efficiently folded it along the narrow ledge. The space now comfortably rigged, I clambered up and stretched out squeezing myself against the drafty windowpane. Beneath the window, the hissing radiator emanated its warmth making me snug in my haven.

With the first winter snowfall, the inside sheet of glass became frost covered. I lightly touched the window with my fingertips and pressed my warm mouth to it. The taste was musty. Ice crystals formed into refined designs of ferns and branching trees. As the heat rose from below to meet the cold air, clear spots spread in the glass, each shape splitting into smaller identical shapes admitting peepholes to the outdoors.

I watched an arcane yet familiar procession. The ragman moved by pulling an old cart filled with assorted rags and bits and pieces of clothing. His hoarse cries echoed through the streets. I could just hear what he was calling out, "Any old rags... rags!" The word "rags" was drawn out, "raaaaaaahhhgggssss," so that it unfurled in all directions, the sound trailing away at last to nothing. Darting in and out of shadowy doorways, scrawny feral cats pounced on scraps in the gutters and then cagily slunk out of sight. An occasional car moved slowly along spewing fumes, and the knife sharpener mournfully calling out his trade wheeled his buggy past secured windows.

Safe on my shelf, I stared out at my world of cement and poverty. The first snow had thawed on contact and turned to slush making inconstant streaky patterns crisscrossing the sidewalks and seeping into the road. In front of my house, a lone maple tree with its scaly, deeply wrinkled bark was bereft of its leafy mantle. The gnarled roots of the tree had thickened into enormous swells heaving up the sidewalk into jumbled blocks. An elderly woman cloaked in a cape wandered aimlessly in her bleak garden, tugging at weeds and brushing snow from hibernating bushes. As the early winter storm gathered speed, the snow hurtled faster eclipsing the raw, blotched ground and scattered, shriveled leaves. Glittery snowflakes gradually collected into small mounds of pure white fluff obliterating the starkness.

My father's voice invaded my secret retreat.

"Where are you hiding? You won't get away this time. I'll make you pay."

I shrank against the window. I could not recall what wrong I had committed or if I had overlooked to do what he had asked. Forlorn tears mingled with the melting frost. As the tiny droplets coursed down picking up others along the way, they formed a slow moving stream, collecting me and carrying me away, disappearing into the window sash.

The effect of comic books on the ideology of children

Eager for company, I hustled from my apartment and up the three flights of stairs to the home of my cousin Ronnie. Rat-a-tat... rat-a-tat on the door with my knuckles, an incessant rapping until Auntie Edith answered the door. She previewed me through circles of thick glass perched on the end of her needle-thin nose. Her prying eyes, one inwardly turned and jiggly, attempted to fathom what I was this time, an intrusive blur of noise or just a mad fool hopping wildly on one foot. Flicking her stubby fingers at me as if I were a bug that she intended to swat or a bothersome fleck of lint, she blocked the entry daring me to cross the threshold. I flashed an innocent smile. Parted from her sewing basket spilling over with socks and shirts needing mending, I was simply a disruption.

Auntie Edith had a stout frame. A gingham apron with a generous check pattern hid fleshy, sagging breasts, a bulky waist, and sulky potbelly. Her broad, serviceable hips were ideal ledges for her chubby, outspread fingers to rest when she was put to the test. Stumpy ankles stuffed into serviceable shoes supported tightly bunched lisle stockings and an unyielding nature. My aunt's appearance always called up the image of a bowl of lumpy porridge with a thickened crust. I was reassured that her current activity was sewing rather than sweeping because in the past she had chased me and tried to give me a sound wallop with the broom stick.

Squeezing by her, ducking to avoid a clap on the head, I called out, "Ronnie, Ronnie, where are you?"

Huffily, Auntie Edith said, "He's in his bedroom. He's being punished."

I always sensed danger at hand in her impatient temperament, hard words, and hardened heart. Ignoring her, I flew down the hall to Ronnie's bedroom where we had played many times. Still in his striped blue and white pajamas, Ronnie was sitting on the floor reading a *Captain Marvel* comic book and other comic books were scattered about. His face was puffy from crying. I looked past him to his bed. It was stripped of the comforter and the linen. The gray and white knobby mattress was made public and in its center was a huge wet stain that seemed to engulf most of the mattress. The twin bed belonging to his younger brother Marc was neatly made up, all the bedding tucked in.

Certain that the bed-wetting was the reason for his tears, I asked, "Did your dad beat you?"

"No! He never whips me." Ronnie's reply was adamant.

"Did your mom hit you with the broom?" I asked, remembering my unpleasant clash with my aunt at the door.

"No, no," he said, acting surprised. "She just told me that I'm in serious trouble and I probably have a mental problem. I tried to explain that it was an accident. She thinks I do it intentionally."

"Are you allowed out at all?"

"I have to stay in my room until the mattress dries."

"How sad… I wanted to play hide and seek."

"I'm probably going to be living in my room forever."

Just then Auntie Edith came in.

"Ronnie has no privileges today."

"Auntie Edith, can't I just stay and play with him?"

She postponed her promise to prolong Ronnie's discomfiture. At last she yielded.

"Okay, but don't make a mess."

Ronnie and I waited until his mother was safely down the hall, the distant clack of heels indicating she was in the front parlor.

"What do you want to do?" he asked.

"Let's play tents."

Ronnie was quite game. Two months younger than I, he was my favorite play cousin, high spirited and adventurous when his mother was not squelching or reprimanding him. We shared our few toys and he had scads of comic books to read including *Blackhawk, Green Lantern, Aquaman, Joe Palooka, Gangsters and Gun Molls, Plastic Man,* the new *Superboy,* and *Batman and Robin.* Today we brushed aside the comics and constructed a system of roadways and tunnels by bridging the twin beds and matching night stands under the removed bedding. After dimming the lights we crawled and groped our way through the passages like burrowing moles. At times we pretended we were in the pitch black underground chambers of the Orthodox Temple down the street or in an abandoned mine shaft. Ronnie began to get careless, bumping into me and following closely down the same narrow space, bringing the bedding down on us so that we were swaddled in sheets and blankets. He clambered over the top of me and then hid under his bed. Calling softly to him, he did not answer.

"Ronnie, where are you?'

After a pause, a barely audible voice whispered, "Under my bed."

I joined him and we lay side by side staring up at the jutting springs and coils holding back our laughter so Auntie Edith would not suddenly charge into the room accusatory and fuming. Ronnie untied the drawstring of his pajama bottoms and reached inside and pulled out his 'pee pee'. He grabbed my hand and put it on him. The sensation was that of a warm wrinkled worm and I gave it a little squeeze, which made him wince. I wondered if he had gotten this original idea from one of his comic books and it made me giggle aloud.

"Shudup," he said insecure with the unpleasant results of his enticing experiment and alarmed that the noise would bring in the disciplinarian. I crawled out from the hiding place, dust balls clinging to my hair and wetness sticking to my hand. I felt weird. We never played tents again.

The popular notion that sleepwalkers
never hurt themselves is far from true

The ritual of sleepwalking started again. I rambled around the house in the darkness moving ghostlike from room to room tripping over furniture, which jarred me to wakefulness. I made it as far as the front door only one time. Intercepted by my mother who was alerted by the rustling noises, I surfaced unscathed. Night terrors began to disrupt my sleep accompanied by aches and sharp twinges. One night the pain seemed real. It began somewhere around my mid tummy and snaked down toward my right leg. When I summoned my mother, she expressed genuine trepidation; her face showed her anxiety and her body began to tremble. By the time my father was fully roused, the stitch in my side was gone, as if a magician had conjured it away. Thinking that he would berate me, I neglected to confess that I was now pain free.

Sleep disturbed, my riled up father snarled, "This is probably another one of your more popular imaginary inventions."

Nevertheless, the die was cast. My mother was certain that I was ill and the gravity of the situation dictated a trip to the Montreal General Hospital.

On the way to the hospital in the taxicab, I cuddled next to my mother in the back of the *Packard* listening to the noisy static along with the dispatcher's voice that came from the cab's radio. "Pick up on Cavendish" sounded like "Pig done vanished," and I forced myself to stifle a laugh. The seat was cold and knobby and I began to wonder what I was doing riding along Côte Des-Neiges Road at this late hour and why I was not in my warm bed. I squashed my face into my mother's lap and felt the consoling touch of her hand but was unable to suspend the uneasiness.

From the emergency room we were directed to the consultation office of Dr. Fordham, the admitting surgeon. My father hastened ahead and I walked slowly dangling like a rag doll from my mother's coat sleeve. I was unprepared for the surgical specialist. He was a tall, heavyset man with eminent nose, bushy brows, and clear-flashing eyes. I guessed his age to be about sixty, but he moved around the room with the brisk efficiency of a younger man. Wearing an elegant but slightly frayed wool suit, he seemed tolerant and amiable. Only his eyes revealed his indifference. I quivered under his gaze feeling like a fly caught in a spider's web, the worst imaginable about to happen. Gesturing me to a cracked plastic straight chair, I sat down on the edge as he settled cozily into his leather swivel chair at his desk. He dutifully took stock of me. In an edgy and patronizing voice he asked, "Caasi, what brings you here?"

I stared into his shrewd eyes stanchly fixed on me and wavered in my answers suspecting he would perceive my inaccuracies and contradictions.

As Dr. Fordham's civility began to lag, he opened my medical chart and jotted brief notes in a tight scrawl that looked like squiggles to me from where I could peep at them upside down. Then he knitted his brow, drummed his fingers on the desktop, picked up his unlit pipe, sucked on it, put it down, and pivoted in his chair. He did not examine me; instead he came around from behind his desk, inclined his head and confidentially spoke in my mother's ear. From the faltering look on her face, I knew a serious decision had been made.

"The surgery is relatively simple and will be over in short course. Our doctors are the finest."

He said this explicitly for my benefit, but I did not wish to hear what he was conveying. My father, who normally asked all kinds of questions delving into details wanting to know the how and why and what, sat mute, an expression of doubt coupled with resignation on his face. Rigid in thought and motionless, my mother was beset by fear. I could hear my own breath in audible gasps, although neither the doctor nor my parents seemed to notice.

I lied, I made it all up, I'm fine, there's no pain. The words refused to come out…

I cried as I was undressed and put into an ill-fitting hospital garment tied slackly about my neck and waist. In short order, I was placed on a gurney overlaid with a thin sheet, and wheeled to the operating theater. Wringing her hands in nervous concern, my mother tried to soothe me.

"Don't send me away, please Mama"

"It'll be over soon." My mother used compassionate tones to reassure me.

"Please take me home, I'll be good."

As the anesthetist began the ether drip, my mother's grip on my arm slackened, her tears vaporized, and her white face faded away.

Several days after the operation, the report from the pathologist read, "Normal appendix".

A friend is he that loves, and he that is beloved

I was pampered for two weeks after my operation. The lavishness confirmed the success of the falsehood and my imagination went on holiday. Petted and tenderly cared for, I forgot the indignity and sin of my lying and grew to have an unqualified sureness in the necessity of the operation. Any momentary unrest quickly dissipated in this unforeseen but welcomed doting. Spoiled by luxury, the truth lay hidden in the containers of sugary confections and pleasurable rewards.

The doctor had advised my mother to encourage me to get out of bed when the surgical incision pain had lessened, but my relatives who came to visit counseled me to stay put. They sneaked a quick look at my scar, still red and angry looking, and made sympathetic, cajoling noises, and gave me presents of sweets and books. Kathy breezily popped by for a short stay bringing me one of her own jigsaw puzzles. We fitted the pieces together to make a jolly clown-like puppet wearing a party hat and springing out of a checkered box. With our heads close together bent over the puzzle, I sniffed the scented autumn wind in her hair, the piquancy of ruby ripened leaves. When Kathy said her goodbye, I was suddenly rankled by the observation that I had inadvertently barred myself from being outdoors.

My father ritually checked my temperature each evening, first dipping the thermometer into rubbing alcohol, wiping it dry, and then shaking it with a whip like motion to bring the temperature down below 98 degrees Fahrenheit.

"Caasi, open your mouth," he instructed.

He popped the cool glass rod under my tongue and I tightened my lips around it.

"Don't bite it," he cautioned, "the mercury inside is poisonous".

The thermometer tasted medicinal but I didn't mind the routine. My father sat at my bedside and read a daily installment from the newspaper, a quirky story about animals. He was nice to me, no scolding, and made me laugh until I complained that the cut on my belly hurt. I asked him to show me how to read the thermometer. As I gingerly rotated it, the line of mercury indefinably appeared and then went astray. I practiced repetitively until I was able to spot the marking where the narrow shaft of mercury ended.

"98.6," I yelled out with glee.

A glimmer of a smile came to light on my father's face, but like the mercury, it slid away and withdrew.

"Okay, enough for tonight, go to sleep," he said.

I heard an unimagined tenor of affection in his voice

My mother gave me a gift of an inflatable doll called a *Schmoo* made popular in the *Li'l Abner* comic strip. Bright pink in color with circular black and white eyes, it stood three feet tall on large flat clown feet. When I punched it, it keeled over and then puzzlingly righted itself. I was amused by this creature and put it into my bed at night. Its silly face was gentle and loving. I thought of it as a person rather than an 'it' and named him Oliver after the overly roly-poly movie character Oliver Hardy, finding both irresistibly funny and ludicrous. My deep attachment to Oliver absorbed and absolved me.

At the end of my convalescence while playing with Oliver, he ruptured and his air hissed out, shrinking him to shreds of pink rubber. Looking at the deflated remnants of Oliver lying on my bed, I knew I was decisively being punished for my deceit. My quaint, amicable friend was lost to me forever.

Dear Mother, is any time left to us

The blustery Montréal winter set in. A barrage of snow cascaded down; dense white curtains of uncountable snowflakes flitted fitfully. The wind whipped up a frenzy of drifts and mounds. Icicles resembling long spears and spiked witches' hats hung from the roof. At the front door, the delivered bottled milk froze and separated, the rich yellow cream rising out of the narrow neck into lid-capped columns. The howling of the wind at the windows and the creaking of the walls caused me to shudder. It was far too cold to play outdoors.

I joined my mother in the kitchen as she was preparing to make my favorite food, lokshen kugel. She was fussing with an elegant but unreliable contraption. Perched on curved legs with enameled green and ivory white doors, the stove's conduct was inscrutable making my mother peeved whenever she used the bake-oven. She placed a fresh supply of wood kindling in the stove's bottom section in an attempt to raise the temperature to the correct degree. It decided under the present circumstances to behave; the fire began burning fiercely, emanating warmth.

Enthralled, I sat at the kitchen table playing with small heaps of raisins, sugar, and cinnamon and watching as my mother skillfully peeled three apples, paring each in one lengthy strip to form a twisting red-green ribbon. Then she assembled sugar, softened butter, four eggs, orange juice, vanilla, cinnamon, cottage cheese, and sour cream and whisked the ingredients into a custard-like consistency. On the stovetop, a pot of water and broad egg noodles blithely boiled; a surge of steam magically lifted the cover. My mother retrieved a noodle and held it suspended on the tine of a fork. After blowing on the noodle, she offered it to me.

"What do you think, dear, is it mushy or just right?"

I genially nodded my head. My mother snatched the pot off the stove and poured the contents into a colander waiting in the sink.

"Mama, why are you rinsing the noodles in cold water?"

Her hands stalled as she considered what to say.

"So they don't soften further. It's better for the kugel if the noodles have a little firmness."

Pleased with the sharing of her culinary secrets, she never objected to my questions, explaining the vagaries of why she always sieved the baking soda and flour together, poked holes in a potato before baking, and held a matchstick between her lips when she diced onions.

My mother added the noodles, raisins, diced dried apricots and apples to the mixture, poured it into a *Pyrex* dish, sprinkled the top with sugar, and set it in the oven to bake for fifty-five minutes. It always seemed like an eternity until it was ready. I sat patiently at the table constructing a winding path with the blend of sugar and cinnamon. Filling it with golden raisins, I pretended I was Dorothy following the yellow brick road in the enchanted land of *The Wizard of Oz*.

I watched my mother scrupulously tidy up. Her dark brown hair was pinned neatly in a bun at the nape of her neck, and the heat from the stove put sunspots in her cheeks. As she moved past, she caressed my arm and gently smiled. Her hazel brown eyes were glistening with pleasure. She was happiest in the kitchen, a simple apron protecting her pale print dress, a comfortable focus and purpose supplanting the joylessness and despondency on other days. Familiar with her pots and pans, wooden spoons, ladles, pastry brushes, and cookie cutters, she radiated a glow of contentment. My father never bothered my mother while she baked. He stayed out of the kitchen reading the *Montreal Gazette* in the parlor. If only he would stay away forever.

"It's ready. You can have a piece while it's warm."

"Thank you, Mama. I love you."

One must have a mind of winter

Parc Mont Royal in the heart of the city was a favorite seasonal recreation area. In the winter the patchily forested mountain slope steep enough for skiing and tobogganing, was crowded with romping children. After an overnight snowfall, the ground was decked out in an unsullied, downy mantle of white but for a few weeds and slender stalks poking through. The sight of fresh snow prompted my father to arrange an outing for me and my cousins Marc, Ronnie, and Philip, and my friend Kathy. My mother insisted I dress for the frosty weather in a wooly sweater and flannel cuffed leggings topped by a cumbersome snowsuit. Knitted hat and scarf, mittens and boots, completed the insulation. I felt awkward in all the wadding but as soon as the first draft of frigid air hit my face, I was thankful for her attentiveness.

My father's route took us down Av Coloniale to Av Des Pins and then turned up Rue St. Urbain and over to Rue Marie Anne. Merrily, the group straggled along through the streets pushing one another into snow banks vying for the popular position behind the toboggan. The wooden slats braced by crosspieces clattered over the bits of coal scattered like black marbles on the icy sidewalks. My father, having smoothly waxed the bottom of the toboggan for swift gliding, scowled as the rough trek scratched his efforts.

As we reached Av Du Parc, the first glimpse of the mountain was always thrilling. It seemed huge. At the top of the run, the descent appeared to stretch for miles, a carpet of glistening white bordered by a rare fir, spruce, or pine. My father arranged the five of us according to size and weight, tightly lacing each of us in place with crisscrossed ropes that attached to the sled. He was unusually cautious retrieving lost mittens, tugging on boots, tethering and bundling arms and legs, and fastening the parts together like trussed chickens. I begged to be the lead person. Winking at me, he granted permission and Marc and I exchanged positions. He tied me in at the front, placing my hands on the curled ledge for balance.

Expectancy mounted to a fever pitch. We took off with one hefty push. Pale flakes of snow craftily whipped across my eyes driven by the gusting winds. My father controlled the direction and speed by shifting his weight and trailing his foot, a steering rudder at the rear. The ride was a series of roller coaster undulations picking up speed over the bumps, slowing in the troughs, and careening through bales of snow.

I held my breath the whole way down. Shivering with excitement, I let out a whoosh of delight. My face was cold, my cheeks a ruddy red, and snow bonded with wayward strands of hair turning them into miniature icicles.

"Please, Daddy, just one more ride?"

My cousins picked up the plea and began to chant.

"Just one more, just one more..."

My father seriously considered the request. He lined us up in marching formation, Philip, the tallest in the lead, and Marc in the rear. Calling out an army cadence, he paraded us up the hill. Our boots sunk into the deep snow and the wind churned around us lifting the lightest flakes into the air to rise and fall on the currents and eddies. Walking was difficult but I never whined. The prospect of a repeat exhilarating turn downhill caused me to ignore my frozen fingers and my snow-crusted eyelashes.

At the crest my father reiterated his sensible warnings.

"Hold on to the rope, keep your boots tucked in, and don't let your scarves trail."

All the kids faithfully did what he asked. No one dared to anger or defy him. They enjoyed the excursion and he did not seem to mind. On the way home, I hitched a ride on the toboggan. I could hear the crunch of the packed snow under my father's heels as he laboriously pulled the cargo. I watched his back straining with the effort. He seemed so confident.

What price bananas?

My father had erect military posture and a long stride for a slightly built short man. He walked as if dogs were at his heels. When I was a baby, he would lift me unto his shoulders carrying me wherever he had to go on foot. Now it was tiring to keep his pace, and I had to run to stay with him. If I tried to lock my hand in his, he shrugged off the close hold and increased his speed often leaving me trailing sluggishly in his wake as if I were a ship unmoored and set adrift. As we neared Sunday market on Rue Rachel, I was soon lost in the crowds among the stalls.

The market was always mobbed. It was the best place to buy fresh and the shoppers jostled one another in their frenzy to get the sought after bargains. I had to avoid being trampled by a belligerent butcher carrying a huge side of a cow preparing to carve it up into steaks and roasts. A Hassidic Jew in black hat and side curls angrily denounced the price of a dozen bagels. The noise level was clamorous, voices screeching above other voices. I covered my ears to subdue the volume.

Many local farmers brought their produce to sell; the hanging scale pans registered the accurate weight of each head of lettuce or sun-ripened tomato so the price could be gauged and bargained. Vendors exhibited their catch of pike, haddock, carp, cod, and mackerel on beds of ice, a fascinating array of fish. Their silver scaled bodies and fins still quivered as bulging eyes blankly stared and mouths gaped. The chicken breeders killed and koshered the fowl in the open market. The air was a secular mix of fresh baked goods and fermentation, chicken entrails and pickled cucumbers, salty herrings and cinnamon sticks. In the cold numbing winter, the smells were curiously friendly; in summer, the heat called forth rancidity.

I found my father tirelessly sorting through a hillock of fruit handling each as if it were a priceless gem until he collected a dozen assorted ones. In the sack were six navel and six blood oranges, the ones with crimson colored flesh.

"These oranges are newly picked, boxed, and shipped here," explained my father.

"Is this good?" I held up a spherical tangerine for him to check.

He competently rotated it in his palm.

"Not bad. You see…it's all about the casing. You have to feel for the thinnest, flattest non-leathery skin."

I believed him because he made the best orange juice, never acidy, squeezing out half-cut navel oranges with the presser-bar until all the pulp was extracted and then putting it through a mesh strainer.

We passed to the next booth and he decided on flawlessly shaped Macintosh red apples, a very fine dessert apple for early winter use. He noticed some bananas imported from a tropical island, a rarity at the market, and asked the vendor their cost. After some haggling, he bought three and continued with the remainder of his shopping.

My father carried home two bags of selected fruits and vegetables. Obediently, I followed him with a prized salt pretzel in my hand picking my way through the liquefying snow, avoiding slippery sidewalk ice. The street people and shop windows bustled by as I scurried along trying to lengthen my gait to match his. In the shadowed corner of a building, I glimpsed a crumbling feeble old man urinating into the street. I tried not to look and cast my eyes down but not before I witnessed his unzipped trousers. Inquisitive, my head turned ever so slightly as I dawdled, a subtle motion that proved to be my undoing. Every sense stirring, my wholly observant father took in the scene; his single glance blazed with rage and scorn. In two paces he reversed direction and with a lurching, sinister twist wrenched my arm. The pretzel and my wanton curiosity perished in a puddle of slush.

A cold coming we had of it,

On a bitter frosty Sunday afternoon late in February, I was fidgety from hours confined indoors. The pleasing ring of the telephone halted my reclusive roaming about the house and the voice of my friend Vinnie was a cheerful intrusion.

"Hello, Caasi, what are you doing?"

"Not much of anything," I lamented.

"I'm bored," Vinnie replied.

"Vinnie," I asked in a low voice, "is Roland's head stuck in his books? If so, can you get away… maybe to go skating with me on the rink in Parc Jeanne-Mance?"

"I'm not certain," she answered charily. Then with more assurance, "I'll try."

Like conspirators, we planned our escape exacting a pledge from one another to meet for some fun. She was seldom able to dodge the ever-watchful eye of her brother and impossible for me to escape my father's tether, but he had left earlier without explanation and had not yet returned. My mother was sitting at the kitchen table, her face serene and thoughtful, wrapped up in writing a letter to her younger sister in Boston. As I sneaked by, she reached out to detain me holding my arm for a moment with placid tender composure. Releasing the soft grip, she turned her concentration to the sheet of paper.

Without glancing in my direction, she said, "It's very cold, dress sensibly for once."

How did she know I was going out, I wondered? No matter, she wasn't objecting.

"I will, Mama," I assured her eagerly.

She looked up at me for a moment; the easy compliance she heard in my voice baffled her. I smiled reassuringly and fled to the bedroom to change into a skating outfit. Once before when watching at the rink, I secretly coveted the stylish look of a young girl about my age. Gliding across the ice in a costume of fur-collared jacket, velvet vest, short filmy skirt, and sequined pink tights, her thin shapely legs stretched

83

into white figure skates. She gracefully twirled and did spins, a sylph unfettered by gravity. I was desperate to copy her. Ignoring the padded snowsuit that would have protected me from the cold, I layered a generous moth- eaten vermillion colored mohair sweater over a pink pajama top and thin flannel leggings, tied my mother's woolly muffler around my neck and pinned a pair of formless mittens to my sleeve. Shuffling through my father's dresser drawer, I discovered a pair of his shrunken green army socks which somewhat fit by bunching the ends around my toes before forcing my feet into my boots. The preposterous attire, exempt de bon sens, was a profusion of vanity and envy; it duped me into believing I looked elegant and slender.

As I hurried the ten-block walk from my house to the corner of Av De L'Esplanade and Rue Marie Anne, the selfish afternoon sun hid behind dark clouds and the wind blustered without pause. The starkness of the landscape reflected winter's bleakness. The skates hung over my shoulder tied together by knotted shredded laces. Remains of snow crunched under my heels as I stomped over coarse and uneven parts; I slipped and lost my balance on a slick of black ice, the steel edges of the blades roughly slapped my face already raw from the cold. My clothes were truly spare for the brunt of Montréal's atrocious winter.

At long last I reached Parc Jeanne-Mance. A rickety fence enclosed the park's skating rink, and an old wooden shack riskily leaned against the boards. The hut was plain and dilapidated but an acceptable sight. Impetuous blade marks scarred the plank steps leading to the weathered door, crisscrossed gouges in the random formation of fallen pick-up-sticks. I stumbled up the steps hoping to find the place warm and dry, but to my dismay, the windows were frosted, and the log burning stove gave off little heat as no one had bothered to add wood or stoke the fire. Deep grooves splintered the floor, and the place had a curious smell reminding me of the inside of an icebox when the milk sours.

After thawing my fingers, I sat on the unstable wooden bench prudently lacing the skates, an old pair of hockey skates in bad condition, hand-me-downs from my cousin Philip. The cracks and creases in the boot leather resembled the furrowed lines in the faces of the old men praying in synagogue. When I tried to stand, my ankles wobbled dangerously in skates too big for my feet. For support, I held onto the bench until I daringly stepped around the hut. My breath came out in short puffs, wisps of fear floating and drifting around the room rising and falling with the wind blasts that penetrated the wall crevices. As I waited patiently for Vinnie, the sun dipped lower in the sky and dusk dawdled around the edges; the cold inside became pervasive.

I needed to move about to keep from freezing. Carving new gouges of my own, I walked in my skates down the fissured steps. Unsteady and timorous, I tightened my grip on the banister. Knowing Vinnie would look to find me out on the ice when she arrived, I ventured there. The rink was a minefield of ruts and bumps, the ice having frozen and thawed in the drawn out winter months before the approach of spring. Bashful at first, I skated around the perimeter shunning the faster skaters. The vision of the dainty ice-skater gliding and jumping propelled me to the center of the rink. Wavering, I balanced on one blade and tried to stroke smoothly into a slow pirouette. It was impossibly difficult and I returned to faltering on both skates inching my way forward or back, crudely inept. Several French speaking boys old enough to be in high school were playing hockey. I steered clear of their corner of the rink. A puck spun out of control striking the fence and careened into a snow bank adjacent to where I stood rocky on my skates. The impact of the puck sprayed me with a cover of snow. I hoped to be unseen but the boys spotted me and lined up linking arms forming a human chain. I could overhear fragments of what they were saying, laughing and ridiculing me.

"Une jeune fille, grosse et stupide."

"Elle sait a peine patiner."

They realized I could barely skate and sensed my fear and isolation. They started a chant.

"Une bébé, pauvre enfant."

"Une bébé, toute seule."

"Laisse-moi tranquille!" I pleaded, hoping to get them to leave me alone.

They skated once around the rink shrieking with merriment, a line of attackers just missing me as they swooped by weaving and skimming. Picking up speed, they raced faster and faster. The scrape of blades cutting and slicing was frightful. I heard the assaulting noise as they knocked me to the ice flat on my chest. My air burst out in an explosive hiss like a punctured balloon, and then I was suffocating, unable to breathe, and frantic. Torn in the fall, the edges of the holes in my leggings covering my knees were stippled with blood. The boys completed the turn and skated back to finish the trouncing. In desperation, I rolled over out of reach of their slashing edges of steel. Sprawled out full length on my back, the hard cold ice was an unjust and fateful finale.

Shuttles of trains going north, going south, drawing threads of blue,

Employed as a brakeman by the Canadian National Railway in Turcot Yard, Montréal, my father was in charge of coupling and uncoupling rolling freight cars from the engine as they were routed unto different tracks. The wooden boxcars weighed up to fifty tons, crammed to capacity with cargoes like coal, timber, construction materials and chemicals. In the closeted space between the cars, my father applied the necessary pressure to engage the lever of the brake-apparatus to retard the motion of the wheels. His duties also included the proper setting of the couplings between cars and watching for signs of overheated axles as he guided the trains from one track to another in switching operations. The work shifts were protracted and the tasks were perilous; sometimes he labored eighteen hours at a stretch. He took pride in his job and often regaled me with descriptions of the hazards he faced.

"It's worse in winter," he explained. "The brake-gear is iced over. As the car grinds to a halt, the possibility of slipping is ever present. It requires skill, strength and balance. Cold numbs your hands and you can be temporarily blinded by smoke and sparks issuing from the wheels."

I listened to him in awe, a mix of admiration and fear riveting me.

"And you never want to drop your leather gloves. The icy steel can rip off your bare skin," he concluded with a flourish.

Though he was a merited employee, my father was dismissed from his job without warning or negotiations. As the cost of labor was the largest itemized expense, the CN was reducing the work force in an effort to meet union demands for a wage hike. Faced with the threat of a nationwide railway strike, the first ever in Canada, the Liberal government enforced the cutbacks.

"Do you know what Prime Minister Monsieur St. Laurent said?"

My father's voice was scathing and caustic as he directed this question to my mother.

"The CN would never be any good unless it was shaken up."

"So you're part of the shake-up," said my mother, her tone soft with sympathy, her demeanor pliant.

"Why the hell didn't they fire some of the drunken switchmen or immigrant section men? A worthless, unskilled scum will probably replace me in this dangerous post. But he can be paid a few cents less per hour."

My father's anger and indignation were insidious. He resentfully moped about the house aware that his career with the CN had ended. Unpredictably idle, he became sullen and aloof; his perpetually glum face altered to an obstinate scowl.

I felt sorry for him and offered to call his boss to plead his case. He laughed cynically.

"It won't do any good. The damn fools who run the CN need to learn their lesson. After a few recruits trip up and get caught between cars in the dark, they will beg me to come back."

Not fully grasping the futility of his situation, I persisted in my desire to help. Nervously I dialed the telephone in the kitchen hoping the operator could assist me in locating the number of the railway yard office.

"Please connect me with the foreman… the man who is the boss at Turcot," I implored.

"Quel numero voulez-vous?"

The operator was unable to make sense of my request. I gave her a rambling explanation regarding my father's jobless plight. Annoyingly she asked in French, "Qu'est-ce toi veulent-il?" not understanding my words.

In my gullibility, I was crushed by my inability to get my father rehired.

"The operator keeps asking me, what is it you want? It's not possible to reach the head man to tell him to take Daddy back," I wailed.

My mother soothed me.

"Don't fret," she said. "It's all for the best. You'll understand when you get older."

She lavished me with gentleness and affection, and in these sweet moments she seemed her true self. Somehow I identified how dearly her proficient reserve must cost.

His Mind was so elevated
into a flattered Conceit of himself

Weeks elapsed and my father was not required to return to work; he rarely mentioned his previous employment. Instead he began to search the 'help-wanted' columns in the *Montreal Star* and *Gazette,* scattering the papers informally over the coffee table in the parlor. *Lucky Strike* cigarette butts mounted up in the ashtrays, and a perpetual smoky haze wafted from room to room. After scanning ads and placing unproductive telephone calls leaving messages that went unreturned, my father gave up the search and busied himself with something he enjoyed, repairing watches, setting diamonds, and fabricating rings. With this new preoccupation, he seemed more relaxed and less given to moody outbursts, so I believed.

"Daddy, how did you learn to fix a broken watch? I asked.

"It's a funny story," he said.

"Tell it to me."

"When I was your age, I took apart my father's pocket watch to see how it ticked. Then I couldn't put it back together again. Your grandmother Ada was irate. You know how she almost never gets mad. That day she was really mad. Not that I blame her. The watch was a valued keepsake of your grandfather Isaac. After that I decided to learn how to repair watches and other pieces."

My father now turned to his work in earnest. His skills provided a small additional income. Set free from his responsibility to the CN, this arrangement at home was to his liking. He cultivated a loyal group of clients who arrived on a daily basis at our house with their valuables to be repaired. Protracted hours of finicky delicate work involving fixing a tiny gold clasp on a cultured pearl necklace or restoring an heirloom gratified him. He had infinite patience with these fragile objects and treated them lovingly. Adhering to a pedantic routine, he spread a white linen cover on the enamel top of the kitchen table, smoothed out the wrinkles, and then fastidiously laid out his jeweler tools. The variety was captivating: pliers, camel hair brushes, two pairs of tweezers and a magnifier, a gas burner for soldering, tubes of glue, diamond files, watch bands, fine silver wire, tin metal boxes, and small squares of paper tissue. Focused in his efforts, he resisted any disturbance. I tried to peer over his shoulder to watch him, but his response was swift and noxious.

"Scram! You'll knock my arm. I'll misplace the diamond I'm setting in Mrs. Finklebaum's brooch."

"Can't I just play with the little finger ring sizer?" I asked.

"Go amuse yourself elsewhere!"

"But I like to watch you work," was my final entreaty.

Now distracted, he turned to glare at me and raised a threatening arm. I recoiled from the intimidation and fled to find my mother knitting in the parlor. Flinging myself in her arms, overturning her basket of skeins of wool, I burst into tears. I cried non-stop telling her about his brusqueness without perceiving the reason for it. She listened in silence patting my head and drying my tears with the corner of her apron. Her gentle touch quieted me and lightened the disappointment of the moment.

Mrs. Finklebaum arrived with pretentious airs, gaudily dressed, an affected woman sufficiently rotund to show no angularity of outline. Thinking her a strange character, I followed her into the kitchen. She filled the offered chair, her loose fat soft flesh uncontained at the edges. She had the conceit of a fool and the complacent smile of a clown. All the while keeping one eye on my father, she managed to sit winking at me. Her chubby hands gestured frivolously as she asked my father's advice on trifling worries. Playing upon his vanity, her flattery and wheedling penetrated my father's thoroughly unsociable guise. If he merely winced, she paused to discreetly pull down her skirt that seemed to hike above her dimpled knees by its own volition.

"Oy veh," she groaned, as if this were a catastrophe and readjusted her ample bottom on the chair. With a capable eye, she appraised the ornamental diamond centered pendant surrounded by an inset of pearls exquisitely presented on blue velvet. She plied him with honeyed words.

"Such fine work... Mr. Lichman, you're a genius."

Savoring her compliments, he showed her the August birthstone ring he had made for me.

"It's a peridot, pretty nice, eh," he boasted, "set in 22 karat gold. It resembles an emerald and sometimes is mistaken for one."

"But she's far too young for a ring of this quality," said Mrs. Finklebaum, making the little clucking noise with her tongue, "Tsk- tsk".

My father handed me the gold ring.

"You are a good-natured man," concluded Mrs. Finklebaum with a sigh. She made a lame attempt to rise from the chair and had to rely on my father's help to make it to her feet.

"Many thanks...and I'll pay next time."

Although I suspected my father was showing off for his client, the fact he had given me the ring was what counted most, and I polished the transparent lime green gemstone with a soft duster until the facets radiated sparks of light. Observantly I revered it dreading the horror of its loss and having to deal with his wrath.

And yet my father sits and reads in silence,

Showing no outward signs of relief, my mother was secretly unburdened about my father being fired from the brakeman job. She was only too aware of the constant dangers related to this occupation. An unfortunate incident involving a CN excursion train that failed to take the siding and collided with a transcontinental standing on the main line made her concern credible. Several of my father's co-workers were severely injured by fire breaking out in two gas-lit wooden cars. Many passengers perished in the flames. New worry hinging on how my father would support us in the future displaced the transient respite of knowing he was safe at home. Indifferent clients were slow or negligent in paying for his work and money was in short supply.

Our meals became simpler with inexpensive lunch menus of deviled eggs or sardine sandwiches, vegetable soup, and fruit or *Jell-O* for dessert. Dinners were often spaghetti and meat balls with tossed salad of shredded cabbage or marinated tomatoes and cucumbers and crackers with spreading cheese and olives. Rarely did we have my mother's delectable baked chicken or pot roast with corn bread squares and buttered rice with freshly steamed peas and green beans. I longed for my mother's delightful pastries: her apricot rolls filled with nuts and raisins, almond crescents, and rugelach, little twisted pastries with chocolate chips. To placate me, using just one egg along with sugar, baking powder, *Crisco*, vanilla, and flour, she baked cut-out cookies in the shape of gingerbread men decorating them with red, green, and white jelly beans. In her valiant efforts to instill moments of sweet pleasure and hope into the dark uncertainty of the days, she covered up her sense of defeat.

Early one morning my mother looked markedly confident. I noticed the care with which she brushed her dark hair, fixed it firmly with a rhinestone comb, and set her russet tam at a jaunty angle. Without a word, she left the house neatly dressed in her faded *Harris Tweed* coat adorned with a delicate blue scarf and her worn leather purse secure in her grip. Several hours later she returned and had an animated discussion with my father explaining that she had spotted a tiny vacant shop for rent at a reasonable fee on Blvd. St. Laurent near Rue Marie Anne.

"You have to settle into something permanent and stable," she told my father simply.

"Something will turn up," he replied gruffly.

"We are running out of money. How will we live? Even before the loss of your CN job, money was scarce. Now the situation is dire. Please try."

I overheard my parents talking, their voices conciliatory then shrilly rising as the exchanged words grew bitter. After the initial tirade, smoothed by my mother's eloquence, she successfully influenced my father to consider leasing the shop to open his own business, a small jewelry store.

For my father, the concept of starting a new enterprise and having to contend with rent, inventory, and sales was unappealing. Grudgingly he agreed after she vowed to deal with the customers, to keep the shop in order and allow him to focus only on repairs and wholesale purchases for retail sale. He canvassed all of his contacts in the trade and obtained merchandise on margin, guaranteed only by the promise of profits to the risk-takers and his good word. My father was an honest man.

On the weekend, my mother permitted me to visit. Two display windows flanked the entry from the sidewalk and a simple sign above the door bore the words: *Watches, Fine Jewelry and Repairs.* Rings jeweled with precious and semi-precious stones, watches in white and yellow gold, and diamonds of faultless quality rested on little satin pillows arranged to attract passing shoppers. There was a myriad of items including silver-plated place settings in wooden boxes lined with red felt, heart shaped lockets, charm bracelets, lustrous pearl necklaces, *Bulova* clocks, earrings, money clips, and hatpins. The sparkling pieces promised success. My mother had worked industriously to make the place brightly attractive and conducive to buying; the shop gleamed and the countertops were spotless. Her gentle mien and patience were apparent, and she was gracious to the clientele and pleasant even as they fiercely bargained to reduce the price of an object.

The door chimed when I entered the store causing my mother to eagerly glance up. There was never a bustle of crowds or lively activity like in the markets; just a few purchasers were there, sales were limited and profits paltry. My father's commitment waned rapidly. He distanced himself by reading the *Montreal Star* and *Gazette* in stony silence and then disappeared for hours offering no explanation. Delaying repairs to the items left in his care and his quick temper were noticed and reproved. He hated the obligation of being somewhere he had to be and committed the store to failure before the first month had passed. Gradually sorrow and tears replaced the expectant spark in my mother's eyes; a reflection on what was done and left undone.

I continued to visit simply to keep her company and play make-believe salesgirl while my mother pretended that the shop was profitable. My father was forced to sell the goods to satisfy the creditors and the stock of merchandise shrank as the nightly arguments between my mother and father intensified.

My father continually griped.

"I never had a knack for dealing and I hate the routine of accountancy and commerce," he protested at the close of each day.

"I understand," said my mother in disheartenment, "but we are hanging over a gulf of debt."

"The shop was your faulty initiative," he answered reproachfully. "I never should have agreed."

"Maybe if you didn't take off to play poker in the afternoon..."

My mother never finished her sentence. Her words were cut short by a loud thud, a sound similar to that produced by a blow.

My father conclusively declared bankruptcy and their fighting ceased. A dispirited mood displaced the optimism and the musical door chimes rang a melancholic tune. Dust gathered on the showcases and the few remaining boxes of jewelry. Poverty returned, linked to the family like the tarnished silver-plated chains.

Then, the sudden call for her

On occasion when I passed Sandra's house a few doors down from my own as I moseyed along toward Rue Roy, her big redheaded father invited me in to keep his daughter company. Dressed in a workman's shirt and checkered overalls, an old suede jacket, and half-laced boots, he appeared imposingly hefty. He was always going or coming, a carpenter toolbox in his hand. He held the door open for me and gave me a brief nod and a flippant grin as I slipped by. His booming Irish voice followed me.

"Yrr a gud kid, Sandra likes you."

Sandra was a tub of a girl having inherited her father's girth. Her coppery colored hair was styled in a short bob, and her curtly trimmed forehead bangs and flat face made her decidedly plain. She attended a privileged Christian school and was old enough to have sweat stains on her blouse underarms. The cap sleeves were cut from the same exquisite fabrics she wore to disguise her blossoming hips. Organza skirts of egg-shell blue or pink and green polka dots flared out from her portly waist. Firmly grounded in her clunky patent leather shoes, her officious bulk entitled her to be conceited. She spoke hardly at all, and when she did her conduct was cheeky or sullen. During the time frittered away in her home, I followed her around, favored by the opportunity to visit yet uneasy in her presence.

Lacking nothing, Sandra's house was decorated in flamboyant excess. Three chirping canaries swung on perches in an ornate white birdcage in the drawing room. Twin *Chesterfield* sofas upholstered in cockatoo patterned chintz with a plume of yellow feathers and matching cushions completed the illusion of a sunny aviary. The adjoining dining room had a sideboard of solid maple shelves garnished with flowery cups and saucers, china plates, and wineglasses in a peacock blue color.

Sandra's mother, Molly, cut me off as I started up the stairs. Wiping her hands on her apron and examining me with a critical gaze, she seemed targeted on not letting me pass. Her birdseed-like eyes were tiny brown and flitting about skittishly. Dark smudges took shelter under her eyes. Hair sprouted from her head in tufts of different lengths with bald patches in between. The longer hairs were tucked behind her ears disclosing in profile a beaked nose, sunken cheeks, and a skinny neck. Ever in the kitchen preparing sumptuous feasts for the family, she was painfully thin, looking as if she never ate a scrap of food. Under her immaculate bib apron was a housedress of nondescript fabric and color, a startling contrast to the ornamental parlor. Meekly taciturn with her daughter, she did not hesitate to order me about taking delight in the pronounced and immediate effect it had on me.

"Don't overstay," she forewarned, "Sandra has homework to do and dinner is at five."

I could smell the sumptuous odors of a stewed dish of mutton, potatoes, and onions escaping from the kitchen, and my mouth watered and hunger pangs twisted my stomach into knots. I was never asked to stay to dinner nor did Sandra ever share her treats.

"I'll go home whenever you tell me to," I agreed.

She gave me a buck-toothed half smile and limped back to her cooking mumbling something about her rheumatism and maddening neighborhood children.

Sandra had her very own room with a canopy bed, a coral and white striped feathery silk comforter, and a closet crammed with toys and pretty clothes. A door from the bedroom led to a protected balcony where she kept a collection of dolls and a splendid doll house. It was a two-story Victorian cottage with pink siding, a shake roof, lace curtained windows, painted green flowerboxes, a porch, and a hinged front door ornamented in pink and green stars. I did not believe there was another equal to Sandra's little doll house. The exactitude of the miniature tables, chairs, sofas, armoires, rugs, and chandeliers was staggering. Flower vases, picture books, clocks, and prints beautified each of the rooms.

We went out on the balcony to play handling the breakable items with care. Sandra quickly tired of this pastime and left me alone. The profusion of dolls was irresistible: dolls clothed like infants, dolls with rolling eyes and lashed lids that opened and closed, and a doll resplendent in a ball gown having an evening doll's face and wig of real yellow hair. There was a boy doll dressed in a sailor suit similar to that of a seaman with a satin-collared blouse, a black bow, flared white pants, a braided jacket, and a spry velvet hat. I lost myself in playacting. With proper etiquette, the dolls and I attended social occasions. I spoke to them in hushed tones meant only for their ears, and in turn they spoke to me in voices not unlike my own. The pretense was focused and intense with picturesque imagery and cordial give-and-take. The sailor doll was the good father, the fancy doll was the beautiful mother, and I was the loved baby. It was a utopian world for me and I experienced a sinful joy.

Bored and fancying my friendship again, Sandra claimed me calling my name twice. I reluctantly left my doll life; the magic departed and the dolls were now lifeless and lackluster. As I replaced the small scale playthings, the outside balcony became noticeably smelly and swarmed with flies from the decomposing garbage in the alley below.

In the center of Sandra's room, a genuine swing seat made of redwood was attached by ropes to ceiling hooks. Her father had crafted it for her birthday using a carpenter's plane to remove chips of wood and to create a decorative motif. Then he worked with a sanding block to smooth the surface area and make it splinter free. Sandra had bragged to me how her father had fashioned the swing and how much effort he had put into the task. She was now entertaining herself by twisting the two ropes round and round until they were tightly coiled and then promptly letting go so that the seat spun turbulently. When it steadied, I asked permission to sit on the swing and Sandra pushed me. I gently sashayed to and fro like a chintz curtain in the breeze at an open window. Sandra caressed my hair. Then her pudgy hand slipped down the front of my jumper sneaking past the elastic waistband of my panties. She continued a gentle motion of the swing as her five plump fingers pretended to play piano between my legs. Impertinently fondling me, she became more insistent and confident. I felt strange and jumpy, but was reluctant to stop swinging. I needed the family of dolls.

The reproch of pride and cruelnesse

I sensed that it was going to be a good day when I woke to the sound of my mother's musical voice. It traveled to my ears softened by distance; the words and timbre pared to a silvery toned murmur. Busy in the pleasure of baking and the prospect of company in the evening, my mother was singing in the kitchen. These occasions were a precious rarity.

There will be blue birds over... The white cliffs of Dover... Tomorrow, just you wait and see...[*]

I could almost see the blue birds with a flash of sky on their backs promising spectacular secret things. Laughter dallied in the air and I joined the frivolity by spinning around the bedroom like a top until I became dizzy and flopped back on the coverlet. It was Saturday, a no school day, a chance to spend time with my mother. I hugged my pillows luxuriating on the bed and examined the fissures and chinks in the plastered ceiling. The light streamed in through the cracked window making distinct textured patterns beneath which I lay in cozy comfort. I surveyed the room with its tall oak dresser and long beveled mirror on the side slightly fogged. Two small drawers adjoined the mirror and below the vanity in the dresser base were long drawers with brass pulls. My parents' bed used most of the space with two night stands appended to the scroll designed headboard. A straight-backed, fine grained wooden chair was loaded with coloring books, a box of building logs, paper dolls dressed in their modish outfits, a little leather pouch filled with marbles, and a jumble of richly colored wooden pick-up sticks.

A whiff of cinnamon and yeast drifted into the bedroom. So delectable, it had the power to irresistibly draw me to the kitchen. All my play toys were obliged to now wait.

I bounded down the hallway wearing only one slipper and kicking

---

[*] *There'll be Blue Birds over the White Cliffs of Dover*
Melody by Walter Kent, Lyrics by Nat Burton, Published 1941

the other one along. To save the time it might take to unfasten buttons, I somehow managed to pull my seersucker blouse over my head. Awkwardly hopping, I tussled with my underwear and thin blue and white striped bloomer shorts. Bypassing the bathroom, I was aware that I was supposed to first brush my teeth, wash my face, and comb my hair; I was in too much of a hurry to stop. *Later... later*, I said to myself.

"I see you," my mother said, not taking her eyes off the kneading board, the heel and palm of one hand working in concert with the drawing out, folding over, and pressing of the other hand. The dough was being shaped and reshaped. It was hard work and my mother's face was rosy-cheeked from the effort. On the kitchen table were ingredients for the pastries: flour, packets of yeast, cream cheese, butter, sugar, finely chopped pecans, raisins, ground cinnamon, and a jar of apricot jam.

"Don't you touch," she cautioned.

"Eh, what's up doc?" I said insouciantly.

"Where did you pick that up?"

"Cousin Philip heard it in a *Bugs Bunny* cartoon. He told me it can be used to say hello and to find out what's going on," I mumbled, hungrily inspecting the assembled appetizing ingredients.

My mother laughed.

"Okay my silly girl, I'm baking cheese and apricot pastries and your favorite cinnamon and raisin swirls."

"Are any ready yet?"

"No," not yet. It takes half the day. At the outset, I make this light dough with flour, water, salt, and yeast. Later, when the dough begins to rise, I mix in the cinnamon, raisins and sugar..."

I interrupted. "I want the first one."

"On three conditions: Get cleaned up, tidy the bedroom and tonight you and Shira must play together nicely."

My jauntiness fled replaced by instant gloom. I remembered it was my mother's turn to host the family Saturday night poker game, which alternated among the homes of various aunts and uncles. My Aunt Malka and Uncle Chaim were bringing along my cousin Shira so we could amuse one another. This news cast an evil spell that robbed the day of its luster. I did not even remotely care for her. My dislike for the plain, chunky, monster bordered on hatred.

Shira was three years older than I and robustly built with short sturdy fingers. Her face was spiritless with translucent skin showing tiny red-violet veins. This oddity was part of a deceptive ruse that suckered the parents and relatives into always referring to Shira as that sweet insecure child. Nothing was farther from the truth; she was in reality tough and feisty. She had quizzical darting eyes, high cheekbones, and a wide nose with flared nostrils and churlish lips. Thick brittle hair, frizzy and kinky, was tamed into curls by hours of brushing. Dressed in frilly sheer fabrics with satin ruffles or finely shirred lace, she towered menacingly over me in her elegant finery. Adept at deluding, she was never marred by a scraped knee or a dirt streaked arm to suggest any defects. An aura of cool disdain kept her remote and inaccessible. In play, she refused all suggestions. It was too cold for a walk, building card houses was stupid, marbles were for boys and, of course, the candy store was off limits because, as she delighted in saying, "My parents don't allow me to eat candy." Shira was also brainy, which made her nasty and critical, and worse for me she delighted in torture, something I never told my mother.

Obedient to my mother's requests, I splashed water on my face, brushed my teeth, ran my fingers through my tangled hair, and finished dressing. Later, I would have no choice but to put on something showier than the tousled attire I was wearing. Poking around in the stored cleaning supplies, I found the broom, some absorbent cloths, and a bottle of lemon oil for polishing. I began to spruce up the room. I sorted and organized my toys, dusted the bureau, dresser and headboard, and even went so far as to wipe all the furniture with lemon oil to bring back its sheen. I swept the floor, shook the little scatter rug out the window into the back yard to free it of flecks of fiber, and sensibly made my bed, fluffing the pillows and folding the top sheet over the pretty quilted bedspread. One pick-up stick fell to the floor but other than that minor oversight, I made the bedroom quite presentable. I hastened to join my mother in the kitchen where I could leisurely earn my reward of her company and baking. The anticipated gladness seemed to require hard work.

The tune accompanying my mother's activities changed.

I'll be seeing you...In all the old familiar places... That this heart of mine embraces...All day through... [*] I believed it to be her favorite song, yet her voice was tinged with sadness. She seemed to lose herself in a daydream of an impending storm, and her eyes dampened with unshed tears and her hands began to tremble. Hesitating briefly, concealing her disarray, calm was restored as she reached the final phrase, *I'll be looking at the moon...but I'll be seeing you...* [*]

Uneasy with the silence, I watched her baking progress, my mouth watering with delight. I had to make do with a glass of orange juice and a bowl of *Cheerios* topped with a sliced banana. While eating my breakfast, I read the ad on the *Cheerios* box. For two mailed in box tops I could get the 'Moon Rocket Kit'.

"Mama, can I send for the reward?"

"It's, may I, please? And the answer is no."

"But I want the rocket."

"No, my dear, it's just a piece of junky plastic."

My mother wiped her floured hands on her apron and scooped up some raisins from the little knoll on the table plopping them into my cereal.

"This will make up for it."

I stopped pestering so that I could hang around in the kitchen watching the process and helping her or possibly hindering her. She never demurred.

In the early evening, the invited aunts and uncles arrived: Uncle Saul and Aunt Rosie, Uncle Morris and Aunt Bertha, and Uncle Chaim and Aunt Malka. Hugs and kisses were exchanged at the door as coats and hats and scarves were doffed.

"Caasi, say hello to Shira," my mother urged.

"Shira, say hello to your cousin," Aunt Malka prodded.

We avoided greeting each other despite the goading of my mother and Aunt Malka.

---

[*] *I'll Be Seeing You*
Music by Sammy Fain, Lyrics by Irving Kahal, Published 1938

"Emma, don't mind Shira's behavior. She's shy," said Aunt Malka with noticeable pride.

Shira hid behind her mother and stuck her tongue out at me.

The adults went into the parlor where the card table was set up just to the side of the coffee table on which stemmed candy bowls replete with handmade fudge, mixed nuts, and assorted licorice were arranged. Pastries heaped on a gold edged platter garnished the sideboard. A server teapot, coffeepot, an enameled water pitcher, frosted glass tumblers, and daisy design porcelain creamer and sugar bowl with lid were grouped on one side of the goodies. Mismatched dessert plates and china cups and saucers completed the display.

Shira and I peeped in for a few minutes thoughtfully eyeing the sweets. My mother's sisters relaxed on the floppy couch and easy chairs and their conversation was animated and spiced with gossipy tidbits as the men settled down to the matter of playing poker. My mother, the flawless hostess, soon offered her guests assorted delectable baked goods and was on the go serving cups of steaming coffee with cream and sugar or glasses of tea with lemon.

Bored of watching, Shira and I went to the bedroom. We sat on the edge of the bed; my legs swung freely as Shira apathetically planted hers on the floor. I twisted strands of my hair and tried to tie them into knots. Shira picked at little crusts on her nose which made her sneeze again and again. We both fidgeted and did nothing. After five minutes of uneasy silence Shira said, "Your dress is ugly."

She then pranced about the room showing off her silk frock belted with a rainbow colored sash tied in a perfect bow.

Ignoring her garish display, I asked her a question.

"What's your favorite subject?"

"Mind your own beeswax," came her quick retort.

I shot her a look that said you have a big yap and you are a weirdo. I would have enjoyed kicking her in the shin if I were brave enough to do it.

Shira mumbled, "I brought my *Anagrams* game."

I hesitated before replying, "I'll play." It was not that I disliked the word game. I did not even mind that Shira always won the game when we played. She was older and her spelling and vocabulary were more developed. It was the unpredictability of her responses. For my cousin, the only motive in the game was victory and in the winning, her aplomb was reinstated. With each win her smugness and coercion mounted. She also enjoyed pinching me every time there was even a hint of a possible unfavorable outcome.

We set the game up on the rug. All 126 cardboard letters were placed face down in a little heap to the side. Seven letters at random were drawn and set face up in the middle between us. To decide who went first we played the odds/evens game. I picked "Odds" and Shira, "Evens." Then we each made a fist, shook it and said "One, two, three...shoot," and stuck out one or two fingers. The total was an odd number but Shira accused me of cheating.

The rules of *Anagrams* were to form words. The first player to make and keep six was the winner. You could steal your opponent's words by adding one or more letters and reshuffling them into words of your own. Simply adding an 'S' to make the plural of a word was not acceptable.

Shira started the game. She made the word MEN and a second word RAT. I pulled the letter 'A' and changed MEN to MEAN. Shira glared at me. We continued the game and words accrued in front of both of us. The word TON changed to TONE and then to STONE. Back and forth, the words were made and stolen. No word was safe. We each had five words of our own. It was close to the end of the game, a battle for the last word. As I picked the letter 'C', I checked my rival's words. Shira had the words, BRAT, CORD, FOOL, HOST and RULE. Intensely, I studied all the words. A 'G' could have changed HOST to GHOST; a 'D' added to RULE would have made the new word LURED. The 'C' was difficult. I could not figure out what to do with the 'C'. Suddenly I saw the possibility. I changed RULE to CRUEL and moved it out of her group and into mine, which gave me a total of six, two more words than Shira's four. I had won the game.

Shira's irksome face turned a vivid cerise and the veins darkened to a navy blue. Her eyes narrowed in fury and she lashed out not with words but with a deft strike. Grabbing my little finger that rested on the last word, CRUEL, she twisted it hard. Not until we heard a snapping sound did she let up. All I could manage were timorous whimpers and choked sobs as waves of dizziness overpowered me. 'CRUEL' had won but the reprisals were ruthlessly vindictive.

A cold spring:

For two weeks the sun could not be enticed to emerge from its hideout. Gaudy yellow and purple crocuses poked their blooms through the dirty beige remnants of winter snow. Snagged in sidewalk cracks, light green stems fought their way up. The meager splash of color was a welcome contrast to the steely gray skies. The sprouting buds on the mottled branches of the ancient maple tree stayed a glum umber brown. Sap dripped from bore holes in the tree, drop by drop, onto the soggy sable-colored earth. As the temperature inched above freezing, curbside drifts melted into licorice slush. A foul mix of winter dregs and muck cascaded down the block. At the point of unbearable, the sun dodged its confinement painting the sky silver and opal, touched here and there with faint yellows and lavenders, reflections of the hues of the spring flowers below. Patches of dry sidewalk, weary from the mountain of winter drifts for many months, eagerly displayed their bareness.

Coaxed awake from restless sleep by the even notes of a lingering song, I climbed on a stack of books, the heavy dictionary precariously balanced on top. Curious, I peered out the bedroom window. From my perch I could look out on a fenced-in narrow space with grubby snow sheltering a nest of withered leaves and derisory cast-offs. A crushed garbage can lid, its silvery edge just showing, sodden newspapers, slabs of cardboard, and crinkled cigarette butts were visible. Stuck on the top of an old fractured broom handle was one of my missing woolen mittens. A single undersized birch tree with puny limbs had survived the wintry blasts. Leaf shoots were beginning to form in the faintest trace of lime green. Sitting on an upper branch was a small bird. I had never seen it before nor did I recognize it. *Was it a sparrow, a starling or perhaps a meadowlark?* I jumped down and opened the dictionary to 'meadowlark' finding the following passage:

Mead·ow·lark (mèd¹o-lärk´) *noun*

Any of various songbirds of the genus *Sturnella* of North America, especially *S. magna*, the eastern meadowlark, and *S. neglecta,* the western meadowlark, having brownish or buff plumage, a yellow breast, and a black, crescent-shaped marking beneath the throat; noted for its singing while in flight.

The bird on the lone spindly birch faithfully matched the dictionary illustration and description. Beguiled, I watched the meadowlark take wing singing all the while, an exotic contrast to the screeching of common black crows in the alley engaged in a quarrel over some shredded, shapeless object. The joy of my small sighting warmed and refreshed as if spring had announced itself only to me. My obligation to read the dictionary had proven resourceful. I planned to tell my father that evening about what I had learned if he seemed in a receptive frame of mind and not cross with me.

What a glorious start to the day! Hurriedly I brushed my teeth and patted my hair in place. Slipping on a pair of jeans and a scratchy woolen sweater, I draped a red and yellow silk bandana over my shoulder, and completed the eccentric outfit with a metal skate key on a chain dangling from my neck. My valued possession, a pair of strap-on roller skates waited for me behind the bedroom door. Not minding that I had salvaged the skates from my Aunt Gittel's trashcan, having been rejected by my cousin Philip because they were useless to him and rusted, I could tell they were an exact fit for me unlike his hockey skates.

Checking the skates, I suspected that the red-orange coating was just surface and the steel was free of corrosion and still durable. I poked around in my father's jewelry repair supplies and borrowed a sponge, a small brush, and silver polish, and carted everything outside. I sat on the bottom step in front of the house. Diligently working on the metal, I cleared the rust from all surfaces. Then I shortened the foot plate and maneuvered it to my shoe size tightening the front clasps with the key and spinning the ball-bearing roller wheels to make sure they were smoothly turning.

Shivering from the morning damp and impatient uncertainty, I strapped on the skates adjusting the clips and practiced skating until I could glide smoothly and steadily in control and unafraid. Slender shafts of sunlight settled on the metal clamps tossing off glinting silvery wings. Unmindful of the sidewalk rubble, flaws, and unevenness,

I skated up and down the block becoming more confident and daring with each venture. I picked up the pace and began to soar, the silk bandana waving in the breeze, *Wonder Woman* in flight, elated with energy and expectation, leaping over the bumps and lassoing the sun with my golden lariat.

Like as, to make our appetites more keen

A new and disconcerting habit began to complicate my life. I could not stop eating sweets. Homemade fudge and store bought chocolate covered marshmallow biscuits had become my best friends. I hoarded my pennies for red and black jellybeans and *Tootsie Rolls*. Although not allowed to chew gum at school, I ignored the rule and long-winded admonitions by defiantly chewing squares of *Dubble Bubble Bubble Gum*, hiding behind an open book or raising my desktop to avoid being noticed. Deviously, I applied an insincere smile and narrowed my ever alert eyes into innocent slits. Mrs. Bessner was astute and not fooled by my trifling attempts to deceive her. She strode down the aisle, clasped my upper arm in a vice-like hold, and dragged me to the classroom door shoving me into the hallway.

"You are an insolent and badly behaved child," she asserted, staring angrily at me as her grip on my arm intensified.

Unapologetic, I stomped away, disrespectful and unperturbed. Neither reproof nor grave censure could persuade me to give up sugary treats.

"I won't let you back in class, and you'll miss the lessons and the homework assignment," she added this finality and slammed the door.

"So what," I said to the barricading door.

Mrs. Bossy, as I had nicknamed her, would later regret her conduct and invite me back after some thought. She had shown how uncaring and dismissive she could be; the contrast of my boorish behavior and her rashness was negligible. To justify my ill-manners, I focused on what I liked least about her. She treated me differently than the Outremont and Côte Des-Neiges girls and favored her niece Sarah who delighted in tossing about her carrot color curls and crossing her eyes at me each time I was severely admonished. Most offensive was Bossy's plain look of disdain that altered her round uninspired face. As she tightly clamped her lips, the tiny hairs at the corner of her mouth stuck straight out like whiskers. Even her mousy brown hair parted in a strict line down the middle piqued me, more so when she anchored it into an inflexible bun with pearl studded combs. On the hottest days she dressed in suits, the jackets tightly buttoned across her ample bosom all the way to the neck and the skirts gripping her protuberant bottom. Looking ready to explode from the confinement of her body within four walls of fabric, she was a force to be reckoned with. No wonder she used her knuckly wrinkled hands to maul me.

The solitary afternoon meandered pointlessly about in the school corridors, a witness to my lonely pacing. I had nothing to do. Uncommonly did a student get excused from class; no one came by to applaud me loutishly blowing bubbles of grand proportions. For amusement I counted the linoleum squares, tried to have a quick look through the narrow gaps in the doors of the second and third grades, and visited the washroom to peel away the gum stuck to my lower lip and my collared blouse. Time dragged on monotonously and it was very quiet in the hallway, too quiet...

I could not quell my craving for sweets. The few stray coins on my father's side of the bureau found their way into my pocket and were squandered on candy. There was no possible way I could understand what I was doing and why I kept up my stealthy acts. My mother seemed not to notice my eating habits or the missing box of *Cadbury Dairy Milk Bars*. She was blunted into impassivity by the heavy weight of dejection; it clouded her awareness and made her unresponsive. When my father was present, their unspoken words alarmed and perturbed me. Not suspecting the real cause of my own wretchedness, I knew it only as an empty and hollow place, one that could not be filled.

Dutifully, I ate my dinner meal obsessed with dessert and shamefully craving more. I favored all the chocolate confections: chocolate cream soldiers, chocolate chip cookies, chocolate coated raisins, and cherry chocolates. The chocolate was secretly comforting and made my isolation more bearable. Later, after too much, the excess gave way to peels of loony laughter or pettish tears. What I desired most could not to be attenuated or bribed by licking the cookie dough off the mixing spoon. Craving comfort and finding none made me liable to fits of unreasonable hunger. I was desperate to be held and reassured, to be told that I was loved, and at night to be rocked to sleep like a baby in my mother's arms. I was infected with longing. The sugary treasures were not capable of assuaging my impoverished soul.

One Sunday morning I rose early. Alone, fearing detection, I foraged in the unlit kitchen. Without making a sound, I opened the grocery hutch hunting on the shelves among innumerable labeled jars and tins. Gawkily, I tipped over the white porcelain sugar bowl with its delicate pattern of pink and yellow roses and green leaves. My heart beat wildly believing I had cracked the lovely container. Instead I had managed to only spill some sugar. Licking the tips of each of my fingers, I plucked up the tiny grains one by one repeating the system until all traces of my carelessness were eaten. Tucked behind a box of *Kellogg's Corn Flakes* was a can of *Planters Cocktail Peanuts*. Using the little metal can opener, I managed to cut into the top of the lid moving with the turns halfway around the tin. I then tried to pry it open further but slashed my thumb on the sharp serrated edge. The gash was deep. Blood seeped down the sides of the can smudging the picture of a peanut in a top hat with a monocle and a cane. I ate the salty peanuts with my uninjured hand before calling out for help.

The hooded Bat Twirls softly by

The oppressive July heat thickened the air. I slept poorly at night fitfully tossing on sheets of sweat, at last falling into a transient slumber only to be roused by tired and sultry breezes. Moments before I awoke, I had a calming dream about a lake. The stately firs bordering the lake were seamlessly reflected as the mist rose in puffs of smoke. In the stillness of early morning, the surface was flat and silver-white. Standing on the sandy shore in bare feet, I felt the gentle lapping of the water as it crept in and out tickling my toes...

As a release from the unhealthy slums of Montréal, we had one week of planned vacation at Lac-Paquin in the Laurentian Mountains. Buoyed by the secure escape from the city streets replete with fermenting garbage, I could scarcely contain my elation... my first venture out of the city to an unspoiled and peaceful place.

In my unrepressed eagerness, I irritated my father by repeatedly asking, "When are we leaving for the lake?"

"You'll leave when you leave," he said with finality.

At last the day arrived for the trip. François, a farmer from Val-Morin, had agreed to drive us to the lake in his open truck, the kind used for hauling farm equipment or crates of produce. Each Saturday, François arrived in Montréal to sell his farm-grown crops at the Rachel Street Market: lettuce, tomatoes, carrots, radishes, cucumbers, and squash. By Monday morning his truck was empty for the return. He and my father had become acquainted at the market, my father praising the quality of François' vegetables. They had developed a friendship of sorts, the two men discovering a similar passion for handicapping races, disputing the jockey weight carried by the various competing horses and judging their merits to find the superior horse and potential winner. François was easily coerced into chauffeuring my mother and me to the lake, a few kilometers west of his own property in Val-David.

With his usual scrupulous care to detail, my father packed the indispensable items for our stay. It appeared as if all the contents of the house were loaded on the flat bed of the beat-up truck. Cooking pots, dishes, groceries, bedding, clothing, firewood, mosquito netting and other necessities were boxed, stacked and fettered with rope. I hovered about like a bothersome gnat.

"Don't forget my fishing pole, books and crayons... and bathing suit... please."

I wanted to make certain they were not mistakenly left behind.

The heavily bundled truck clumsily pulled away from the curb lumbering under the weight like a tough old sow. Entrusting François to deliver us safely to our cabin, my father was staying behind in the city to attend to some odd pieces of work as he was now devoting his time to wholesale jobbing of jewelry dealing as a middleman with the merchants. We expected him to join us as soon as possible toward the end of the week. In the rear view mirror I could see him standing motionless in the grimy street, hands firmly planted on his hips critically eyeing the bulky cargo until we turned the corner.

Jammed in the front cab with François, who spoke no English and smelled of fresh mown hay and manure, I held fast to my mother's hand. We were quiet during the ride gazing at the passing landscape inhaling the serenity. As the truck sped along, I felt my heart beat in consonance with the clatter of the wheels removing me from the clamor and dirt, the insufficiencies and neediness. My mother's face gradually lost its wariness as if she too had become sufficiently replete. She slumped in her seat, her form composed and her breathing rhythmically serene.

The road climbed northwards twisting and winding through green hills and ploughed farm fields. François sat easily in his seat, his body relaxed and his right hand resting on the wheel. Ahead lay mountains covered by dark green fir trees disappearing and reappearing with each turn. Even as he paid attention to his driving avoiding the deep ruts and potholes and slowing somewhat around curves, he glanced at the view admiringly, a look of innocent disbelief on his face as if he had never seen it before.

"Incroyable," he exclaimed, his gaze following the gilded streaks extending across the meadows into the blue-shadowed hills. At times I sat forward watchfully trying to catch a better glimpse, but the crazy lurching rocked me back in my seat and the side to side motion bumped me against the door or jolted my mother from her reverie. She steadied me with a firm hand, swept back the wisps of hair trailing over my eyes tucking them behind my ears, and then smoothed the creases in her skirt before settling in again.

Casually controlling the steering wheel, François reached over us to rotate the handle rolling down the window and then broke out in a huge friendly grin. His gold- capped front teeth glinted beneath his drooping mustache and an unlit *Pall Mall* cigarette dangled from the corner of his mouth. At times my mother glanced at François' leathery tanned face, perplexed by his perpetual complacency and good nature. The draft from the window teasingly romped through my hair cooling the nape of my neck. We wended our way through Ste-Therese past St-Jerome. The scenery unfolded as if I were turning the pages of a picture book; dense foliaged oak trees, lime green pastures prospering with wild flowers, and grazing sheep and cattle all blending into a multihued patchwork quilt.

"Look at the cows, Mama, they have white faces."

I was excited by everything I noticed.

"And there's a coal-black baby cow."

My mother laughed, her eyes crinkling, sending forth a shower of hazel sparks from the darker brown tones.

"A calf, dear," she said, "and it's quite young."

At a small village market near Mont-Gabriel, François stopped the truck for a smoke. He bounded out of the cab to first stretch his legs and then offhandedly struck a match on the front bumper to light his cigarette. We climbed down in slow motion, unfolding as if we were packaged. Raising our arms skyward, we let the dampness escape as the hot sun dried the sweat to tiny grains of salt. I tried to smooth the wrinkles out of my shorts and tugged at them. They were stuck to my underpants. My face was ruby red with the heat; my sleeveless blouse was rumpled, and my socks were sticky. I took little notice and followed my mother into the country store.

Behind the counter resting her elbows on a sac of flour was an imposing figure of a woman. Her thinning hair was wound in tight pink rollers in an almost unbroken halo around her head. Her face was wide and her cheeks were puffed out almost obscuring her sly hooded eyes. Questioningly she looked at my mother and then transferred her gaze to me. Somewhat pleased by our intrusion, a small twinkling of light appeared in her slitty eyes, and she widely yawned in greeting offering a view of crooked, misshapen, and mottled teeth. Coming forward from behind the counter, she inelegantly wiped her fat hammy hands on the front of her flowered apron. The pattern was tainted by an unhealthy mix of brown coffee, yellowish tobacco, shades of Neapolitan ice cream, and green pickle juice.

Grunting, she finally asked, "Tu veux?"

My mother purchased two bottles of *Coca-Cola*, icy cold from the cooler. She paid the woman who now grinned and settled down in the tottering chair by the door to capture the afternoon breeze.

We unpacked a little lined breadbasket stored in the truck. Nestled in a bed of ice chips were three sandwiches protected by moisture proof wax paper and several peaches. My mother offered some lunch to François who graciously accepted and then handed me one of the egg salad sandwiches and the purchased drink.

"Mama, could I please have a bag of potato chips?"

She nodded with a smile knowing I would never ask if my father were present, and disappeared into the store returning shortly with the coveted chips and an orange *Creamsicle*. Sitting on the stoop, I unwound in the sunshine slowly licking the frozen treat to reach the center vanilla ice cream, and when that was gone I scraped my tongue on the flat stick. I was contented yet eager to arrive at the lake. The air was crisp and tangy sweet. It was beautiful in the country, a startling contrast to the city, and I imagined waking in the morning to new pastures fresh and green as parsley.

Just past Sainte-Adèle, a distance of seventy kilometers from Montréal, we were almost at Lac-Paquin. François veered off the main highway onto a soft deeply furrowed side road with barely enough room for two cars to pass.

"Nous sommes au lac," he simply said.

The path to our rented cottage was bordered by an uneven fence. Overgrown with weeds, posts missing, and its white paint blistered and flaking, it was charming in its state of disrepair. Carpets of moss green farmland edged a shimmering expanse of lake painted with fiery streaks by the setting sun, and the tops of the tall firs captured the last of the sun's rays, their leaves tinted yellow.

The cabin was a primitive structure made of pine walls, each corner anchored to four flat rocks raising it slightly above ground level. The area under the cabin was filled with dirt and sod partially eroded by rigorous winters leaving clefts under the walls where rodents could hide. A sagging corrugated tin roof continued out over a porch screened by wire mesh to keep out the mosquitoes. Bats tended to nest on the upper ridge beam. My mother and I were frightened having heard stories that bats retire by day to dark recesses only to emerge at night blindly swooping down on thin wings to entangle their long fingers in one's hair. We begged François to inspect the inside before moving in our possessions.

"Bats, comprend tu?"

I flapped my arms and ran about shrieking in a simulation of terror trying to get François to understand. At first he misunderstood but when I pointed to the rafters, he got the message.

Shaking his head, he said, "Chauvresouris, non… Elles ne sont pas ici."

François laughed reassuringly, his eyes twinkling like two crescent moons in his sun-scarred face. He continued to unload and carry boxes, cheerfully talking to himself in French. "Le travail est presque fini; à la bonne heure".

François, having completed most of the work in good time, left me still concerned about the bats in spite of his good humor.

"Mama," I wavered, "maybe we'd best search the place."

The interior was one large room; the kitchen and alcove were partitioned from the two small bedrooms and bathroom by ragged maroon colored drapes clipped to the rafters. My mother scrutinized the cabinets and poked a stick into the eaves near the summit of the roof as I climbed on top of the beds and checked the struts and beams above. We found no phantom vampire forms in hiding. It was dark when the truck took off. François bid us goodbye with his cheery, "Au revoir et bon chance." We punctually settled in for the night, tired, relieved, and happy beyond description.

Morning was my mother's favored time. After the breakfast dishes were stacked on the sideboard to dry, her desire for fresh air carried her into the garden and led us along the pathway to the lake. The wind was invigorating and tart like grapefruit. Being with my mother beside the water full of the play of sunlight, I was spilling over with joy. I loped along ahead of her and then in a rush ran back to smother her with kisses or lagged behind to pick poppies, a rare Blue-Eyed Mary, and yellow buttercups, offering her the precious bouquet from a child's pure heart. In those days I did not think that one day I should forever regret her loss. She tickled my nose with a sprig of mint leaves that she had pinched from the dark green plants sprouting along the pebbled country trail.

"See the whorl of petals," she said with delight and reverence. She proffered her open hand sheltering a cluster of the tiny leaves. "Take a sniff."

I inhaled the fragrance and committed it to memory without the knowledge of having done so, planting the verdant leaves and aromatic scent in my brain inseparable forever from the outstretched hand of my mother. The gaiety of the languorous summer day was as clear and blue as the sky. It reached into the dark recesses of my being with incandescent bliss.

Startled, two bright yellow-breasted birds with black and white streaked wings rose from the hedges and settled on the green orchard grass. They had been hunting for food in the dense undergrowth where the dew still dappled the leaves. My mother glanced at the sun shading her eyes from the brightness, her face crimson from the warmth of the day.

"We'd better start up the mountain before it gets too hot."

Pocketing the mint for the after-dinner dessert, she wended her way slowly on the steep path lined by tall lush grasses, their tips straw colored. The old dirt trail was full of bumps and potholes; it followed the ascent up into the hills curving around boulders and short drop-offs. Passing my mother, I bolted ahead swinging my basket enjoying the climb as the sapling spruce, fir, and maple made their appearance. Raspberry bushes, hundreds of them, were tucked between the young trees, and I began to pick the succulent berries, one at a time, releasing each into my basket, and popping a random one into my mouth. Stooped over, moving from bush to bush, my mother and I occasionally nudged each other and laughed, delighted with each newly discovered fruit laden clump.

On our way back to the cottage, we wearily trudged along. Canopied branches shielded us from the glaring sun, and our path was strewn with thin shafts of sunlight. Thirsty and sapped from the efforts of the morning, we were in high spirits even as our legs faltered.

In the evening my mother and I sat side by side at the oblong, rickety wooden table covered with a red-checkered oilcloth. In the center she had placed a Mason jar with my wild flowers, the glorious blossoms and leaves cheering up the gloom of our cabin. We rushed through dinner eager for the long-awaited reward of the freshly picked raspberries topped with whipped cream and decorated with the sprigs of mint. I ate slowly not wanting the bowl to empty, not able to recall savoring or appreciating a similar taste. To dispel the evening chill, my mother arranged dry firewood in the cast iron potbelly stove and lit the kindling. Within minutes crackling flames danced about visible through the clear mica window of the stove, and the smoke magically spiraled up the flue exiting via the chimney in the gable-end wall. In the warm coziness of the room, I sketched and colored pictures of the views remembered from our hike: crested mountains tinted with lavender and distant billowy hills of blue with patches of sap green and beige under a whitish sky and wispy clouds. My mother went out to sit alone on the fenced-in porch, her sighs masked by the squeak of the rocker.

Before our return to the city, my father arrived to spend the final days with us. My mother's anticipation was apparent as she fussed and preened most of the day. I watched them in their greeting catching a whiff of softness in the country air as they gently embraced on the dusty road, the lake glistening in the background. I wished it could always be this way.

And indeed there will be time

At the lake I made friends with Claude, a young French Canadian boy, whose grandfather owned a farm near Lac-Theodore. Claude hiked over to visit me in the mornings. I watched him crossing the meadows, his lithe wiry body easily covering the distance, his bare feet hardly pressing the tall grasses into the dirt. He dressed in a raggedy, sleeveless undershirt and cut-off patched jeans. His longish black hair was slicked back leaving a few unruly, sweaty strands curling at the neck. I could see his eyes as he drew near, round and dark as two small lumps of coal. They were beguilingly deep-set above the arch of his cheekbones, and his long, delicate eyelashes cast spidery shadows on his ruddy cheeks. He had tiny, very straight white teeth and thin lips the color of red crayon. I looked sallow next to his tawny glowing skin; my city whiteness covered me like cotton wool.

It was fun spending hours with Claude even though he spoke no English and my French was minimal. We played in the shallow end of the lake, neither of us being a competent swimmer. Claude hunted for a frog and proudly carried it over for my inspection, a challenging smile on his face, and I grimaced and in the end poked at the slimy creature. He found a salamandre d'eau, the water salamander, with its broad flat nose, bulging eyes, and slender body ending in a tail. We excitedly turned it over to examine its brightly colored red belly full of yellow spots. I gradually got used to worms, slugs, grasshoppers, and other squiggly things, and took childish delight in toying with them.

One afternoon we followed a rocky mud-caked stream bed marked on the sides by gnarled tree roots and overgrown with thistles and stinging nettles burgeoning on a trail that led past a grove of weeping willows to open farmland. Cows grazed in the sunlight on the cropped grassy fields near orderly ploughed rows of shifting shades of brown-beige soil. We skirted Claude's grandfather's farmhouse and threshing machine, careful of its blades, and walked through the horse stalls to the cow barn. The fresh hay smelled sweet. We picked our way around manure piles and climbed the ladder into the loft. Claude and I watched his grandfather and older brother milk the cows tugging the bulging teats until a stream of white froth hissed into the buckets. The cows impatiently twitched their tails.

As the hot sun streaked in through the wooden rafters, we lay on our backs in the hay looking up at strips of sky, the caress of heat making us dreamy and sleepy. We napped together just like that not saying a word or stirring on our straw beds. Only once did Claude put his hand under my blouse to touch the skin of my chest. My breasts were small, just starting to bud, and still unshaped, so that his curious probing seemed harmless and funny. The year before, Marty from my class at school had subtly done something similar, but his purpose was wicked and humiliating.

I gazed at Claude, his lanky frame in repose, the sun and shadows creating a languid tableau. He seemed so satisfied in the unsuspecting nature of a child's mind, ignorant of the world of cruelty and cunning. He thrived in the simplicity of summer days of innocence. I ran my fingers along his sinewy arms and legs, touching and sharing common life, till its ordinary quality gave me the thrill of a new life, one to hold on to for a brief moment.

Now that the lilacs are in bloom

Unstoppable billows of heat lolled about in the city emptying the streets. In despair of the solitary summer that loomed ahead, I randomly wandered along in the forbidding alleyways pulling my little red metal wagon on its tin wheels, searching for discarded toys. Under a rickety staircase, I found my reward: a wooden rattle with a clown painted face, a green hat and green body, and one swinging green and white beaded arm that clacked when I shook it. Not minding that it was missing the other arm and one white leg and green shoe, I rushed back to the house to see if anyone was around to share my find. No one was out of doors. I sat on the stoop, lonely and fretful, as the shimmering waters of Lac-Paquin, its treed shorelines, and grassy knolls gradually faded from my memory, a rich tapestry growing plainer, withering in the sun. The brilliant colors slipped away like silk threads unraveling.

Something mysterious was happening in my neighborhood. I spotted notices posted on doors up and down the street, small placards with a word in bold lettering: **QUARANTINED**. Tying my wagon to the maple tree, I rushed up the stairs to ask my mother to explain.

"Mama, what do the signs mean?" I asked.

"Some of the children are sick with fever and a red rash. They have to stay indoors not to spread the illness." Her reply was evasive not to frighten me.

My mother was anxious about the outbreak of scarlet fever in this part of the city, aware that children rarely fail being harmed by it. She discussed the situation with my father, and he concurred to send me for a stay at my aunt's home, one of my mother's sisters, until the danger passed. My relatives were notified and without qualms accepted the little 'package'.

My uncle arrived in his fat, luminous *Packard*. It was a dazzling new car with gleaming curved bumpers, white-walled tires inset with chrome hubcaps, polished mirror, and a glittery hood ornament. With a grand gesture he opened the door for me. I stepped on the running board and shifted into the seat, yielding to the sensation of creamy soft leather on bare arms. In an instant, I was transported into a fantasy world. I stroked the polished wood dash and charily turned the shiny radio knobs astounded by splendid music pouring out. As my uncle drove the car, I watched the dinginess of the street recede to an indistinct blur. Intoxicated with the air of freedom, I sat placid in silent wonder. Uncle Saul's voice intruded into my daydream.

"So, how's everything?" he asked.

"Okay," I answered.

"You look good, a little color in your face."

I glimpsed at my uncle in profile, almost a stranger to me. He had a huge head, bald save for a few stands of hair that lay across the top in neat thin rows. His nose was protrusive, made more noticeable by a small wart on the end, and a well-groomed moustache hid his upper lip. He energetically chomped on an unlit cigar, his jaw moving from side to side. Always dressed in a formal suit, stiff collared shirt and tie, he appeared jittery, as if he were ready to attend a company meeting or confront a client. He drove the car smoothly but his fingers tapped nervously on the steering wheel, little clicking noises rhythmically in time with the music from the radio and the wheels skimming along the roads. Lulled by these sounds, I forgot to talk and act in a polite fashion. There was little to say and less to ask. I remembered suddenly his fondness for sweets.

"Uncle Saul, do you have any *Chiclets* in the glove box?"

"Aha, you little devil, you remembered."

I was rewarded with a smile and a fresh box of candy coated peppermint chewing gum in exchange for letting him pinch my dimpled cheeks. It was his pattern whenever he had visited in the past, and I considered it a small price to pay. We followed Av Du Parc and turned on Av Du Mont Royal heading to Hampstead with its luxurious homes and spacious flower filled gardens extending down to wide avenues bordered by stately elms. A few miles along, the homes became more modest, but all the gardens were lush with blooms.

Uncle Saul deposited me at the front door and shuffled back to his car to drive off, my expressed gratitude trailing limply after him almost not noted. Auntie Rosie greeted me with a hug, clasping me tightly to her ample bosom, almost smothering me in her Brussels lace trimmed dress and dangling chains of gold trinkets. She released me offering her soft cheek for a kiss. A cherry almond scent of *Jergens Lotion* was on her smooth skin reminding me of my mama. Looking me over through her thick bifocals, she assessed my state of well being.

"Just look at you. My you've grown and so pretty."

Blushing, I managed an unsure reply, "Thank you, Auntie."

"Only from such children can one derive naches," she said with prideful pleasure as she ushered me down the hall to the guest bedroom. I placed my tattered suitcase on the chest at the foot of the bed aside the neatly folded linens. On the burled walnut bureau and nightstands were delicately stitched doilies and needle worked runners. An unworn silk nightdress was draped over the back of the nearby rocking chair. Not wishing my aunt to see me shyly trying to contain my ecstasy in awe of this perfection, I started to unpack. Sensing my timidity, she left me alone to settle in. I opened the windows to the garden. The fragrance of lilacs wafted in the breeze. Bursting gems of pastel pinkish violet, white, and purple blossoms hung from intertwined branches. I reached out and selected a cluster plunging my face into the delicate perfume. Slips of sunlight filtered through the leaves painting patterns at my feet. The room was awash with beauty.

At dawn, I was the first to awake. Enjoying the soft warmth of my cozy bed and the deep silence of my room, I lay quite still, the rosy morning light trickling in through the lace curtains. In the comforting tangle of my rumpled blankets, I nested like a robin's egg waiting for the day to hatch. When I heard stirrings from the adjacent rooms, I leaped out from under my coverings and pushed the curtains aside to face a blaze of gold stretching across a lucid space.

After lunch, my cousin Myrna offered to spend the afternoon with me. She was my aunt's only daughter. Myrna had one older brother Nathan possessing a proper mustache and having made partner in an import/export firm, and a younger wise guy brother Arnold who thought he knew more than the rest of the family. Myrna, on the verge of womanhood, was engaged to her sweetheart Edward, a college professor. I openly worshipped her nature in its refined graciousness and genuine amiability. She possessed a classic elegance, her movements graceful and fluid, yet she dressed simply and in good taste. The beauty of her face was highlighted by a smooth honey brown complexion with a rosy glow. When she laughed her eyes were sphinx-like, amber and shiny like two jewels.

She posed the question I slyly hoped to be asked.

"And what do you want to do today?"

I readily replied, "See the neighborhood shops."

We left the house walking on Clanranald and then turned at the corner in the direction of Decarie. Not a murmur or sigh of wind stirred the dejected leaves on the trees as the sun punished the day with its heat. We passed a barbershop, a hardware store, a shoe store, and ultimately a drugstore with a soda fountain. The temptation of ice cream drew us inside and we mounted the high stools to rest our elbows on the cool counter. I swiveled around and around on the cracked red leather seat until Myrna tugged my sleeve.

"Behave yourself."

"I'm sorry," I said trying to contain my exuberance.

Myrna smiled and the incident was forgotten.

"You can order anything you wish."

"May I really?"

The sundae set in front of me made me whoop with amazement. Two scoops of ice cream, vanilla and strawberry, were drenched in chocolate sauce and decorated with walnuts and marshmallows. Foamy whipped cream topped with a maraschino cherry completed the presentation.

My thank you was a faint murmur.

I ate it all. I felt delirious. It was far better than the licorice pieces I occasionally snitched from my grandmother Ada's dresser drawer and as delectable as the raspberries and whipped cream my mother had served me at the lake. I planned to save all my pennies, hoping to go back, but I knew it would take forever to accumulate the needed twenty-five cents.

My aunt and uncle's home had a refrigerator inside the kitchen. Everyone sat down to dinner at the same time. The light-hearted banter flowed easily. My uncle pontificated on some trade and industry prob-

124

lems; my cousins Arnold, Myrna, and Nat ignored his bluster and chose to tease one another, and my aunt urged food on me. I ate in small bites, chewing with my mouth closed. I felt like a 'sneak-in' at a movie theater, not having paid admission, undeserving of the images of pleasurable words. I never joined in the discussions, at times hectic, chaotic, and circular in which all opinions were voiced and no resolutions were found. Uncle Saul sternly lectured waving his fork in the air for emphasis. The boys typically made smart-aleck remarks which riled him turning the wart on the end of his nose deeply red. Bursts of laughter eased the controversy. My cousins settled into trading nonsense and enjoying the tender brisket, Auntie Rosie's specialty. She roasted it in a honey colored sauce made of brown sugar, lemon rind and cinnamon, on a bed of raisins, apricots, pitted prunes, potatoes, and carrots. In concert the family all declared, "Delicious!"

Auntie Rosie was a true baleboste. She defined the word by being an excellent cook, a thrifty shopper, and a particular homemaker; she dedicated herself to caring for her children and teaching them to be righteous. I watched her prepare tantalizing meals in the kitchen and traipsed after her to see what I could learn. She bestowed considerate treatment on me out of the kindness of her heart, urging me to go out to play in the garden or to read one of the many books readily available from the collection on the bookshelf in Uncle Saul's den. I was more content just staying close by sniffing the heady scents in the kitchen. I patiently chopped dates into tiny morsels to combine with cinnamon, vanilla, nutmeg, cloves, mace, sugar, and chopped pecans, the mixture needed for Auntie's supremely good date bars. After dinner I helped with the dishes cautiously drying each *Wedgwood* fine bone china dinner plate, bread and butter plate, soup bowl, dessert plate, cup and saucer, and serving platter and lid. The cupboards for the china and crystal were edged in whitewashed wood with inset panes of clear beveled glass. The dining table was of the same whitewashed wood with matching chairs. I stood on a kitchen chair wisely removing my shoes so as not to mark it up and placed each dried item back on the shelf approving the visible arrangement. I worked in slow motion as I was concerned one might drop from my hand, and I would be blamed for breaking up the set. My shyness and diffidence were palpable. I flitted from room to room, a firefly, unable to settle down like the fine dust on the polished mahogany furniture and the ebony wood grand piano. I was the unique guest, polite, mindful and silent.

When I returned home, the clustered lilacs were replaced by flocks of pesky chickens. Just below Rue Roy, the neighborhood specialized in poultry houses where the broiler chickens were slaughtered and the laying hens were raised for eggs. In the mornings often before sunrise, I could hear the cheeky roosters' shrill crow. During the day, the clucking noises of the chickens as they fluffed their feathers and shook their bodies was disconcerting, but their frantic squawking when butchered crushed me. A perpetual snowstorm of feathers clogged the air and the sidewalks were stained with scarlet splotches, a contagion of the dreaded fever. As I turned the corner to Rue St. Dominique, the pervasive stench tore at my nostrils. I began to run chased by an infuriated urgency, desperate to avoid the massacre of the chickens. Disconsolate, I yearned to retrace my way back to the lilacs.

The beams, that thro' the Oriel shine,

They all said it was the worst summer. The heat rose from the sidewalks in steamy curlicues. There was no relief from it. The street was quiet as if the abnormal warmth had cordoned it off for the day. Without the hint of a breeze, not a leaf moved on the maple in front of the house; the neighboring dogs quit their yelping and sought shade under scraggly bushes or crawled into toppled garbage cans to lay panting and whining. I had nothing to do and no one to talk with. Returning to the stale brooding solitude of the house, I hoped my mother was well enough to play with me. Ever since our return from the lake, she was listless and morose.

I found her resting on her bed, an ash white drawn look on her face, a cool compress across her forehead, and her eyes tightly shut squeezing out the bright sultry morning. Earlier she had confided that she had an overpowering headache and wanted only to be left alone. Not intending to disturb her, I patted her arms resting on the light coverlet spread over her. She stirred and murmured, "Sorry, sweetheart." Even in repose, lines creased her brow and tugged the corners of her mouth. Her sleep was erratic, split by wakefulness and quiet shedding of tears.

I overheard fragments of telephone discussions she had with her sisters. Pretending not to notice, I tried to process what she said in her soft voice. *Weighing heavily on my mind, overwhelming* and *tired all the time* recurred in segments of the conversation usually punctuated by, *What shall I do, where I can go? It's hopeless.* Sensing that her world was crumbling at the edges and incapable of reaching through her confusion of pain, I pulled away.

My father had left for the day to visit his wholesale suppliers. I safely poked around in his coin box and found ten pennies for the bus and three dimes for the admission charge. Packing my swimsuit and bathing cap in a brown paper sac, I left the house walking to Av Du Parc. Amazed at my own daring, I hopped on the bus, got off at Rue St. Antoine and made the Rue Wellington connection to the city of

Verdun. The route was not unfamiliar because I had traveled it twice before with my cousin Philip and his older brother Doug. The Wellington bus was fully crowded. Lurching to the motion of the wheels, the huddled bodies reeked; an acrid stench like spiky cactus stung me. Dismayed, I invoked the memories of Lac-Paquin, the fragrant rich smell of pine and the early dew on the scraggy grasses. Refreshed and comforted, I lasted the ride to Verdun's outdoor swimming pool.

The wait at the gated entry was interminable. Public pools were always teeming with children and a new swimmer was allowed access only when one left. The line of children moved in measured countable inches as the minutes slowly stretched on, invariable and without rationale, wearing me numb. I began to doubt if it would ever be my turn to buy a ticket and pass through the iron turnstiles.

Feeling peevishly alone, I decided to talk to the girl behind me.

"Do you think we'll get in?" I asked.

"Sure, everyone gets in," she gaily answered.

The air was stifling and the sun, a cruel fireball of mischief. My feet in thin-soled sandals were burning from the searing hot sidewalks making me to shift from foot to foot, quick, jiggly, hinge-like motions resembling those of a marionette. I seemed to be dancing on wires controlled by a puppet master. Without warning, I collapsed into a blood-red hole and plummeted down a limitless tunnel into thick coal tar.

When I surfaced from the black pit, I was lying on a cot in a peculiar place. The sun poured its checkered light through the stained glass windows onto the white tiles. The flat polished surfaces acted like prisms breaking the light up into all the colors of a rainbow. A scowling face smelling of chlorine spoiled my dreaminess, her snappish voice dragging me back away from the lovely violet, blue, green, yellow, orange, and red reflections.

"I'm a nurse. You're in the first aid room," she announced with authority, and handed me a glass of icy cold *Orange Crush* soda.

"You fainted outside, probably heatstroke."

"I'm sorry," I said in apology.

"Lie still for fifteen minutes. Tu est un peu malade."

The nurse left to chastise some boys who were roughhousing poolside. The door was ajar and I could see children diffidently wading into the shallow end or jumping into the midst of the pool, rising and shrieking, noisily splashing in the cool wetness. I wanted to join them and asked the nurse if I could pay my thirty cents and go swimming.

"C'est impossible," you are not well, she said.

"But, I waited outside for two hours."

"Non," she bluntly restated.

"Oh please let me play in the pool... please," I begged, even as I knew I was destined to lose in this war of words

She did not relent and left me just as I had thoughtlessly deserted my tearful mother. Shielding my face from the blinding truth, I wept in earnest, tears that deserved more tears.

Since she must go, and I must mourn, come Night,

Facing the wide glare of day, my mother sat in her chair at the open front window waiting for night to fall. The inexorable heat and stench of the city excluded even a whisper of a breeze to offer relief. Motionless for hours, my mother looked almost formless as if all her energy had taken leave of her without permission. At times she cooled her brow with a dampened hankie or fanned the air parched by the sun. I fetched a frosty glass of lemonade and set it on the sill careful not to startle her. She sipped the tart beverage and then held the glass against her neck seeking comfort from the cold. The only sounds heard were the occasional whine of a passing car or squeal and screech of wheels.

Aroused by the displeasing street noises, she left the parlor moving gloomily about the house as if in a trance. Disruptive thoughts seemed to take root in her mind littering her path with sighs of grief. I followed her pensiveness from room to room. Helplessly I watched her chafe, and her inevitable progression toward a fated collapse was a real concern. In the kitchen she seemed not to notice me clinging to her skirt as she considered the brilliant yellow, orange, and violet tablets in the medicine vials. She culled the best as if the most colorful ones could disperse her depression. Worried by her unremitting secretiveness and curious reveries, I listened hearing only her desperation talking to me in muffled tones. Other mornings she rose early, the cool dawn giving her ease, and breakfast appeared on the table like so many previous mornings, and her voice was musical and loving once more. I was content with such random consolations aware of their impermanence. When she experienced alarming sensations of choking, unable to catch her breath or speak, my befuddled father vented his fear in outbursts of rage. Denunciations rang out cutting the silence like a knife.

"It's those damn pills. Your doctors are idiots."

Attempting some meek adjustment, my mother cut back on the prescribed dose in an effort to dislodge all notions and regrets that were overtaking and consuming her. I detected no visible effect, not even a ripple of improvement. A sense of impending disaster frequented my dreams at night. In the dreams, I watched a wraithlike figure slip away below the surface of a lake and drift soundlessly down and down to a murky bottom.

One afternoon, as the sun sagged under storm clouds and the sky became darkly shaded, my mother, no longer absent or dazed, emerged from her brooding.

"Would you like to go shopping with me?" she asked.

Her voice, which had previously trembled with emotion, surged with renewed vigor and doused me in a vivid rush and wild gust of gladness. She brushed her dark hair, applied a trace of rose to her lips, and put on a summer dress all the while urging me to hurry so that she could catch the day before it skidded from her grasp. We set out for the dry goods store on Rue Villeneuve passing hastily through the market stalls tempted awhile by the fresh smelling baked goods and tart, bright green Granny Smith apples. My feet scarcely touched the pavement as I skipped along, irrepressibly happy in the release from the baleful angers of the house and my binding fears.

On display in the shop window were all sorts of linens and silk items, delicately stitched draperies, tablecloths, tea towels, and flowery hatted mannequin heads. Inside was conspicuous clutter. Cartons and boxes lay scattered about randomly. Bolts of textiles were layered to the ceiling. Each cabinet drawer was stocked with silk stockings and undergarments; wire hung dresses swung from every conceivable knob or hook like colorful flags fluttering in a reckless breath of wind.

The dressing area was protected from prying eyes by a shabby curtain on a drawstring. I went in to change out of my shorts and top and my mother appeared with her selections for me: two new pairs of satin panties, one in baby blue and one in pink. I tried each on in turn, the airy fabric touching my skin with a fine silken caress. Flinging the curtain aside I danced around the shop in the pink panties joyfully brazen, ebullient, and silly. Several shoppers temporarily paused to witness the commotion and shook their heads disapprovingly. My mother scolded me for my flamboyance.

"Caasi, stop your prancing and get dressed this minute."

I flung thoughtless words at her.

131

"Mama, you're crazy!"

A hurt look crossed my mother's face as she retreated into her protected place of forbearance. If only I had suspected the impact of my brash words. These few words revisited shredding me with the sharp talons of enormous hawks.

We are such stuffe

The overpowering hot summer days showed no signs of letting up. The air was sultry, the shriveled leaves drooped, and around the maple tree the dry congealed soil split and cracked. I idled outside for a short time sluggishly tossing my ball against the wall. Disgruntled, I climbed the stairs to sit in the open doorway. Seeing the mopey look on my face, my mother suggested that we go on a picnic. The old wicker basket came out of dusty hiding and was filled to the brim with all the pleasurable goodies. She hastily dressed in a sleeveless summer cotton outfit, loose fitting and unbelted, and a pair of open-toed sandals. A floppy straw hat added to her look of sweet disorder.

"Hurry and get ready," she firmly implored suggesting she might change her mind if we did not leave without delay. I rushed to slip into a gauzy chemise and darted to meet her waiting at the door. We shared the load of the basket, each carrying one handle, reaching the corner in time to watch the bus come around the bend lurching and twisting. No one alighted and we clambered aboard, the doors closing behind us with a snap. I smiled out the window at the squalid houses and the vulgarity of the streets knowing I soon would be in a charming place. My mother sat quite still beside me, her eyes turned absently toward the window. As the bus bumped along, she seemed distant from me as if she were gripped by secretive thoughts taking her to a remote far away place, one I had agreed not to enter.

Within the hour, we approached the banks of the Saint Lawrence River, the brownish-ochre mud flats scorched by the blazing sun, and started across Pont Jacques Cartier, an elaborate steel bridge connecting Montréal's waterfront to Île Sainte-Hélène. The river below swallowed the sunlight, its surface choppy and rough and its depth indeterminate. As we went from city to island, concrete blocks and barren soil were transformed into lush, leafy greenery. We stayed on the bus until the end of the line and then set out on foot to follow a trail that wound along the edge of the craggy rock walls bordering the river. There were mossy hills, low bushes, shade trees, and picnic areas on the cliffs. We spread out our blanket on the windswept heights above the level of the fast-moving water; I imagined it was the picture perfect spot Mother Nature had invented just for us. Vibrant yellow, pink, and purple wildflowers speckled the grass creating lacey patterns of color. I walked about barefoot on the luxuriant carpet amid flapping amber-brown Monarch butterflies and collected flowers for my mother to weave into bracelets.

At lunchtime, she opened the basket and displayed the contents: hard-boiled eggs, smoked salmon, cheeses, crusty rolls and two bottles of *Pepsi*, as well as potato chips, *Brach's Chocolate Covered Cherries*, and black licorice twists, snacks I was never permitted to have at home in my father's presence. It was such an amazing array of delicacies; I wanted to cry out of sheer joy.

After the feast, we lay looking up at the unclouded blue sky, partially eclipsed by the branches of a gnarled oak. Sunlight trickled down in fleeting golden designs as my eyes wavered in advance of sleep. The stillness of the air made us indolent in silent, gilded contentment. Lying together on the grassy bed, it was quiet enough to hear the distant rush of the rapids. Drowsy, we dozed in the hot midday sun.

Unsettling dreams suspended my tranquility. This time the details were clearer, and I could not escape from their grip. My mother seemed very small, almost doll like, and she was playing far below the rocky ledge. The river was angrily raging driven by a blustery gale. The powerful waves savagely snatched her from the shore. I stood on the steep face of rock trembling and sick with terror incapable of diving into the blackness to save her. I woke with a start, my heart constricted with fright. At my side, my mother was facing the river, oddly peaceful; her gaze drifted to where the currents tossed foamy waves about, and the sunshine dipped in but was not reflected. When I sought out her eyes, I noted a vague unease.

As the afternoon wore on, she proposed a swim in the river. I was sorely tempted as the air was hot, and I had learned how to swim the past summer at Lac-Paquin. The descent from the cliff edge was sharp; protruding, scraggy boulders cascaded precipitously into the water.

There was no shallow part or beach where I could have waded in ankle deep water. Some words of caution played in my head.

"Dad said it wasn't safe to swim here...the rapids...they're dangerous..."

My mother offered no response as if my contentions were unfounded. Wordlessly, she gathered up the picnic things. When we arrived home, my father was ill-tempered. It was then I failed to tell him of my mother's erratic suggestion revealing it much later when it was too late. That paltry duplicity besieged me in years to come.

Thou'rt gone, the abyss of heaven

One unforgettable, unforgivable Sunday in early August, I woke to a cloudless sky and sun streaming through the voile curtains. Brushing aside the sheer net fabric, I enjoyed a fleeting look out the window into the courtyard at the back of the house. The lone birch tree was in late bloom, green leaves pasted all over its slender twig-like branches obscuring the blemishes and knotty whorls. The morning was already muggy with heat and humidity. Dressing quickly, I put on a pair of shorts and a little halter-top. Without stopping to fasten my sandals, I scampered out of the bedroom down the hall and into the kitchen to greet my mother. She had been secretive these last weeks, slipping out of the house, not saying where she was going, returning at odd times, even late in preparing dinner. It called to mind only one possibility; I was certain her inexplicable actions hinted at un cadeau, a gift, for me.

"Mama, hi Mama, do you have something planned for me? You know the reason… a special day will soon be here."

She was sitting languorously at the kitchen table her back to me. I expected her to turn in my direction and give me one of her priceless smiles, the kind that softened my heart and made me want to hug her in a protective embrace. She seemed reluctant to face me and spoke in a voice lacking in vibrancy.

"I do have a gift for you. You may open it now."

"Do you really want me to? My birthday won't be here for another week."

In my exuberance I paid little care to her flat lifeless tone. My glance went directly to the enamel tabletop. Centered was a white box tied with a yellow ribbon and a bow made of loops of ribbon; a garland of wildflowers was pinned to the corner, the sweet smelling pink and white clover we had picked together on Île Sainte-Hélène.

"Thank you, thank you, Mama."

I adeptly worked loose the ribbon and put the garland on my wrist to wear as a bracelet. Opening the box, I discovered under the tissue a cream colored eyelet cotton pinafore embroidered with tiny yellow daffodils, the most charming frock I had ever seen. I clutched it and held it against my body lovingly caressing it. I kissed my mother on her cheek and right there in the kitchen impetuously changed into the dress and twirled about. I was elated. My very own pinafore, brand new, never owned by another!

"Can I wear it today, can I? I mean may I please... oh say yes Mama." My overjoyed words toppled out.

She nodded distractedly and her hands trembled as she patted loose strands of her hair neatly into place, inattentive to my nagging insistence.

The morning should have been out of the ordinary to match the new dress, but it dragged on commandingly hot and monotonous. I played hopscotch in front of the house until lunch and read my *Nancy Drew* mystery books borrowed from the library. Feeling isolated, I asked my mother's permission to walk to the nearby YMCA to be with my cousins and other kids from my block. She approved with a small wave of her hand. As I skipped past my mother seated in the parlor, I caught her reflection in the mirror of the credenza. She was so still, her elbows resting in her lap, her face nestled in one palm, her eyes cast down. Unlike the blithe garland of flowers encircling my wrist, her image enclosed me in sorrow. At the front door I briefly halted, introspective, compelled to go back. Uneasy and fearful, I wanted to linger and comfort her, but I was eager to show off my gift to the group at the 'Y'. My footsteps took me farther and farther away leaving her alone to find some measure of peace.

It was dusk when I returned from the 'Y' and saw no visible light coming from the front parlor window and the house repressed by inauspicious shadows. I plodded up the steps clunking loudly to announce my arrival only to find the door locked. How odd I thought and then a flash terror seized me. My hands chilled in spite of the undiminished heat of nightfall. In doubt of what to do, I climbed up on to the roof of the basement compartment to reach our window. The window was generally left ajar in the summer to invite breezes into the house but I found it latched. I hopped down taking care not to dirty myself and remounted the front steps to check the front door once more pulling and twisting the handle. It stubbornly refused to yield. I peeked through the keyhole squinting with one eye to get a clearer view. My mother was not at home at nightfall as she always had been before. It was getting late, far too late. I felt as if I were stepping off a precipice into a vast expanse of dread.

Suddenly my father arrived to witness the dark unwelcome horror of the empty house. His anger was fierce.

"I told you never to leave her alone. You should have been with her. You left her. You left her alone," he shouted.

"I didn't intend to, honest. I only went to play. I asked her permission."

"She's been going somewhere all these past weeks. Didn't you notice?"

Unalterably, he persisted with the questioning. Crying miserably, I tried to defend my careless neglect.

"I thought she was out shopping."

"Fool!" He spat out.

Unlocking the door, my father methodically searched the house, and then wildly tore from room to room. He raged. He paced the hall. He called her sisters. He called the Jewish General Hospital. Lastly, he called the police station. With each passing moment, his fury intensified and my fear took the form of a monster. I hid from it in the space under the sewing machine. My father found me there and dragged me out by my hair.

"What did she say? Where was she going? How did she look? How was she dressed?"

He interrogated me over and over again asking the same queries.

"She was at home. I don't know where she might have gone. I'm not sure. She didn't tell me anything."

He struck me across the face. The force cut my lower lip and blood trickled down like red teardrops splattering the yellow flowers on my new dress. I watched as the crimson pattern spread eclipsing my earlier happiness.

A severe knock on the open door interrupted the beating. Two uniformed policemen entered and paused as they scrutinized me and my father, their faces somber. One officer was carrying a purse and a woman's shoe.

"Monsieur, je fait a contrecœur de vous dire"... said the French speaking policeman, his voice faltering.

"What he's trying to say with great difficulty," interrupted the second officer, "is that a fisherman who was out in a boat on the river today saw a woman matching your wife's description. She walked into the water and disappeared in the rapids. By the time he got to where she had gone down, there was nothing he could do. We found on the cliff this purse and one shoe. The identification in the purse led us here."

The cry that came out of my father was more animal than human. The pain and suffering were excruciating. He wrenched the items from the policeman; briefly regaining his composure, he thanked them for their courtesy. They departed in bewildered haste.

I was caught in a whirlwind of grief and terror. There was no mind or mouth or voice to evince the cries that shrieked and heaved inside. The worst of my dreams had happened. My mother had succumbed to her despair. She was nowhere to be found and would never again return home. My father turned to me. I reached out to be swept up in his arms, to be reassured, to weep, to rail, and to scream *no* a thousand times. Instead he hit me, hit me over and over again until I was an open sore scantily covered by a bloody, shredded dress, one that never would be worn for my eighth birthday. The news of my mother had ripped out my heart and my body did not matter. I wanted him to pummel me to death.

"It's your fault," he said. "It's your fault."

I lost myself among my mother's clothes in her closet. Her rosewater eau de cologne melded with the pungency of the mothballs and gradually lessened. I pulled her muskrat fur wrap over my head. In the dark, the muskrat's beady eyes accused me. I saw my mother's torment as she was swallowed up in the currents. The black, turbulent Lachine Rapids of the St. Lawrence River off Île Sainte-Hélène had taken my mother from me. That part of the river was the deepest and coldest. It could drown a city.

Valediction: Forbidden Mourning

The day of my mother's funeral should have convened strident un-availing winds howling through the bleak emptiness and furious gales whirling into a mad delirium. Instead, the skies were clear and fair, and brisk fall-like gusts of wind scattered the cloying August heat. The air was alive with promise as uninvited death sack-clothed our house and sprinkled ashes on our heads. My father was immersed in sorrow. Relatives from both sides of the family lingered in consolation. Of all those close to me, there was but one face my eyes wished to see, one voice my ears longed to hear, and one touch to keep me from breaking like glass. Sitting on my bed in a quiet stupor, I could hear the rabbi from the orthodox synagogue on Av Laval groaning and praying. I watched him through the open door. His hunched shoulders were cloaked in his white taffeta tallith prayer shawl with black stripes and embroidered-fringed border. He seemed smaller than I remembered, shrunken in seriousness, his cheeks sallow and pallid. Clasped tightly in his wrinkled old hands were his tephillin, two small leather boxes containing strips of parchment. My father had once shown them to me in synagogue, and I remembered them as holy, not to be played with, containing inscribed verses from the Torah. The chanted Hebrew words called to me from a place of sadness. The poignant piercing mourner's prayer rose from his mouth in solemn repetition as he swayed and rocked. His black yarmulke, a cloth skullcap, nested on his graying bushy hair that sprouted out in a berserk way and then plummeted into a rough matted beard. It was curious, this outsider moving freely to and fro in strident mourning while soundless hear-tache rooted me. I could not weep.

My father's sister Mildred found me alone in the bedroom.

"You're going to our house in Sainte-Anne-De-Bellevue for the day," she told me.

Surprised and shaken by what she said, I defied her. "I thought I was supposed to be at the funeral."

"No, you're too young."

I looked at her obediently groomed hair, her face rather pointedly oval, her eyes uncompromising, and an expression of meanness on her firmly fixed jaw.

"She's my mother. I want to go," I stated bluntly.

"What's best for children is not attending."

She ruled from her sanitized world. Having made that statement of fact as if it were written in some Biblical text, she paraded out of the room, her proper solid heels tapping a leaden dirge.

My Uncle Alfred, Mildred's husband, was obliged to drive me to their cottage. He and my aunt lived on the campus of MacDonald College where my uncle taught undergraduate students in the biologic sciences. Under normal circumstances, I loved the ride with Uncle Alfred past Côte St- Luc, Dorval and Beaconsfield into the countryside. He was a favorite uncle related only by marriage, a scholarly biologist, gentle and simple, far too fine a person to be married to this snapping turtle of a wife who smacked him down with her rebuffs.

He let me out at the front gate.

"Here's the key. Maybe you should lie down. You look so tired."

The dark grief in my eyes and my silence put Uncle Alfred on edge.

"You'll be fine," he said, more to reassure himself than me. He made a move to clasp my wrist in a shy attempt at comfort, but I pulled away. Reaching into his jacket pocket, he removed a handkerchief inserting it into my hand. It was damp with my Uncle's tears.

"Mildred means well," he called out as he got back into his car for the return to the city.

Distracted and obsessing, I thought about Aunt Mildred and her unpleasantness secreted by her cordial words. Her methods were transparent to me, and I wondered if my uncle was aware of her pointless affectations. Prone to hysteria, nagging outbursts, and constantly talking nonsense, she was not a likeable person. I vowed never to forgive her intrusion and her decision to keep me from the raw and painful goodbye. This was not the first circumstance in which I derided insincerity. It troubled me to realize that I was becoming competent in vile deceit; the face I showed was innocent yet my heart snarled with intolerable loathing.

Surrounded by farmland and orchards, I spent the early afternoon watching the lambs at play and eating green apples until I had a stomachache. Fleeing through the manicured gardens feeling an insane need for my mother, I ran past a vine-covered gazebo and saw her sitting on a bench smiling and holding out her arms to me. I flung myself into her warm comfort bursting into insatiable tears, craving a treasure house of tears from which there was no return.

Her image evanesced as a puff of smoke from the burning fire of memory. Her soft embrace was replaced by the rugged bark of an elm tree. Its broad curved branches leaned over the green lawn, the scattered early leaves of imminent fall, and the snow-white swan in the pond. Having been banished from ever knowing or seeing my mother's resting place, I hated every lovely thing. Excluded and forbidden, I felt as if I had entered a restricted room in a never-ending corridor of rooms, the one of lost love. My inner voice whispered and circled about like the pale swan in her watery nest beginning the sad lament of an ending without end.

Year, if you have no Mother's day present planned; reach back and bring me the firmness of her hand

It was a humid muggy mid afternoon in late August. I loitered in front of the house clad only in a loose sleeveless top and shorts. To evade the heat, I retreated into the cool shade of the house. In the parlor, the burgundy velvet drapes were drawn excluding light from the room. All the mirrors were draped in ghostly sheets so there were no reflections to multiply the heartbreak. Each room was performing its own memorial service in the shloshim period, the initial thirty days of mourning. All of my mother's relatives had departed. Only my grandmother Ada and my father remained to grieve.

I could scarcely identify my father. He looked like he had aged twenty years. His unshaven face wore a mask of thunder clouds and his eyes were darkly narrowed and deeply sunken from lack of sleep. He was dressed in the same clothing from the day of my mother's funeral: the doleful suit jacket with the rent in the lapel, his rumpled, sodden shirt and unpressed trousers, and his black socks. Sorrow held his tortured body in the chair as if cosseted, a mute display of unfathomable bereavement. It seemed to be scouring his soul causing him to shrink into an inaccessible, bruised portrait of a man. My grandmother's tear soaked face seemed blurred around the edges. I knelt by her chair and wrapped my arms around her small frame. I dearly loved my grandmother and always affectionately called her, Bubbe, but I was wordless in the vastness of loss. She contained her sorrow for a moment as she softly spoke Yiddish words of solace. The flood of tears returned in gusts like a violent summer storm drenching her pastel cheeks.

Dejectedly, I wandered about lost in a maze unable to escape the pull of my mother's presence made more compelling by her absence. Every niche held a secret, every corner clasped a memory, and sounds of whimpering seemed to strew out of the idle kitchen. *Was she hiding in the cellar doing the weekly laundering?* Simply opening the door to the basement and inching down the creaky stairs frightened me, but I was enticed by the possibility of finding her there, of confirming it had all been a stupid mistake. A surge of aloneness embraced me in a cloying stifling hold. I pined for my mother's touch, her loving fingers that swept impish strands of hair away from my eyes, smoothed my wrinkled middy blouses, and tied the laces of my clunky shoes. At night before bed, she never failed to brush my hair accurately counting aloud one hundred strokes, untangling the mats and releasing the gloss. Then tucking me in, she traced a quick kiss across my forehead, unable to linger for fear my father might notice her softness and vulnerability.

Where are you Mama? In the duskiness of the cellar I could see her clearly, a tired beaten-down woman, hair silvering at the temples, and moisture refining the flush on her cheeks. She was attending to her task of filling the porcelain tub with assorted soiled clothes and bedding. The noisy agitator was churning as she was urging the sheets through the wringer to squeeze out the water, the weight of the saturated pieces too much for her to manage alone.

"Mama, you're back," I called out with relief.

"Keep your hands out of the basin, don't splash water on the floor and don't act silly. You're supposed to be useful, not make it harder for me."

My mother leniently scolded me but her twinkling eyes softened her words. Her sweet-natured laughter danced around in the dampness. The washing machine sat patiently in the middle of the floor attentive to her efforts.

Suddenly, the cellar door opened sending Spartan shafts of light cascading down the stairs, and my father's unmistakable tread could be heard on each step. Terror took on shape and sound. My father strode directly over to my mother and smacked her across the face. I felt the sharp stinging pain. It made no sense. She had not done anything wrong. I watched in sorrow as she did not cry out. I imagined her throat was clogged with tears. Rasping, she collapsed into the corner chair, a broken reed.

I could hear my own sobbing, plaintiff wailing howls. They gyrated about like the frenzied agitator spewing the images into a fine mist until I could not make the distinction of what was real or what was past; it was too curious and sad. Turning the handle of the wringer, it spun around purposelessly and I spun with it. Hiding my bruised cheek, I scrambled up the steps into the bright heat and emptiness.

Back in the street again, I waited for evening shadows to drape the neighborhood in protective folds. A shrill clang of a bicycle bell attracted my attention, but the cyclist was a high school boy Jean Paul from Rue St. Christophe who rode past my house on his way to church choir practice. "Laisse- moi passer!" he crudely barked and grossly picked his nose. Overlooking his insulting gesture, not even caring, I moved aside to let him go by. Expectantly, I examined the driver of a slow-passing car hoping it was one of the policemen arriving with reliable news of my mother's absence. I expected him to say, "Je te fais mes excuses. C'est un malentendu. My apologies, it was all an inadvertent mistake, a repellent error."

The apparition of these faces in the crowd

The heavy-hearted days of grieving had passed, but my father and the house were steeped in unalterable sorrow. He declined to speak and glowered at me when I entered the dusky parlor where he was still sitting shiva long after the traditional time of mourning. Meals were neglected and I was obliged to fend for myself most days. My morning cereal was eaten dry as the milk had soured and was hastily poured down the drain. The overly ripe bananas turned spotty brown and further darkened as if sun-baked; the insides were an inedible mush. Slices of vitamin enriched *Wonder Bread,* colorfully packaged, were now stale and moldy and only the few fruits in the icebox that had not spoilt were usable. I opened a tin of *Campbell Tomato Soup* remembering to dilute it with one can of water and stirred the mixture as it heated to a rolling boil. I ate the soup with a side of *Premium Soda Crackers* spread with peanut butter.

One early evening, my grandmother Ada stopped by with fresh eggs, bagels, cottage cheese, and a container of pot roast for dinner. The succulent smell when she removed the lid was unbearably appealing, and only then did I know how hungry I was. The roast was tender and juicy, browned to perfection with carrots, onions, and baby potatoes. My grandmother and my father sat together in the kitchen while he dined, but I dared not go in to join them. His arms like long tentacles reached around the house to circle me in his unquenchable wrath. When he finished his meal and returned to the parlor, my grandmother prepared a special plate for me and watched over me as I slowly savored every morsel. Together we cleared and washed the dishes and stored some leftovers in the icebox.

"Caasi," she said, "a little something for you."

On a plate was a slice of her delectable honey cake frosted with a fluffy mix of egg whites and honey, moist and smelling of cinnamon.

"Thank you," was all I could manage without tearing up.

"Sit, eat," she urged.

"Bubbe, can you stay the night?" I asked her, my mouth full of cake.

"No, Mamaleh," she replied, replacing my name with the Yiddish expression of endearment, 'little mother'.

I knew her dislike of walking home in the poorly lit streets. Her failing eyesight made the short distance a source of consternation. Not wishing to impose on her, I hugged her warm body cherishing the fragrance of yeast and vanilla, an integral and definable part of her goodness.

The front door clicked as she left leaving me alone with my thoughts. I could not escape the inconsolable sense of being an undesirable reminder discarded by my father to placate his loss. He had disposed of me as dispassionately as I had gotten rid of the curdled milk. The unbridgeable disparity of his fiction and my truths held me in a stultifying grip, unfettered only by falling into an exhausted sleep.

The next morning, swept away by a strange wildness, I ventured from my house. Without any plan, I boarded a streetcar at the corner of Av Des Pins and Av Du Parc. The September air was crushingly hot; a steamy haze brooded over the city landscape. My blouse stuck compliantly to my back and sweat trailed down the undersides of both arms to the wrists drawing streamlets in the light layers of dirt. Uncomfortable in my own clothes and skin, I moved uncomplainingly about on the wooden seat until the streetcar picked up speed. We passed Parc Mont Royal and in a gradual upward climb connected to Côte Ste. Catherine. The open windows invited a temperate flow of air to glide across my damp neck in bracing relief.

At Rue Plantagener, carefree families with picnic baskets clambered on chattering gaily in French. The green fields and wildflowers of Île Sainte-Hélène and the serenity of my mother's face returned for a moment only to be dismissed by mean-spirited tricks of memory. I tried my best to enjoy watching the cars, houses, and trees whiz by but everything ran together in a drizzling splash of colors. Sitting by myself, I felt my mother's presence in a silent yet tangible roar. I clasped my hands in my lap to lock the portal on my secret grief. The streetcar slowed to a screeching stop; the conductor pulled the lever to open the doors and a large crowd of newcomers squeezed in thoughtlessly shoving and mingling with the descending mob. I offered my seat to a frail woman tinged with age wearing a mottled babushka, stringy hair dangling, and her arms burdened with papered parcels. In the ensuing confusion, I felt myself being lifted and dragged down the metal steps to the curb. Without cause, I was standing on a corner, one that I failed to recognize.

The sign read 'Côte Des-Neiges'; it was the wrong place to get off and I was miles from home. Frantically I reached for the familiar grasp of my mother's hand but she was not at my side. It was inconceivable that I should be there without her. I pursued the streetcar and caught a glimpse of her desperate face pressed against the glass of the rear window. The overhead cable sparked like Dominion Day fireworks sending showers of luminosity into the air. In an instant, a jagged flash of lightening crashed and a violent thunderstorm cracked open the sky releasing chilling rain. As the tram sped away, my faint cries trailed behind the silver tracks as they receded into the distance.

Not in substance or in shadow was my mother ever to return.

Meanwhile.., Within the Gates of Hell sate Sin and Death

The events of the recent weeks revisited in a drowning flash soaking my light thin shirt with tears and sweat. I leaned against the maple tree in front of my house taking comfort in its solid presence even though the rough textured surface was insensitive to my plight. The street was queerly silent. Most of the neighborhood kids were at Parc Lafontaine. I was loath to join them even though it was not too far a walk along Roy Street to Amherst, a distance of merely ten blocks. Before...I could not think of the time before without giving in to distraction and the violent uproar of abandonment and loss. The very air around me was in disarray like the passage of waves in shallow water.

In happier days, my mother had taken me to play in the park. As she rested on a bench reading her book in the shade of the huge poplar trees, I climbed on the memorial statuary or waded in the cool waters of the pond. It was fun to chase the numerous squirrels or pester the park keeper tending the plants in the greenhouse. The reassurance of my mother's company made the park a wondrous place. Now I was lost, foundering like a ship sunk at sea or struck upon a rock.

I looked in both directions and had a sense of someone approaching. A seedy looking man in torn beggarly attire staggered and lurched along. His furtive glancing about settled on me and targeted me in a queer disconcerting way. My body became limp and my skin clammy. Screened from the warmth of the sun by his impertinence, I began to shiver uneasily. His indecision altered to a leering grin, mocking and slimy, unmasking spittle on his split lips and rotted teeth. Crassly mumbling incomprehensible phrases and obscenities he moved closer. Chained by an invisible hold, I was fixed to the spot anchored by fear I could not shed. His arm thrust out toward me before I could duck or move or turn to run. I reached into my hair where his vile hand had passed to find a sticky gob plastered to my scalp. Gum... I recognized it was chewing gum. My baby fine hair was caught in a sickening vise.

The man was gone in an instant. My father had witnessed the assault through the parlor window and rushed into the street. He tore after the intruder, his urgency driving him, energy pumping his legs in the chase, but the man was already too far off and moving too fast disappearing around the corner to Rue St. Dominique. Averse to further pursuit, my father gave up the search. I watched his slow recoil. He was panting from the effort. At a distance his pace seemed measured and deliberate and his anger calmed. As he drew close, my bewildered eyes saw the look on his face, his brow deeply grooved in fury and his eyes wild and fierce. I covered my own to hide the unbidden tears and then presented my dishonored palms to him. He struck me. His voice was the second strike, swift, vicious and savage.

"You little whore, you invited that!"

I meekly followed him into the house. He ripped off my shirt and tossed it down the cellar stairs unto the heap of dirty laundry. Finding a pair of shears in my mother's mending kit, he used it to cut a wide swath across the top of my scalp, gum and hair falling to the floor in one abscission. The unprotected bare white patch implored to be forgiven. It took months for the new growth of hair to cover the bald part. Years passed before I outgrew my father's sin.

One would think,
that every Letter was wrote with a Tear,

Hitting me became my father's customary method of dealing with the mundane tribulations of day to day and taking care of an eight-year old. He was incapable of shedding the regrets and remorse that remained as close to him as the clothes on his back. I was trapped in the gorge between the peaks and ridges of his misery. He found the familiar doling out of physical blows mitigated for a while his conflicted emotions. It seemed not to matter what I did or said; his measures were quick and deliberate and the act became easier and recurring. He invented new ways to trounce me; when his hands tired, he used his belt. The sound of his leather belt being ripped out of the loops of his slacks, a snapping, popping, or whipping noise, sent me scurrying into the furthest corner. I could not elude him. His face was an ashen and sallow mosaic with inflamed cobalt blue eyes. Bare sharp utterances of censure forcibly split off like shattered bits of granite

"You are to blame."

I heard the words as if spelled out letter by heartrending letter. Held accountable, I listened but did not argue with him. The small but seemingly vital secret I had hidden from him was magnified in my mind by his charges. He was unable to concede that the brutal and unconscionable handling of my mother had caused her to spiral into desperation. There was no truth or truce between us.

With each beating, the heat of impact reddened my tender skin; swollen purplish raised marks stippled my chest. Tears welled on my lashes and uncontained sobs at last slowed him down, and he lowered the thrashing belt to dangle in remorse and contrition. To make amends, he spread *Vaseline* on the welts and ineptly blotted my tears with *Kleenex*. I turned my face away from his hands, now disconcertingly gentle so that he would not see my eyes burn with scorn and disdain.

His censures rang in my ears, the words making their mark again and again, allegations corrosively carved in my mind, drop by drop, into tunnels of contempt.

Part III

1948-1952

How easily our little world can go to pieces!

As time passed, whole days, the tender reminder of my beloved mother continued to touch my mother's sisters with deep regret and remorse. Before the fall start of the school year, I was invited to attend my cousin Howard's wedding in Boston. I wanted so much to continue my attachment to the family and to satisfy an earnest obligation to my mother. My relatives helped with the needed arrangements. Aunt Rosie and Cousin Myrna suggested I accompany them on the trip in Uncle Saul's car, and Aunt Ethel insisted I stay with her and my cousins Howard and Rita while in Boston.

A few years back, Rita's family had visited in Montréal at my Aunt Rosie's home and I had taken an instant liking to her. In fact, I idolized her. Rita was everything I was unable to be: happy, talkative, mischievous, and vivacious. Her face was plump with smiles and in her company my impassive shyness was transformed by her blustering winds of affection. Together we were impishly outrageous. We tied the tail of Rita's English bulldog Winston to a rocking chair. With each arc of the chair, Winston's tail flicked automatically sending us into howls of naughty laughter. When we were scolded for that prank, we dressed him in dolls' clothing complete with bonnet covering his bullhead and muzzle, a sweater and scarf folded around his short hefty body, and booties on his paws. Winston was good-natured and allowed our antics without flinching or barking; he tagged along wherever we went as we searched for new rascally things to do.

I spoke to my father of the proposed trip to Boston assuming an air of casual indifference knowing full well if I seemed overly eager, he might immediately say, "No." He behaved as if I had not mentioned it at all. Inexpressively tinkering with the stem of his watch, he elaborately wound it in a forward and backward motion between his thumb and forefinger. He walked away and out of the blue said, "I'll think it over." Those few words were sufficient to buoy my spirits. Considering it was family, I firmly believed there was a chance he would permit me to go.

Ahead of the scheduled drive, I cleaned the house working zealously like an army of ants. I scoured the cracked porcelain tub in the bathroom, polished all the mirrors, and using *Spic and Span*, washed the kitchen linoleum with a scrub brush scrunching down on my knees to clean under the water heater. The sink in the kitchen was blocked and refused to drain. I tried the plunger to no avail. Bucket by bucket, I lugged the slimy water to dispose of it in the toilet until the sink was completely emptied, and then I rubbed the discolorations with steel wool removing all but the rust marks. I fretfully waited until my father came home. As soon as the front door opened, I tugged him by his coat sleeve urging him to follow me into the kitchen.

"Look, Daddy, look how clean everything is!" My voice squeaked with pride.

He scrutinized my visible efforts and made no reply. Bottling up my tears, I hid my pinched washerwoman's fingers behind my back and disguised my crushed heart with a sweet smile.

The long-awaited day for the trip arrived. I packed my clothes in a plain paper shopping bag, party shoes at the bottom, and every other piece including socks and underwear, neatly ironed and folded, placed above. Occupying its own hanger was my lovely dress for the wedding borrowed from Cousin Myrna and altered to my size. It was a softly finished Empire fashioned taffeta dress. During my fittings, I proudly paraded in front of the mirror enchanted by the crisp swishing sounds of the taffeta.

Freshly bathed, I dressed in a sheer, crisp, blue/white dotted Swiss blouse and pleated, navy blue wool skirt, perfect for traveling. I gathered my light brown hair into a neat ponytail and smoothed the wisps of bangs on my forehead until they lay flat. Primly and expectantly, I sat at the very edge of my bed listening for the sound of my uncle's *Packard*. When the front bell rang, I raced to fling open the door. Uncle Saul and Myrna stood on the top step bundled up to ward off the autumn chill.

"Ready, kiddo," said Uncle Saul.

I had no chance to reply. My father shoved me aside.

"Go to your room," he said to me, his voice terse.

Between the mad poundings of my heart, I paced to and fro. Beads of sweat, tiny as dewdrops, formed at the back of my neck and slid unhindered into my embroidered dickey collar. Short bursts of conversation, unclear words rose in timbre until they were discernible roars assailing my ears.

"Let me make it clear, I won't permit Caasi to go," bellowed my father.

My tenuous glass of hope, now emptied, crashed to the hard floor shattering into slivers, sharp and cutting. I sunk to my knees among the shards as the steady hum of the car's engine grew faint and distant.

Truth, we say, is not found exclusively in the possession of those with a high 'intelligence quotient'

Returning to school after the senseless solitary horror of the past six weeks, my mind was unreliable to deal with my teachers' well meant but poorly delivered sympathy or the weird stares from class-mates. I was in a fishbowl drowning in snide and idle gossip.

There was a noticeable clutched-up jumpy atmosphere in my third grade classroom. Our teacher, Mrs. Adderly, generally as expressive as a window mannequin, keenly walked about the room looking feve-rish, her bony frame twitching with curbed agitation. At last, easing into her chair at her desk, she said in a tremulous voice, "Class, come to order."

All chattering promptly ceased cut off by the plain request, and there was a collective inhalation of breaths. The door opened and two men in almost matching broadcloth suits and pinstriped ties pompous-ly walked in, one bristly mustached and the other stiffly lame. They had the worrisome impact of administrative types familiar with com-mand.

Mrs. Adderly clapped her hands twice to gain our undivided atten-tion.

"Boys and girls, these gentlemen are from the Provincial Board of Education. Please say hello to Monsieur Herissons and Monsieur Le Lièvre."

"Hello Monsieur Herissons and Monsieur Le Lièvre," we chanted in unison.

"For today, we will be examining your ability to answer simple questions of logic. It is not a test that required study," announced Mrs. Adderly.

She paused and turned to Herissons.

"Perhaps you would prefer to tell the class more."

Clearing his throat, Monsieur Herissons puffed up and then said with exaggerated outward show.

"We wish to measure the I.Q. of children in the third grade."

All my classmates looked at him quizzically, then looked at one another and said nothing. Monsieur Le Lièvre limped around the room accurately centering on each desktop small booklets and shiny yellow sharpened number two pencils.

"The Province is interested in documenting the numerical, pictorial, spatial, and conceptual ability of all of the students at your age for predictive purposes," said Herissons, pleased with his prodigious rambling, certain we were incapable of absorbing the obscurity of what he said. His words were muddled rubbish.

Mrs. Adderly finished up with the specifics.

"For accuracy, you will have exactly one hour. There are four sections and you will use fifteen minutes for each. At the end of each time period, you will go on to the next section, but you cannot return to the previous, even if you have failed to solve all the problems. Is that understood, class?"

"Yes, Mrs. Adderly," we chorused.

"You must not speak to one another, glance at another student's notebook, or ask for help from me. Now if you are clear with this, write your names and your birth dates in neat block print on the front page. Are there any questions?"

"No, Mrs. Adderly."

"You may begin," instructed Mrs. Adderly, as she set her time clock on her desk.

I stared at the first two questions in bafflement.

1. Two ducks and two dogs have a total of fourteen legs.

    | True | False

2. Two of the following numbers add up to thirteen: **1, 6, 3, 5, 11**

    | True | False

They were harmless math calculations far below the level of my skills, but the sum of the activity of my mind was zero. I moved inattentively from page to page unable to see the point of the simplest concept, randomly checking true or false, oblivious and uncaring. Sorrowing, I lost my way in a thick fog of disorder. Chewing on the end of my pencil, I stared out the window and watched orange, red, and yellow maple leaves flutter by drifting soundlessly to the ground doomed to shrivel and die.

I wanted to tell Mrs. Adderly that the test was wrong for me in the critical juncture of bleak days without hope, and dreams without clarity of meaning. How could the Province judge my brightness or dullness when I was being crushed by the power of darkness?

Several weeks later, my father received the results of my I.Q. exam accompanied by a request from Mrs. Adderly to come and discuss my low score; he discounted her summons and refused to comply.

"Dad," I asked, "how did I do?"

"According to this report, your intelligence is equal to that of an aardvark."

I laughed for the first time in weeks.

"Not good, eh?"

"Estimated by intelligence tests, general ability is largely hereditary, the so-called specialists say. By that standard, I must be an armadillo," My father caustically replied.

"Now I know why you're crusty," I blurted out jokingly.

"Not bad for a little dimwit," he said and smiled.

"If my I.Q. is low, will it matter?"

"What matters is you were given an imbecilic test at an imbecilic time by imbeciles.

Children, leave the string alone!

My cousin Philip, three years older than I, lived in the same apartment building on the north side of the four-unit complex. Whenever I spotted him, he was eagerly bustling about generally looking for mischief. A crop of untidy yellow curls, blue green eyes iridescent as polished marble, pronounced cheekbones, and sensuous full lips made him particularly attractive. Although older, he was only several inches taller than I. His body was compact and athletic. Whenever he was bored, he was an insufferable show-off flexing his forearms to display his muscles or prancing around shadow boxing. Never walking at a regular pace, he was always in a hurry and breathless as if he had just completed a race. He had a devilish daring spirit and a brash endearing presence, and it was hard to refuse him any request, risk and peril put aside. I worshipped him.

We did not often play as he was busy endlessly scheming. On rainy days or when he needed amusement, we got together in his parlor, comic books scattered willy-nilly scanning the advertisements for stamps by mail looking for rare finds. In spite of our age difference, we shared a common hobby of collecting and trading stamps. He sent away for stamps and was obliged to pay for them on arrival. I was skeptical; my suspicions soon were confirmed that he was deceitfully gypping the mail-order companies. In return for my silence with respect to his fraud, Philip gave me duplicates of stamps that he already had and an occasional first issue or commemorative stamp. I felt a twinge of guilt accepting his gifts. They were dishonestly gotten but he laughed at the sober look of aversion on my face.

"Caasi, take them, they're for you," he insisted.

"Are you sure it's okay?"

"Sure I'm sure," he said.

Philip was blasé about his stamps tossing them into a box, but I stored mine in a protective album mounting the squares and rectangles in neat rows like little boxcars. We amassed a group of collectibles from far away countries, names I was unacquainted with like Lithuania, Paraguay, Hungary, and Nippon. I was captivated by the array of pictures: locomotives, dogs, buildings, weapons, flowers, dour profiled heads of state, miniatures representing an unknown world. We admired a unique one featuring a Jamaican hummingbird and another, a sea eagle from Senegal. Using a magnification lens to capture the details, Philip looked for 'stamp mistakes' such as paper folds, flaws in printing, or errors in the perforations that made the stamps valuable. I treasured my album with the glued-in stamps, not realizing that the adhesive residue on the back rendered them worthless. I never planned to sell my collection.

One day after we finished sorting and exchanging stamps, I tired of the finicky chore of pasting and appealed to Philip's good-nature.

"Do you want to go to the candy store?" I asked

"Why not," he answered in his cavalier way.

We walked to the corner of Rues Napoleon and De Bullion, Philip rushing on ahead as we neared the little shop. The partially deaf owner did not hear the little ding-a-ling of the bell as we entered, and he remained in the rear behind a drawn curtain. We were free to wander about examining the displayed sweets surrounded with the temptation of licorice pipes, *M&M's Plain Chocolates*, toffee apples, fruit jujubes, caramel chews, *Life Savers*, and gumballs. I saw Philip cunningly slip a *Snickers Bar* and some *Tootsie Roll Pops* into his pant pocket. He signaled to me to nab something for myself, and I impetuously stole a peppermint twist. Just then the proprietor came into view from the back, drunk, dirty, and untidy, smelling like a cellar. He cursed us, his eyes flaming.

"Riffraff! Mon Dieu! Why do good-for-nothings come here?"

My hand holding the two pennies' worth of candy began to sweat melting the peppermint stick and lining my palm with red and green sinful stripes, squiggly strings of shame. I was tongue-tied, inarticulate with fear, and appalled by my crime. My sense of right and wrong turned inside out. We headed for the door and ran away from the shop, Philip assertively laughing in the sport as we darted for home.

"Good girl," he said, congratulating me on my speedy cunning.

I could not bring myself to eat the candy.

No! Pay the dentist when he leaves A fracture in your jaw

It had been bothering me for at least three weeks, but I was afraid to tell my father. The right tooth in my mouth ached, the lower molar next to the pointy canine one. A slow flow of pain throbbed in my jaw and kept me wakeful and worried at night. An innocent draft of air felt like a cutting scythe. My fondness for sucking on the wax coke-shaped bottles with colored sugar water inside and eating marshmallow biscuits persuaded me that I had caused this tooth to decay. I imagined flashing a toothless grin when one by one my teeth rotted and dropped out. Fear of my father's reaction could not contain the sensitive sharp stabs.

"Dad, I have a sore tooth," I said, letting slip what I had kept secret as if it were an offense.

I had chosen an importunate time. My father did not look up from his reading of the business section of the *Montreal Star* concerned with the market fluctuations of his stocks. It was impossible to gauge from his reaction whether his portfolio was profitable or losing money. He was stony faced, resistant, and holding fast to his positions.

"It hurts a lot," I bleated.

"Go to Docteur Trudeau," he said, vexed by my barging in on his line by line detailed scrutiny of the little symbols. The low, high, bid, and ask prices appeared to be speaking to him in a reverential and affectionate language.

"I hate Trudeau. He scares me and I don't trust him."

I balked but did not back away. My father slowly lowered the newspaper pages from in front of his face so that he could squint at me over the top. His eyes, narrow in assertion, scrutinized me with an uncommon degree of severity.

"He's a dentist. You don't have to like him."

The tone and the look indicated our discussion was over.

Docteur Trudeau was located on Av Henri Julien near Blvd. St. Joseph, a substantial ten-block walk. Buckling on my parka, I stuck my feet into dilapidated rain boots and left the house, the gusting wind prickly against my face. The streets were still sheeted with ice by the nightly frosts, and there was no morning sun to conciliate the chill; the cold breached my thinly layered parka like hammered in nails. To postpone the arrival at his office, I made no effort to fight the blustery weather and dawdled along buffeted by the elements. Stopping at the front door of a two-story nondescript brick building, I tried to peer through the leaded glass panes but my view to the inside was distorted. Unwillingly, I turned the knob stepping into a cubicle size lobby. There was a smell of must and stale air that told of damp and imperfect ventilation, of smoke and of mittens drying on the sputtering radiator, and of the unsavory stench from the uncurbed breath of sickness.

It took all my composure and willpower not to bolt. On the wall above the mittens, the directory was encased in a framed box and the doctors' names were mounted in small black block letters, some put together in a proper line and others precariously sagging. I traced my finger down the dusty glass cover spotting Docteur Trudea (the u had descended to the bottom of the frame), Dentisterie Général: Suite 201. Pressing the little buzzer in the panel adjacent to his name to announce my entrance, I trudged up the narrow tenement staircase in the gloom and damp finding little niches and ledges in the coarse-grained brick walls to hold on to so as not to trip on my fright.

Docteur Trudeau's door was ajar and I walked in without knocking. No one was present in the small antechamber, so I sat down in the middle of the sagging sofa, and stared at the seedy wrecked carpet, the details long-trampled into an ill-defined pattern. The gnawing pain in my tooth reminded me of my aim. Emitting the smallest of sighs, I succumbed to the interminable wait counting slowly backwards from one hundred by threes. And in the hush, I heard the ticking in my head of the wall-mounted *Bulova* clock, the sounds in English and French, no-non… non-no… no-non…

A port-colored corduroy curtain fluted in tiny grooves separated his living quarters from the waiting room and dental office. Pushing it aside, Trudeau materialized cloaked in a cloud of smoke, a cigarette loosely hanging from his mouth, indifferent to the ash collecting on the end. A large haggard looking man, his sloppy brown hair was streaked with gray, and his bulbous nose had pronounced blood vessels matching the purple-red of the corduroy. It seemed as if too much cold had withered his face and indented his rheumy eyes. The front of his white jacket was splattered with flecks of blood and the sleeves exposed frayed edges with flagging threads jiggling about loosely as he moved his arms. Sullenly, he motioned me into the treatment room and indicated the dental chair working the foot pedal to let it down to accommodate me. I clambered into the chair and tightly compacted myself resting my head on the little leather pillow, my distrustful eyes watching as Trudeau hung a fabric bib about my neck pinching my skin as he fastened it in place with a metal snap.

"Ouch," I cried out.

Unmindfully, he proceeded with adjusting the chair slowly tilting it until I was lying flat. I was now helpless and truly scared. A bright overhead lamp shone directly into my eyes stunning and blinding me, but not fooling my sense of smell. Docteur Trudeau stank of liquor. A foul, gasoline like odor of alcohol fumes bombarded me. His big chunky-fingered hands were shaking as he swung his instrument tray into position and stubbed out his cigarette. On impulse, I turned my head to see the display of probes, drill bits, extraction pliers, retractors, and gauze sponges. At the edge of the tray was a metal mould filled to overflowing with cigarette butts. I was beginning to feel sick to my stomach.

"As tu mal aux dents?" asked Trudeau.

"J'ai la douleur dans ma dent."

I pointed to the affected tooth.

He looked at it using a small mirror fixed to a curved handle, then tapped it with the blunt end causing flares of sharp pain to shoot through the side of my face and my body to rise up out of the chair in agony.

"You don't like it? Ni moi non plus."

"Not me either," he kept repeating in sing-song fashion as he lumbered over to the sink. He speedily washed his hands, dried them on the mucky towel hanging from a hook, and returned to my side. He was suddenly holding a giant syringe in one hand and grasping the corner of my mouth with the forceful fingers of his other hand tasting of antiseptic soap, nicotine, and whiskey. He tugged my lips out of the way and injected the contents of the syringe near the bad tooth. At first the pain was deadly, but then miraculously it slipped away until only a faint, imperceptible memory of it remained. I tried to say, "Merci beaucoup," but my tongue was numb and my words faltered together in uncertainty.

Docteur Trudeau left the room without any instructions to me and I stayed put, only moving my eyes to catch allusions of what there was to see. On the wall above the sink was a poster of a young boy looking miserable and downcast, his swollen cheek wrapped with a huge bandage extending from under his neck around his head. From the distance, I could not make out the printed words below the picture, but since he was a fat kid, I was certain it proclaimed how he had indulged in too many sweets and caused a monstrous cavity. Right above my head adjacent to the light was a drill joined to something that resembled a belt driven engine. That sight reclaimed my terror and I squirmed vulnerably in the chair shifting to examine the brown stained porcelain bowl with the *Dixie* paper cup on the edge, the running water swirling around under the ledge funneling down to the drain. Propping myself up, I took a sip of water and spit into the bowl. There was some blood mixed in the spit. I felt dizzy and lay back clutching my hands together feeling icy fingers holding each other for comfort.

Docteur Trudeau reappeared. His awkwardness and unsteadiness had increased, and his liquored breath was even more potent than before. After tapping the anaesthetized tooth and hearing no moans from me, he picked up the pliers. Cradling my head against his chest, he grasped the tooth, twisted it, rocked it, and then tugged it forcefully. I heard a snapping popping sound and then saw the results of his efforts on the instrument tray, my enamel tooth with its smooth edges, indentations, and grinding surfaces standing on little roots, a plucked pearly white flower.

"C'est tout," he said. "Go home."

He inserted some gauze into the now vacant gum, lifted me out of the chair and ushered me to the door clenching my arm like a cold leather strap. I stumbled down the stairs and walked home in a bitter, drizzling rain, my face pinched and wan, huddling within myself. Blood saturated the sponges and frothed from the corner of my mouth, trickling down my neck and staining my collar.

My father was waiting for me seeming not to notice my ghostly appearance and the smeared streaks of blood on my face.

"Well," he said, "did he put in a filling?"

"No, he pulled it out."

Unable to choke back his anger my father roared, "Damn that Trudeau, doesn't he know the difference between a baby tooth and a permanent one?"

Scarce had she ceased,
when out of heaven a bolt...struck

In the late afternoon before the frost settled in and the meager light of a watercolor washed sky signaled dusk, the neighbor kids gathered on the street for a game of hide-and-seek. They were just faces to me; I rarely spoke to them even though most lived nearby in shoddy adjoining apartments. Ritchie was a regular and enthusiastic participant in our childish games. He must have been at least four or five years older than the rest of the group but he looked no more than nine. He always wore a baseball cap, the brim pulled low over his brow. Attached to the belt loops of his pants by leather strings was a beat-up fielder's mitt.

Once when we chanced to talk on the street, he showed me his collection of baseball cards. He prided himself in knowing all the names of the players on the *Montreal Royals* team.

"I bet you didn't know the *Royals* are the farm team for the *Brooklyn Dodgers*," he bragged.

"What's a farm team?"

He eagerly explained, "The *Royals* are in a minor league and the *Dodgers* are in a major league. It's a big thing for the guys to suit up in the majors."

All this baseball stuff sounded great.

"I have lots of autographs! Jackie Robinson, Duke Snider, Johnny Podres, Ed Roebuck... " He rattled off the names of his heroes.

Ritchie had an impact on me. I wanted him to like me and not think I was just some silly girl. My father had mentioned the name of the stadium where the *Royals* played. It gave me a chance to show Ritchie I knew something about baseball and even pretend I was a fan.

"Do you go to *Delormier Downs* all by yourself?

"Sure, why not?"

"So, who's your favorite player?"

He showed me a card of Chuck Conners. I could see why he was awed. Chuck was everything Ritchie hoped to be someday: handsome, over six feet in height, weighing 210 pounds, hitting twenty home runs, and batting in 108 runs in one season. Watching Ritchie sort his valued baseball cards, I could not help but notice the smooth, chiseled look of his face as if he were sculpted from marble. Thin, with indented cheeks and colorless lips, he was a wisp, a puny, undersized slip of a boy. Dark rings under his eyes gave him an aura of tragedy as if he were flickering and fading away. His arms were well-built but lean and his slender fingers had clean nails, not bitten to the quick like most of the other boys. Clothed in a lumpy woolen sweater and tatty flannel pants patched at the knees, he seemed shabbier than the rest of the common ruffians. The rough worn shoes spoke of abject poverty.

As the countdown began for hide-and-seek: 99, 98, 97, 96... I took off like a shot. A door under my house led to coal chute sliding into the cellar. There among the coal storage bins was a coveted, restricted hiding place tucked behind the lit furnace. The sparks cast flame-tipped shadows on the dark walls scarred by cinders. The thrill of the wait and the keyed up peak of pleasure just before disclosure made me delirious with excitement.

"Where are you? I can hear you breathing..."

I identified Ritchie's voice and faintly heard the soft motion of his footsteps on the cold cellar floor. He found me crouching in the secret niche, quivering and tightly drawn up. Outlined by the glow from the furnace, he fumbled around in the half-light until his hands rested on my body. His slim fingers wrote pointless scribbles on my chest. My skin tingled as if tiny needles were tapping out an indefinable coded message. I squirmed dizzily under his touch with an answering blast of wild heartbeats and the sharp intake of breaths. Round and around the sounds echoed in the leaden air scattering the soot.

"You're it now!" Ritchie jubilantly called out.

There are other circuitous erections of stone

My grandmother tried to be firm with my father, watching out for him as if he were still the precocious young son in her grocery store of many years ago. He responded to her nudging like a spoiled brat fortifying her image of him. Their conversations at the dining table took on the identical ceremonial format whenever we visited in her old apartment on Av De L'Esplanade. She first served my father tea in a glass, and he helped himself to two cubes of sugar holding them in his teeth as he sipped. Then she pushed a plate of treats in front of him chosen from her freshly baked challah, sugary coated lemon bars, and swirled vanilla-chocolate cake. Initially he took no notice of the confections but eventually he sampled the challah, unable to resist the traditional egg bread topped with poppy seeds. I was already stuffing myself on the lemon bars hoping I would have room for a piece of her cake and covertly eying the sliced candied fruit, halvah, and bowls of mandarin oranges, filberts, and walnuts.

Speaking to him in a mix of Yiddish and English, my grandmother said, "Vohveh, vos hert zith, what's new?"

Her name for my father was his own garbled word from his baby days when he tried to say Evan, his given name.

"Not much."

"Nu, when are you going to get a job?"

"I don't know, Ma," he truthfully answered.

She switched back to Yiddish to express her consternation.

"Es tut mir veh."

"Voden, so what else?" he said noncommittally.

"Vohveh, you have to look after your life now," she pleaded.

"I'm doing what needs to be done," he said. "Don't nag, Ma."

Talking to my father was like talking to a wall. My grandmother looked over at me. I knew she was wondering if her son provided me with nutritious meals and attended to my health needs. Incontestable in his grim declaration to raise me as he saw fit, he had steadfastly refused her offer for me to stay with her on a temporary basis. She did

169

not suspect the intolerant state of affairs in which I lived from day to day, the privations, the battering, and the restrictions. When she spotted bruises on my arms, I was always quick to say I had injured myself while playing.

"And a warm overcoat, Vohveh… you're walking around in rags."

"It's almost spring. I'll get one next winter."

"Vos about a new jacket for Caasi?"

"Her old one still fits."

"Why are you so stubborn?"

"Takeh? Really?"

"Ya."

"You know me best, Ma."

"Vohveh, your teeth, you'll lose your teeth if you don't see the dentist."

"I'll go, Ma."

"Wen?"

"Sometime soon."

Circling in this way, their talks always ended in frustration for my grandmother and procrastination for my father. Never acting disparagingly to her, he simply was unreasonable. He loved her as a good son loves his most precious possession and hoards it, craftily dallying with it, covertly putting it on display, but primarily just delighting in ownership. As part of his contrivance, he spiritedly resisted and was unbending. He paid no heed to her concerns even as he respected them.

Let us seek The forward path again

In the early part of April, the Hebrew month Nissan, 5709, Grandmother Ada began her preparations for the Passover holiday. To honor the precepts of Orthodox Judaism and its traditional observances, she cleaned out her kitchen of all the chometz, wheat, barley, rye, oats, and other foods prohibited on Pesach. Even the eating utensils were stored in a remote closet because she did not have a back yard in which to bury them, the method established in the little Jewish townships of Russia, the shtetlach. After her kitchen was koshered, she wrote out her shopping list for the Pesach foods in preparation for the first two nights, the Seder-evenings.

At the end of the stark winter, daylight was still scanty and spare. The afternoon chiming of the antiquated grandfather clock summoned the frugal sun from the sky leaving a passing note of frost in the air. Readying for her trip to Rachel Street Market, my grandmother enclosed her head in a shawl folded around her throat, tightly buttoned the Persian lamb collar of her wool coat, and snuggly laced her sealskin boots. Under a canopy of clouds, she walked the one-half mile to the stalls where she gossiped and bargained with her favorite vendors. Lugging by rope handles two heavy cotton sacks of groceries, she trudged back. As she mounted the stairs to her fifth floor apartment, on each of the landings she paused and rested for a brief spell to catch her breath. Slight, plump, and in uncertain health, she was drained, the strain of years taking its toll. Yet she resisted complaining. She once had told me of the many hardships she endured as a young woman living in Irkutsk, a small spot on the map of south-central Russia.

"We had to flee from the Cossacks. They burnt our village, our little shtetl. We were poor. Life was hard."

Even as she spoke of the misery in her village, her face was sweetly cherubic, as if the divine presence of the God of Israel dwelled there, a description she would have disallowed. She was truly virtuous, a humble soul. I loved her for her gentle thoughtfulness more than for any other reason.

On Seder-day, my father dropped me off at the front entrance to her building, electing not to visit, preferring to avoid one of those roundabout sessions with his mother. The grimy snowdrift at the door was dappled ash like a dust heap, wasting and blowing away. As I walked up flight after flight to the top floor, the perfume of piquant scents and spices whisked past me carried by the airstreams in the corridor.

My grandmother had been up since dawn preparing the Seder food. Gefilte fish were steaming in a boiler on the stovetop next to a stewpot of bubbling chicken soup. Roasting in the oven was a brisket with carrots, prunes, and sweet potatoes. Watchfully reaching into the cupboard above the stove for the Pesach china and cutlery, my grandmother wore a fine mist on her forehead and a warm glow on her face. Amazingly organized and neat in her small kitchen, she was the hub of the activity that proceeded in the evening, a complete four-course dinner for twelve adults and four children.

I fitted my jacket and knitted cap onto a wire hanger in the overstuffed hall closet and sniffed my way to the kitchen. My grandmother's apple sponge cake in the oven, checked with a toothpick, was too moist to come out.

"Maybe half an hour more," she said.

"Bubbe, how do you know when it's ready?" I asked.

"It must..." she searched for the word in English, "vi zahgen, how do you say, jump up to touch?"

"That's right," I answered finding her expression charming and funny.

The chocolate-dipped macaroons and crunchy pecan nut cookies were cooling on a wire rack, and I made a motion to snatch one but was impeded by my heedful grandmother.

"Caasi, later." She tried to be firm but as I stood there with imploring eyes, she gave in and I was awarded one cookie.

There was still time to complete the last of the small tasks. I trailed behind her as she rubbed the worn brass taps in the bathroom into a burnished glow and lovingly polished the distressed cherry wood credenza.

"Bubbe," I asked, "may I help?"

"No, Mamaleh," she replied.

She set the can of furniture wax down and pulled me to her bosom cradling me in the aroma of lavender, vanilla and peppercorns. I hugged her tightly, her strength and affection nourishing my starved life.

"But I want to do something," I said plaintively.

"Watch, lernen zith, learn."

The old *Naugahyde* sofa in the parlor was lumpy and puckered by small grooves and ridges, the pillows grumpily sagging from wear. In need of tuning, the piano was missing a few ivory keys, some had yellowed with age, and edges were chipped like teeth desperate for repair. Hung framed prints of water lilies and landscapes hid from view the nicks and gaps in the walls, and the cabinets were crammed with books and newspapers. The clutter and deficiencies went unnoticed. Her presence and her grace made the rooms opulently palatial.

"Come, let's sit."

I could tell she was worn out and I nuzzled next to her on the sorry couch full of knobs and prodding springs as she pondered the news in the *Jewish Forward*, her glasses slipping down her nose in her intensity to track the events of international import. When she finished reading, we returned to the kitchen in time for her to rescue the sponge cake. It was superbly golden and she placed the tube pan on a stand to cool. Fussily wrapping the carp and whitefish skeletons in the newspaper for disposal in the incinerator, she laughingly said, "Gut-nacht dogim." Thinking her comment witty, I echoed her, "Goodnight fish," as I tossed the packet down the chute.

In the evening, we took our places at the dining table for the Seder service. I sat with my cousins in my fetching new dress. Bubbe had purchased it for me to wear during Pesach without informing my father. In pale pink, it had cap sleeves with a delicate floral design, scallops around the neckline, and satin belting around the waist. I warded off the astonished glare of my father and sat in prim and ecstatic obedience.

The head of the family, my grandfather Shimon, who I simply called Zeyde, orchestrated the Seder. Wearing his stern black silk yarmulke, he read from the *Haggadah*, the book containing the text of the Passover service. Before him on the table, three matzohs, unleavened bread intended to recall the hurried departure from Egypt were resting on a plate under a royal-blue and gold embroidered velvet matzoh cover. Zeyde poured the first glass of wine reciting the blessing. A tiny portion of parsley, karpas, dunked in salt water was passed around to each family member after the fashion of free men in ancient times who ate greens dipped into liquid. I thought it tasted like seaweed and I chewed it distrustfully choking it down with one gulp hoping to avoid my father's eagle eyes.

Attentive to the reading from the *Haggadah* when fine, familiar words electrified me or faking interest when the passages dragged, I sipped the sweet *Manishevitz* grape wine as Zeyde refilled our glasses and concentrated on the blessings. Giggling inappropriately, I felt slightly tipsy, and my father frowned at me but said nothing. The Pesach cloth, snowy white and crisply starched was soon stained with carmine red spots from spills. Crumbs scattered about as we ate matzoh topped with charoset, a tasty mixture of finely chopped dates, raisins, walnuts, pistachios, almonds, pears, and apples to which cinnamon, apple cider vinegar, and wine had been added.

Standing at the foot of the table, my grandmother listened patiently to the youngest grandchild ask, "Why is this night different from other nights?" the first of the 'Four Questions'. The halting Hebrew words mispronounced by the little lilting voice smoothed the weary creases in her face. Sighing with contentment, she disappeared into the kitchen to complete the final details of the food presentation. Occasionally, I watched my father's face; his quiet criticism of Zeyde, his stepfather, was evident, but he held himself in check and joined in the Hebrew narration of the exodus of the Jews from Pharaoh's enslavement. The story always seemed new to me. It had a magical quality and I was drawn into it as though I too had been brought forth from Egypt.

Grandfather Shimon resisted our pleas to shorten the service waving his words above our heads like a baton. Behind the thick lenses of his glasses, his magnified eyes focused on the text, which he chanted in a deliberate and sonorous voice. He was an educated and principled man, a private teacher of the Hebrew language, a substitute cantor in the temple and when needed, was available to form a minyan, the congregational quorum of ten.

The marriage between my grandmother and my grandfather, both widowed, had taken place when my father was in his teen years at least a decade after the demise of his own father. I rarely saw Zeyde's family, except for his unmarried daughter, my favorite Aunt Helen, and the others usually only at Seder.

My young cousins and I were antsy as the Hebrew passages moved along slowly. When it was time for the recitation of the ten plagues, we became animated putting our little fingers into the wineglasses and placing a drop of wine on our plates to represent each of the plagues. Our lively voices rose with each one pronounced, "Dam, zehfardehya, kinim... blood, frogs, lice..." an excessive litany of misfortunes visited upon the Egyptians. Then we slumped into boredom as the everlasting procession of, "It would have been enough, dyānu...," wove its way around the table. Zeyde prepared the korech, a piece of matzoh folded over bitter herbs accordant with Rabbi Hillel, as a memorial to the destruction of the Temple, and in recognition of servitude and freedom.

In his flawed English he said, "Here's a samvitch."

As with one voice, all the children laughed an irascible, cranky laugh. My grandmother, sensitive to our tedious impatience, appeared at the entrance to the dining room, her thinning hair now neatly parted in the middle and gathered back in a bun, her modest dress covered with a generous apron, and sensible orthopedic shoes on her feet.

"Shimon," she said, "the children are hungry. Skip a few pages."

Generous platters of food appeared, shulchan orech, the festival meal.

"Ada, genug, enough already, sit," Zeyde encouraged.

She joined in the singing of the Pesach songs: "This is the kid (goat), the little kid, my father bought for two zuzim, a little kid, a little kid..." and "Ehchod mi yoydeya, one, who knows one?" "I know one, one is our God..." numerous choruses until we dissolved in merriment. Then we searched for the afikomon, the middle matzoh Zeyde had split in two and hid one-half before the Seder. I hoped to find it and be rewarded with a quarter.

We all pitched in and helped with the cleanup and the dishes. Jostling for coats, hats, and scarves, and with repeated goodbyes, Zeyde's family departed to return to their homes. I filled the ornate silver wine goblet for the prophet Elijah and placed it on a side table at the front door, and my father sunk in the luxury of the padded easy chair reading his newspapers. Fatigue inescapably snaring her, my grandmother rested at the table scooping up specks of matzoh and pieces of shelled walnuts. As I walked past her on my way to the remaining macaroons, she caught hold of my arm.

"Oy veh, my plants!" she said. "Mamaleh, I forgot."

I rushed into the kitchen to get the watering can out from under the sink and filled it to the brim carrying it over to my grandmother. She was upset with the dry and hardened soil in the planters. After watering her thirsty ornamental plants, she gently wiped the foliage with a damp cloth. The dark emerald upright leaves had yellow and silvery-white stripes on the leaf margins. During the summer, the plants sat on the window ledge overlooking the alley below. In angled sunlight, the stiff variegated forms cast filigreed shadows on the brick, the only greenery in a forest of apartments.

"Mamaleh," she said, turning to me when she was done, "you're my hope. Like my plants, you will blossom and give me naches, make me proud."

A ruffled faraway look crept across her eyes. Leaning against the sill, her prim apron limp with exhaustion, her nylon stockings wrinkled at her swollen ankles, she sighed, a deep-drawn quiver from her heart. Tenderly she patted my cheeks with her wrinkled sensible hands thickened like the leaves of her plants.

The windows are small apertures...innocent of glass

In the months that followed, my father surfaced from the gray vapors that had enshrouded him. The change was startling in that he seemed almost expectant, and there was an air of wildness and edginess that I had never before witnessed. The telephone rang at odd hours, even in the middle of the night, and he alertly reached to answer the call and spoke in rapid fluent French. Hurriedly leaving the house, he was away for undetermined stretches of time, even returning early in the morning of the following day and offered no explanation. I learned the harsh lesson of unsuppressed emotions tumbling out. "Where were you?" and "I was worried" received the same impassive response, "It is of no concern to you." I adjusted to my father's wacky routine; it was his preferred state of disorganization and involved some risk. At this stage of my young life, I was quick-witted enough to be aware of his penchant for gambling. In plain view on the work space next to the inert sewing machine were decks of blue and red *Bicycle* playing cards and scattered poker chips. Any further questions I dared to ask he answered speciously and our conversations were forced and artificial.

Unwilling to assemble his life in any normal scheme, he was bent on structuring mine. A stickler for punctuality, he enforced rules and regulations by which I had to abide. Our proximity to my elementary school allowed for me to walk to school each morning and return home for lunch, and then go back for afternoon classes. I had to be at our front door within minutes of the final four o'clock bell. Each noonday when I arrived promptly at thirteen minutes past the hour, my father disdained any form of greeting but instead propelled me to the kitchen where a bowl of hot vegetable soup, a sandwich, a glass of milk, and sliced fruit waited for me on the table. My set place with the provided spoon and paper napkin was a clearing in a shambles of newspapers, harness racing daily forms and intricate sheets of handicapping statistics, torn tickets from two dollar bets that did not pay, unopened letters, ten and twenty dollar bills, and loose change.

Under his watchful eye, I ate in awkward silence. As the weeks cycled, the silence became chameleon like in its contrary behavior. At any given moment it was a tightfisted silence in which I could hear my heart pound, and in the next, the eerie silence of being alone in a crowd, or the pale blue weighty silence of wading in deep snow up to my waist. It was also the black spinning silence after a mistake or the silence of shameful retreat from memories all too sorrowful.

Beholden for the care he took to provide me with simple prepared meals, I was nonetheless distrustful of him and always on guard. The authoritative demands were persistent and not to be tampered with or disputed; I was terrified of the slighting and rage that could surface with the merest alteration.

One sunny lighthearted day after the sounding of the noon bell, I rounded the corner from Duluth to Coloniale and bumped into Benjamin, a boy in my fourth grade class who had transferred to my school. In class he was a model of perfect behavior, polite and respectful. The other children thought him unapproachable. He was not one to seek favor by fawning or flattery, and he had already earned the unlikely nickname of 'Benny the crummy penny'. I had noticed him in the school courtyard at recess leaning against the rails of the fence reading a *Hardy Boys* book. He had a slender build, his dark bristly hair stood straight up in exclamation points, and an animated color stained his cheeks. I stared at him insolently expecting a sneer in return, but his eyes smiled at me in an innocent and gentle manner boring deeply into me as if he had found an opening to my mind.

At lunch break we strolled along together for a short distance and then stopped to talk.

"I read the *Hardy Boys* mysteries too," I bragged.

"You do, wow!"

"I like Frank best. He's smart."

"I'm reading the *Secret of the Caves*," he explained. "Frank and Joe get tangled up with a mysterious hermit."

"I haven't read that one yet, but I borrowed *The Tower Treasure* from the library."

"Maybe we can trade sometime," he said.

It was a harmless conversation peppered with shy giggles. I

clutched my class notes to my chest as if to protect me from the astonishment of our connection. I wondered if he could be a friend with
whom I could exchange ideas, discuss books, and share idle amusing
trifles. I prattled silly nonsense, twisting strands of hair around nervous fingers, shifting about restlessly, unused to the easy give and take
between acquaintances. Benny seemed not to notice my skittishness
and offered to walk me home. I glanced at the watch on my wrist and
the realization of the time struck.

"No, you can't," I exclaimed.

Without warning I sensed my father's furtive but aggressive approach. Wordless, he grabbed me by my hair unbalancing me and began to pull me down the street as the heels of my shoes inelegantly
scraped along the pavement. My notebooks fluttered to the sidewalk,
pages of my childhood wasted and spent. Benny got down on his
knees to collect them; the bewilderment on his face added to my disgrace.

The Deserted Village

I hated when my feet grew to a size five shoe. My brown leather laced *Oxfords* blatantly walked ahead of me stepping on all the sidewalk cracks I was supposed to avoid. A tyrant's hand seemed to be working overtime in an insidious and sinister aim coercing me out of my immature and sheltered child's world. It was as if I had grown years older in one day. Other changes became noticeable. My chubby round face took on definition as it narrowed, and my features became more striking with almond shaped eyes, a delicate slender nose, and a sharper profile. My body lines curved in the intangible transition indenting at my waist and flaring slightly into hips. Silky black hairs like tiny streamers sprouted in the hollows under my upper arms and round nubbins noticeably poked against my washed-out middy blouses. Inhibited, I crossed my arms every which way over the front of my chest to level the mounds but they refused to obey and lie flat.

I was unable to find any measure of calm to lull me to sleep at night; in vain I tussled with the uproar of disquietude and doubt. My daytime insecurity clambered into my nighttime dreams. Powerless, I roamed through fearsome dark woods chased by furry bears that ultimately captured me, their heavy mass squashing and beating me down. I awoke in cowardly fear to find thin strands of hair on my lower belly above my thighs. Breathless and my heart hammering wildly, I was overcome by the invasion of change and no one was available to explain away the gravity of the new symbols. There had to be some secret that was altering me or perhaps I had done something wrong to bring this about. I looked to my mother's untenanted bed and all the traces of her to find the key to unlock the mystery. Her spurned robe fastened to a hook behind the door, her hand mirror dim with the absence of her image, her hair brush and the untouched jar of *Pond's Cold Cream* on the night stand, all evidence of her was disbelievingly mute. In the tumult of this shadowy scene and altered events, the tortured remembrances sat in judgment of me.

One morning following a distressing sleep, my panties showed spots of scarlet. I hid them in the bottom drawer of my mother's bureau thinking to let her know if somehow I could summon her, and praying my father would not chance to look there. I suspected God was punishing me and assured Him I would be good and stop pulling the legs off spiders, but it did not seem to make a difference or provide comfort. Pitiable and left forgotten in a desolate village, my transformed body flowered as my heart withered in the abandonment of my mother's affection.

Part IV

1953-1957

It mounts at sea, a concave wall

One of my father's methodically researched investments paid off. He had bought shares of common stock in *Rayrock Mining Company*, and the value predictably rose encouraging him to sell some of his assets. As chance and opportunity impulsively held hands, I was destined to profit and have fun from a surge in precious metals. Feeling flush, my father made the hasty decision to take me by train to Old Orchard Beach in Maine to vacation for the month of August. The ocean and the sun drenched beaches seemed to have a claim on him. He spoke glowingly about the vastness of the Atlantic Ocean, the mighty waves, and the pristine stretches of wide hard packed sand. His expansive praise of the coastal region of Maine was an acceptable sign that he was emerging from the torpor and listlessness in which he seemed to have lived in season after season over the past four years. I was able to breathe freely again unchained from his moroseness and meting out of abusive punishment. Both traits appeared to be waning and had fallen off considerably influenced perhaps by some newly agreed upon sensibility.

Preparations for the journey were simple. I rashly stuffed my father's durable *Samsonite* leather case with summer beach apparel. In the bottom space I placed my father's bathing suit and items of clothing he designated, his shaving kit, shampoo, laundry and bath soap, and beach towels. Layered on top was my bathing suit, shorts with little tops, a poplin sleeveless dress, a middy blouse and a full circle skirt, and a pair of sandals, my fancy slip nightgown with narrow ribbons down the front, a brown glass bottle of *Coppertone Sun Tan Oil*, and an iron. I prepared a boxed container of sandwiches and snacks, and my father arranged for our tickets at the Canadian National Railway Central Station on Rue Dorchester. The CN connected Montréal to Old Orchard Beach on the old Grand Trunk Railroad line in Maine enabling Canadian visitors to flock to this popular resort. My father's willingness to go made me more confident that he was pardoning me.

In my state of fidgetiness on the train, I struggled with the long hours on the polished wooden bench with my nose pressed to the glass window at my seat, while my father, inattentive to my excited chatter, unsociably read his newspapers. When we reached Portland, it was only a short remaining distance of about fifteen kilometers to our destination. At seven in the evening, just at the time when the sun was dipping in the sky preparing to close down the day, we arrived at Old Orchard Beach.

One quick step off the train and I could already taste the salty ocean spray, sniff grilled hot dogs and fried clams peppering the air, and hear the squeals of the thrill seekers on the *Rocket to the Moon* ride at the pier. We leisurely walked from the station along Grand Avenue bordering the oceanfront past picturesque cottages, seafood diners featuring lobster and shrimp, an ice-cream parlor, a candy store, a bowling alley, and shop windows crammed with shells, beach toys, postcards, and souvenir ashtrays. At a small market, we made a brief stop to pick up provisions for our stay. As the hour was getting late, my father moved expeditiously through the narrow aisles, and assorted fruits, breakfast cereals, freshly baked bread, canned beverages, milk, cheeses, and kosher luncheon meats filled two paper bags. He tossed a pomegranate at me remembering that I loved picking out the sweetly sour seed casings of this fruit once it was opened by scoring it with a knife and breaking it into segments. With a cry of delight, I added the purple red apple-like fruit to the purchases as he paid the salesperson. Frivolous and frolicsome, I was a world away from the lifeless, dull, and torrid streets of Montréal.

Our accommodations were at the modest *Sofia's Guesthouse* on York Street where my father chose to stay for budget reasons; kitchen privileges allowed us to save money by cooking in. It was a quaint establishment with only nine rooms for rent and regularly patronized by an eclectic mix of characters. Sofia, a tough wiry New Yorker, a busybody, and a stickler for practical rules and etiquette, pasted detailed notes all over the house. Under each light switch was a reminder to turn it off, a message on the refrigerator warned the guests not to dawdle with the door ajar, and a long list of 'dos and don'ts' was fastened to the outside wooden stall shower. With all her finicky habits, our hostess nonetheless identified something good in her boarders and was attentive to all. The only room available to us at this late booking was airless and hot during the day, but she reassured us that the evening sea breezes cooled it for sleep.

The morning brilliance stirred me to expectant wakefulness. I rose early before the sun's intense heat baked the sidewalks and breakfasted on grapefruit wedges and buttered toast with jam. I yanked on my pink and white gingham strapless bathing suit with the ruche waist and brief skirt, charmingly trimmed with lace edging, and capably doused my vulnerable skin in *Coppertone*. Packing a blanket, a thick towel, some fruit, a book, and a deck of cards in an oversized canvas tote, I hurried to view the ocean for the first time. Transfixed, I paused at the edge of the sand, golden and amber grains, soft and dense with tiny crystals and shell fragments, an infinite beach that stretched for miles in both directions. Except for a few stalks of wild yellowy grasses growing in secluded inlets and watchful gulls standing on sandbars drying their damp feathered wings, the beach was undisturbed, flat, and broad. The smooth buff colored expanse sloped down to the water's edge to meet the surge and thud and low bellowing hoarse insistent murmur of the Atlantic Ocean. The wind rose and flung some grains of sand in my face stinging my cheeks. Dropping my beach bag, I raced without reserve stumbling and tumbling along the grainy wet sand into the shallow foamy water.

The churning ocean lifted me out of the discontent and sorrow of my life. The waves embraced my ankles, bubbles spreading over my legs. It was cold, but so alive, exhilarating and soothing at the same time. I thrashed about and flopped around in the froth ducking the rising of the waves against the shore and swimming in the breakers feeling the force and drag of the incoming tide. My heart leapt up with the whitecaps and fell back with them forgetting its own sadness and soothing itself in secret harmony with the sea. I waited for the waves that rose to a concave wall catching them at the peak of their curl. Then with a crash I was carried along in their overpowering clutch to shore, readily tossed and twisted like a toy. Lurching to my feet, I gasped with fear and delight rubbing salt and sand from my face. When I tired of the rides, I swam outside of the roiling peaks and gently floated on my back in the ink-blue water, arms spread wide held by the sea. I closed my eyes and the hot yellow sun turned a velvety red against my eyelids. Suspended in the rolling rhythm of the waves, I ignored my father's screaming voice. Without looking, I knew that he was standing on the beach gesturing for me to come back in.

"Don't make me ask you again. Get over here. You are out too far."

Exquisite days followed in monotonous splendor. I staked out my spot each morning in front of the *Hotel Normandie*, an elegant two-story white building with charcoal colored roof, and wood columns. On the screened-in shaded porch, a motley group of old-timers tucked into spindle wooden rockers, catnapped, or pleasantly arced back and forth conforming to the motion of the waves. Neatly unfolding my blanket on the sand, I secured the corners with my sandals, books, the towel, and beach bag. This vantage point at the *Normandie* seemed to attract other kids my own age from nearby lodges, and we shared our lunches and sun tan oils, played games, planned evening activities, and gossiped. As the plaid wool blanket collected sandy wet footprints from our frequent dips into the ocean to cool off, it became bristly against our sun-broiled skin. Several times during the day, we lazily rolled off our backs and gathered up the lotions, magazines, decks of cards, beach balls, and collection of half-eaten fruit, and dumped the whole lot on a towel. We then allowed the blanket to billow in the breeze like a sail or vigorously shook it. This dalliance sent us collapsing down, sun-bruised and desiccated, not unlike ocean seaweed scattered on the surf-beaten shore.

The salt scent tarried in the air and crystals of brine stuck to my lashes. I lost the dark circles under my eyes, and the sun danced lights in my hair. My skin cast off the city pallor and before bed each evening I slathered *Noxzema* over the burns on my shoulders. When I was evenly bronzed, I applied moisture creams to keep the tan smooth and gleaming. I fancied this relaxing life of sunbathing and loafing and could have lived at the beach forever.

In the evenings, my father was preoccupied in the gaming room at the hotel playing poker. Reliably, I stopped by to wish him good luck. Alternating puffing on an *Export-A* cigarette and picking up his dealt cards, his right hand with the nicotine yellow stains between the second and third fingers moved adeptly. He looked so serious wearing his inscrutable poker face behind the spiraling plumes of smoke choking the air. He could bluff or bid the value of his cards as he chose and collect the winnings afterwards with little remorse. His mind seemed refreshed by the discipline of the game, and he had perfected offensive moves to counter the trickery. Tolerant to my presence, the other players at the table concentrated on the cards and the stacks of red and white chips that were pushed toward the growing heap in the center of the green felt cloth. The only sounds heard were the grunting and wheezing of the old fat men, the scooping of the chips by the winner, and the kvetching of the loser. My father, with his sense of humor, turned to the angry whiner and said, "Sol, if you always lose so much money, why do you stay in this business?"

In his winning mood, my father's spirits were high, and he tossed quarters to me to splurge on *Skee ball*, one of the arcade games. Happily unleashed, I wended my way past rows of lamp lit cottage windows arriving at the pier, a long steel structure on wooden stilt-like supports extending over the water. The sky changed to a rosy pink as twilight dismissed the day deepening slowly into a dark mercurial blue night. Under a vague and ghostly moon, the gay carnival atmosphere beckoned. Everything was bright and loud; red neon lights and boisterous laughter spun together on the rides. I stopped for a moment to watch the activity at *Noah's Ark*, the two carousels, and the *Jack and Jill Slide*. Hoarding my money for the games, I elected not to ride the merry-go-round of wooden horses and instead strolled along on the pier. An array of concession stands and games flanked the boardwalk: a shooting gallery with little ducks on a chain conveyor belt, a gypsy mannequin head selling fortune cards, pin ball machines, and a penny toss into crockery, nifty gambits to provide amusement and unload one's pockets. As I unhurriedly ambled along unable to take it all in, the competing gruff shouts of the carnival barkers enticingly rang in my head.

"Everyone's a winner!"

"Test your skill… three darts to break a balloon."

"Cotton candy… get your pink cotton candy."

"Knock over the milk bottles and win a giant panda."

The glow from the stall lights exploded into a shower of diamonds over the dark ocean below before plunging into the frothy surf that pounded the pilings. Beams of silver shot across the water glistening incandescently then fading into luminous sparkles buried beneath the waves.

I paused to talk to the operator of the *Rocket to the Moon*, a good-looking man in his twenties. Business was slow this night and the un-occupied passenger cars reeled about futilely, no shrieks of pleasure or fright piercing the air.

"You Montréal girl, yes?"

"Yes," I timidly answered.

He had an engaging look. His eyes were the blue of distance where one might float between blue and blue. Mesmerized, I would have al-most forgotten who I was had I not averted his gaze. Self-consciously kicking the tips of my sandals at the wooden planks on the boardwalk, I shuffled my feet in exquisite awkwardness.

"My name, Konrad."

"I'm called Caasi."

"I work Montréal," he said. Job no good. I make ladies' purses in factory."

His English was spoken with an accent, one I was uncertain of, but his mouth and the texture of his voice were sensuous.

"You're from somewhere else?"

I posed the question in a timorous voice. Konrad took no note of my bashfulness.

"Brother in Gdansk say, Konrad, you go America. Make new life."

"From Gank..." I struggled with the pronunciation.

"In Poland... country with Communist government. You know Polish People's Republic?"

"A little," I lied and blushed.

"Not good there...not so good here."

He said this matter-of-factly rather than in a discouraged way.

"I come to beach. Work in amusement park. I want to be circus performer like in Gdansk. I was magician and juggler."

Sneakily, he reached behind my ear and held up a shiny quarter placing it in my palm, and closing my fingers around it. He continued to grip my hand. I giggled and squirmed. It seemed as if my hand were ablaze sending sparks flying through my body, the flames nimbly spreading melting me into confusion.

Releasing me from his hold, Konrad said, "I shut ride down."

I watched his brawny arms work the levers. *Rocket to the Moon* slowed to a grinding halt as I whirled unsteadily. His blonde mane of unkempt hair reminded me of radiant sunshine rippling in the water. Sweat and salt and cigarette smells exuded from him. His cotton T-shirt and jeans were tautly molded to his trimness and his feet were bare, browned by the sun. I was drawn to the rawness and plain unpolished nature of the exotic foreigner from across the sea.

"C'mon, we go beach."

He grabbed my hand and we raced down to the dark wet shore directly under the pier. He lit a cigarette exhaling the pungent tobacco smoke and offered one to me. I shook my head no. Our conversation was like the single match he struck, a brief flame stifled by my adolescent shyness and the awareness of his eyes on me. The smell of fried clams and taffy mingled with the smoke and salty ocean air, and I filled my lungs with the elation of the moment, the wind on my face, and the man's bold grip on my unruly curiosity.

Abruptly, he dropped his cigarette to the sand, grinding it under his heel and spun me around pulling me to him. He kissed me hard, full on the lips. His tongue slipped into my mouth, warm and probing. Flustered, I pushed him away, not ready for the speedy advances or the mystification of intimacy. Thinking I was inaptly violated, I turned and ran the length of beach back to our lodgings; the compact press of sand, cold and unyielding under my feet, silently rebuked my every step. His arms around me, the pressure of his lips, the taste of him, and the enchantment; this illicit mélange had to be rejected.

In the tiny bathroom of *Sofia's Guesthouse*, I groped for the light switch and worriedly scrutinized my face in the murky mirror to see if there was a perceptible change to brand me as a bad girl. Finding nothing, I washed my mouth out with soap. The taste was vile.

I went into the kitchen to find some juice or *Pepsi* and met Mrs.Gitlitz fussing at the stove stirring a pot of cocoa. She was wearing tight rollers in her hair, spots of pink calamine lotion on her mosquito-ravaged face, and an ankle-length chartreuse bathrobe over her stumpy body. She looked like a globular apple resting on chubby suntanned feet stuffed into slippers. I tried to avoid her inquisitive probing eyes and generous mouth that chose never to stop talking, but she was delighted with my presence and insisted I join her at the table.

"So tell me, how's by you?" she asked, sliding a plate of hazelnut cookies in my direction.

"Okay."

"Just okay? A scheina meidl should have boyfriends. You're a pretty girl."

She patted my hand conspiratorially.

"Just between you and me, you must have a boyfriend, yes?"

My guilt rose to the height of a tall building and toppled over into stones of ruins. I jumped up and fled the room leaving the startled Mrs. Gitlitz to drink her cocoa alone.

"Don't bang the screen door," she called after me.

I am a parcel of vain strivings
tied By a chance bond together

My father's Canadian dollars were being slapped away by a string of bad luck poker hands he was dealt nightly in the back salon of the *Hotel Normandie*. I was worried that he would revert to his cranky and capricious self replacing the more agreeable sunny disposition he had displayed since our arrival at Old Orchard Beach. To my relief, the gambling losses did not seem to alter his state of mind. At breakfast, after a marathon night of extravagant high stake betting, his eyes were merry and lively.

"Winning or losing is not the issue," he declared. "It's all in the strategy."

He spoke about 'game playing' as if it were a reflection of life itself. I could not quite grasp the parallel but my perplexity about my father and his thinking only led to more confusion. *What then did it matter to me?* He was satisfied with his proclivity for gambling as an exercise or experiment; the test was the worthy victory, not the results unshakably abandoned to the whim of destiny.

"We're going to Biddeford today... to shop for new clothes for you to wear to school," he announced.

Without notice, he had made preparations to splurge the last of the investment profits on a fall wardrobe for me. I was shocked into silence and had an impulsive urge to reach across the table and hug him around the neck, but I had not embraced him since I was a baby nor had he touched me as a child except in brutish anger. Savoring the moment, I watched him sip his lemon tea, his eyes absorbing all, a playful smile on his lips, intangible connections reaching cautiously out to me, slippery and gossamer. In that fanciful, impractical timelessness, the enormity of the distance between us was swept away.

Mrs. Nussbaum entered the kitchen to prepare her breakfast. She had newly arrived for her holiday and Sofia had assigned to her the most exclusive room, the one with the private bath because she had been a recurrent seasonal visitor with Mr. Nussbaum until he had passed away from a stroke. The widowed Mrs. Nussbaum had taken an instantaneous liking to my father and appeared at breakfast to impress, dressed in finery, a patent departure from the rest of us in casual beachwear. She strutted around the room in her colorful cotton shift made from fringed rectangular pieces reminding me of the dhurrie flat woven rug in the lobby of *Hotel Normandie*. Her mahogany-dyed hair fell wild on her forehead almost to her eyes set too close to her coarse nose. Though fastidiously powdered, her underlying complexion was chalky and speckled with moles, and beneath her red lipsticked mouth, her chin sloped to a heavy colorless neck hanging in folds. A thin breathless voice and expertly manicured long fingernails were a sharp contrast to her stout frame. She batted her lashes at my father, cooed at me, and installed herself at the table, almost knocking Mrs. Gitlitz from her chair.

"Biddeford, how charming," commented Mrs. Nussbaum picking up the threads of the conversation.

"My father's taking me there," I said, with a touch of arrogance.

"I know all the lovely shops..." she said, letting her words trail away apparently hoping to be asked to go along.

My father was enjoying the scene, hardly flattered and singularly unimpressed.

"Mrs. Nussbaum," he asked with abject complacency, "were you aware that the Grand Trunk Railroad was the first connection from Montréal to Old Orchard Beach?"

"Not until this moment, Mr. Lichman."

Her displeasure was apparent. Mrs. Gitlitz reveled in the obvious rejection of Mrs. Nussbaum's overtures and plunked her dentures into her cocoa in careless delight, while the imperturbable Sofia directed our attention to the latest sign posted under the kitchen light switch: 'Turn off before leaving room'. My father was not to be enticed or drawn in by any personal discussion, however remote, or any social involvement. *Poor Mrs. Nussbaum, I thought, you have definitely picked the wrong man to pursue. He has turned your lights off before you ever had a chance to turn them on.*

We returned late from Biddeford carrying bulky packages of fashionable clothes tidily folded in tissue, a day's effort at the fine boutiques respecting the merchants' advice on a trend-setting collection for the discriminating young person. My father was fatigued; it had been tedious for him to wade through the infinite choices of fabrics, colors, and matching accessories, and he was unused to the fancy notions and impulses of a teenage girl. I was giddy from the excesses, bubbling with joy. I put on my new lemon- yellow, fluffy, angora sweater, and lavender and yellow pleated wool tartan skirt, coordinating socks with frilly cuffs, and penny loafers.

"Dad, what do you think?" I asked as I pirouetted about.

"Fine," he said without looking up.

Then he stared at me peculiarly, as if a stealthy spray of pain fingered his face. His piercing blue eyes, the color of the Atlantic Ocean at sunset had surrendered their blaze of gold and seemed to drift into a morass and fog of uncertainty.

"I don't want you going to the *Normandie* any more and hanging out in the lobby," he said.

"Why not?" I asked, unable to subdue the crossness in my voice.

"Those college kids who work there are rowdy lunatics, that's why not."

"Okay," I lied, "I'll stay here and read on the verandah."

Right after dinner my father went off to bed, morose and silent. I was less than sympathetic, eager for him to retire. As soon as he was fast asleep, I thrust aside my unread fiction book and brushed my shoulder length sun-streaked hair into a peek-a-boo hairstyle like the femme fatale actress Veronica Lake, put on some peach lip gloss, and pinched my tanned cheeks until they glowed. By this age, my well-formed body and narrow waist were swish and appealing, and I walked with a natural rhythmical movement. I was dimly aware of the changes, noting in the mirror my heart shaped face with sparkling emerald green eyes, and a softly sensuous mouth. My focus was on sneaking over to the hotel in opposition to my father's directive. The bellhops and busboys from Bowdoin and Bates, though on duty, openly flirted, playfully teasing me. Moving away from my cloistered and repressed life, these new sensations were alarmingly pleasurable, my first girlish use of seductive charms to entrance. Lacking the poise of maturity, I appreciated their glances and their banter but avoided their hands.

It was my one wonderful vacation. My father stayed out of my way most days.

The terrible mournfulness...
of the truth gnawed within her

There was a great sense of letdown and discontent following our return to Montréal from Old Orchard Beach. It was as if we never went. My father's jocular mood vanished and he disappeared for unaccounted hours into the intense swarm of the city. The Atlantic Ocean, the tang of salt in the air, and the azure skies shaded with blush pink and clouds of feathery gold became an imprecise memory. Thin streaky corkscrews of heat and gritty back streets and alleys smelling of gasoline fumes and putrid garbage replaced the gleaming beauty of coastal Maine. My carefully acquired sun-bronzed luster blanched in the cramped stench and sordid wretchedness.

A few weeks remained before school was to begin, but the excessive heat falsified the end to the summer. It stayed hot, blisteringly hot. There was not much to do to escape it so I chose to visit my grandmother. The building in which she and Zeyde lived on Av De L'Esplanade was across from Fletcher's Field, a park bordering on Av Du Parc. I climbed the 188 counted steps to her apartment. Inside was intolerably muggy with the windows tightly curtained in an unsuccessful attempt to exclude the heat. Bubbe, dressed in a sleeveless cotton frock patterned with orange blossoms and her requisite linen apron was pleased to see me. She clasped me tightly to her bosom burying my nose in the delightful aroma of vanilla and almond. Out of the corner of my eye I spotted the cookies, almond curls, dusted in a light coating of sugar cooling on a rack.

"Vos new?" she asked, while patting my cheeks.

"Nothing much," I answered, gazing longingly at the cookies.

"Avi gezunt, your health?"

"I'm okay, Bubbe, just lonesome."

"No friends to play vit?"

"No one's around."

Looking at my dejected face was more than she could bear.

"Cookies later," she promised.

195

"Oh goody!"

She went into the kitchen and put the kettle on to boil and prepared a large jug of *Lipton* tea. The ice cubes merrily clinked as she stirred them into the amber color tea. Reaching above the sink up to the small shelf held in place by china brackets, she removed a variety of glass mugs. From the refrigerator she withdrew a jar of homemade cherry jam.

"Breng blanket from hall closet," she said.

I found an old but serviceable comforter that smelled of mothballs. Taking my hand, Bubbe tugged me out the door, and we went down the apartment steps in halting fashion to the street below, she carrying the pitcher and clinging to the banister, and I prudently balancing the jam, the coverlet, and the cups. A blast of hot air assaulted us as we stepped outside the building. Screening her eyes from the glare of the sun, she scanned the park across the roadway searching for an unfrequented place. Sycamore trees with deeply ridged dark brown trunks and knuckled flaring roots ringed the park. The old trees topped with spreading crooked branches and large leaves afforded sun and shade. We walked on tough yellow-green grass speckled with dandelions withering in the sun and spread the blanket at the base of the tree on a patch of soft earth and clover. The faintest of breezes rustled through the huge leaves.

We passed the afternoon lolling in the park drinking tea sweet-flavored with her delectable cherry jam. Since I never had much to say, Bubbe talked to mitigate my modesty. She regaled me with her life story. I never tired of hearing it. There were always slight variations because of her problems with the English language and stringing together contained memories. Sometimes I asked her specifics that she was unable to recall and some questions simply went unanswered. I regretted that I knew so little of my heritage. My father admitted to nothing. Occasionally he used a Russian phrase or in anger cursed the Kazaki, the Russian Cossacks. Other than the occasional outburst, he was guardedly silent.

"I vas born in Russia, I think 1898," Bubbe began. "A long time ago… mein family lived in small village, a shtetl, called Irkutsk. You know that part."

She paused to wipe some jam from the corner of my mouth and swipe strands of straggly hair out of my eyes.

"Our house vas simple. Not orem, poor. Nischt reich, not rich. The land nischt our own, but mir voynen nischt farmers. Mein father vas educated man, scholar. He made gelt as scribe. Kenst tu scribe?"

I shook my head, no. She explained that her father's work was to interpret the law and was concerned with writing and the keeping of accounts for the tradesmen. He was a man of God and righteous. He directed her to read and write in the Russian language as well as in Yiddish. The story continued to unfold with fascinating detail. At times, I had to ask her to translate the Yiddish words because I was already forgetting my parochial school teachings.

"Tsar Nicholas II vas ruler of Russia. Our shtetl lived quiet. Work for some, charity for others. We observed the Shabas. The frum, pious men vent to shul, synagogue. The women koshered chickens and blessed the candles. In 1917, Revolution came. Country now... in konflikt. Lenin and his Bolsheviks made terrible things happen in Moscow and St. Petersburg. In mein shtetl, the Russian peasants grabbed land. There vas bloodshed."

Bubbe sipped her tea and looked to the sky. Vapors of gold hung in the air. Under an awning of leaves, the day had become almost too agreeable for the rest of her story. She paused wondering if she should finish.

"Go on, Bubbe, tell me more," I pressured.

She explained to me that a drought generated famine and millions died of starvation, hunger and cold. The Kazaki, who were loyal to Tsar Nicholas, went crazy when the country was Bolshevik.

"They vas meschuge, crazy, before, now vorse. By dark nacht, they rode on horses, set fire to villages, both Russian and Jewish. I forgot to tell you, I married at fifteen. It vas tradition, so yung. Your grandfather, Isaac, l'hasholem, vas elegant mensch. He died wen your father vas six. A krankite, a sickness. The pogroms, oy veh! Our shtetl vas island with tsores, trouble all around."

My father had defined for me pogrom. I knew of the massacre of the Jews in Russia, battered down as with a thunderbolt.

"They used fire to destroy vitout pity."

My grandmother's eyes welled with tears. The story was unsettling. In Yiddish, she expressed her grief and dismay at the devastation. Her refined voice soared above the irrational flames and floated on the strewn ashes. Her words took on color, shape, and size, and spoke the despair for all those lost in vain.

"Wen Stalin took Russia in 1927, mir farkoifn, sold everything. Many days by oxcart, mir arumforn, travel, and then on ship to Canada, just me, mein bruder, your father, Mildred and Cora. Other mischpoche, family, and shtetl were farloirn, lost.

The sadness was zu fil, too much. I shared her grief and her loss. It somehow made my loss more bearable. She was so strong, my little grandmother. She wanted me to be strong.

My game was now quite the reverse
from what it had been at starting

To excel in sports not only required natural talent but confidence, skill, strength, and pluck. I was small for my age, well proportioned, but lacking in athleticism, especially stamina and speed. Conscious of my weakness in these merits, I made no effort to conceal my character failing. Repeatedly let down and dissatisfied with my performance in gymnastic exercises and group sports, I became intimate with defeat. Complaisantly I accepted being on the sidelines for most competitions or listed as a spare only in the event of disaster on the girls' basketball or track team. Had the school issued ribbons for last place, I would have garnished all. In the annual interschool 'Field Day' contest, I participated in the 200-meter race, longing to perform well just this once. At the starting line, I surreptitiously eyed the competitors from Montreal High and Strathcona High. The girls were lanky, their frames towering above me and their legs lean and strapping. They wore snug fitting shorts and smug defiance. Before the race began I was the loser.

"On your mark...get set...go..." I made an earnest dash for the first 100 meters and then jogged lumpishly to the finish line, out of breath, my face sweaty and blotchy. Not looked up to or respected, I reasoned that I was ungainly and graceless. It was both an unsettling and settling decision and pushed me to surpass my classmates in what I could master. Sullenly and arduously, I concentrated my ingenuity on absorbing science, mathematics, and art. Math was to my way of thinking, clean and pure, and I could recall with ease geometric figures and solve high level algebra problems. The numbers refined and measured me with precision. Art possessed the intangibles of light, reflections, and illusions insistently probing my mind yet acting as a balm to my disordered thinking. At home, with the math book propped against the milk bottle on the kitchen table, I pondered the complicated equations as I gulped down my *Rice Krispies* and reveled in getting the answers correct. The logic in the accuracy was a comfort. The beautiful books on art I obtained from the library and obsessively read in the late hours of the night expanded the boundaries of the impossible.

Pointlessly, I still dreamed of being slimmer and taller and doing a well executed leap to gracefully sink the ball into the basket. It was not to be. My courage existed only in the abstract. Clumsy and awkward adhered to me like repentant pals. I competently trained with the basketball team but wasted the games on the bench ruefully watching the action. In badminton, I fared somewhat better until the real competition of the intramural games where I finished next to last in my grade level and disappointed once again our gym teacher, the imperious Miss Duffy.

My enduring appreciation of the skill and superiority of the professional athletes on the *Montreal Royals* baseball team now included the *Alouettes de Montréal* football team. I had followed their exploits that won them *La Coupe Grey* in 1949 against the *Calgary Stampeders*, even remembering the final score, twenty-eight to fifteen. Later on, I became a big fan of the quarterback Sam Etcheverry and his talented receiver Hal Patterson. I listened to radio broadcasts of the games and visualized what was happening on the field. Enthusiastically, I read the sports section of the *Montreal Star* thrilling in the details of Etcheverry's completed passes, a feat I could only imagine as I never attended a game.

Out of interest, I scanned the upcoming events, and spotted an advertisement for the *World Series of Basketball Tour* featuring the *Harlem Globetrotters* against a team of College All-Americans. As a bungling player unable to hit the rim of the basket from the free throw line, I instinctively admired these talented athletes, not readily understanding that the Harlem players were black and facing the injustices of racism and segregation. Immersed in the daily uncertainties of my life, I was inattentive to the politics of the time. I was simply thrilled to know that they were booked to play in the *Montreal Forum* indoor arena located on Rue Ste. Catherine. Having overheard the boys in school deferentially describe the *Globetrotters'* basketball genius and court antics, I wanted to watch them in action.

With the usual fluster, I asked my father's permission to buy an admission ticket. Unpredictably, my father seemed not to mind my going to the basketball game. He was rather taken with the fact that the manager of the *Globetrotters* was Abe Saperstein, a Jew, who was steadfast in his efforts to erase prejudice and discrimination. If I had put in a request for consent to see the *Montréal Canadiens* hockey team play, my father would have strenuously objected. When I had even hinted of wanting to see Maurice 'The Rocket' Richard play, his comeback was the usual no with the ritual embellishments.

"Hockey is a game of riotous toothless ruffians."

"But..." I never had a chance to complete my dissent.

"Do you want to get hit on the head by flying beer bottles? Fights break out. You'll get stomped on in the riot."

That issue was retired, never to be revisited.

On the night of the game I was excited and anticipatory. In leaving the house, I ignored the cautionary warnings from my father.

"Watch out for perverts," he said. "You need eyes in back of your head and stay on your guard."

Obediently, I gave him the requisite reply, "Okay, Dad."

The forum was packed to the rafters. All 9000 seats were filled. I was sitting way up but I could still view the action well enough. The *Harlem Globetrotters* came on the floor with a fanfare of lights and music. The first thing I noticed was how tall and limber they were. Dressed in the colors of the American Flag, they were wearing shirts with stars, shorts with broad bands, and circular striped socks. Some wore kneepads. The agility and comedic routines were astonishing. The players were six-foot rabbits in the way they cavorted around the floor. Down on one knee, twisting turning, eluding, and dribbling took place in rapid fire precision. The ball rolled down an arm, around a shoulder, in back of a head, and bounced off a head to another receiver. It was remarkable and funny. There were no-look passes and ingenious hand-offs and shooting prowess from the half-court line, amazing hook shots, and beautiful floating slam dunks. One of the players picked up the ball and tucked it under his arm and ran it like a football for a touchdown. The hilarity and entertainment was abundant. I would have loved to sit close to the floor because the players interacted with the audience, specifically with the kids.

Perched at the edge of my seat not to miss a spellbinding moment, I laughed loudly with the favorable crowd. Suddenly, I was struck by a ghastly pain in my head that turned my stomach sick. Never before had I experienced this. Halos of white and garlands of diverse colors circled the court lights. As my vision became fuzzy, the sport stadium dimmed and blurred as if I were viewing the scene through a dusky shade. The throbbing was ferocious. Convinced I was on the verge of blacking out, I mustered the energy to grope my way past the cheering fans in my row, foundering and stepping on toes until I reached the aisle. Somehow I managed to find my way to the exit door, and I plunged into the frosty night air on Rue Ste. Catherine. The beams from the street lamps and shop windows and traffic blinded me. Disoriented, I started to dizzily walk and had to lean against the sides of buildings as I slowly wended along. The pain would not abate. In a panic, I got on a passing streetcar hoping it was heading to Av Du Parc and turning north in the direction of home. I stayed on the streetcar as long as I could, but waves of seasickness forced me to alight in the middle of nowhere. I was in a dark residential area.

I felt the discontent of strangeness of not knowing where I was or unable to predict or clearly visualize. Alone and helpless, I felt disconnected from the world. The stars of earlier had turned off their lights and the night sky was tarry black, heavy with gathering rain clouds. I was inside a kettle drum and whoever was banging would not stop. Swaying and weaving, I slipped on a patch of weeds at the edge of the sidewalk, barely staying on my feet. Intuition headed me in the direction of home. As the rain clouds burst wetting me through to my skin, my head continued to pound with rampant fury. The roar churned with the remembered yells of the appreciative crowd at the forum. They had thumped and clamored their approval for one of the favorite players, chanting "Goose"... "Goose"... every time he scored.

The wind was cold and sharp and got under my thin jacket settling between my shoulder blades. I hugged myself for warmth, my arms encircling my chest, my fingers hanging on to my arms like a last hold on sanity. A man shuffled past me in the dark, possibly a vagrant wandering the streets. My body stiffened with alarm, but he kept on going in clothes about to fall apart. I saw he was a religious Jew with his black hat, disheveled beard, and long side curls hanging in front of his ears. He merely glanced back at me with his rheumy eyes and hustled away reeking of garlic and poverty.

How I made it safely back escapes me. Taunted by the paucity of memory from this short-lived evening, one that had started with promise and ended with pain, I climbed the stairs to our apartment now dreading the confrontation with my father. I had reached the limit of tolerance. I somehow managed to unlock the door, the key shaking in my hand. My father emerged from the kitchen, a dishtowel in his hand and a querulous grimace on his face.

"You look like a mangy dog. Go to bed," he ordered.

The Pangs of Love

Kevin was my first boyfriend, not literally a boyfriend, more like a friendship between a girl and boy exploring new harmless pleasures in the simple and unspotted days marking the end of childhood. We met by chance in the school corridor during a break between classes, Kevin leaning with the casual slouch of youth against his locker as I fussed with my hair gathering it back through an elastic band to shape it into a curvy ponytail. From the start, with "So, how's school?'' we hit it off.

"Fine," I answered, "I like it."

"Good," said Kevin, "eighth grade is hard."

"I got assigned to the advanced math class in second term. I'm the only girl in there," I giggled.

"You must be a math whiz... God... I barely scraped through!"

"I hope I don't flunk out," I said with a wry smile.

The bell rang for the next period. Kevin grabbed his books from his locker and started down the hall to his class. Then he stopped and said without turning around, "Catch you out front after school."

The day crawled on hands and knees; the hands of the clock moved snail-slow until the closing bell sent me scampering out to meet Kevin on the sidewalk at the bottom of the stone stairs. I spotted him in the crowd of students, tall, probably close to six feet in height, something I had not been conscious of when we stumbled upon one another at the lockers. There was elegance to his posture as he stood amidst his classmates, the way he held his head regal and poised reminding me of the fairy tale prince charming in *Snow White*. I could tell he liked me from the way he smiled when our eyes locked, a smile the color of honey. He was brassy handsome, his thick dark hair sleekly combed and greased into a bit of a duck-tail with a few loose strands on his neck, prominent cheekbones highlighting his big brown eyes, and an engaging cleft in his chin. We were noticed as we began walking away together from the school. I felt the envious stares of the other girls piercing my back, specifically vindictive Becky who had dated Kevin for a while until they broke up the previous month. She was a ninth grader, a tough looking, full bosomed girl in voluminous crimson folds of cashmere, her long raven hair worn like a trophy.

Kevin was oblivious to the intrigue and gossip. He picked up our conversation where we had left it settling into a smooth rhythm without choppy half-sentences that hung in the air on an updraft of reluctant pauses. I could not recall a time in my entire life of being able to talk without stammering, blushing, biting of hangnails, or toe scuffing.

"Your math teacher, Mr. Hartman, coaches the senior basketball team," he said.

"Oh yeah?"

"The guys call him 'Hard-man' cause he's so tough."

"It's scary in his class. He made me go to the blackboard to figure out an equation with two unknowns. I felt so at risk. I dropped the chalk."

"Did you solve it?"

I laughed, "I'll never tell."

"Bet you did," Kevin said, seemingly proud.

"Maybe," I teased.

"Hey, I made first string this year... no more benchwarmer for me."

My heart did joyful cartwheels conscious I was walking home with this great-looking senior basketball star.

"You gonna come watch me play?" he asked.

"Sure," I said.

He took my hand and tucked it into his as we strolled along in no hurry to silence the echoes in our hearts. The March air was brisk, typical of early spring, but the sun dawdled on our backs. We walked on slushy lawns admiring the yellow, pink, and peach-shaded tulips springing out of the ground, leaves folded one within another for protection from the old snow. Spears of crocuses and frisky daffodils rose out of the hard dirt along the brick foundations of the homes.

My shoes were thoroughly wet and my toes were starting to freeze. These pangs were no rival for the tempestuous tingling of my fingers in his hold. I glanced up at him just as he pushed away a stubborn curl that had gone awry, but it rebounded as if it were untamable. He ignored it and chose to adjust my collar in a responsive informal manner, raising it up about my neck to fend off a sudden gust of wind. His touch was gentle; his smile was a blend of ingenuousness and cockiness. I smiled back finding myself growing demure. My shyness and silent ways deviously slipped in, and I became aware of the cold, my thin coat, my red runny nose, and my inexperience.

In a detour down an alley, Kevin tugged me close and kissed my chapped mouth. The fine hairs above his upper lip surprised me with their softness. I put my hand into the deep warm pocket of his duffel coat. It was like a smoldering furnace. I wanted to climb in, dissolve, and disappear.

The grossest errours, if they...be but new, may be perswaded to the multitude

"Dad, I got 100% in my geometry exam, "I said, hoping to hear some words of praise.

"Did no one else write the test?"

He squinted at me, his face deadpan, not giving me a clue as to his true reaction.

"It was the final and I scored the highest," I bragged.

"Well, you know what I always say; it's easy to be a big fish in a small pond. Wait 'til you hit university."

"Yeah, but for now, may I have my hair trimmed?"

"Geometry and hair, some new math mischief, eh?"

"C'mon, please Dad. My hair is long and the tips are splitting."

"I advise against it."

"There's a beauty parlor on Rue Bousquet near Parc Lafontaine and Bernice from my class had her hair bobbed and it's adorable, all crinkly towards the ends and they charge only six dollars," I said in one breathless rush.

"I'll cut it for you for free."

"You're being nutty, can't I have my way just this once?"

"I'm warning you, you'll be sorry. Mark my words."

"Thanks, Dad," I said demurely.

The visit to the salon started with some niggling skepticism. The shop was located in a basement flat accessed by a short flight of crumbling stone stairs. An earthenware pot trailing scarlet geraniums badly in need of watering guarded the entry. I was already tainted by my father's parting words and in general was disposed to mistrustfulness. The drooping leaves and withered flowers hinted at doubt. Glitzy lace curtains adorned the one small window of the front door, the first pleasing sign. However on entering, a curious mix of peroxide, hair spray, nail-varnish, and perfumes assailed me. It was a nauseating odor and one that I was ill-prepared for. It should have been the definitive cue to turn and run. Before I could make my escape, the stylist, Marie-

Noel, owner of the shop, ebulliently greeted me. Her flattery beguiled and cajoled me.

"Quel bonheur! Une jeune fille charmant. This darling girl has luckily found her way to my shop."

She waltzed me around the room hanging by turn onto my arm and royally presenting me to the women seated under the hair dryers.

"Regardez ladies," she said, and clapped her hands for effect.

Deafened by the noise from the blowers, hair wound in tight pin curls, heads totally confined in netting, and reading magazines, they paid me no notice. Marie-Noel tossed her head about sassily and beamed at her clients nodding condescendingly if she noted them fidgeting in the heat of the dryers. She behaved as if she were in a sophisticated melodrama of glamour exhibiting to a captive audience of simple folk. It was an effective tactic accomplished by her winning, well practiced smile and her engaging character, a mixture of Southern verve and Québec guile. Her lustrously radiant hair was parted down the middle, and her hair-do was cropped very short on one side; on the other side, misbehaving curls were drawn high, secured above her dainty ear with gemstones. As she dragged me about, her pretty hands with manicured and polished fingernails left little indentations in my arm. In my childish trust, her hands held a guarantee of talent. She showed me pictures of the new vogue craze in *Mademoiselle* and described the latest trends in New York and Paris. Leery yet naively trusting, I was drawn to the assured notion that the modern sculpted look complimented me. My father's common sense reasoning still rustled in my ear, but her persuasion addressed my feelings and imagination and won me over.

With a foolhardy stroke she first lopped off my ponytail as if trimming a superfluous branch of a tree then snipped my hair short and blunted my bangs. It was impossible for me to augur the damage as she swiveled me in the chair scissors whizzing like hummingbird wings. After the shearing, I stared at my mirror reflection laden with distress and overcome with disgust. Scattered about on the tiled floor were long strands of filmy pale blonde and light brown cuttings.

"Formidable!" Marie-Noel gushed, "très chic!"

I was devastated. Without a word, I placed the money on the counter next to the rollers, combs, and nail-varnish and ran from the shop. I arrived home, skin ablaze and spotty, and eyes puffy red from crying. Shutting myself in the bathroom, I could not be induced to budge from my hiding place until my father threatened to break down the door.

"That," my father scornfully said examining me from all angles, "was hacked with a sword and is fit only for *Prince Valiant.*"

He was right. The clipped and severe cut did not suit my heart-shaped face. In a state of dread, I anticipated the Monday morning scoffing at school. The comments from the girls were more degrading and insulting than from the boys. Falsely extolling their own vain qualities, I was easy prey in their need to slight and to vilify. I could not distance myself from the spite and acerbic words and regarded myself as something of little value. My short hair became my shortcoming. I hated the severe 'warrior look' but there was no recourse and nothing to rectify this defect but prudence.

Over the long waiting months, my hair grew to its original fullness gloriously hanging to my shoulders, the color of sun burnt grass invested with streaks of amber and six dollars worth of gold.

Ladies, like variegated tulips, show;

My Aunt Helen, my father's stepsister, was a solitary myopic spinster who played the piano. I attended Helen's recital one Sunday at the home of her music teacher, listening to the doleful strains of Beethoven and Chopin, gazing dreamily out at the rain pounding the pavement below. The ever present metronome indicated the exact tempo of the music, its clicking sounds adjusting to the sharp rattles of the parlor window, the pulsing rain, and the lazy sighs of the pensive hour. After the recital, we walked together on the slick streets huddled under a single umbrella sharing the same mix of impetuosity and irascibility that came out of the dreary afternoon. Then our outlook lifted and we joked and teased one another.

"How's your boyfriend Barney?" I asked.

Helen was vulnerable to being harassed by my childish black humor, and I took advantage of her sweet nature.

"His name is Bernard."

"No, it's *Barney with the Goo-Goo-Googly Eyes*.*" I kept at it mercilessly.

"Bernard won't bring you candy cigarettes ever again. He's sensitive about his crossed eyes."

"Okay," I conceded, "his eyes are just wiggly."

Helen scolded me then erupted in howls of laughter. The wind inverted our umbrella, and we dashed along hysterically, rain and tears washing down our faces.

"I swear I will not call him *Googly Eyes* anymore. Cross my heart and hope to die."

"That's good of you, you little beast."

"His eyes do jiggle though," I added.

"Stop it, enough!"

"Helen, why do you date Barney... I mean Bernard?"

---

* *Barney Google With the Goo-Goo-Googly Eyes*
Lyrics by Billy Rose 1923

"I won't lie to you. There's no one else."

"You're not going to marry him, are you?"

"No, Caasi, I won't."

Reassured, I reached for Helen' hand and we skipped along Rue Durocher dangling the useless umbrella, sliding with careless neglect on the wet leaves underfoot. On Rue Ste. Catherine, passing a theater, I noticed the lighted marquee display. It announced in bold lettering, ***Because You're Mine***.

"Helen, let's go to the movies." I said excitedly.

She was not hard to convince because we had gone together to see *The Toast of New Orleans,* Mario Lanza starring with Kathryn Grayson. His magnificent tenor voice and Clark Gable-like charm had entirely enchanted us.

The movie was wonderful and we left the theater singing, *The brightest star looks down and envies me, because you're mine...*[*]

Helen checked her watch.

"If we hurry, I can get home in time to fix my hair. Bernard is picking me up at seven."

"Helen, may I sleep over tonight?"

"Bubbe won't mind in the least," she answered amiably.

Helen always took great pains in preparing for her dates with Bernard. She was aware of her defects. Her narrow face continued into a pointy chin, the delicate skin thinly covering the hollows of her cheeks. Glasses with thick lenses, too heavy for her fine nose, willfully coasted down, and she had a custom of pushing up the bridge piece even while playing the piano. Her hair was wispy and mousey brown. She combined peroxide with her shampoo to lighten the plain brown shade and add thickness and body to her hair. When damp, she tightly pin-curled it, letting it dry bound up in this mode. No sooner did she remove the bobby pins, did the ringlets droop into straggly filaments of spun silk.

She arched her eyebrows with a dark brown pencil, daubed rosy

---

[*] *Because You're Mine*
Written by Nikolaus Brodszky, Lyrics by Sammy Cahn 1952

spots on her ashen cheeks, and applied scarlet lipstick to her slender lips tracing outside the lines to make them appear fuller. For all her immense effort, when she returned from her evening with Bernard, her face appeared lengthened in desperation and the blush on her cheeks was livid with defeat.

"Did you have a nice time?" I yawned with tiredness.

"He's no Mario Lanza," she answered, her voice striking a flustered note.

She sat on our shared bed, her frail shoulders hunched in disappointment, and she pulled her sweater close, a gesture concluding her stifled evening.

"You shouldn't have waited up so late," she said.

Even as deep-drawn breaths of uncertainty, weariness, and longing defied her woeful lips, she implored me to yield to sleep. Outside the casement window, faceless shapes and forms of things unknown vaulted the fire escapes. A maze of metal lattices stretched to the sky and I unendingly climbed the grates. I could not leave my sobs behind, the lingering notes echoed off the brick walls, a somber Polonaise.

Helen stroked the back of my neck, little deft strokes with her slender fingers, comforting me until my dreaming stopped.

What is our innocence,

We moved to Rue Chambord in the north end of Montréal. The arrangements were entirely conducted by my father without my knowledge or consent. Scouting out the area, he had located a recently constructed duplex, and the owner agreed to a modest rental fee for the top flat. On departure day, in the furniture laden van sitting on padded cushions propped up to the exposed frame of the old parlor easy chair, I had qualms about deserting the Av Coloniale address. It was as if I were being disloyal to the alliance I had forged with the dilapidated old place and dust infested walls battered by my cries and yearning. As the truck trundled along, I cast away my childhood home with each passing mile, but the covenant with my memories was unshakeable.

The modern interior was tiny: two bedrooms, a kitchen, and one bathroom. A picture window in the kitchen faced east coaxing in the disobliging sunlight on gloomy mornings. The bedrooms were carpeted in aquamarine and the walls were freshly painted white. In short order, I appreciated the uplifting new setting, but the added distance to school was a cause for concern.

To arrive promptly at school by eight in the morning proved to be a difficult task. I coped poorly with the early day shambles of messy hair, grungy sweaters, careless dragging shoelaces, and loosely scattered homework pages. As I straggled, the hands of the clock moved with swift and unerring regularity, a tiresome reminder of my lateness. After classes let out, the lengthy streetcar ride followed by a one-mile walk home wore on me. The streetcar schedules lacked consistency, and on snowy days I started hitchhiking rides. At first I excused it out of necessity and thought it amusing, but then it became ongoing. I was not unaware of the lurking peril; more dangerous was the irresistible lure to do it all the while in fear of my father divining my rebellious deceit.

The same car came by on a daily basis. I noticed it because it was a flashy red *Buick* convertible with red and white leather upholstered seats. The driver was a man in his forties, attractive in an eccentric way, but possessing a forbidding profile, his jaw hard and angular. His minty green eyes hinted at an evil intent. When he pulled over to the curb, he stretched his arm across to reach the passenger door handle opening it from the inside with sly invitation. His thinning hair was freshly trimmed as if he had just left the barber shop, but his face was covered with the stubble of several nights giving him a rough quality. I believed him to be a corporate executive in his posh light brown vicuna topcoat, shimmering silk shirt, and expensive looking wool gabardine trousers. I was undecided and suspicious of this character, yet I jumped in the front seat with my exuberance and frosty pretense. I never asked *who are you and why did you stop for me*, suspecting his answers might be subtle and inventive.

We rode along Rue St-Denis in stylish comfort, the heater fan blowing hot currents on my chilled face and fingers. The radio was tuned to a station playing popular songs. *Kiss Of Fire*, a Georgia Gibbs hit started up, and he fiddled with the knob to increase the volume. The rhythm was fast and sultry. *I touch your lips and all at once the sparks go flying... Those devil lips that know so well the art of lying...*[*] There was only the slightest movement of his eyes in my direction. I pressed my winter dry lips together in a tight bond as I watched his hands on the leather covered wheel driving the car with proficient ease. *Just like a torch you set the soul within me burning...I must go on along this road of no returning...*[*]

At the signal light, he shifted his arm to rest it across the top of the seat and his thin long fingers drummed to the beat of the music on the radio.

"What time does school let out?" He asked.

Not answering, I had an unbridled urge to jump out of the car, but the light changed to green and we sped off again. A welcome intrusion of a jingle commercial for *Lennox Warm Air Heating System* came on. Then the music changed to Perry Como serenading *No Other Love*

---

[*] Music written by Ángel Villoldo, Argentine musician
  Premiered Buenos Aires, Argentina, 1903

*...Only my love for you**. My notable, unknown driver hummed along picking out the lyrics he knew, exuding self-possession. I felt at risk and on edge. The cloth-topped warm interior became more and more like a smothering enclosure as I wondered what I had gotten myself into.

The man started waiting for me after school, parking his car several blocks away at the intersection of Av Du Mont Royal and Av Du Parc, and each time I spotted him, it was always the same reaction: recognition and surprise. I ignored his waiting presence but he flashed me a sweet almost melancholic smile showing wholly white teeth and beckoned me to come. Drawn in his direction, I yielded to the temptation, squelching my father's warnings of men and their perversity. The man did not act familiar; never so much as touched my hand, but the quirkiness of our relationship enveloped me in a fog of doubt. Searching for proven signs of his kindliness and willingness, I insisted he always let me out at least a quarter of a mile away from my home. He tolerably agreed.

One stormy afternoon, the howling wind whirred past my ears blowing fine snow on my face in numbing blasts as I neared the accommodating car. During the ride, my *Buick* driver insisted that because of the squally weather he walk me to my front door. He parked the *Buick* at the corner of Rue De Normanville and Rue Everette, one short block away from my door. He extended his gloved hand to help me out of the car, but I declined the offer. We walked side by side through the drifts, and as we vigilantly stepped over a bank of snow, he suddenly reached over and took my elbow, a gesture that was supposed to be fatherly. His hand latched confidently to my elbow, and the urgency of his fingers was intense and too familiar. Steering me along, his firm clutch, rigid and inflexible, was like a clamp at my throat. I choked out squeaky words, snippets of fear.

"I can't accept rides from you anymore. My father will kill me if he discovers what I have been up to."

"We just won't tell him, will we?"

Solidly planting my boots in the mounting banks of snow, I with-

---

* Music by Richard Rogers; Lyrics by Oscar Hammerstein II 1962

215

stood the wrong of that demand and refused to go any further. The man slowly let loose the constraint on my arm and withdrew, then staggered away, his footsteps imprinting ill-designed lost opportunity in the fresh powder. I took off for home, light and unburdened, noting with blissful relief that the convertible had moved far down the street almost out of sight. Between the tread of the tires, a line of black oil trailed on the white innocence.

We should all come home after the flare, and the noise, and the gayety

Each Friday noon until one, Mr. Alexander, our principal, let the students mingle socially in the gymnasium with a provided decent phonograph player, a collection of 45's and a granted permission to dance. The records were a mix of ballads, pop, doo wop, rhythm, and rock: *You Belong To Me*, *Cry*, *Earth Angel*, *Smoke Gets In Your Eyes*, *Little Darlin*, *Come On-A My House*, *Honeycomb*, and *Party Doll*. Mr. Alexander resolutely believed that a supervised setting would discourage us from indiscreetly leaving to buy cigarettes at the corner store or disappearing to make out in the wooded slopes of nearby Fletcher Field.

Surprising him most of all, his plan was an unqualified success. When the buzzer sounded to end morning classes, we eagerly gathered in the gym; the boys good-naturedly fidgeted and ambled up and down, while across the span of floor, the girls assumed a cautious demeanor. Feigning nonchalance and disinterest, each girl scanned the room with radar eyes to settle on which guy might have the courage to ask for a dance. Most of the boys went to the noon parties stag. Social life was less complicated for them, not the way it was for girls who had to wait until gauged and chosen.

Jordy was the sought after dance partner. His quick tempo step patterns in the jitterbug were embellished with swinging arms and acrobatic flips over his side. When it suited him, he performed the rumba, samba, and mambo with rhythmical hip movements or shifted easily into the Charleston with jive kicks. He was fun to watch but the coup de foudre, the stroke of lightening, was to dance with him. Jordy had taken me out on the floor on successive Fridays, but this noon he was disgracefully flirting with Donna, a curly haired, creamy complexioned and bright eyed student from the tenth grade. I watched them together, Donna wiggling her hips provocatively and Jordy smoothly whirling her about never missing a beat. When the blaring of the music stopped, she swayed leaning against him with a possessive attitude. I turned away in disgust unable to conceal my vexation, on the verge of tears.

My mortification was observable and attracted the sympathy of Jean-Christophe, a senior, who suffered the awkward dilemma of being French-Canadian in a school primarily attended by Jews. I was unimpressed by the distinction though others critically assigned him the pejorative term, shegetz, a Hebrew word for a non-Jewish boy literally meaning rascal. He had a keen sense of the comical and salient disparities of his situation and kept apart from the crowd. Distinguishing himself as a swaggering bully by wearing his hair long, a scarred black leather jacket with an eagle on the back, tight navy-blue denims, and motorcycle boots, he was a decided contrast to the more conventional and fashionably neat look of his peers. His appearance was not a barrier to being thought of as a hero of the ruffian breed. Reticent and shy, never getting into trouble, I found him savagely attractive.

Jean-Christophe sensed my dismay because he was suddenly at my side holding out his urging hand. At that moment, all I wanted to accomplish was to make Jordy jealous. I offered no resistance and welcomed the chance to strut my stuff. Jean-Christophe was not the smooth Fred Astaire type dancer but he had flare. As we danced to *I Only Have Eyes For You*, his grip was firm and sure. We made eye contact and he held me close within the limits of respectability for a lunch time event. There was a sensual aura emanating from him that made me breathe hard, turned my knees to *Jell-O*, and caused my hand to sweat within his. As the music continued to pour out, *I'm Just A Fool In Love With You*, *There Goes My Baby*, and *Jezebel It Was You*, I wanted him to take me far way, to hold me hostage in shadowy places, and to feel his mouth on mine. I was drowning in his enormous eyes, black as a starless night.

The tempo changed and he was twirling me around to *When the chimes ring five, six and seven/ we'll be right in seventh heaven... we're gonna rock, rock, rock 'til broad daylight**, and the room revolved like the hands of a runaway clock. The 1:00 P.M. bell clanged

---

* Performed by: *Bill Haley & His Comets*
Written by: Jimmy De Knight; Max Friedman

and shrilly blew us apart. We stood regarding each other, his expression honest, openly divulging his caring without saying a word. I realized it was not a spur of the moment thing but feelings he had from before, overlooked and unappreciated as I had desperately vied for Jordy's affections. My heart urged me forward to give him an enticing smile, to show him I was charmed, and to suggest we meet after school. With stanch force, winds of condemnation blew in my head; my father's words intruded, rattling from one side to another, rolling thunder denunciations of this liaison.

What, his intolerance screamed, you want to go with that French shegetz? They're all hooligans, you hear me hooligans. You're crazy. I'll beat you within an inch of your life. You'll never leave this house ever!

I managed a hazy, uncertain smile and then hung my head averting his eyes, my gaze shifting from his face to the hand with which he still held mine. It was only then I noticed caked dirt under his fingernails.

Fates That weave my thread of life
in ruder patterns Than these

Rosalie, who sat across the aisle from me in class, had a steady boyfriend Bruce, and the two were always together at recess. They talked in a confidential and familiar way as she saucily stroked his hand, and he predictably responded with a knowing smile. On passing them in the hall, it was instantly clear that they cared for one another, and by ignoring all other students, they basked in an enviable whirl-pool of oblivion.

During French class, while we were doing uninspired conjugations of the verb "vouloir," to want, Rosalie passed me a wrinkled message interrupting my daydreaming. I read the scrawled words.

"Whad ya do Saturday nite?"

"Nothing, just nothing, and you?" I whispered.

Rolling the paper into a hard wad, I tossed it on her desk eluding the notice of our French teacher Miss Loisel, diligent and tireless in the repetitions of "Nous voulons, vous voulez, ils veulent…"

Her reply returned on a sheet of paper compactly folded. On it she had drawn a heart- shape and scrawled a note with bunches of symbols for love and kisses.

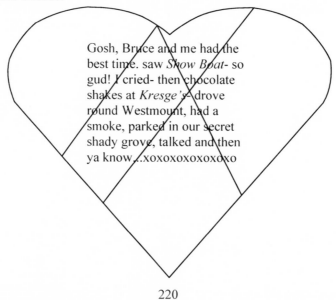

Gosh, Bruce and me had the best time. saw *Show Boat*- so gud! I cried- then chocolate shakes at *Kresge's* drove round Westmount, had a smoke, parked in our secret shady grove, talked and then ya know…xoxoxoxoxoxoxoxo

I directly read the short but graphic details and begrudged her joyfulness. My hands trembled in the effort to control the urge to crumple the paper or rip the heart to shreds. Before slipping the note back to her, I corrected her sentence grammar error to 'Bruce and I' as well as her spelling errors.

Rosalie looked at me perplexed and then mouthed the word, "Jerk." She turned her back to me facing the girl on the other side of the aisle. I began to conjugate vouloir aloud. My heart was covetous; I could hardly stand it. A bundle of sighs rebelliously rushed out from my lips. Je veux, I could not get past je veux. I wanted what Rosalie had, a boyfriend, fun, wicked conversation, and innocent fondling, but I knew it was not to be no matter how hard I wished. Aware of the fact that my father never permitted me to date, I fabricated excuses. When asked out by the immodestly endearing and know-it-all Jordy, bold lies ingeniously tripped off my tongue putting obstacles in his path. The inventive fictional story made my vanity so much the more visible, but averse to confessing the truth, I simply could not say that I was not allowed out in the evening.

Confident that an exacting monastic life of reading, obedience, and prudence shielded me from all youthful misfortune, my father's disciplinary tactics made me miserable, an effect I doubted he grasped or was sympathetic to. Yet I was loath to deceive him and sneak around, a supposition made salient after my close call with hitchhiking. The exacted penalty for detected infractions far surpassed the imagined joy of holding hands with Jordy or sharing another kiss with Kevin. The fervor of an exclusive relationship was replaced by dull, uneventful Saturday nights looking after my cousin Toby's eight month old son. Mindless of ideas and having no other options, the prospect of earning one dollar and twenty-five cents for five hours of babysitting plus a fifty cent tip was a healing token and welcome reward.

Saturday evening at 7:00 P.M., Toby's husband Sterling arrived in his *Chevrolet* to pick me up. Leroy, a silky, fair-haired, droopy-eared Cocker Spaniel bounded from the car shaking with glee and jumped up bestowing wet kisses on my face. Sterling took liberties with Leroy's affectionate and compliant nature and taught him to do all sorts of silly tricks for amusement. Overjoyed, the dog performed but seemed not to

understand the '**no**' command and raced wildly around in circles enthusiastically barking. Sterling semi-seriously disciplined the dog and
then slipped him a biscuit. Other than appearance, dog and master
were remarkably similar. Instantly charming and endearing, Sterling
was good-humored with a roguish streak and a stream of ribald jokes.
Tall, slender with dark wavy hair, mischievous eyes, and dimples, he
was friendly with everybody, quick thinking, and nonsensically inventive. As I fended off the nuzzling dog, Sterling evoked riotous laughter
from me with his inability to restrain his dog.

"Leroy down," he said.

"Leroy, **no**, behave! You are pestering Caasi."

Leroy quit mid-leap and flopped down to sit on my shoe obliging
me to drag myself and the dog into the car.

Toby greeted me with a set of instructions to follow about baby
Neil's care, a list of telephone numbers, and details of their evening
plans to ensure I was clear on what to do in case of any and all emer-
gencies. This routine was repeated each Saturday that I was hired.

Worriedly she asked, "Are you absolutely sure you can manage?"

"I'll be fine," I said placidly.

"We're first stopping off at Mel and Elli's and then dining at the
Kon Tiki. We'll bring you some egg rolls if we're not late."

"Thanks."

"Don't answer the door."

"I won't."

Opening the door to the refrigerator, she pointed to the baby's bottle filled with formula on the top shelf.

"Warm the bottle in the little pot of water on the stove and be sure
to test a few droplets of milk on the inside of your wrist. It mustn't be
too hot."

"Okay."

"And don't give the dog treats."

Toby's incessant fussing with trifles did not exasperate or ruffle
me. I was grateful to be somewhere for the evening in a fine home im-
bued with a plentiful sense of family and normalcy. I gazed at her admiringly as she completed her preparations for her social time out.
Dressed in a smart looking silk shantung suit, she artfully applied the

practiced touches of makeup and twisted and twirled her thick hair into a coiffed pouf on top of her head fastening it with a black leaf
shaped barrette with gold speckles. Scrupulously adjusting the seams
of her silk stockings at the back of her legs, she slipped into a pair of
trendy pumps dyed royal blue to match the color of her suit. Almost as
tall as her husband Sterling, they were an unusually comely couple,
their differing ways playing a role in their substantial happiness.

Unmindful of Sterling's fitful urging, Toby stepped away in her
own good time calling out final admonitions even as the door latched,
and the click of her heeltaps distanced to silence. Without a respecta-
ble waiting period, I investigated the contents of the food cupboards
espying cellophane packets of chocolate bridge mix, licorice allsorts,
gumballs, cinnamon hearts, and other assorted candies. The freezer
contained a carton of Neapolitan ice cream. I scooped out a sizeable
portion of the chocolate/ vanilla/ strawberry layers and fringed it with
chocolate rosettes.

Leroy tracked me to the living room, his pink tongue lolling out in
submissive expectancy. I let him lick some ice cream from my fingers,
which made him ecstatic, and he curled up on the couch beside me as I
watched television. Leroy heard the baby cry out in his sleep and startled bounding up, his hair bristling and his eyes wild. Releasing the
spoon, I sped into the bedroom and lifted the warm little bundle from
his crib cradling him in my arms. Seeming to accept me, baby Neil
stopped crying almost at once, his little bow mouth making quaint
sucking noises. As I positioned him against my chest with his head
nestling at my neck, I felt less alone and tenderly protective, feelings
before wanting in me. Carrying him into the kitchen, I skeptically lit
the gas flame under the pot. As soon as his formula was warm, I fed
him, burping him per Toby's instructions. He drank just under two
ounces; his eyes fluttering like butterfly wings as he soon tired. Wrapping him snugly in his blanket papoose style, I held him close and
rocked him until he drifted back to sleep, thinking unsuitably that I
was luckless in love, yet baby Neil was precious and adored.

I settled back in front of the television to watch my favorite show
The Honeymooners starring Ralph Kramden, the stubborn blockhead
bus driver, and Ed Norton, his loyal, honest, clumsy sewer worker

friend. As I went along with the absurdities of the plot and their hare-brained get rich scheme, the sounds ricocheted off the furniture and roamed about in the trivial tedium of the living room. Ralph threatened his wife Alice: *You have just said the secret word... Alice, you have just won a trip to the moon!* Recorded studio laughter boomed from the set and a single wailing voice asserted itself. The outcry was my own. The tenuous hold on my indomitable hope had splintered and snapped, and I felt the sadder and the lonelier for the thought.

The hockey game started next and the evening slipped into solitary periods. The ice cream melted unattended, its usefulness thwarted. I tried to absorb the announcer's voice calling the action, his words excitedly clamoring, "Puck in the corner... digging it out... shot on the boards... big rebound... picked up... passed... loose puck in front... Maurice Richard grabs it... firing ... **he scores!**" The thunderous cheers of thousands of fans for the *Montréal Canadiens* swept through the Forum mounting to a crescendo. A breaking wave of half-buried longing came down with a rush on my adolescent ache pining for the company of only one.

At midnight, the television test pattern came on. It steadily eyed me in the dark of the room, a vacuous flicker of sooty gray cinders and charcoal picture elements woven into plain invariant threads impervious to the hour. It was Sunday again and another Saturday night had passed without a date.

Go in thy native innocence;

At the prompt hour of six in the evening Daniel arrived. I was slow in the process of getting ready brushing my precisely waved hair to smooth radiance and dabbing on *Wild Orchid* lipstick. Unhappy with my selection, I changed to a color called *Exotic Pink* and applied a smudge of black eyeliner under my lashes and touches of blush on my cheeks to create a look of sophistication. It seemed impossible to contain myself within my skin; my exhilaration was disobedient and my underarms were damp despite the dusting of powder. An evening out, excluded before from my life, summarily arranged without a hitch. My father was trusting of Daniel, his one favored nephew, eight years older than I was.

Showing no impatience with the delay, Daniel was properly courteous to my father. They talked at length. My father chuckled enjoying Daniel's seriousness in detailing his expeditions as a pilot employed by a small charter airline company to deliver supplies to lead, zinc, and silver mines on Baffin Island. As I rashly fretted, concerned with trifles, I overheard snatches of concentrated description, but I was unable to focus on the content. Phrases fell by the wayside, drifting and floating in the downdraft of my blithe vanity.

"... arctic climate," Daniel was saying, "...depending on wind conditions... my approach from...indented coast or over ice-capped mountains... flying... foothills with sparse-growing sage... treeless monotony... you just don't wanna go down... worst fear...wings icing...damn...only walruses, birds and beluga ..."

My father let Daniel ramble on without interruption, evidently attracted to Daniel's love of adventure, fierce courage, and stubborn obstinacy based on ethical standards. In my bedroom, engaged in my own immodest flouncing about and mirror reflection, none of this seemed relevant. That my father was suitably influenced and had loosened his protective leash on me for this evening mattered most.

Daniel continued the discourse with some bawdy tale of the workers at Iqaluit and the scarcity of tobacco.

I emerged from the bedroom dressed in a pink cashmere cardigan, unbuttoned at the neck, and a close fitting cerise color woolen skirt. Daniel noticeably paused in mid-sentence seemingly dazzled as if the parlor was at once rose-painted or the color of ripe cherries. My father, probably more engaged with the future of mining in the Northwest Territories, seemed not to notice Daniel's gawking and appreciative stare.

Politely helping me on with my coat, Daniel informed my father of our plans.

"We have dinner reservations at *Moishe's*."

"Order her a fancy steak,"my father said. "She likes to eat."

The two men laughed in some man-type camaraderie. It was good to see my father affable and on his best behavior.

We stepped into a chill night without a moon, and through a thin cloud cover, the stars appeared small and insubstantial. I felt a mix of elation and inexpressible sadness. As we walked to his parked car, I shivered in the cold air; Daniel placed his arm possessively across my back firmly holding me at the waist.

"Caasi, you look great," he said, his voice silky with admiration.

"Thank you."

"Definitely not the same kid I once babysat."

"Don't even mention that, Danny," I said coyly as my lips formed a childish pucker.

Grinning, he gallantly opened the door to assist me and tucked my coat around my knees. As he slid into the driver's side, the overhead lamp stayed on long enough for me to see that his flint gray eyes held tiny sparks. We drove through the darkened residential streets in nervy eagerness to reach our destination, Boulevard St. Laurent, with its brassy lights and glittering neon signs. It was the beginning of a night of magic and newness.

Daniel turned the car keys over to the valet at the curb, and in an eager rush, we scooted up the stairs to the expansive dining room at *Moishe's*. Pure white linen covered the tables enhanced by matching silver place settings and crystal wine goblets. Muted by glass shades, the small curved flames of the glowing candles were crescents of moonlight in the room.

Innocent flirtations wafted in the air with the smoke from Daniel's cigarette.

"Would you like a cigarette?" he asked, as if it were entirely natural.

"I might," I said with a touch of insouciance.

Danny lit the cigarette and handed it to me. I put it to my lips and without thinking drew in the smoke resulting in a spasm of coughing. Red-faced, I handed the offending cigarette back. This time Daniel instructed me how to carefully and slowly inhale so as not to end up gasping and choking. Attentive waiters in their dark formal jackets delicately changed ashtrays and ignored my fits of coughing. The wine steward, his jolly face florid with pleasure, applauded Daniel's selection of an imported Pommard to compliment our charbroiled filets.

"A fine full-flavored wine, an excellent choice."

Daniel described the wine to me all the while the man twittered about and delayed leaving.

"It's a red wine from the vineyards in the Côte de Beaune region of France."

I nodded approvingly, astonished by his elegance. His carefully groomed curly hair, slender face, and impeccably attired charm were seductive, and though I had never sinned, I began to wonder if I might.

Discreetly, our waiter displayed an attractively labeled bottle of deep red wine, uncorked it with a grand gesture, and poured a small amount into Daniel's wine goblet for him to taste. Daniel reacted favorably.

"We'll have another bottle of this excellent Pommard." He twirled his crystal glass to make his point.

The room was tilting about; strobes of light flashed and Daniel's gray eyes softly regarded me with indulgent fondness. I casually sipped the wine and felt absurdly dizzy and overpoweringly ardent.

As we both drank wine but ate sparingly, our mood shifted to silly. Daniel attempted to balance the salt and peppershaker on end, resting each on one grain of salt. He borrowed others from adjacent tables and laughed unpretentiously at our impervious waiter who chose to ignore the row of precariously perched shakers while clearing the plates. My feelings were whirling around, and I felt nothing but the implicit pressure of Daniel's hand on mine in that restaurant amid the crystal, lamps, napkins, ashtrays, and words never said.

The ride home in his car was close and intimate. I snuggled against his fine wool topcoat while the windshield wipers crooned. He parked around the corner from my apartment house and turned off the motor. A flurry of snow sheeted the window insulating and isolating us from the whole world. As he reached for me putting his mouth on mine, his tongue slipped into the warm recesses, and the scent of his after-shave was sweet with desire. I lightly placed my hand on the back of his neck encouraging the embrace. His skin there was hot and his curly hair was now limply wet. Groping for my breasts, his fingers tentatively reached under my sweater to massage and rub my nipples making them stand up pouting and firm. I tried to hold him back but my body was smothered in wool and conflict.

"Don't Danny." It was a softly spoken plea.

Oddly enough he stopped.

How can she foresee the thick stranger

Shirley, my closest friend in high school, possessed the elegance and classiness I lacked, she having matured into an enviable figure of poise at only fifteen and one-half years of age and I still unable to discard my shy and nervously taciturn ways. I commonly visited her home after school to vicariously enter her privileged orbit. She was movie star pretty with long streaming hair of true wheat-gold nonchalantly pulled back and coiled in a chignon or French twist. A few strands of hair irresponsibly slipped from the fastenings charmingly framing her narrow face and dimpled chin. Her eyes were oval shaped, sea green dappled with blue, the color of my prized marbles I played with as a child. In profile, her distinguished nose showed a sharp bump in the center, yet overall it flattered her face and added to her mysterious composure. Shirley's family was prosperous and she possessed a wardrobe of fabulous clothes. At times, sympathetic to my attire of mundane ill-matched outfits, she generously offered to share with me. I had nowhere special to go and certainly no dates, other than the one evening affair with my cousin Daniel. I resignedly inspected her closet jealously fingering each piece of clothing on its hanger, a picture perfect assemblage of beaded sweaters, crisp-collared blouses, silk dresses, fine tailored woolens skirts, and complimentary cashmere scarves.

On select Friday nights, Shirley invited me and her boyfriend Gabriel, and classmates Leah, Freda, Paul, Greta, and Ben, for an evening of fun. She had an extensive record album collection and a surprising connection to folk music and music of the West Indies. Self-taught, she played the guitar and knew almost all the folk songs of the early 50's and sang the lyrics accompanied by the music. She held us under her spell by her rendition of hit tunes by *The Weavers, If I Had a Hammer*, and *Tzena, Tzena, Tzena*. The music influenced her nature and as she strummed, she switched to Woody Guthrie's *This Land Is Your Land* and inspired us to join in: *As I went walking that ribbon of highway, I saw above me that endless skyway, saw below me that gol-*

den valley, this land was made for you and me*. We did not know that
some of these ballads were activist comments on the plight of migrant
workers and the urban poor and downtrodden. Simply loving the music we wore ourselves thin on the popular songs: *Blowing Down That
Old Dusty Road, Kisses Sweeter Than Wine, Do Not Forsake Me,* and
Sixteen Tons.

The only edge I had over Shirley was my consummate attention to
my school studies and near perfect scores. Her grades improved as I
helped her with the assigned homework pressing her to pay attention.
One hour was all she could tolerate, and then her thoughts drifted to
Gabe and his motorcycle. She snappily closed the books, propped the
mirror on the texts, and tweezed hairs out of her eyebrows to shape
them. She was vivacious and rebellious and in my fondness for her, I
gave up on the tutoring, leaving X and Y unsolved, and joined her in
practicing the calypso, playing Harry Belafonte's single recording *Ma-
tilda* again and again driving her mother crazy.

One day after school, I paid a casual visit to her house to help her
ready for an upcoming history exam. We ended up putting on makeup,
reading *True Romance*, and listening to albums. As the hour grew late,
I tarried hoping to be invited to dinner, hovering expectantly like a
Dickens' orphan sniffing the delightful cooking odors issuing from the
kitchen. Shirley implored me to stay, and I was easily influenced. The
house was warm and comfortably furnished with plush couches, silk
shaded lamps, and handsome curtains with tassel tiebacks. The elegant
dining table was set with handworked crocheted linens. Shirley's
mother, a dumpy frowsy housewife with scowling eyes and tightly
clenched lips, made me feel ill at ease as she apprehensively moni-
tored her husband who appeared to be feasting on me instead of her
roasted chicken and mashed potatoes. I tried to pay little in the way of
attention to the family behavior and tension at the table being more
interested in the delicious food. The meal ended with a scrumptious
cream cheese frosted carrot cake for dessert after which I was overly
full, edgy, bored, and tired. I wanted to depart but the lateness of the

---

* Woody Guthrie, singer-songwriter and folk musician
  Lyrics written 1940 based on an existing melody

hour made it prohibitive to walk the distance alone.

Shirley's father offered to drive me home and I happily accepted. He insisted on my sitting close to him for warmth because the heater in his new *Chrysler* was mysteriously not working. He regularly swore at the vehicle.

"This damn car's going back to the damn dealer."

The curses paved the way to petulant sighs, snorts, and forced exhalations. His cigar breath notched out circles in the frosted windows admitting light from the street lamps in pockmarked designs. Edgily he ran his thick fingers through his thinning hair patting the strands into place and then proceeded to roll his dark waxed mustache beneath his abundant nose. His fleeting look in my direction, his cautious staging and expressionless face, disguised the wickedness in his eyes.

"So, how many boyfriends do you have?"

Startled, I said the truth, "None."

He gave me a broad smile and a knowing frisky wink. He looked so antique to be playing a fool.

"I don't believe it… you're a pretty thing…and desirable."

His flattery was subtle and warped and his voice stone dead yet somehow obscene with lust. I shrank away from the daunting hulking form and wedged myself in the corner confinement of the front seat. While driving and holding the wheel with one hand, he used his free hand to stroke my hair and then made a premeditated move downward to explore the front of my chest searching for my breasts hidden under my coat. I felt the blood drain from my cheeks as I was seized by fear.

"Stop it," I shouted.

Unrelentingly, he continued his fumbling and undesired caresses, and suddenly I discovered his assertive hand between my thighs trying to pry them apart. I grabbed the defiling hand and violently jerked his thumb back causing him to yelp with pain.

"Damn you, you little shit," he said as he pulled to a quick stop at my house.

"Get out!"

The family dinner rose in leaden lumps in my throat.

Am I then the sport, The Game of Fortune, and her laughing Fools?

The game played swiftly with early scoring. Lightly snapping back and forth, the white-feathered shuttlecock crackled through the air charged with electricity. I bent to pick up the bird to set up for the next serve. My chest felt tight from the effort as if bound in a plaster cast. As I tried to normalize my breathing, my own sharp intake of air rustled in my ears. Dressed in my white square neck middy blouse and short navy bloomers, the required demure court attire, sweat soaked my waistband; circling my thighs, the tight elastic pinched and nipped. Even though the tally in the game was convincingly in my favor, I was susceptible to that familiar nervousness, the inconsistent feeling of being both inside and outside of my body. The floor started to pitch and heave and the walls twirled and turned as if I were in a revolving barrel that had plummeted off a loaded truck. Pointy barbed shafts of light pierced the high grated windows of the gymnasium maliciously blinding me. In my mind a troubling image lurked that I was to suffer *The Slings and Arrows of outrageous fortune**; or was it *To be, or not to be** for me this day? I cheered myself on with the remembered soliloquy, but the slippery edginess slithered back in, a sneaky devil in my head.

I was worried. A failure at most sports, never qualifying for the cheerleader squad and hurtfully being called by my classmates 'bookworm' or worse, I wanted to win this match, to hold a sports trophy in my hand, and to outrageously brag...

Just two more points, just two more I kept saying to myself; hang on, you can do it; you will be the senior girls' badminton champion.

My opponent Thelma was an excellent competitor, aggressive, long-legged, and naturally gifted in athletics. The gym teacher Miss Duffy pinned all her hopes on her for an interscholastic track and field

---

* *To Be or Not to Be*
William Shakespeare's *Hamlet,* Circa 1600

victory. It seemed to be an off-day for Thelma, her thoughts elsewhere, probably on her boyfriend Allan who had recently dumped her
for voluptuous Becky. We had played before in tough matches, my
wiliness and sizzling smashes making up for my lack of speed and po-
sitioning for returning the high lobs.

There was no spectator courtside; only Miss Duffy was officially
present to referee and supervise the final match. Miss Duffy was not a
favorite of mine. From the time I entered high school, I was the target
of her Monday morning Moorish mind and Irish irascibility. Whenever
she ordered laps around the gym, I lagged behind the faster runners
breathing too hard, swallowing air and grumbling of having a cramp in
my side. She thought me lazy and unmotivated. I simply was not a
sprinter. As my pace wilted, she confronted me, grabbed my arm with
a twist, and dragged me off to the side for a public lecture. Unable to
master a single vault on the pommel horse, she berated me until it
seemed as if a crimson pencil of disparagement spattered her face
bright red. Contorted with fury, Miss Duffy's frizzy saffron hair trembled. Her parchment thin face with transparent cheeks revealed a fine
and delicate bony structure seemingly incapable of such vehemence.
Most disquieting were her eyes, the palest ink blue as if diluted in the
chemistry lab with only a mere residue to prove the color.

*My God... nine to nothing, the score was nine to zero. I was way
ahead.* The game was going according to my degree of skill and the
months of practice I had invested. As I was about to serve planning a
swift low angle one over the net cross court, Thelma asked for a recess. I lowered my racquet and looked questioningly at Miss Duffy.
This was not the usual behavior in a final. Miss Duffy held up her
hand and motioned for me to wait. Thelma went to the sidelines and
the two of them quietly spoke, their heads nodding in synchrony and
sympathy, scruples chucked away. The injustice rankled; it festered
into bitterness, fretting, and chafing. *What disclosures were they exchanging?* I imagined the worst. Miss Duffy was aware of my liabili-
ties, my ungainliness, and my foolish and pathetic attempt to defeat the
invincible. Had she prearranged that her talented student was not be
beaten or excelled? Whatever was said was enough to set Thelma off
into peals of laughter and she returned to her side of the court staring

across at me, haughty with arrogance and disdain. The badminton racket shook in my hand and I tripped over my shoelace botching my serve.

In a shrill voice Miss Duffy called out, "You're so clumsy. Just like a baby elephant!"

Her jeering words caused my fingers to loosen their hold on the handle of the racket and untied the remnants of my focus and composure. Thumping wildly, my heart raced erratically and my arms and legs seemed made of putty. Knowing what I needed to do and craving the victory so badly, my tenacity failed me in this crucial test of wills. It was as if I were on a hill in a runaway car, no brakes to curb the descent, falling prey to *The insolence of Office, and the Spurns That patient merit of th' unworthy takes.* *

I lost the championship match, Thelma defeating me by a final score of eleven to nine.

---

* *To Be or Not to Be*
William Shakespeare's *Hamlet,* Circa 1600

Oh my love my darling I've hungered for your touch

After a lengthy but lively discussion, Shirley and I crafted a provisional plan. Confident and cunning, she was certain it was a fait accompli.

"Just think," she said, "who wouldn't just die to spend an evening with 'Miss Top of the Class' and 'Miss Gorgeous'?"

Being the mathematician, I computed the probability of two fine-looking guys willing to trade a *Montreal Royals'* baseball game for the honor of our company.

"The chance is $1<0<1$," I announced.

"Don't be such a smarty-pants," she scolded.

Her romantic affair with Gabe, the motorcycle boyfriend, had been touch-and-go for the past weeks and had then permanently gone down the road. She was eager to make good use of the free time in her newly unattached state.

Still skeptical, I said, "I'm not sure of the plan you've devised."

"Ah, c'mon, music, dancing, maybe… getting to second base, what more could they want?" she asked with a smile.

"Shirley, you're awful!"

I wondered if she had ever gone all the way with Gabe, but I did not dare ask or even want to think about it.

We made a list of eligible candidates to invite, detailing their good and bad points and graded them with pluses.

1. Jack: terrific build, just broke up with Barbara, possibly not in good humor ++
2. David: good natured but too fat ++
3. Joel: handsome, super-intelligent, not a sports fanatic ++++
4. Jordy: sensational dancer, smokes too much, sneaks off to the racetrack during school hours +++
5. Carl: great choice, suave, thick curly hair, rich, new car ++++
6. Allan: shy, bad acne +

7. Michael: dreamboat, polite, best-dressed, had already dated Eileen, Marilyn, Faigie, and probably half the Latin class girls but never more than once +++++

I argued in favor of Jordy but Shirley was obstinate.

"Your dad hates him."

"I like him."

"Jordy, here at your grandmother's, are you crazy?" What if your dad found out?"

My grandmother had offered to let us use the front parlor for a Saturday night small party thinking it was a chance for me to have a social life. To her way of thinking, dishonesty was not a sin if my father was unsuspecting and I did nothing harmful.

"Es is nischt sein gescheft," she said, "not his business."

Respectful of my grandmother, I did not want to do anything to jeopardize her or her home so Jordy was a no.

"Michael then?" I asked.

"Too much of a playboy."

"Joel?"

Checking the list, Shirley crossed out the 'nos' with one sweep of the pen. Joel, my chemistry lab partner who brushed up against me as I reached for the Bunsen burner, was my latest crush, a secret flame I had not yet shared. Crossing my fingers in desperation, I hoped Shirley would not veto him.

"I'll vote for Joel for you if you think Carl's a good choice for me," she said.

With a sigh of relief I agreed. We decided on Joel and Carl saving Jack, David, and Michael as alternates if our strategy went awry.

"Okay, Shirley, but you're doing the telephoning."

"God, you're such a baby!"

Shirley had been around and savvy to a lot of things I was innocent of. Relying on her quick wit and experience, I expected her to reel in the two boys in some original and ingenious way.

On the afternoon of our planned event, she lugged over her makeup case, fashionable clothes from her closet, her record player, a stack of 45's, and four bottles of beer snatched from the refrigerator in

236

her basement recreational room. We sorted through the records and picked popular ballads and a few rhythm and blues for dancing: *Only You* and *The Great Pretender* by the *Platters, Ebb Tide* by Vic Damone, *Earth Angel* by the *Penguins, Blue Moon* by Mel Tormé, and *Sh-Boom* by *The Chords*. She switched on the record player and put *The Great Pretender* on the turntable, lowering the needle with care into the first shellac groove. We rehearsed dancing, Shirley pretending to be Joel, instructing me how to provocatively rest my head on her, or rather his, shoulder and easing me into a few simple steps.

"Ouch," she cried out, "you stepped on my toe."

Feeling silly, I started giggling.

"Stop that."

"Sorry, I'm just no good at this."

"You're so bashful. How are you going to handle dancing with Joel?"

"I don't know."

"Just move a little and act sexy. That's all there is to it."

"Zei gut, girls" my grandmother said, which was her way of telling us to behave properly as she and Zeyde took off for the evening to visit their friends Norma and Barry Friedman. We heard the dull clunk of the closing of the front door and made a mad dash for the bedroom. Our clothes were heaped in disarray on my grandmother's bed. Sorting through, I decided on my fawn colored double-ply cashmere sweater, a black velvet rope- twist with furry white puffballs, a narrow white cinch belt with a yellow buckle, and an ankle length flared brown felt skirt and flat shoes.

"That won't do." Shirley said. "You look like a dappled tabby cat."

Assessing me with a critical eye, she snatched off the twist, draped a filmy fringed scarf about my neck, and insisted I wear her wide patent belt, slinky black silk jersey skirt ending at the knees, and one inch black patent heels.

"Now you look smart," she said approvingly.

She gathered up my hair snugly pinning it at the crown, and letting it fall in ringlets and curls swinging freely and bouncily. Working on my willing face, she applied liquid makeup, finishing powder, eyeliner, eye shadow, blush, and lipstick.

"A dab of perfume and, voilà, the new you!"

The old beveled mirror in my grandmother's bedroom reflected my new elegant, detailed, and classy exterior. I was slow to be on relaxed terms with the alluring and trendy look, a marked contrast to the mounting surge inside.

We heard the hall clock chime the quarter of the hour.

"My God, it's almost eight," Shirley said, "hurry up."

Using my grandmother's good china bowls, we filled them with chips, mixed nuts, squares of cheddar cheese and crackers, and placed them on a cloth covered folding table.

"Here's the sour cream," Shirley said returning from her search in the refrigerator. "Read to me the directions for the *Lipton's* onion dip."

A faint trace of lemon oil lingered in the air; the hardwood floors and furniture were rubbed to spotless perfection. A last minute inventory reminded us that the table was missing glasses, napkins, and ashtrays. I plumped the sofa pillows and then lowered the lighting in the table lamps to create carefully nuanced shadows as if the room were candlelit. Shirley, at ease, unburdened by doubt, flopped into the occasional chair as my fingers distractedly played with an ivory paper cutter on the dining room sideboard.

"Stop looking like a scaredy cat," she commanded, "it's no big deal."

As soon as the bell rang, Shirley flung open the door, a seductive expression on her face thrilling the boys and making them eager and uncontainable.

"Hi Joel, hi Carl, c'mon in."

Shirley hugged each of the fellows in turn and helped them off with their jackets, which she tossed with gay abandon unto a dining room chair. Turning to me, she whispered in my ear, "Joel's wearing the new sexy men's lotion *Woodhue* by *Fabergé*; you'll love it!"

The evening passed negligibly for me. I glanced at Shirley from time to time noting how playful and coy she was moving blithely around the parlor or pretending, in a display of passion, to fall into Carl's arms. Joel and I retreated to a corner to talk but our conversation either lagged or burst forth in short abbreviated circuits and detours, electric sparks that were promptly eclipsed.

When the silence cut sharply between us, Joel finally asked me to dance. I could hear *The Platters* singing, *Only you can make the world seem bright, only you can make the darkness light**, and the rhythm and pulse of the sounds took over. Joel held me tightly against his muscular chest, his face smelling freshly fragrant. Suddenly incautious, I rested my cheek cozily in the nook of his neck. Blissfully and wantonly enticed by the sway of the music and the pull of desire, I unwound in his arms. Joel rested his hand on the middle of my back and caressed my soft sweater, then moved down to my waist and continued the slide until he caught my bottom in a firm grip. I felt a rod-like hardness between us, and he held me in a hot embrace, rubbing against me with a sense of urgency. The song ended and Shirley changed the mood and the music to *Sh-Boom*. In the dim half-light, Joel's face blazed red with sheepish embarrassment.

---

* Pop song composed by Buck Ram
Recorded by *The Platters* 1955

I never knew any of these forward sluts come to good

Mr. Alexander was a meek disciplinarian. When I routinely arrived late for class in the morning, his only rebuke was a warning. He used his stern voice but beneath the hard deep timbre was leniency and compassion. Much to his chagrin, I failed to alter my bad practice of breezing in after the bell.

"Young lady, next time I will punish you," he declared searching out my concession with his serious eyes. The twin linear frown lines above his nose extending into his brow deepened as he spoke swallowing his displeasure so that he never disclosed it in words.

An imposing figure, he towered above me, but he had no consistent resolve. His serge suits hung limply on his frame, a size too large, and his snuggly knotted tie drooped outlandishly under his jutting Adam's apple. Unable to straighten his knees, he seemed plagued by some type of arthritis and his stooped ill-shapen shoulders made him vulnerable. Determined to avoid garnering his anger, I pledged to try harder, which satisfied him, and he advised me to scurry off to class not to incur the less forgiving wrath of the teacher.

At the approach of the end of senior year, my collective grades were excellent and the possibility of scoring well in the provincial examinations was promising. Mr. Alexander sent a note to my home room class to appear in his office. I delayed until the end of the day. Sorrow-laden, I halfheartedly tapped on his office door believing he was going to make good on his threat to assign me the chore of washing the lockers to remove the scribbling put on by the school pranksters. Instead, he caught me off guard with a formulated plan, well thought-out in his deliberate and measured way.

"I want to submit an application on your behalf for a scholarship to Radcliffe College in Massachusetts," he said.

I was shocked.

"Why...I mean how did you know I wanted to attend there?"

Good-humoredly he answered, his eyes twinkling, "Oh, I have my ways."

"Do you really think I'd qualify?" I asked falteringly.

"Why don't we just complete the necessary forms and find out."

The waiting was riddled with edginess plucking holes in my mind. I vacillated between zeal and the hindrance of pessimism and apathy. Attending to my needs and those of school was performed mechanically in a hazy abstract of garbled thoughts and pondering. *Did I remember to brush my teeth, did I have bus fare, would the university judge me suitable, had I made my sack lunch, did I have my homework assignment complete, and was I deserving?* I sank again into the pattern of flustered sleep, perplexing dreams of ancient stone buildings overgrown with ivy crumbling into rubble and dark-green leaves, layered with dust crawling and creeping over the wreckage. I tried to free myself of the images, but my days took on a suspenseful and contrary ambiguity.

Passing the lockers near the school entry, Mr. Alexander detained me.

"I'm so sorry, I didn't intend to be late," I said with a pitiful whine.

"I'll let you off the hook," he said, "only because you've been granted a Radcliffe scholarship, mind you, a full scholarship."

His voice was heavy with unguarded pride.

"Oh my," was all I could come up with.

I was beyond ecstasy, an award of this magnitude given to a Canadian student by a prestigious American university.

Mr. Alexander requested a conference with my father to discuss and confirm arrangements. I passed the message to him, my face shiny with simple eagerness, and the words scarcely able to come out of my mouth without blundering. My father offered no protest and agreed upon the set date and hour for the appointment. The session took place in Mr. Alexander's office. I tolerantly waited in the hallway outside the thick paneled door, my heart thumping in my chest, the weird visions from my nightmare laden world holding me fast. My alarm grew by the moment as I heard my father's voice obscured by anger escaping as if from a crypt. Each sentence was a scourge.

"Did you think you could arrange all of this behind my back and expect my approval? It will never happen!"

He burst out from the meeting leaving the door widely ajar, his face contracted in fury. Time had not altered my father still crippled by lack of restraint, his ever-present torment deterring him from all reasonable prudence. Disinclined to let me be free of his control, he grabbed hold of my arms shaking me into a limp cloth doll as he sputtered a barrage of irrational phrases, each one landing a whip-like strike.

"I know why you want to go there...to roam freely round the campus... you bold-faced little slut! Well, you're not going...not now...not tomorrow...not ever..."

Mr. Alexander heard the appalling utterances and witnessed the scene. The school corridor was bleak with outrage. As my father strode away, my decent and beloved principal regarded me with quiet sympathy and constrained apology. Wordless, I turned and walked to the exit, the trodden path pitching and rolling in the turmoil of shell-torn air.

The most important formality
connected with the graduation

Almost completely detached from the aims of my original motivation, I became jaded at school, only attending classes because it was required in order to graduate. The end of the school year was fast approaching, and there were provincial exams to take to qualify for entry into university. Startled out of my disinterest, I settled into a practice of study into the late hours, and applied effort to review the year's work. In class, lulled by the sound of the teachers' hushed or verbose voices, I nodded off to sleep only to be sharply awakened by an unsympathetic slap of a book on my desk. The perversity of my fate daunted me; fighting the battle out with my father took a strange and unanticipated turn. At home, I distanced myself from him, comforted in the persuasion that I had the upper hand if I denied him access to what I was doing or thinking. Rarely was he about but when present, the solitude was rendered yet more insistent by the silence. The daily monotony of soundlessness treaded an unworn path between us.

The preparation for finals paid off and I was able to score well in all the major subjects. Only in art did I flounder and was unable to produce a little gem in the allotted time. Shaken by this, I conceded that I was not immune to the instability at home, and of the two of us, my father was more practiced in obstinate and fractious opposition.

Celebrating post examinations, the graduating class was obsessed in planning the formal dance. The girls were busily shopping for glamorously beautiful prom dresses. Animated discussions revolved around dresses made from fabrics such as organza, taffeta, tulle, and satin and adorned with sequins, rhinestones, lace, and embroidered appliqués. Even bright colors of turquoise and tangerine were considered. Rosalie brought her dress to school to preview. It was feminine and innocent with a fitted bodice, and the multilayered skirt over nylon petticoats was large and poufy. They all raved over it and wondered how to find its equal. The daily frenzy continued with having shoes dyed to match and locating beaded bags, jeweled clips and headbands, getting their hair coifed, and even having their nails manicured with colored polish applied to compliment their lipstick. A rock band was hired to perform live music. The fellows were ordering their tuxedos, bow ties, and flowers for the girls, and arranging for sharing cars or borrowing dad's car. The prettiest of the girls had already been booked for the dance by the most popular boys, and as I waited to be asked it dawned on me that inevitably I would not be attending. Never in the past had I been able to sustain a relationship because my father had purposefully disrupted any prospect of dating. I contemplated asking my cousin Daniel, of whom my father approved, but the others would most likely notice the age disparity. I was not in the mood to further withstand a storm of censure and ridicule.

In an offhand manner, Joel stopped me in the hall as I was engaged in poster painting for the decorations for grad night. He motioned for me to meet him away from the others so that we could talk undisturbed. Stammering, he began his rehearsed speech and then more fluidly he managed to string coherency into one line, "How about going to prom with me?"

"Yes," I answered without pause. Then a whole raft of doubt thudded in my head like a judge's gavel rapping on my conscience.

"My father may not permit me to go," I offered up the response that I had sedulously omitted for four years.

Joe, momentarily confused and taken aback, recovered, and in a forthright deed said the inconceivable, "I will ask him on your behalf."

At home in the evening, the anticipated shrill ring of the telephone put me in a continuous stream of fears and hopes. I could not configure my father's mood as he sat and read his newspapers after dinner while I cleared the table and washed the dishes. The hour was close to nine when the telephone jangled. I startled with alarm but made a pretext of being occupied. Disturbed from his relaxation, my father answered with unusual formality, "Evan Lichman here."

There was a minute of absolute noiselessness in the room as my father listened keenly. He said nothing at all until Joel had completed his presentation and request.

"Joel, you sound like a fine young man, and I am most impressed with your formal request to escort my daughter to the graduation dance."

My heart skipped several beats as I heard his modulated voice.

"I will tell you something I have repeatedly told Caasi. She is not permitted to date while she lives in this house. It is the law here and there is no deviation. In essence, Joel, the answer is no."

Part V

1957-1958

So spring has sprung, so what say I

In the opening lecture in which the professor had defined the study of physics as the science of matter and energy and of interactions between the two, I was lost in the ether, a land wherein Archimedes and Ptolemy wandered. Not only was terminology difficult, but also the ideas were hard to conceptualize and therefore impossible to absorb. Nor could I even make it to class on time. It was scheduled at 9:40 A.M. and my English class let out at 9:30 forcing me to scamper along the slippery ice covered path to the Science building at the north end of McGill's campus characteristically arriving minutes late, half-frozen and huffing. I climbed the steep steps of the raked auditorium to the top middle row ineffectively trying to be inconspicuous. Settling into my seat, the nearby students were bothered by the unbuttoning of my coat, pocketing my mittens, dropping my colored pencils with a clatter, and the rustling of my texts and papers. Professor Maxwell took note of the flurry. I was a vexing windy gale of interruption of the serious composure in the room. From the lecture podium looking up at me over the rims of his bifocals, he griped under his breath sardonic words heard by all, "Late again, mademoiselle; maybe you should be in Home EC Class." The stifled laughter appeared to vaporize into long thin fingers of luminous gas like blades of fiery grass singeing my face and eyelashes.

Professor Maxwell projected complex illustrations of principles on the screen: Momentum is the product of the mass times the linear velocity of a moving object: ($\mathbf{p} = m\mathbf{v}$).

"Lines that govern position, length and direction, namely vectors," he intoned, "are used in the calculation of a quantity having both direction and amount. Like velocity, momentum is a vector quantity, possessing a direction as well as a magnitude... clear? Let's move on."

Yes... clear, significant, properly emphasized, and totally incomprehensible to me.

New images appeared as I was still scrambling to copy the diagrams and narrative from the introductory section. My brain told me this was hopeless, an impossible science to master, yet my pride pushed me to stick it out. The diagrams were intriguing from the standpoint of illustration but their interpretation problematical. As I looked around in dismal dismay, sitting next to me was a gorgeous man, strongly built, all muscle and very intense. He seemed to be following the lecture and even asked a question of the professor, which indicated his complete awareness of the presentation. My note taking was confusedly hodgepodge. I gave up trying to record and instead paid attention to the masculine hunk beside me. He became a desired object, all the more because he appeared unattainable. Crossing and uncrossing my legs, I succeeded in distracting him and he glanced my way, our eyes meeting in a direct line. I flashed him my best smile, flirtatious and innocent at the same time, and it traveled at the speed of light to warm him in its glow. His reaction was substantial and he actually blushed. *Maybe this was a classic example of momentum.*

After class, recognizing I had a break until chemistry at 1:00 P.M., I decided to wait at the exit doors. When my newest target came into sight, I sidled up to him and obliquely commented.

"Tough stuff."

"Not so bad," he answered.

"You seem to understand it. Your question about the conservation of momentum was way ahead of the class."

"That so?" he said modestly.

"Even the easy parts are beyond me,"I admitted

"I could help you, if you like," he offered.

Was I dreaming or was my very own hero offering to tutor me?

He introduced himself as André and we made arrangements to meet in the library twice weekly for coaching sessions. As we shook hands, I appreciated what a firm grip he had, and my slender fingers were almost crushed in his persuasive hold.

Tuesdays and Thursdays at 4:00 P.M. were the hours of the beginning of my instructions and romantic pursuit. André was patient, an excellent teacher, totally serious and committed to his undertaking of getting me to pass the mid-term with at least a B grade. As we pursued the vagaries of electrical charges capable of attracting and repelling one another, I was somewhere in between falling in love and setting my heart on winning his fondness. The connection between magnetism and electricity kindled my flame of passion as the seemingly naive André focused solely on drumming scientific principles into my head.

After the tutorials, he had to leave to pick up his gear at *Currie Memorial Gym* and suit up for football practice. An athletically talented junior, he had qualified for a fullback position on McGill's *Redmen* team.

"What's a fullback?" I asked him, not entirely familiar with the game.

"I do offensive blocking, hitting the opposing player and bringing him down," he explained.

"Sounds rough. Can you get hurt?"

"Nah, I'm too tough. It's my job to protect the quarterback."

Weeks of instruction and study went by and gradually I started to master the physics material we covered. Curious to watch André in action on the football field, I ventured over to *Molson Stadium*. He was strikingly handsome in his padded red uniform with the white lettering, and when he threw a block and tackled, his brute energy was intimidating. At the end of the workout, he trotted to the sideline sapped from the effort, peeled off his helmet and ran his fingers through his short-cropped sweaty blonde hair. As André and I walked away earnestly talking, the pretty cheerleaders eyed us, unaware that our conversation concerned electromagnetic waves. A celestial sheen of envy followed us.

I could not wait to give him the news.

"André, I got 86% in the midterm exam."

"Très bien," he said, his eyes lighting up.

"Thanks to you!"

"You were good and worked hard." He refused to accept the tribute.

Well, I did pay attention, I thought smilingly, and it wasn't just to physics.

"Hey little girl, I got you a ticket for tonight's game. We play UBC."

The happy coincidence of having planned to stay after hours in the chemistry lab to review the experiments for my final worked to my advantage. My father would not grill me if I came home late, and if it was really late, I could say I missed the bus. In matters of love, logic and common sense were tossed willy-nilly and indiscretion superseded telling the truth.

The evening was a blur of rowdy crowds, cheering, stomping, celebrating victory, and drinking from flasks. When the game ended I met up with André outside the men's locker room. He was freshly showered and shaved looking sexy in a navy crew neck sweater hugging his broad shoulders and his tight corduroy slacks revealed more than they concealed. We tramped through the snow to the apartment of one of his teammates. Replete in our friendship, thrilled with his win and my grade, we held hands, singing repetitious choruses of *Alouette*, a French song popular on campus. Nearby, the small flat on Rue Pierce was jammed to the rafters with noisy merrymakers whooping it up. André handed me a paper cup of *Molson's* ale and a warning.

"Don't drink too much. You're not used to it."

I nodded my head indicating I faithfully intended to do as he instructed.

"Behave yourself."

He ruffled my hair and then ambled off to accept the usual back-slapping congratulations and enjoy the high voltage craziness that a sports event caused. Conversation was impossible in the near-riotous commotion and I was not on familiar terms with the elite group of juniors and seniors. Feeling elated and daring, I boldly downed three cups of beer one after the other. An intriguing buzz ran through me. Floating on infatuation and alcohol, I wove my way unevenly through the smoky film to hunt down my quarry.

"C'mere André," I mumbled.

Grabbing the sleeve of his sweater, I pulled him into the small back bedroom away from the party and put my arms around his strong neck pressing my body closely to his. He easily lifted me up like I weighed no more than the football and gently set me down on the bed. Our kisses were full of longing and desire, yet for all his strength and all my weakness, pure and unsullied. I held him tightly not knowing where we were going, totally enamored but warily insecure and inexpert. André prudently detached himself and cupped my face in his large callused hands intently staring at me, his blue gray eyes brimming with reflective reason.

"You're still so young, not ready for this."

I rubbed my fingers across my wet lips tasting a bitter dose of reality; André's example of conservation laws of physics was a most important and universal truth.

Frenchmen, for us, ah! What outrage

Using his grimy handkerchief, Sidney wiped his spectacles lenses splattered with grease specks and other grungy spots. Placing them on his nose, he perked up, his bulging bullfrog eyes leering at me. Mondays and Fridays, from 2:30 P.M. until 5:00, I was stuck with this amphibian in chemistry lab. Working next to me at the long countertop, in impeccable penmanship, he precisely recorded the details of the experiments in his leather bound notebook, which he hid in his briefcase when completed. His prissy know-it-all pretensions incensed me. Fastidious in his reports, he was an untidy heap and an unappealing mess with musty ill-smelling clothes. I would have ignored him entirely but for his older brother Hymie. The extravagant parents had gifted Hymie with a brand new *Oldsmobile*, and he loved to show it off in a smug self-satisfied way. With his warty skin and noticeable pores, wide spaced teeth, and irritating tics of both eyes, Hymie was equally repugnant. Living on Rue De La Roche not too far from my Rue Chambord apartment, he had offered the twice weekly lift home, which I gratefully accepted wondering what price I would pay for sitting in a car cramped between a frog and a toad. They were uncannily similar: uncombed hair hanging in a fringe about the forehead, clammy faced, bulbous ears, protrusive jaws, and incessantly vocal in resonant croaking voices. Opinionated on every issue, they leapt unwanted into conversations as if their minds had long hind legs and webbed feet. There was something about the speckled green smarminess of the brothers that made me see red.

Riding in Hymie's car, I was pleased to discover that he was a skittish driver and gripped the wheel with both hands so that he was unable to relinquish his hold and try to slip an arm about my shoulder. I could sense his intent in the way his head swiveled and his eyes seemed to pop out twitchy with anticipation when I slid across closer to him making room for Sidney. Caution inhibited him. Meanwhile, I slunk down in the seat and pulled my coat over my head to avoid being seen by other students as we exited the parking lot. Neither Sidney nor Hymie seemed to take notice of this eccentric behavior. They were earnestly engaged in interminable discussions of their strategies to enter McGill's School of Medicine. Hymie's acceptance for the fall term had arrived early on February 28th; the letter was prominently displayed on the dashboard. Sidney's long-range goal was to apply in his senior year. Mama's good little boys were both intending to be doctors.

Holding a beaker of potassium permanganate crystals in one hand and a printed circular in the other, Sidney in his devious way asked, "Are you signing the petition?"

"Don't bug me," I said, "I'm right in the middle of writing the method for today's project."

Ignoring my sharp retort, he needled, "I dare you to sign it."

"What's it to you, Sidney?"

"Just curious."

"You're just a pest! Give it to me."

I snatched the sheet of paper.

"I see you didn't sign your name," I said.

"No, little teacher's pet, I'm not that stupid."

"Sidney, it's just a petition circulated by the *Nationalist St-Jean-Baptiste Society*. Can't you read?"

"Dumbbell, it's a communist front organization."

"What nonsense are you spewing? The intent is to get enough signatures to christen the new CN hotel *Château Maisonneuve* in an effort to defend Quebec's cultural heritage."

Sidney snorted, laughing convulsively, amused by what he was about to say. Tears coursed down his face and snot ran from his nose.

"Your opposition will do no good... hah hah hah... Queen Elizabeth sent a letter agreeing to have the hotel named for her."

"Liar, liar, your pants are on fire," I chanted.

Grinning with elation he retorted, "I'm telling you the truth. Buckingham Palace already notified the CN."

"In any case, I'm signing. Maybe it can be changed. Queen E has sufficient acclaim; let this tribute go to one of the city founders."

"If you put your name down," he warned, "you're in for trouble."

"Good," I said wickedly, "I love trouble."

I tossed some camphor balls into a glass jar filled with water and sealed it with a lid. Sidney, hunched over his manual, industriously recorded the day's procedural observations and conclusions. I opened the jar and stuck it under his nose. Disconcerted, he flinched and bolted from his chair. The volatile crystals filled the room with the strong characteristic odor.

"There's the proof of the experiment, molecules move and are in motion."

I stuck my tongue out at my adversary and flounced from the room. Outside the building, hordes of students were streaming down Rue McTavish to Rue Sherbrooke chanting, waving signs, and singing; I joined the throng in choruses of *Frère Jacques*, *Sur le pont d'Avignon*, and *Auprès de ma Blonde*. A bus came by grinding to a halt at the corner of Rue Peel and we crammed aboard refusing to pay the fare. Several burly students threw off the driver leaving him fuming at the curb. One student driver took over and headed in the direction of the home of Nathan Gordon, chairman and president of the CN. We broke into refrains of *La Marseillaise* howling like fearsome protestors taking a stand against tyranny. At the top of our lungs we sang the rallying lyrics as if part of the uprising that had destructively stormed the Palais des Tuileries, the royal palace in Paris.

"Allons enfants de la Patrie, Le jour de gloire est arrivé!" *

We posted ourselves under President Gordon's window chanting our demands for the Québecois name for the hotel, and objecting to his bias that the *Queen E* would symbolize unity between the two language groups.

After growing hoarse with our censure, we gradually disbanded and I returned to school to pick up my texts and homework. I was tired and somewhat deflated knowing I had not honestly cared about the naming of the hotel *Le Reine Elizabeth* or *Château Maisonneuve*. My participation in the rally was provoked by my urge to spite braggart Hymie and prudish Sidney, one on his way to medical school and one who intended to apply. The mix of courses I was taking, physics, Eng-

---

* National anthem of France
Written and composed by Claude Joseph Rouget de Lisle 1792

lish literature, chemistry, scientific German, and calculus, a program conceived by my father, was not advancing me closer to my undeclared ambition to study art. Listening to the unclear sounds of the past and the unformed sounds of the future, my day of glory was not yet destined to arrive.

Of a solempne and greet fraternitee

I hurried to a lecture in English literature dreading it because I was running late and had failed to complete my assigned pages from *Chaucer's Canterbury Tales*. Tasked by the reading of the lines of poetry in *The General Prologue*, I had stayed up until one in the morning struggling with the antiquated language and the subtext references; I stopped at the worthy Knight who had fought against three bands of pagans as I fought to keep my eyes open.

The wind gusted fiercely in my face as I crossed the open patchy snow covered area between barren trees just starting to bud. Ahead, I could just discern a huddled group of men shoving each other and laughing, obviously having a good time. As I scurried to the building entry, André caught hold of my arm.

"Wait up ma petite fille," he said, "why the hurry?"

"I won't make it to class and I'll end up way in back where one can't hear a word."

"Give it a break," he chided, "school is for fun too."

"It is, since when?" I said with a trace of cynicism.

"Since right this minute! Hey guys… this kid needs a diversion."

André turned to his friend Julien.

"Why don't you invite my cute chick to your frat house party tonight?"

Julien looked directly at me, assessing my merits, scrutinizing me like a bug under a microscope.

"Yeah, you'll do just fine. The party gets going round nine. It's on Aylmer near Prince Arthur. Just bring those rosy cheeks."

They all laughed. I guessed it was some off-color joke, and with stately rebuff I put down his impertinence. This provoked more merriment and I ended up blushing and ducking through the doorway into the building. I consoled myself that out of a chance encounter with André and his entourage outside the faded cinder granite walls of the arts building, I was invited to a fraternity party. It held the promise of an evening with a group who defined for me glamour, romance, and excitement, and my first entrée into this privileged college society.

The professor was reading aloud line forty-six as I tiptoed in through the access door at the rear upper level and sat in the top row. Though eloquent and resonant, his voice barely reached me in the vaulted height of the amphitheater, and I had to strain my ears to capture his words.

"Trouthe and honour, freedom and curteisye."

He explained for the benefit of the impassive faces, "Integrity, generosity of spirit and courtesy."

It seemed sensible and I put my mind to the recitation trying not to let my thoughts digress to exploring the plan in store for me later. When the class concluded, I found it difficult to recall the Knight's expedition and realized I had been inattentive and had merely made a deceptive show of interest in Chaucer's poetry. To redress the lapse in concentration, there would be many tortured nights of tedium in store for me.

I passed the day in the library progressing to line 205 wondering how I would ever finish in this sluggish manner. Mentally depleted, I collected my books and went downstairs. The hallways were quiet, forlorn, and lonely, most of the students having left for the night. I sought a place of refuge, the ladies' bathroom in the basement. Feelings of resignation and discouragement conquered me as my mirrored reflection showed dark defeatist eyes and cheeks robbed of their bloom. I considered not going to the party. Two contradictory thoughts argued with one another: *Would a mere freshman, a no-one, fit in with this well-heeled group? What of the lost opportunity, and when would this happen again, if ever?* Deluding myself with strategies, I hid the pallor with a touch of pan-cake makeup and powder rouge, applied a shimmering shade of pink to my lips, snuggly tucked my sweater in, and hiked the waistband of my tartan skirt to just above my knees. I scampered up two flights, shedding weariness with each step.

The night was clear and frosty cold. Only dimly aware of the darkness of the sky and the large number of stars, I walked in a troubled trance the short distance to the frat house. Torn between going home to emptiness or worse, an angry father, I chose to disobey him and my own misgivings. I felt a sadness of a sort, a stale sadness, which no amount of gaiety and moonshiny illusions could dispel.

The stairs creaked under my feet as I climbed to the landing. The open door beckoned and I was enticed into the sensual heat and hubbub like helpless iron filings unable to resist the pull of a magnet. Elegantly dressed young men and tastefully attired beautiful girls were mingling, chatting, and smoking in easy shared intimacy. For a brief moment I felt shabbily out of place giving way to childish rage and malicious envy of their refinement, unable to summon Chaucer's generosity of spirit and courtesy. The feeling quickly passed as a clustered group pulled me in while hands talked and touched. Shrill voices, clinking of beer bottles, and high-spirited laughter reverberated and amplified to include me. I trembled with the thrill of the favorable reception.

The crammed room became blazing hot. My face shone as if rubbed with a polishing cloth and pinpoint drops of sweat shimmered on my forehead. My angora sweater stuck to my skin like wet fur on a rabbit. Someone shoved a *Labatt Blue* at me and I slowly drank the light-tasting beer licking the froth from my lips. With each sip I ignored the lateness of the evening, discarded my integrity and my redundant texts lying at the door, and forgot about my father who would be suspect of my failure to return home.

In a moment of lucidity, I wondered of the likelihood of his finding me; part of his routine was to monitor my activities and spy on me. When walking between classes, I believed I saw him lurking on the campus behind the engineering building, and at other times I attributed the sightings to my overactive imagination playing tricks on me. But the possibility always existed and the dread of discovery impinged upon me with chilling stealth.

Abruptly, I was whirled about by an invading icy gust of air. My father stood framed in the doorway. His rigid form taut with fury attacked the room like a blitz. In two forceful steps he crossed the distance and grabbed my arm, his fingers pressuring into my skin like sharp pointed daggers. Not a word was uttered, there was no need; his gruff and malevolent look spoke for him. He half-guided half-pushed me to the exit as the bewildered fraternity and sorority crowd split to let us through like the biblical parting of the Red Sea. I prayed for the wall of waters to hurl me into the depths, a disclosed pretender submersed in the onslaught.

Stamp we our vengeance deep, and ratify his doom

My eyes circularly luminous and expectant like those of a great gray owl perched on the top branch of a fir tree reacted in surprise to my father's unexpectedly phrased reaction.

"You can go, he said, it's about time."

My grandmother also caught the improbability of the words.

I posed the simple request at her dining table over tea and poppy seed cookies, my insurance against his usual disinclination.

"Dad, I was wondering, is it okay for me to go on a date with Larry this Friday?"

"Which Larry?"

"The one whose grandfather owns the big chain of grocery stores."

"Vohveh, you know vos she means, Schulman's markets," said my grandmother.

My father smiled, a queer quirky smile suffused with quiet venom. His jaw muscles tightened and quivered and his lips curled into a sneer.

"I know," he said, "only too well."

"So is it okay?" I persisted.

"What does Larry do?" he asked.

"He's studying at Sir George William College. I think economics or political science, something like that."

"Why not at McGill?"

"He wasn't accepted."

My father laughed convulsively, a deep, unbridled, guttural laugh from his personal hideout, a perverse laugh squeezing tears from his eyes, a resounding laugh taking on a life of its own.

"Vohveh, genug, enough, tell her yes," negotiated my grandmother on my behalf.

Croaking out the words still consumed by his ironic laughter, he cackled, "You have my consent, it's about time."

"Vohveh," my grandmother interjected, "it's good for her. The Schulmans are rich."

She was secretly hoping for a match for me, some family of afflu-ence, a way of climbing out of the pit of poverty. Not daring to give utterance to a thought of this nature, she would never have voiced this hope of hers preferring to guide me in my own choices in all issues.

At first, my father's reaction was a mystery to me, his easy uncon-ditional permission bordering on endorsement. Gradually, a picture began to form in my mind, an assemblage of word memories. Larry's grandfather, the grocery store mogul, was the one who had induced the ruin of my grandmother's small store, bankrupted her, and disrupted the family. This act irrevocably altered the course of my father's life. Hired as a delivery boy for bobkes, a handful of small change, there was insufficient money for him to go to McGill even on scholarship and pursue his deserved education. My father had never forgotten or forgiven. The injuries done demanded not only reparation but also vengeance. My grandmother, not one to hold a grudge or speak ill of a living soul, had long ago put aside the transgression.

And now, the grandson had innocently entered the picture. Larry, a weakly banal and tedious branch on his family tree, not particularly gifted or ambitious, preferring the social life to studies, was fervently pursuing me. Unnerved by the initial phone call to my place inter-cepted by my father, he relied on wistful messages left for me at my grandmother's apartment. Not finding a way to contact me directly, he played hooky from school showing up on McGill's campus trailing along behind me on my way to class to ask me out in person. I turned him down successive times, finding him not at all likeable. He was dull, beyond dull, a hapless product of a wealthy, high-living family.

My capriciousness seemed to boost his advances. Expert at getting what he wanted, he kept trying, and in a moment of weakness I yielded to the pleading of his quick marmoset eyes. His face blushed readily, the smudge of his success spreading to the roots of his reddish brown hair and continuing down over his thin humped nose, fair cheeks, and pimpled chin. Cringing, I wondered what had compelled me to give in. I decided to use Larry's persuasiveness to my advantage, as a test to see if my father was ready to untie the tether that bound me to school and home.

There had to be a devious explanation for my father's capitulation.

I knew his calculated behavior and there was no place in his character to be docile. Did my father suspect that I cared little for Larry? Was he presupposing that I would lead the boy on, be bold enough to seize satisfaction for the grievous wrong the grandfather had caused our family and do so by breaking the grandson's heart?

Incredulously, my father offered me a sum of thirty dollars to purchase a new dress. This display of magnanimity and pleasant disposition was puzzling, and in disbelief I forgot to thank him. Added to my saved babysitting money, I pocketed forty- two dollars and fifty cents, enough for a total fashion statement.

After hours of browsing and serious contemplation in *Eaton's* store on Rue Ste. Catherine, I found a feminine princess style dress of rayon linen in a lovely shade of oyster shell pink and a dainty tote bag and pumps. The dress was sleeveless with a mandarin collar, and a row of tiny fabric covered buttons extended from the neck to the tight fitting waist. The tea length skirt flared softly over a petticoat of layers of nylon chiffon and tulle, and the hem was trimmed in rose point lace.

I showed the outfit and accessories to my father who nodded with approval saying, "Not bad. Any money left over?" Then he laughed and walked away.

Friday evening at seven, I dressed with care enjoying an expectant sense of well-being so intense it made what was to follow trivial. For a full ten minutes I brushed my hair to a sheen letting it fall loosely unpretentious to my shoulders. I had become expert with makeup and perfume; my skin tones were creamy peach and my glossy fair hair released a scent of hyacinth.

I asked my father to answer the knock when Larry arrived so that I could make my grand entrance. He cooperated with the plan and formally ushered Larry into our apartment.

"Caasi, Larry has arrived," he called out cordially.

All very proper, I answered, "Thank you, Dad," and glided into the room.

Astonished, Larry blurted out, "You look marvelous. I love what you've done with your hair." Then he blushed. To my regret, he looked the same as at school except for his impeccable attire, a fawn-colored serge blazer with large gilded buttons, a crisp-collared moss green shirt, chocolate brown wool trousers, and tasseled penny loafers. Polite and formal, he passed my father's usual inquisition. His social skills were well honed. My father easily dismissed him with a few words, "Back before midnight, eh?" and that was it.

Larry drove a new '55 *Chevrolet V8* convertible, two toned, part aqua blue, part white, a dream of a car. It was early evening and as the sun vanished, the clouds flushed with splashes of rose, gold, and orange contrasting with the dark bluish hue of dusk. We headed in the direction of the stately houses with cobblestone driveways, orchards, and manicured hedges. Following along Rue Sherbrooke, we angled off on Côte-Saint- Antoine, and then took a circuitous path to Forden Circle. Larry's home in Westmount was a mansion, a veritable royal castle overlooking a park of neatly trimmed and well-groomed foliage.

"Do you mind if we stop for a minute?" Larry asked.

"Fine," I agreed, trying to drum up enthusiasm.

"My mother wants to meet you. I told her so much about you, how smart you are, and how pretty."

How weird I thought! He needs his mother's pre-approval for his dates; probably to protect the family name from persons of low social status.

We found Larry's mother in the glass-enclosed solarium. Porcelain vases held bouquets in a showy array: tulips, lilies, daffodils, narcissus, gladiolus, and delicately whorled roses in full bloom, variously colored green-white, yellow, red, pink and dawn-tinted. A seductive overpowering fragrance greeted us. Mrs. Schulman did not. She was busily chatting on the telephone, her elbows propped gracefully on the marble counter of the bar, a tray with a Martini shaker and two iced Martini glasses nearby.

We waited patiently until she finished her small talk related to her Siamese cats Sasha and Zelda and their jeweled collars. She replaced the telephone in the cradle. Careful of her lacquered nails, she lit a cigarette with an ornamental, engraved, silver lighter, and narrowed her eyes in her appraisal of me.

"So you're Larry's girlfriend," she alleged, sweeping her hand up along her smooth coifed hair in a chignon.

"A friend," I said, "it's our first date."

"Welcome to our family."

She came around from behind the bar dressed in a tea-gown made of a combination of white Alençon lace over yellow silk. The swags and flowery scallops made her appear as a floating floral arrangement. By contrast her voice, gravelly and coarse from smoking, was barely sweetened by her gushy praise.

"Larry didn't exaggerate. You're a little doll!"

Turning to her son, she said, "Don't forget to invite Caasi to Sunday brunch. Grandpapa will be here and also your uncles, aunts, and cousins. I'm sure the family would like to meet your girlfriend."

"Yes, mother," said Larry, his face an alarming shade of red matching the blood-red tulips.

Mrs. Schulman dismissed us with a wave of her hand. Affairs of greater importance needed her attention.

"Sasha, Zelda, my little babies, where are you hiding?"

Two buff-colored felines with narrow heads, large ears, and slanting copper orange eyes cunningly stole into the room and adeptly leapt on to the glass cabinets holding the crystal glasses and bottles of liquor.

Mrs. Schulman stroked their short hair and purred, forgetting our presence.

As we exited through the gilded wrought iron gates, I heard her husky voice calling loudly behind us.

"Larry, she's a prize."

"My mother loved you," he kvelled basking in the light of her endorsement.

I hated Larry's mother, hated Larry, envied their wealth, and thought their house disordered, their cats indulged, and their money ill-gotten.

Larry was a most conscientious date; he hovered close all evening, immoderate in his pampering. Circumspect and emotionally distant, I seemed to inflame his desire. My indifference and cutting dry humor stirred his passions. The words I uttered were gems, sharp, entertaining, and witty. He lapped them up like Sasha and Zelda at their milk bowls. I talked rings around him, flirted shockingly, pulled back, incited him, and as a final coup dumped him into an abyss.

"Thanks for the lovely evening," I said. "I can't make it to brunch on Sunday. I forgot to tell you, I have a boyfriend, you've probably heard of him... André, McGill's football hero who plays fullback... so what if he's a shegetz ... he's terrific."

Triumphantly, I dished out the ultimate lies and insults and rejoiced in it. Larry blanched from the scorn and displacement, his hopes crushed, his heart shattered by my casual cruelty. Severe punishment for crimes perpetrated on our family was long overdue. Maybe my grandmother could forgive the Schulmans, but it was not in my father's nature or in mine. I was my father's daughter after all.

Rain out the heavy mist of tears

The strain of final examinations began to take its toll. After class, the long hours of study in the library left me tired and wanting. Words blurred on the pages of the texts as if secreted by a gritty film. I slammed my books shut and decided to go home. Although afternoon spring weather promised hazy sun, the skies were lusterless. As I hastened to the bus stop, the air caught a wintry chill and it began to snow, thinly at first, then thickening. Retreating into my lightweight serge trench coat and folding the lapels under my chin, I waited on the corner of Rue University and Rue Sherbrooke, unprotected from the shifting gusts. As the wailing wind blew the coarse snow in bursts, traffic proceeded at a snail's pace, frenzied windshield wipers useless. It was growing late. Wind-driven snow flurries plunged my world into limitless white. In spite of the cold, I was unaccountably hot and sweaty.

Impatient and frenetic, I tramped around in ever widening circles. My head throbbed with a fiery, perverse, and unendurable pounding. The frost elicited a myriad of colors changing the snowy drifts into a lattice of red, yellow, green, blue, and purple ice crystals. At length when the bus pulled to the curb, my legs could just carry me up the steps. Throat aching and body trembling, I brushed the snow off my face and dabbed my eyes with my damp mittens. Refusing to go away, the strange crystals glowed and sparkled in the dismal damp of the heaving bus.

I made my transfer at Jean-Talon and dozed fitfully until I came to my stop. Avoiding the sidewalks, which were almost impassible, I trudged along the snow-rutted road, slipping clumsily on the unseen ice patches. Instinct led me to the duplex on Rue Chambord. I stumbled up the stairs to the top floor, unlocked my door after several failing tries, and lurched in falling to the floor. On hands and knees, I crawled to my bed, shuck out of my wet clothes, and lay down pulling the blankets over my limp, frozen, and burning body.

I drifted into a bottomless sleep, roused by noise. In my pain and

266

delirium, the uproar was magnified ten-fold and deafening. My father, on arrival, was forcefully blowing his nose and stomping his boots. He came into my room to see if I had made it home safely in the storm.

"Dad, I'm sick," I whimpered.

The soreness in my throat and the searing tightness in my chest reduced the words to unintelligible whimpers. He came over to my bedside and placed his hand on my brow.

"You have a fever," he stated.

"Dad, please, I'm really sick, I need a doctor."

He looked at me as if I had requested a priest for confessional.

"There's no need. The flu is self-limiting."

"I think I'm going to die."

He found my proclamation amusing, and snorted a dismissive laugh.

"More likely the doctor will kill you."

Removing his sopping wet black felt fedora, grungy top coat, and motley scarf, he draped them over my desk chair and left the room returning soon with a thermometer and a glass of warm milk and honey. I patiently held the thermometer under my tongue while he rummaged in the bathroom cabinet. Finding a bottle of *Bayer Aspirin*, he extracted two tablets.

"Your temperature is 105 degrees Fahrenheit," he announced handing me the pills.

Propping myself up in bed, I tried to swallow them, gagging and coughing as one got caught in my throat and began to melt leaving a caustic, scratchy, and acidity taste. To no avail, I choked out little pleas for the doctor; submissively I slumped back on the pillows.

Sleep once again claimed me and chained me. The raging fever made me delusional and I began to dream, vivid dreams, confounding and frightening...

...I was outside again and a heavy wind tore through the tops of moaning trees. Lac-Paquin was laid out before me, a huge expanse of black water, storm tossed whitecaps flinging foam high in the air. Mist had settled upon the surrounding hills and unrolled itself on the lake. In the middle of the lake, my mother sat in a rowboat, the loose oars deeply dipped in the water. The boat appeared to be anchored. Swirling about, slips of low lying clouds were as opaque as fog. Knowing how terrified she was of boats, it seemed unfit for her to be out alone on the lake. I called to her to come back to shore but she ignored my cries unresponsively gazing at the churning dark waters. A steady soaking rain wet my feverish skin. I waded into the lake and began to swim in the rough current. My arms were limp and lifeless and each stroke bore me no closer to the boat. I began to sink beneath the waves sputtering and gasping and rolling about helplessly as they wild-hurled me back to the watery shore. Dripping wet and discomposed, I tried to raise my head to see the boat. It was lost in the blur of distance and a stream of tears blinded my eyes.

"Mama…"

The word failed on my lips. She was gone…

…A tall man with black curly hair dressed in a flawless white coat took my pulse at my wrist. He seemed familiar, a large version of a childhood acquaintance. Appearing very scholarly, he had an ivory name tag pinned to his coat pocket, which read in burnished-gold lettering, Dr. Irving. I knew him. It was Irving from the seat behind me in grade school, no longer pimply-faced, and his eyeglasses appeared to be mislaid. His look was grave with misgiving.

Placing a moistened cloth on my forehead, he said, "I am returning your kerchief."

I tried to thank him but he disappeared, shrouded by the steaming mist…

…A battered old truck was parked on the shore. Sitting behind the wheel in the cab, François, smug and cheery, was placidly smoking a cigarette. The truck was laden with crates of bats tenaciously clinging to the slats, their wings beating in an irregular, uncertain, and jerking motion. Fear engulfed me.

François asked, "A quoi bon sortir puisqu'il fait mauvais? What is the use of going out if the weather is bad?"

He laughed and the truck trundled away…

…The mist cleared and a faintly radiant sun became visible. Flowers blossomed from the reeds forming a garland and floated on the becalmed waters. The vibrant multicolored blooms lacked fragrance; joylessly they glided below the surface. Lakeside, Mrs. Schulman, her face veiled in peau de soie, walked on the sand in high heels, her cats in procession behind her.

"You missed your wedding," she said. "Larry still cries himself to sleep at night."

I wanted to say how sorry I was.

"I'm late for my manicure appointment," she resolutely announced.

The cats snarled and hissed.

"They lost their jeweled collars," she explained, her voice now tremulous carried away on the wind...

..."Mamaleh," my grandmother pleaded, "ask the four questions."

I tried to tell her I was too old for this Passover tradition. She sat beside me on the bank, her firm hand clasping mine. The exquisite pleasure of her nearness made me weep anew.

"Sha," she said, and stroked my head to comfort me. "Don't be narisch... foolish. Du bist crank. You are sick. It's okay to cry. You can water my plants with your tears."

I could not bear for her to leave, but the dream floated to the surface of my mind forsaking and releasing me...

"Look who has come back from her coma," my father said.

I opened my eyes to find my father appraising me, a quizzical look on his unshaved face and a trace of relief in his weary eyes.

"You slept for almost twenty four hours; kept me awake with your moans and cries."

"My bed sheets are soggy," I said contritely.

"Your fever broke and you sweated, that's why."

"Am I better?"

"Better, I don't know, but getting well, yes."

Pain is the necessary contrast to pleasure.

It was the random and changeable nature of our relationship that dragged me down. Stressed, stretched, made thin by tension, it seemed as if we lived together in a baleful interlude expectant of an outrage. Words spoken or words held back circled about like numerous birds in our small apartment settling uneasily to be weighed, measured, and at last liberated. Responsive to the implicit nuances, I modified and tempered my choice of words in subtle shades of meaning, feeling, and tone, and expressed no need that might result in an adverse effect or regret. My father and I were contradictions chafing in disharmony.

He was scrupulous in his habits and I was consistently variable. The mornings were a curious contrast. Disordered as always, I rushed about hurry-scurry collecting my jumbled notes, finding my crepe blouse tucked in the far recess of a drawer, my rumpled skirt on a chair under a mass of soiled laundry, and my tortoise shell combs in among the cutlery. My father sat at the kitchen table placidly reading the *Montreal Star*.

"I tolerated this nonsense in high school but a university student should be more disciplined. You've been neglecting your homework and then studying 'til dawn," he said.

His observations were astute.

"Dad, I know, I know," I answered back.

"If you had assigned a certain number of hours each day to your chapters, you wouldn't have to cram at the last minute."

Ignoring his remarks, I continued my harried hunt.

"I've lost my shoe."

"It's behind the floor lamp," he said.

"I'm going to be late again for class."

"I don't know why I ever gave you that *Bulova*. It keeps perfect time for the sake of accuracy. You obviously never look at it."

I had fallen away from the virtuous propriety of my childhood. Neatness and orderliness had served me well in the past, an absolute insulation from the unreasonable and combustible daily sounds of terror. Distracted now with flowering life, thorny and sweetly tempting, I was spending time cultivating friends, playing squash with the pre-med students, flirting over coffee in the cafeteria at McGill, and sneaking out to fraternity parties. Inconstancy, pretence, and lies replaced the faithful folding of clothes and sincere scrubbing of the bathroom. Solitude, once my friend and partner, was now an obscurity. I had changed. My father had not; intrusiveness and threat of punishment was not a deterrent. Once he had told me that he liked children only until the age of six.

"They are manageable and docile," he had commented wryly.

After age six, I imagined he thought of children as noncompliant monsters, an attitude I was sensitive to and had intimately lived with all these years. My rebellious time lagged, not starting until age sixteen. A few digressions along the way were undetected or severely penalized, but as I matured, I deflected the rebukes.

In the evenings upon returning home from school, my father and I met in the kitchen for the one shared meal, the only part of the day reserved for some type of communication. He preferred to do the selective shopping at his favorite small markets along Boulevard St. Laurent. He felt comfortable in the old neighborhood quibbling with the grocers, pinching the chickens to determine plumpness, stipulating on only the lean grades of beef or lamb and picking over the fresh fruit and vegetables to his satisfaction. His ideas about healthy choices for our supper had advanced and his cooking skills had favorably improved. My ideal dinner consisted of lamb chops and thin flat slices of potatoes grilled to correctness in our small broiler oven. I topped the crisp, honey-brown wedges with dollops of butter and did not protest the combination of steamed carrots and peas accompanying the meal.

There was no distinct rhythm or rhyme to the way our contact unfolded after dinner. If luck held, with little said, food eaten, dishes washed and stored in the cabinet, there was a semblance of normalcy and a non-confrontational milieu. Engaged in the daily newspapers, he relaxed putting his feet up on the kitchen step stool, and the tangy smell of his *Export-A* tobacco smoke drifted affably about the room. Audaciously I asked him if I could smoke one of his cigarettes. He pushed the pack across to me.

271

"Go ahead."

Striking the match along the sandpaper strip of the *Diamond* match box, it burst into flame, and I offhandedly lit the cigarette inhaling according to Daniel's instructions when we had dined at *Moishe's*. My one previous lesson proved to be inadequate. A fit of severe coughing wracked my chest and unhindered tears coursed down my cheeks. My father laughed and slyly said, "Want another?"

The very next dinner scene was unaccountably altered. Rehearsed the previous day, the script had changed without notification. His vehement tantrums wreaked havoc among the pots and pans. As insignificant as a dropped potato peeling, a spill of milk, or the clatter of a sputtering faucet set him off. His narrowed eyes, retracted lips, hardened jaw, and taut tendons in his neck participated in violent outbursts of ranting and thundering. The incredulity of the suddenness of the release was as terrifying as the calamity itself, and I ran for cover, hands over my ears, heart pumping wildly, and choking with fear. He refrained from hitting me, but these fits of irritability were equally painful to endure.

There were many taboo subjects. I never mentioned my mother or any of my mother's sisters. He did not permit me to attend family functions and eventually I lost all contact with my aunts and cousins. Not living within walking distance to my grandmother's apartment, I saw her infrequently. She was preoccupied with my father's sisters Mildred and Cora. My Aunt Cora had immigrated to Israel in 1944 and married Efran, a member of the Haganah. Cora and Efran lived in the Sinai on a kibbutz and were active in the defense of Israel. I imagined my Bubbe had replaced me in her heart with her worry over Cora and gentle consolation to Aunt Mildred's newly born children.

My father's irascibility and snappishness was capable of shifting like a prevailing onshore wind blowing sand inland trapping all that lay in its path and then falling off creating dunes of shelter from the wind. In those slack moments or if in a demonstrative mood, my father was a gifted raconteur. No one knew more good stories or could tell them so well. In focused detail with camera-like precision, he regaled me with tales of his youth. In turn, I offered my own recollections to win his favor. We talked in parallel, listening to what was said, but not probing the depths or directly sharing in the pleasure of each of the stories. It was as if we were dining together at the same restaurant but ordering from a different menu.

"You know the towering Cartier monument at the upper end of Fletcher's Field by Av Du Parc, the one that is a tribute to Jacques Cartier the French explorer….on the very top perched on a dome is a celestial figure with angel wings. Somehow I thought I could climb all the way up to reach her, but I only made it as far as the Cartier statues," he reminisced

"When I was little and didn't want to walk far, you hoisted me to your shoulders and carried me," I described fondly.

"Soccer was my sport at Montreal High. I scored the winning game in the finals against Strathcona knocking the ball with my head into the net. The ball sailed right through the goalie's outstretched arms. That was a thrill," he bragged.

"You taught me how to spiral a football, but I had no talent for soccer."

"Did you know I wrote short stories and poems? One story in Yiddish was published in the *Jewish Forward*, a fable of life in the Hereafter populated by men with long red beards. They congregated in gardens bordered with fruit trees bearing exotic, delectable varieties, and overhead, green, yellow, and purple crows croaked… caw… caw…caw…all in glorious *Technicolor*. It was visually impressive," he grandly described.

"Remember the time I painted pictures of an orchestra of animals playing musical instruments? I cut them out and scotch-taped them to the wall."

"Do you recall the sukkah I built in the back yard on Av Coloniale? I covered the roof with pine branches and leaves and decorated the inside with grapes, figs, pomegranates, olives, and dates. You loved to play in it."

"Dr. Gold came to see me when I was sick. I drank the whole bottle of cough medicine," I laughed.

"Those antique coins I collected, many are missing," he reported with a sigh.

"I stole them for bus fare. I shouldn't have," I confessed offering at

273

last a genuine reaction. All the other recollections on both sides, important in their own way, were ignored and retired as soon as they were revealed.

Interpreting his mood, believing him to be mellow, I took my chance.

"Dad, may I change my course work to include art history and architecture in second year?"

Our communication was as precarious as a frozen tree branch cracked by a sudden thaw, the pieces tumbling to the ground. My father snapped out of his reverie; his private disturbances and folly made his pale with fury.

"I told you no before and I'm telling you no again," he sputtered, his voice rising.

The yelling started anew. I cowered like a dog at the sight of the whip crouching in my chair retreating from the storm. A tempest of cloudy distrust and frosty doubt debased me. Trying to avoid his violent tirade, I slipped on the freezing circle of his craziness facing his glacial breath. The sensitive and softhearted part of me began to toughen like shoe leather in harsh winter. I was walking a tight rope, my mercurial balance shifting with each step; the longer I remained with my father and his paroxysms of rage, the more I feared turning out to be like him. Similarities were unfolding, slowly and imperceptibly but becoming noticeable. Quick to condemn, cunning, wily, guarded, cruel, and secretive, the duality of my life was starting to frighten me. The future seemed coldly vacuous and the present was iced-over.

Never calling for my mother in daylight, I found myself crying her name aloud at night.

"Mama, why did you forsake me to settle with this madman?"

I directed my anger at her and then remorse retracted it.

"Where are you?" I pleaded "and why did you desert me?"

I waited for a reply, a signal from the heavens or a symbol of her hearing me. Not knowing where her grave was, I was unable to kneel in the turned soil, clutch the headstone, and demand she return to salvage what had become of me. The impossibility of her reappearing made me steadfast. I made up my mind to leave Montréal, leave my father, and leave my mother's final resting-place to be tended by persons unknown.

With the painful resolution ripping me apart, I tried to picture my mother no longer sad or distraught sitting in her rocker on the porch at Lac-Paquin, a light breeze caressing her, the hot sweetness of the sun warming her face. One distant day I would be by her side.

Time, place, and motion, taken in particular or concrete

The first year of my university education drew to a close in modest and unassuming conclusion. Embarrassed by my mediocre grades, I was acutely aware of my father's timely admonitions.

"Last minute studying is like straw stuffing in a scarecrow's head. It flies out in the first stiff breeze. Day by day, in small bites, ingested knowledge lasts forever."

I accepted his censure realizing that the blame for my lamentable performance could not be shifted or discounted.

"You missed the boat," he said, "but maybe it taught you a lesson. I can't say for sure. No one listens, that's the problem."

What he said was justified. I had not been induced to alter my lackadaisical ways and was stuck with the outcome; a rather sad transcript record was mailed off to the University of British Columbia. If accepted for transfer into the sophomore class in spite of the dismal scores, the execution of my escape plan was going to be tricky. Basically, I needed money.

Scanning the help wanted columns in the *Montreal Star*, I chanced to find a job offer for a summer position in a mill laboratory. The specific requirement was a sound knowledge of chemistry. Convinced that my year of inorganic chemistry at McGill with a final decent score of 84% was sufficient, I made the call to set up an appointment. To modify my youthful appearance, I dressed with utmost care for the interview. Brushed hair conservatively drawn back with a crimson barrette, a crisp white blouse, a poppy floral patterned skirt, waist cinched with a flattering red belt, and glinting leather pumps. With reasoned purpose I left the house before seven in the morning.

It was a long and grueling ride to my destination. One streetcar, two buses, and seventy minutes later, I was rudely deposited on Rue Notre-Dame at the end of the line in the harbor area. Never having been to the port and docks of Montréal, my confidence was shaken. Huge-masted sea-going cargo ships were anchored at quays for the convenient loading and unloading of goods. Stacked on the wharves, crates of brown sugar, ginger fruit, cocoa, vanilla, cinnamon, and exotic spices of cardamom, cumin, turmeric and coriander, had ventured thousands of miles to their Canadian destination. I still had a trek of one mile to the mill.

Hidden from view by a cloud cover of flour dust, the sky was thickly curtained; only resolute bands of amber sunlight pierced the dense layers to reach the sidewalk. An acrid odor of linseed oil polluted the air. The barren street was fiercely hot. My father's perpetual cautions put me on guard watching out for perverts, but I spotted no one, and only the sounds of my own solitary footsteps startled me. A battered sign, rusted and scarred, was posted high on the top of the building spelling out the words: *Ogilvie Flour Mills*. There seemed to be no definitive entry into the building. Heaped burlap sacks, processing machinery, cranes, trucks, and tall grain elevators flanked a storehouse large as a football field. Searching in the dim light of the cavernous space, I saw a small directional wooden arrow with the printed word, 'OFFICE'.

The narrow planked walkway underfoot was warmer than the concrete stone floor. It led me to the mill office without incident. Mr. Stuard, the chief chemist, was busily examining a new shipment of vanilla; he conducted the interview on the run. I followed him around the lab, sidetracked by his *Brylcreamed* hair sticking out at odd angles, his colorless face, hooked nose, skewed teeth, and click-click sounds from his jaw as he nervously twisted his lips from side to side. Disinterested in my faultlessly groomed appearance and neglecting to glance at me, he spoke in rapid, clipped phrases, never pausing to discover if I was following what he said or had questions. He stirred beakers of chocolate of varying shades from milk-brown to deep fudge, sniffed glass containers containing cinnamon, and documented entries in a large ledger. I grasped the idea of the work. My job was to check the purity of the ingredients destined for the cake mixes. In addition to *Ogilvie's* lucrative production of every type of flour, the mill had developed a new line of cake mixes and was planning to release the products based on successful testing.

Finding my qualifications acceptable, Mr. Stuard employed me without references or personal questions. Salary was set at eight hundred dollars for three months of work. My hours were 8:30 A.M to 12:30 P.M., one-half hour for lunch, and resuming work at 1:00 P.M. If all the experiments for the day were completed, he assured me that I could leave at 5:00 P.M. Overwhelmed by the enormous sum of money, I accepted the position thanking Mr. Stuard who merely nodded and held up a vial of vanilla, pipetted a tiny globule on to the tip of his finger and tasted it. He grimaced at the bitterness and proclaimed, "Splendid."

Sorting through files and untidy bundles of loose paper in a cabinet, he produced a cocoa stained manual of instructions and thrust it in my hands.

"Here, take it home, study it."

In this abbreviated form, my job at *Ogilvie Flour Mills* began. For a short time Mr. Stuard followed me about in the lab and when satisfied of my aptitude left me alone in the lab after the first day. The absence of the cyclical click-click sounds plunged the working space into silent attentiveness. The novelty of the experiments entertained me until they became familiar and unvaried. I set about tidying up the lab and within two weeks of my being hired, the counters were cleanly scrubbed, the ingredients were indexed, the flasks were washed and arranged in order of type and size, and the ledger book contained recorded careful evaluations.

A shipping delay put my chemical testing on hold. Mr. Stuard left on summer holiday and so I had no one to ask what more to do. Solitary and bored, work apron tied about my waist, I walked about the complex in a futile manner opening doors to other rooms. Most led to abandoned storage closets or small windowless chambers with an occasional dust covered desk and cloth-draped swivel chair. To entertain myself, I imagined I was *Alice in Wonderland* having fallen down a long way to a curious hall with many locked doors of all sizes. To construe the mystery of the locked doors and intrepidly search out the right door was my deputed task. One door finally led to the baking room and the welcome sight was a revelation and a place of enchantment.

Fragrant, freshly baking cinnamon spice cakes at once banished the tedium of my pointless roving about, and the engaging smile of the baker dismissed the solitariness. Under his tall, round, starched white hat, the baker's rotund face was flushed with rosy color. He was wearing a white double breasted jacket in thick cotton to help protect him from the heat of the massive oven. His body, like his face, was rounded, stocky, and podgy. With a quick deftness and a sure hand, he stirred the cake mixes in large steel bowls, his military precision undermined by an impish quality. The mixing spoon was waved about as he moved along from one bowl to the next, little flicks of batter plopping onto the squeaky clean stainless steel table. Accurately parceling out the mixture into pans, he slid them like curling stones along the floor of the oven talking to them and cheering them on, "Faites comme vous voudrez, je ne demande pas mieux."

I understood enough French to know he was telling the cake mixes to do as they wished, asking nothing better of them.

"Bonjour," I said.

"Il n'y a rien qui presse, no hurry," he told me. "En attendant, meantime, other cake is pret, ready to eat."

Lined up on the sideboard were ten marble fudge cakes, their blended moist chocolate and white excellence begging to be savored. The baker cut a large wedge of cake, put it on a paper plate, handed me a plastic fork, and said, "Goutez." I more than tasted; I ate the entire piece and every last crumb.

We became fast friends humorously struggling with our English-French conversation, but communicating well enough. A faithful employee, the baker had worked at *Ogilvie Flour* for many years providing for his devoutly Catholic family of six children. Never grouchy or reproving, he was a generous mix of stability and friendliness. Including me in his good intentions, he provided a welcome balance to the friction in my life. He let me help him bake the cakes, try new recipes, experiment with the ingredients I tested in the lab, and always sample the end results. In the mill's kitchen at Montréal's waterfront, the unusual chemistry between us mitigated the heat and monotony of the long hours. The summer obeyed the quick motion of the days and the speedy turn of the months, and at its close, I was rewarded with boxes of cake mixes and my eight hundred dollars.

I feel a weightless change, a moving forward

One distinctive, memorable September evening, I skipped past the wooden benches, the marble pillars, and the ticket cages in Montreal Central Station. The ceramic floor tiles clattered under my heels, a sharp, hard, conspicuous sound resonating urgency. There were only a handful of passengers milling about. An unshaven, ancient black man in a striped shirt and red bandana tied around his neck patiently mopped the floor; the meagerness of his smallish, frail figure was revealed by a pair of ill-fitting coarse blue overalls. A mist of disinfectant and the smoky reek of oil and tar infused the air with uncertain prophecies. My heart was beating intolerably echoing in my ears and pulsing down to my feet. The rapid repetitive fiercely ticking sounds of keen expectancy rattled me. I moved forward in a rush of impatient haste to the ironwork gateway of track ten, the loading platform, and the waiting train.

A huge headlight, a glass eye encircled by a thin line of yellow haze like that of the Cyclopes primordial giants loomed in the front of the locomotive. The distortion stopped me as if struck by a bombshell. Through the thick fog, I could barely differentiate the close pack of cars that stretched behind as one long continuous astounding mass of metal. I lost sight of the caboose at the end. Though indeterminate, the diesel looked different from the old steam engine train, the type I had traveled on before to Old Orchard Beach. Caught in the locomotive's beam, I thought I saw hardworking firemen hunched over in their denims; leather gloved, they shoveled coal into the engine sending a huge shower of water crashing into the air. I remembered when my father had taken me to the front of the train to see the engineer in striped cap and goggles, his encrusted hand on the throttle that turned the giant wheels.

"It isn't uncommon to put eighteen tons of coal through in a day or night," my father had stated.

"Wow!" I had exclaimed in awe.

"See the boiler pressure gauge," he further explained, "and below are the brass handles for the train brakes and the reversing gear lever."

From his years with the CN, he knew all the railway technical features, but the knowledge gained by the channeling of his senses had the power to impact. His perceptions were fixed in my mind.

The puzzlement of the past began to clear and I became aware of a clean, quiet, modern diesel cab without dirt and heat and no steam pouring out; a shiny bell was mounted on the top. The conductor set down the metal stool to help me board the painted two-toned gray *Pullman* sleeper carriage car. Safely aboard, he passed my small valise up to me. I glanced down for a brief moment possessed with a sudden urge to wave to a figure on the raised walk along the side of the line or clench a hand in a final goodbye. It was not to be. I felt weak and dubious from the effort of the secret preparations, the months of planning and deception, formerly a rumbling in my head, now an actuality.

Knowing only that I was leaving for good, I prepared a note for my father to find when he returned home. The wording was evasively simple.

"Dad, I must get away from here. I'll call you. I'm sorry."

For a moment I began to contest this arbitrary and possibly flighty act. The clenched paid for ticket offered the firmness of belief I needed, and it was up to the train as my abettor to hasten my escape from the inconstancy and capriciousness that had defined my life for years. Turning away from the platform, I bumped into a genteel black man in a red flat brimmed porter's cap wearing a navy wool vest with gleaming buttons and a stiffly starched long sleeved white shirt.

"Excuse me, Miss," he apologized.

"No, no, it's my fault I wasn't looking."

He escorted me to my berth.

"If you need anything, just ask," he offered courteously.

"Thank you," I answered, tremulous in gratitude.

"Goodnight, Miss."

The sheets were crisp and smooth. I tucked myself in between the tightly folded corners. I hugged the pillow with its familiar scent of laundry soap and starch ironed into the silky cotton fabric. My arms tightened about it unwilling to be parted from the comforting firmness and bulk. Staring at the deepening darkness, I saw my reflection in the layered glass window, my eyes mirroring the implausibility of my actions. Soundlessly, the porter drew the heavy lined drapes of the compartment enclosing me like a worn flannel nightgown. I was safe inside. The rhythmic screech of the wheels sang a sweet lullaby as the station slid backward. The platform lights and the curtained windows of the adjacent train reeled off in a blur, and the track dwindled to oblivion shriveling the past to a mere speck. I welcomed the monotonous hum of the engine, the continual rocking, and insistent clack of the wheels. Entrusting myself to the night, I plunged into a roaring tunnel of sleep.

During the day I sat in a saloon car. There were no happy chatterers brimful with words and wit or young travelers on holiday going west to hike up and down mountainsides. Across the aisle, a prim-lipped woman with the look of church pew stiffness was diligently knitting. She rarely paused except to tug the yarn from her embroidered knitting bag tucked between her knees. Facing her, a man who decidedly was her husband, sighed with each wail of the train whistle, an expression of neglect stamped on his broad bland face, his arms obstinately folded across his ample belly. From time to time she took note of me with conscious precision through her *Benjamin Franklin* style bifocals. Appearing discomfited with what she saw, she set her knitting needles flying so that she might be able to supply all her neighbors with woolen socks. Amused by her prudish dismissal, I turned back to the window enthralled by the sights. We were already past North Bay and heading to Thunder Bay and Winnipeg. A procession of long-walled gardens, provincial towns, children playing in the streets, grazing sheep, and vast stretches of tilled fields filed by; it seemed like an abundant harvest of intertwined earthy-brown, saffron, and forest-green ribbons. As the train crossed the country, each province entered and left provided great landmasses of protection, like mattresses heaped one on top of the other.

At a stop in Saskatoon, I got off to browse in the shop close to the station. Tempted, I bought a small jar of local preserves of a very luscious fruit, like black currant and strawberry combined. Eager to stretch my legs, I followed the tracks and strolled along a path lined with impenetrable bushes thick with soot. In the distance, lengthening shadows of threshing machines crisscrossed the furrowed fields and resplendent sheaves of gold bound with straw were gathered into waiting bundles. A flock of starlings scavenging in the wet and fresh ploughed rows were surprised by the warning whistle of the train; their scattered squawking into the skies reminding me to return to the train.

When we pulled into Kamloops, soldiers on home leave thronged aboard in rain-soaked hooded fatigue jackets, khakis, lace-up jump boots, and arrogant comportment. Raw sweat, sweet hint of pomade, tobacco, and fermented malt liquor scented the air. Loud, fierce droning, high decibel sound intensity crackled through the rail cars as the men vied for any available seat. I removed my blanket from the adjacent space inviting company. A young man's body flopped down beside me, a cigarette dangling idly from his lips, ashes heedlessly dropping on his uniform and rolling carelessly to the floor. His canvas bag jarred me. Leaning toward me he muttered, "Sorry, didn't mean to," inclining his head to make certain I heard him above the clatter of the wheels.

As he lingered, my ear collected the notes of his muffled words and the whoosh of exhaled smoke. The sound waves followed along hollow channels coming to rest in a labyrinth of impulses. I sat motionless staring at the rain pelting sideways against the windows. Under a somber metallic sky, the train twisted and untwisted along the tracks. Ancient wooden trestles bent in the squall as we bridged a roaring river, winds churning swells to white foam and froth. The damp rough fabric of his sleeve daringly brushed my arm cleverly probing my nature to find out how translucently clear and pure it was. If I moved in his direction I would chance his lips, his tongue, and his hard edges. My father had warned me about men who flicked ashes from their cigarettes. I slowly turned my head...

Part VI

2002-2003

The mind can weave itself warmly
in the cocoon of its own thoughts

"Le Métro est simple," said the obliging concierge Monsieur Bouchard gesturing with his pen in the direction of the hotel's glassed entry doors. I glanced across busy Rue De Maisonneuve East. On the corner was the entrance to a shopping mall and an office complex. Noting my mix-up and indecision, Monsieur Bouchard came out from behind his desk and led me to a better point of reference.

"Regardez the sign, it's over there," directed the concierge.

The entrance to the subterranean train system was marked with a plain blue-on- white sign.

"What about the charge?" I asked, new to the details of using public transportation. On my previous visit to Montréal in 1996, I had leisurely detailed my plans to include a rental car for finding my way around the city. On this return, the urgent summons permitted time for simply booking hotel accommodations. A frantic conversation with an *Air Canada Airlines* representative guaranteed travel at the cost of some heated words unwisely said in the fear and frustration of the moment. Casting away the reminder of that flash of irritation, I focused on the practical advice of congenial Monsieur Bouchard.

"Best to buy a book of six tickets. You save maybe four dollars. Not bad, n'est-ce pas?"

He briefly smiled at me turning his attention to the unrelenting jangle of the telephone. In his helpful voice, I overheard him say, "Bon matin, *Auberge St. Germain* ... mais oui…" as I pushed open the door bracing myself against a briskly cold winter wind. The sky was cloudless and the sun bright for December 26th, an appreciative clash with the seasonal forecast. The nighttime snow flurries had left a light patchy residue on the sidewalk punished to a thin paste by the walking traffic. Avoiding the slicker icy strips, I snugged my head in the fur hood of my coat only to have a fierce gust vengefully toss it back. The staunch morning working procession and the solitary stragglers converged into the building. I followed them, my boots inexpertly skidding on the slippery concrete floor. A series of escalators led to the thriving underground rail service beneath the streets and buildings of Montréal, a complex labyrinth of connecting tracks.

In my haste, I took vague notice of a bistro, a *Natureworks* vitamin market, a cigar and cigarette shop, and a passport photo parlor as my legs propelled me along in cautious but controlled insistence. The savory aroma of freshly baked pizza, only ninety-nine cents a slice, and the display of tomatoes, anchovies, and mozzarella on thick, crusty dough was irrationally enticing at the early hour of 10:00 AM, reminding me that I had not had anything but a quick coffee. I ignored the food stand. The modernization of the city, which had unhinged me six years ago, failed to shock or catch me unaware Traces of the Montréal of my childhood lingered in memory, a collection of pitiful unfocused photographs in a disused album embellished in a fresh dust cover. The single glimpse that ruffled me was that of a homeless man, filthy and slovenly, his grizzled beard and matted head of hair nestling on a computer keyboard appended to the wall.

The corridors were inexhaustible reeking of urine and sweat and the graffiti-sprayed tiles were an unclear foreshadowing of what yet might come. The posters on the walls attracted my contemplation even walking at a fast pace. Usually in airport terminals, I paid no heed to the advertisements. Each individual panel in the Métro tunnels affixed itself to my brain: *Musee D'es Artes, Hertz Car Rental, Calvin Klein's* sexy men's underwear, *Optique Boutique* and *Point Zero Montres,* displays of decorative graphic art irrelevant to my visit.

I followed the orange painted stripes down long staircases to the loading platform of the Henri-Bourassa line. Groups of passengers, not milling about, appeared to be of simple trustworthy rationale and averted my impolite staring. I watched them feeling my separateness. The rumble of each approaching train was thunderous. One blue plastic seat screwed to the wall was bare. Gratefully, I flopped into it. I was breathing hard as if I had undertaken to wade through the depths of unknown places without a guide and was being carried away by unsuspected currents.

With portentous shaking, the cars whipped into the station led by twin headlamps, klieg-like lights, making public every wrinkle in the patient, melancholic faces. As the automatic doors opened, the people streamed off and on in less than thirty seconds. I scurried aboard. The train was on route as soon as the doors slid together. Tightly hugging my leather briefcase, I sat nearest one exit to be certain not to miss my transfer at Jean-Talon.

In the seat facing me was a young fair complexioned girl with an unsightly blotch on her cheek. She was eating a slice of the ninety-nine cents pizza out of a paper sac. Oil had seeped into the bag and the stain spread in an ever-expanding circle transferring itself to her brown suede jacket, a disagreeable blemish matching the one on her face. It strangely unsettled me as an abuse might have convened salty tears in my eyes to temper the affront. Impatient and drowsy, I yawned shifting on the hard bench to stay alert. Two hefty black girls, jolly and giggling, one with ribboned pigtails on top of her head and the other with a frazzled ponytail diverted me. They were sharing a portable CD player; each girl had a single earpiece. Rocking and bouncing to the beat of the music, they tapped their *Air Nikes* on the back of the seats ahead of them. A woman in an elegant fur jacket and hat swayed with the motion of the train as she held on to one of the upright poles. Haughtily, she glared at the girls. My focus on the assorted riders of the Métro car was intense memorizing minute details with careful clarity. Like a shadow catcher, one who grasps at and retains trifles, I assessed and catalogued for no useful gain. Preparing as if it were for an inventory at the end of the route, I was not yet aware that I was postponing thinking about why I was here. My mind had numbed itself to the insoluble and shunned discomfiting speculation.

The sight of a sleeping elderly man, his head drooping on his neatly folded *Montreal Gazette* arrested me. Protected from the cold by a rumpled jacket, a moth-eaten muffler strangling his unshaven neck, tough corduroy pants, and well-worn galoshes, he was familiar to me although I had never seen him before. I tried to read the words in the newspaper but the lines of print faded to invisible threads. He seemed a shriveled and obscure figure. His aged formless frame and chapped wrinkled hands with long stained fingers began to jostle and tackily dismantle my stored memories. As the train lurched, his hat with earflaps dipped to one side exposing part of his face. Beneath the rough grayish whiskers, it was the color of plaster. The unseemly hue of his skin breached my paltry wall of defense. I was in Montréal because my father lay critically ill in a bed in intensive care at Le Centre hospitalier de St. Mary.

Want makes almost every man selfish

The transfer at Jean-Talon to the Snowdoin line proved to be simple, and in a few short stops I was urged forward off the Métro in rough, unfastidious fashion. Standing at the corner of Chemin De la Côte Des-Neiges and Rue Lacombe, I stubbornly rejected the idea of asking for directions, certain that if I walked along I should spot it in the residential neighborhood. Within a block, Le Centre hospitalier de St. Mary appeared. Its red bricked exterior and thick walls and turrets at the angles gave the whole the aspect of a fortress. As I approached, the yoke on my heart tightened.

A taxi pulled up in front letting out an elderly infirmed man bundled in a cumbersome wool coat and serious comportment. As he began to slip on a patch of ice, I braced open the front door and offered my arm to steady and guide him into the small vestibule, which led to the heated lobby. Not seeing an attendant at the reception desk, I located the directory and steered the man toward the outpatient department receiving his bristly grunted, "Merci."

A quick turn took me to the women's washroom for a needed time out. The mirror revealed a depleted and haggard face with dark eyes and unattractive black crescents below. Eighteen hours had passed since I had departed from Chicago; apprehension had sapped my energy. Splashing frosty cold water on my cheeks and brow, I then roughly wiped off the excess with some paper towels. The heat from the radiators issued forth in wheezes and hisses. I removed my coat thrusting it over one shoulder as I left the confines of the restroom to trudge to the elevator and ascend to the third floor following the sign for the ICU. The glass doors to the intensive care unit swung open.

At the nursing station, the interns, nurses, residents, and secretaries were engaged in confidential conversations regarding their charges, making notations in charts, typing at computers, or using fax machines. Telephones rang incessantly. No one noticed me or asked me who I was or why I was in ICU. Few of the beds were taken and the row of divided cubicles was not long. As I walked along dubious thoughts weighed heavily on my mind and spirit. I was not prepared to see my father gravely ill. My visit with him in 1996 confirmed that he was in a weakened condition; I should have been equal to the task of handling the news of his decline. That it was my father dying rattled my unnatural calm.

We had lived apart for so long a time. Our connection had strengthened in part over the last six years; as before his letters were still uncompromising. Irrationally, I had donned a delicate bond wearing it without the confirmation that he was agreeably fastened to it. It seemed untimely for him to be in this terminal condition; I wanted him around longer. I was still grappling with the perplexities of his chameleon mind. The earned disclosures were in infant form, and I was creeping rather than striding along on the path to a clearer picture of the man, my father, even now, a stranger. His capricious ideas never ceased to confuse and amuse me, but in patient analysis there was always something to learn. He possessed a sharp visionary mind and a blend of cunning and stratagem. These notable traits served as a reminder to me of his fine intellect. His handwritten sentences, not without chastisement or sarcasm, contained word fluency, astuteness, and cannily crafted humor.

He stayed confined to his flat. He refused to have a telephone installed so we might speak. In his letters to me he alluded to having high blood pressure and a kidney problem; walking to the nearest Métro station or bus stop was not a choice. Restricted in this way, he spent his time reading and monitoring his erratic stock portfolio. Having no respect for the medical profession, he was carelessly inattentive to his health. His decisions dictated this impropriety without considering the inevitable consequences.

I promised to visit in the spring of 2003.

"Hang in there, Dad," I pleaded.

"Don't make plans," he answered, "when you get here, that's when you're here."

I wanted to know if the lilacs were in bloom.

"They're buried under four feet of snow now," he replied.

Deprived of my mother for almost all of my life, I had dredged up my father or remnants of my father, the father who I had hated for so long a time, then forgave and declined to hate. I embraced the longing that he now could be a good father if only he could forgive himself and untangle the past. The threads spun by the lost years, alternating strands uniformly strong and flimsily weak, had woven an unbreakable link between us. Not my father, I reasoned; he was too tough to be in this predicament. I had not projected his death, not wanting a tragic mishap once again. His loss would irrevocably fasten close the gate to my past. Life and death, neither of them exclusive, both joined at the last.

I walked the length of ICU in a shivering state of solitude.

When everlasting Fate shall yield To fickle Chance

I peeked around the suspended drape at each partition, and it was not until reaching the final one that I found my father. He scarcely resembled the father of my recent memory. Only a vague aspect, an imprint, or some eerie configuration of him was unaltered by the passage of time. Lying still on his hospital bed, the covering sheets were firmly tucked up around his neck. His head was thrust back on his pillow, and in profile I identified his broad longish nose. His mouth opened with each intake of breath; in between the whoosh of air he screamed out shrill noises. A few shafts of hair, short and thin, seemed to be randomly stuck to his head. Even in deep sleep, his forehead was furrowed into a frown. I stared at his face, the adverse effects of illness making their mark. He was clean shaven, his skin whitish with a yellow cast. Patchy scattered brown moles spotted the portrait, the only insult to an unusually smooth almost unwrinkled complexion for an eighty-eight year old man. His lips were thin and drawn in a purple line and tightly clenched. He gasped, alarming me, making a new rough strangled sound, and his lips parted for a moment showing two decayed lower teeth.

I circled the bed examining him from all angles and then dumped my coat, purse, and briefcase on the provided folding chair. Slowly I walked over to his side. Oxygen prongs were in his nose and a feeding tube was taped to his cheek

Gently I tugged the sheets down by inches. There were purplish bruises on his jaw and his protruding neck cords were covered with thin, almost transparent skin. A monitor recorded heart rate and pattern. He had intravenous tubing in both arms and an arterial line as well. Both hands were bloated and his fingernails were yellowish-black. It was if I were viewing a sculpted figure battered into ruins.

A sudden deep racking cough roused him to wakefulness. He opened his eyes, still azure, the clear blue color of the unclouded sky, and looked up.

"Dad, it's me, Caasi." I croaked out the words of greeting.

He stared at me for a long time then grimaced in pain.

"What are you doing here?" he asked. His voice was more clamant than expected.

"You're sick, in the hospital."

"When did you arrive in Montréal?"

"Only a few hours ago."

"Did you fly?"

"Yes, from Chicago."

My father closed his eyes as if the talking and the disclosure were a heavy load. I reached under the sheet and grasped his icy cold hand.

"How did you get to the hospital?"

I was astonished by the question because I thought he had drifted away.

"I took the Métro."

This response had an unexpected effect. My father opened his eyes again and fixed me with a suspicious stare. Then a hint of a smile played on his face.

"Well, it's about time you learned how to get around by Métro."

"Dad," I said, "you're in St. Mary's Hospital… sick."

"Why not the Jewish General?"

"The ambulance transported you here."

My dad tugged on his feeding tube with his free hand. Capturing his hand, I dissuaded him and readjusted the tape. It was obvious that he knew little about why he was in the hospital. I was not prepared to tell him how seriously ill he was.

"You shouldn't have bothered to come all this way," he said decisively.

My voice trembled as I tried to reply.

"I wanted to, Dad, you're not well. I thought you might need me."

"I do need you to go to my place...you can get in from the upstairs...my Greek friends live above...on my table is a book of Métro tickets and in the bedroom bureau...bottom drawer is some American and Canadian money. Go now, before it gets dark so you can have some cash."

I turned my face to hide the tears that had welled in my eyes. My father, seemingly undisturbed about his own condition, was worried about my welfare. He set his look of single-mindedness on his face and tightly shut his eyes. His hand reposed in mine as he nodded off to sleep, unshackled from the prison of his agony.

"So you're Evan's daughter?"

I felt a light tap on my shoulder and spun around. A nurse had come to check on my father. She was wearing a waist-length long-sleeved jacket with stockinet cuffs, loosely fitting powder blue cotton pants, and sensible shoes. The hospital's name was stenciled on the pocket containing a surgical mask and latex gloves.

"I'm Emily, your father's day shift nurse," she explained.

Her middle-aged face was pudgy with ruddy cheeks and bright kind eyes and her hair was swept back into a scrub cap, a bonnet-like wrap around hat. The elastic had made little pink creases in her otherwise pale hairline. She flashed a welcoming smile and gave me a quick hug.

"I'm Caasi, Mr. Lichman's daughter."

She already seemed to know who I was.

"Evan told me all about you," she offered.

I tried to suppress the surprised look on my face.

"He spoke of you in quiet times between fits of agitation."

"Did he suspect I would be here for him?"

"I believe he did. I think he was waiting for you. He said that you are an excellent teacher and water colorist, and respected in art criticism."

I blushed hearing her repeat my father's words and took secret delight in the partiality of his description.

"He also mentioned that you teach courses in art education and that you started a program of art methods to help children with social interaction problems."

This added disclosure astounded me.

"How does the artwork help?" Emily asked with sincere interest.

For a moment, I forgot about my father near death in the ICU. Emily wanted to learn about a new undertaking that had become important to me; I answered without hesitation.

"I've tried with some success to mix art and language to reach children whose world is limited. Using simple media like clay, crayons, beads, and glitter, they create visual images. The children seem happier and more confident."

"My six-year old son is autistic," she said with a note of sadness in her voice. "I would like to hold his attention and perhaps even inspire him through art."

"It could help with his communication and behavior. And he may become more trusting."

"Thank you... Excuse me, but I had best introduce you to Dr. Steinman. He just came on the ward to make his rounds."

Distracted by my conversation with Emily, I returned to the pressing problem of my dad. Emily took hold of the doctor's arm as he passed by. She whispered in his ear and returned to the nurses' station.

"Dr. Steinman, thank you for calling me," I said. "Just the sound of your voice was reassuring."

Dr. Steinman was a tall and slender man with silvery hair falling in thinning strands on a low forehead. His face was narrow and every feature was pointy down to his receding chin. Behind his thick glasses, keen searching eyes bore hints of sympathy and fatigue. Dressed in a rumpled white coat, his name stitched shoddily on the lapel, creased pants, and the defining stethoscope swinging from the pocket, he exuded aplomb and skill. I almost felt myself happy in the midst of all my anxiety.

"I don't want to overstate the problem. That said, the circumstances of your father's condition are tenuous," he stolidly said.

Speechless, I listened to the doctor. His words, though clear and specific, seemed incoherent and half-effaced as I resisted the probability in disbelief

He continued in an unruffled practiced way.

"We are treating him with antibiotics, diuretics, and anti- hypertensive medication. He is on morphine to keep him as pain free as possible. His vital signs stabilized on admission but he has started to deteriorate. The fine arteries in his limbs are blocked resulting in decay of body tissue. His kidney output is minimal and although he's dehydrated, because of congestive failure we can't push fluids."

"I think I understand," I said, realizing there was no going back.

"Your father's condition continues to worsen. He may last just a few more days, although one never knows. The plan is simply to maintain him as comfortably as possible. No other measures will be undertaken. The surgeons who have consulted can not in good faith operate considering all his other complications. He is not salvageable."

Dr. Steinman paused to let this information seep in. My face remained expressionless but I held on to the bed rail for support. Dr. Steinman removed his glasses and rubbed his eyes as he proceeded in an unhurried yet urgent manner.

"I hate to be blunt, but I need a DNR order from you."

The room reeled about me with this request. I needed clarity to absorb all that was happening. This was my father who was still an enigma to me and the father who I was not prepared to give up with a 'do not resuscitate order'.

"I want to I think it through."

The words were calm but my heart was racing. I was in an untenable position of deciding my father's destiny. He had always decided his own and for the first sixteen years of my life had decided mine. By signing the order I would at long last set him free from the millstone of blame; would the act of yielding him to the inevitable haunt me? I reasoned that there was but one who would determine his fate and that was my father.

Then share thy pain, allow that sad relief;

When I left the hospital, no rich crimson glow or orange luster burned in the sky after sunset on this late December afternoon. Darkness with a very grave face called for the end of day unfolding evening's dismal drapes. I retraced my steps to the Métro and boarded in the direction of Saint-Michel traveling five stops before alighting at Acadie. Tracking down an open convenience store, I stopped to purchase assorted cleaning supplies: *Lysol* spray, sponges, boxes of *Hefty* garbage bags, *Mr. Clean*, *Ajax,* a broom, dustpan, and towels. It was difficult for me to walk balancing the broom and the over-filled shopping sack. The winter cold had settled in disagreeably severe and truculent making my eyes tear and my nose drip. I moved with measured tread, shuffling along in the middle of the road where the raspy car chains had melted the ice to slush, and staying clear of the snow blanketed sidewalks. Under the snow were dangerous ice slicks. Identical tenements with masked windows and dark landings, untouched by the general jubilant character of Christmas, lined the cheerless street. The road lamps trailed just enough light to depict the weary poverty of the brick apartments. Only two blocks remained to the Birnam address.

The wooden stairs leading to my father's neighbor's flat were steep and slippery. Timidly I pushed the door buzzer. The window of the door was caked with frost. At least two minutes elapsed before a light went on and the portiere was drawn aside. A smallish pinched face with a worried look peeped at me through the window and the door was opened a crack. Hurriedly I explained to the woman who I was, worried that she would keep me out. The mention of my father's name gained me access and Maria, his upstairs neighbor, enfolded me in a warm embrace. Taking the broom and overstuffed bag out of my hands, she ushered me into her modest home, remarkably similar to my childhood house on Av Coloniale. Replete with dark, cumbrous furniture and a table covered with a white lace cloth, the ornate parlor was in flawless condition. I suspected Maria used the room only on exceptional occasions. She pointed to the small floral upholstered divan at the piano. Plainly, she wanted me to sit down and remove my boots. Then shedding my coat, scarf, and gloves, I neatly folded and arranged them seeming to meet with her approval.

"Your father, he's no good?" she asked.

"He's very sick." I considerately replied.

Maria began to cry softly, tears streaming down, which she swabbed away with her apron. Petite in size with thinning salt-and-pepper hair and very black eyebrows, her large, innocent eyes revealed a gentle nature poignantly resembling my beloved grandmother, l'hasholem. My own sorrow stung as I suffered the pangs of an earlier loss and one yet to come.

"My Bobby found him. He was on floor. Not moving. Very cold."

Maria's husband Bobby had noticed that the delivered *Montreal Star* papers at my father's door had not been taken in for three days. Worried, he had checked on my father, only to discover him in the bedroom lying next to the bed, unconscious and skimpily clothed. He acted promptly to call the paramedics. The account was consistent with what Dr. Steinmann had told me in his telephone call.

"Come to kitchen," Maria pleaded. "I make you Greek coffee. To-day I bake fresh."

I followed Maria noting her swollen ankles and how undecidedly she walked as if the pressure was more than she could bear. Her feet clad in felt slippers moved quietly on the wood floors. Appreciatively, I sat down at the table. The covering oilcloth had an ornamental design of bunches of purple grapes on leafy vines. As I warmed up in the heat radiating from the oven, Maria served me a wedge of baklava and dense black coffee, steaming hot, in an espresso cup. Paper napkins, a pitcher of cream, a sugar bowl and silverware followed, accompanied by, "Eat, eat." It was a familiar refrain. I sniffed the delicate scent of flaky pastry, honey, and nuts. The kindness of this plain, unassuming woman overwhelmed me. As I ate the sweet dessert, Maria watched over me relating her fondness for my father. She proudly showed off a beautiful intaglio carved amber cameo of the Virgin Mary. Set in sterling silver and masterfully crafted, she had fastened it to the collar of her dress.

"Your father, he give to me."

"Maria, it is exquisite!"

In one of his letters to me, my father wrote of Maria who was on dialysis for a chronic kidney problem. He showed tender concern for her. Now that he was so ill, she cried freely sorrowing for him when she had cause to weep for her own ill-health. I rose to put my arms around her in our shared sorrow. She seemed tiny and fragile but I sensed a resilient spirit. I gained an inkling of why my father cared about Maria and her family. Their generous hearts freely gave him affection overlooking his oddities and reclusiveness; the quantity he received was in excess of that which he gave.

Disinclined to start the task of sorting through my father's belongings, I reluctantly left the comfort of Maria's kitchen. Thanking her profusely, I lugged my cleaning items down the inside stairs to the suite below. In the shadowy sparse light, I glimpsed the dinghy runner, its nap worn off in the center, flanked by assorted snow, rain, and ski boots lined up all the way to the last step. At the bottom, the handle to the door was broken and it pulled through the insert in the door almost coming off in my hand. A bare light bulb hung from a frayed cord. By simply pushing the door, it easily opened and I found myself in a narrow corridor. There were two other doors, one leading to the garage, which was stocked with stored furniture and boxes, and the other was the front door that I had come through on my visit in 1996. The same lace curtain was strung in the window, flimsy and yellowed with age.

The corridor advanced to the main living space. Little had changed except it seemed smaller. The air was musty and stale. Scanning the room, I was facing a task requiring an army regiment to attack. A sense of frustration washed over me. Fatigue was taking its toll and I had not yet started. My father's easy chair, though resembling a beggarly garment, beckoned; I wiped the dry, fissured leather seat and back, poked the stuffing into the torn padded arms and sunk in. Maria's good nature had calmed my grief but a new storm raged in the stillness of the room.

A conscience thread-bare and ragged
with perpetual turning

Where to begin? I had not contended with so abstruse a problem by myself since preparing for my doctorate in art history. The subject of my dissertation was 'The Evolution of the Classic Modern Movement into Post-Modernism'. I spent long days on the research which extended into months of writing, revisions and references. The work to be done in my father's place seemed equally staggering. My mind faltered under the load. Feeling faint and disconsolate in the cellar's damp disarray, I walked about the cramped space as if in a dream. Childhood fears of squinty eyed rats hiding in the gloom made me cringe. To stay my terror, I examined all the items on the walls. The remembered *Felix the Cat* wall clock in black and white was there. Now its eyes were stuck in one position and its tail dangled limply. Mounted nearby with scotch tape and thumbtacks were articles from the *Jerusalem Post* and editorials from the Montréal newspapers. The mother of Christ painted in oils on wood stared at me from his bedroom. Another area was covered with a large poster of Janis Joplin. The wacky ensemble curbed my inclination to run away. Ensnared, the trials began.

Calling upon ill-defined reserves, I picked up the broom, and with slow deliberation began to sweep the floor and clear a path to the bedroom and kitchen. As I swept, years of accumulated dirt blew up in a cloud. My mouth began to taste of grime and my nose reacted to the dust with many sneezes. As I made headway scooping up the layered refuse, thin sheets of warped linoleum with missing portions and bare boards were exposed. Tucked in the corners of his living room and under furniture were some rat poison pellets. Thankfully, it seemed the rats instinctively had quit the place and I shuddered in relief. When I did not come upon any cockroaches either, I went forward with recharged vigor. I discarded the reams of old newspapers filling four of the large capacity plastic trash bags and lugged each into the corridor. I could now move around more easily and began to attend to the details.

A wobbly bridge table with a folding chair served as my father's 'study'. At this table he had written his personal mail, attended to his bills, and ate his spare meals. The grooved and faded red leather surface was strewn with notepads, loose paper clips and rolls of stamps, ashtrays with coins, vials of medicines, letters, and a large bottle of *Bayer Aspirin*, newspaper clippings, and cookie tins with stock certificates. Sitting at the edge was a forlorn cracked China cup drained of its last remains other than dried tea leaves. The sadness of the room collapsed into the empty cup. I was loath to move it fearful of scattering shriveled leaves of sorrow into the air.

Whatever I judged valueless, I discarded. For convenience, I randomly stacked the surplus items on the tatty runners lying on the nearby dining table. Leaning against a crate overfilled with books on mining companies was the old television set with a bent antenna. Nosily, I pressed the 'on' button but nothing happened. Dropping down to my knees, I hunted for the electrical outlet. It was out of sight behind boxes containing countless pieces of costume jewelry, pins, watches, and strands of pearls. The cord from the TV was plugged in. Finding the connection intact, I tried once more to revive it without success. On my visit six years before, the sound had been turned off but some fuzzy reception from a news channel was displayed. Now it refused to perform. This did not stop me from dusting it and using *Windex* to remove the grime from the screen. I stopped questioning my motives for doing any of this. There was obviously some baser need of my own to satisfy. I washed and polished the leather tabletop until it shone and returned the odds and ends situating them in the exact place as found. The neat arrangement buoyed my spirits.

With this first chore done, I grew bolder and elected to check out the condition of the kitchen. I lamented that choice as soon as I walked in. The kitchen was filled with swarming fruit flies the size of sparrows. Crusted dishes, fry pans and pots were piled in the cracked twin porcelain wash basins under the cupboards. Food remnants from past weeks were scattered on the counters: partly eaten chocolate chip cookies, stale and dry, an old banana still in its casing having turned to mush, a tin of salmon and a few orange peelings. A clothesline was strung in the kitchen from the cabinet hinge to the back of the door. The pegged nondescript clothes drooped in respect like unfurled flags lowered to half-mast. The old *Leonard* refrigerator, model circa 1950, a holdover from Av Coloniale occupied a notable post. I discovered upon opening the door that it was not functional. The shelves were stocked with cans of tuna, sardines and salmon, one jar of mayonnaise and one of mustard, a few oranges, some moldy cheese, rice, butter, eggs, and a tin foil canister of *Orange Pekoe Tea*. Next to the fridge was the brown leather *Samsonite* suitcase, the one my father had used for our trip to Old Orchard Beach. I was surprised that it was only slightly damaged, the clasps still intact, a testimony to its durability. In the far corner of the kitchen near the tiny window was a pantry with the door ajar. A disorganized arrangement of cereals, more cans of *Clover Leaf* tuna fish and salmon, plastic packages of toilet paper, two bags of sugar, a can of *Folgers* coffee, digestive biscuits and a single packet of black licorice was visible. Under the bottom shelf board sat a sizeable carton completely filled with outdated medical textbooks. A second cardboard box was crammed with antique household and workshop gadgets: can openers, hammers, axes, a rusted rough in-dented grater, an orange juice maker, serving tools, an old flat iron, and a maze of wires.

It was not feasible to begin a cleanup of the kitchen, a project that would take more days. The best I could do was dispose of the garbage and spray the room with *Lysol* hoping to block the nasty smell and kill the fruit flies. I moved the boxes to one area of the living room intend-ing to find a dealer in antiques. Wherever I glanced, the years of hoarded stuff coated in a filthy residue caused my eyes to tear. I felt as if I had been transported back in time to the Roman city of Pompeii buried in cinders and ashes after the eruption of Mount Vesuvius. The enforced silence of the tiny rooms and the urgent necessity disturbed me. The silence grew more terrible as if edging toward something un-bearable.

Hours passed. Oblivious, I refused to stop to rest or bother to think of eating. There was a sense of the imperative, of needing to make consistency out of chaos. I was an intrusion into my father's retreat. Aware of his illogical nature, he would have strenuously objected to my interfering with his possessions. He valued them and he alone knew where everything was placed. As I became familiar with his treasures and handled each one, the gap between us lessened. Dr. Steinman had said he could not survive his illness; I had to clear out this abysmal place to which he was never coming back.

Was this diligence for me or for him? Wary of this thought, I dared not allow myself to pause in the effort. *Why had my father continued to stay in these desolate rooms, horrid ones in a sorry part of Montréal?* The contemptible conditions held him captive. Perhaps there was nothing more that he wished for. My father, an intelligent man, a man of character and scruples could not abide his complicity in the loss of my mother. Haunted and sickened by his failings, he consciously chose to live a wretched and meager existence to assuage his remorse. I believed he had paid penance for his misdeeds and should not have imprisoned himself forever in the confines of regret. This awareness choked me and my cheeks flamed as if I were branded with a permanent blot of dishonor. How small a part of life we had shared. I was long overdue in the sorrowing. I would soon be mourning his death.

And that deepe torture may be cal'd a Hell,

Mid-morning the following day, I returned to see my father. Overnight his condition had worsened. He seemed frailer and yesterday's smooth face was paper thin, pale, and shadowed with whiskers. His wrists were strapped with gauze restraints latched to the bed rails. Purple bruises had appeared on his arms; his skin, thin and taut, seemed at risk to shred like old cloth. In his confused and delusional state, he did not discern who I was. I spoke soothing words to him to calm his ordeal, and gradually he gained awareness and became lucid once more. The food tray at his bedside was untouched. It seemed the ICU was short-staffed and there was no one to attend him at this time. I fed him three teaspoons of yogurt and the same of apple juice, waiting patiently between each serving for him to swallow past the feeding tube still in place. Too weak to take in more, he pushed my hand away. After a few minutes during which time I read his chart at the foot of the bed, he perked up and looked at me quizzically.

"So, what do you think of your new president?"

I laughed not only because he was teasing me about my years spent out of Canada in the US, but also it was such an unexpected question.

"I don't trust him," I answered.

"He looks and acts like a weasel," he commented in return.

Sick as he was, my father had not lost his sense of humor.

"Dad," I said, "while I was in your apartment yesterday, I opened a letter from Banque Laurentien. Your account has been dormant for two years. It will be closed unless you initiate some activity. I want your permission to deposit some funds into the account."

"Don't trouble yourself," he stated, glaring at me.

"But Dad, you have over twelve hundred dollars in savings that will be lost!"

That statement seemed to impact him.

"What needs to be done?" he asked.

"I found a dividend check that you received in the mail. It's from

Gold Corp. If you sign it, I will go to the bank and deposit it for you."

I showed the brokerage paperwork to my father. Remembering his precise ways, I knew he would examine it in detail.

"Untie me," he demanded.

I removed the restraints from his right hand and offered him a pen placing the documents on my briefcase. He could scarcely hold the pen in his swollen hand. I winced as I watched him judiciously endorse the check, his handwriting shaky, and his signature drifting down to the right. Dissatisfied and frustrated by this he wrote his name again; the effort of doing this aggravated his pain.

"Don't get lost going to the bank."

These cautionary words said, he slipped back into sleep, the morphine taking over and reducing his agony.

As I passed the nurses' station I was intercepted.

"Your father is so loud at times, screaming at the doctors and staff."

"Where's Emily, his regular nurse?"

"She's off today and I'm responsible for him." The charge nurse, hands on hips, confronted me in this hostile way.

"Just give him the damn morphine!" I lashed out and walked off.

Having mastered the Métro, I now had to transfer to the Parc 80 bus at Acadie. The walk to the bus stop proved treacherous on slush, ice, and charcoal pieces. There was no traction and I slid along the sidewalk into the path of the oncoming bus. Saved from falling under the wheels by smashing instead into the side of the bus, I hurried aboard as the door unfolded and I sunk into the nearest seat. The ride was brief, the bus shimmying along swerving around parked cars past rows of apartment buildings to Rue Jarry and then another balancing act on the ice to the corner of Av Wiseman.

It was a small local branch of Banque Laurentien and unexpectedly crammed full. I counted about sixty people ahead of me and only one and occasionally two tellers at their posts. The line of clients snaked along. Not a word of grievance was uttered. Heat from the wall radiators and moisture from melting snow on wet clothing turned the room into a small steamy laundromat. Sweat caused by the sultry heat trickled down my face and back. I took off my hat and gloves followed by my coat and then shed my heavy sweater. Now all these cumbersome items lay over my arm trailing on the floor. Shuffling, we moved in slow motion as if our winter boots were sticking to the tiled floor. With each step we bumped one another or received an elbow jab, an unwelcome poke of a lumpy parcel, or an accidental kick in the ankle. An odd potpourri of tobacco, garlic, and cheap cologne left a brackish taste in my mouth.

"Unsavory," I grumbled to no one in particular, "at least the line's moving."

I passed the time staring about. The minute examination of the assorted idling people comforted me. An elderly Greek woman with a babushka on her head, her face worn and lined, seemed unperturbed by the wait. A dark skinned man of Muslim origin piqued my curiosity. Atop his head was a circularly wound turban of yards of gold peau de soie and India silk, a rich contrast to his acne pitted face. In a carriage, a fat-legged baby swaddled in blankets blissfully slept. The youthful parents cheekily exchanged kisses, she pulling on the lapels of his coat tugging him to her. A young black girl in an unbuttoned ankle length coat and fashionable hip-high boots stiffly squirmed on her stiletto heels. Swaying imperceptibly, a thin man with a waxed mustache and darned wool hat dozed in place. All the details distracted me and substituted a disorderly collection of faces for the one of my sick father. Almost two hours went by before I could execute the minor transaction. At the end, I accomplished it by angrily demanding to speak to a supervisor to explain why my father could not come to the bank in person. At this point the squandered time and the intrusive annoyance brought me close to tears.

I hustled back to the bus stop, caught the Parc 80 alighting at Av Beaumont, and walked the short distance to my father's apartment. A small, ramshackle house with a yard beckoned to me and slowed my haste. The compacted snow against the fencing radiated a pale violet light. Tangled therein, stiff spreading branches of a lilac tree, a young one, had taken hold in the soil beneath the snow. Smooth dark green leaves were in bloom and clustered buds with greenish tips had opened to sprout young flowers in shades of lilac, light purple, and lavender. It was far too early in the season, with snow on the frozen ground and more to come, to have this explosion of color and fragrance. Ever so gently, I broke off two small blooming branches. The years had not dulled the exquisite memory of violet, white and purple blossoms at my Aunt Rosie's home in Hampstead. In a heartbeat, the early evening was awash in lilacs and blossoms of memories.

Not willingly, but tangl'd in the fold Of dire necessity

The only touch of life and color in my father's place were the two sprigs of lilacs I placed in an antique cut glass crystal vase with a leaf motif. The previous day, I had salvaged the container from the kitchen cupboard. After removing the cob webs and washing it in soapy water, it dawned on me that this was a brilliant sample of early American crystal. The cuts in the glass reflected the lilac colors, and in only dismal light, the lavender tints retained their richness.

The sluggish gloom returned. It settled on me once again as I pondered the filth and squalor in which my father had been living. Entrenched in the past, the relentless changes relevant to starting fresh had eluded him. Completing the clean up task became my priority. The sight of my father's bedroom was yet another reversal. Through my fog of tears, the walls seemed smeared as if painted with smoky brush strokes of distress. The air was sour. Littering the uncarpeted bare board floor were dozens of plastic bags crammed with letters. On his narrow cot-like bed, a matted mess of ripped unwashed linen and scratchy army blankets lay in a twisted knot as if his tortured sleep had wound itself into the covers. I imagined him beneath the sheets tossing and turning as if in an angry sea. Two flat pillows hung over the edge of a thin striped mattress, its meagerness could do little to alleviate his arthritis pain. There were no cases on the pillows, nothing to protect his face from coarse soiled fabric. On the floor, under sagging bedsprings, I found dust, more dust, and cookie tins jammed with papers, jeweler's tools, and boxes containing coins, scrap gold, and junk jewelry. As I arranged the bedding, loose feathers drifted in the air refusing to alight on the unkempt scene.

Two curiously carved wooden dressers and one giant hutch with mirror and shelves, once fine grained mahogany furniture, were now flawed and missing drawer handles. Behind one bureau tucked in the corner was a large floor lamp topped with a porcelain shade in the shape of a bowl mounted on a fluted brass stand with ornamental legs. By standing on the edge of the bed, I was able to grope inside the shade and remove the burnt out bulb. The disheveled light in the room made me wish I had thought of bringing a replacement to brighten this one end of his dusky apartment. My eyes were tired and strained from the hours of sorting in the dimness.

Most of the drawers were filled with jewelry and gems packaged in small brown envelopes neatly labeled or prudently folded in tissue paper. One drawer held his tephillin, yarmulke, and scrolls from mezu-zahs*, Québec Hydro bills and CNR books. It was cluttered but not disorganized. I found in another drawer a tidy arrangement of personal papers: his birth certificate stating he was born in 1914, the twenty-seventh day of August, his passport application which he never completed, income tax returns, his employment record, and a certificate of medical discharge from the Canadian Armed Forces. Frowning, I read about my grandfather Isaac who died of a blood disease, the man I never knew after whom I was named. I gathered up these treasured articles of his past and placed them in my briefcase.

In a brown paper grocery bag, I found all that he saved relating to my mother's life. Pushing aside a container of flowery costume brooches, I sat down on my father's bed and emptied out the contents: a birth certificate from Russia, Emma born the third day of March, 1910, mother Rachel and father Abraham, a mourners' guest book and vials of prescription medication. Her leather purse and chiffon scarf demanded my consideration. The purse was still in excellent condition, the silver handle untarnished, and the leather supple. I lifted it to my nose to catch my mother's precious scent but only the smell of time was trapped in the folds. The sheer chiffon scarf began to shred in my hands into thin filaments of sadness. The pristine purse and the scarf falling into tatters prompted a flood of weeping. In the dense, deepening shadows of the room, my mother's lasting love held me as if I were a child again until the sound of my sobbing subsided to whimpers.

My father's garments were heaped in careless clutter in one small niche of his bedroom. Unwanted in the mass were derelict shoes full of

---

* Pieces of parchment, often contained in a decorative case, inscribed with specified Hebrew verses from the Torah

holes, soles and heels worn down, and foul rags of a neutral tint splattered with brown that made an attempt to pass as dishtowels. Slacks,
falling to pieces, were on top of embroidered tea cosies and soiled
aprons. A shaggy lamb's wool hat, a muffler, seedy scarves, sweaters
with frayed cuffs, raggedy long-johns, protective clothing for
Montréal's winter: not one thing was in wearable condition. All were
useless and had the same stale smell. I filled more trash bags with the
clothes and the bedding, stripping the room of all fabric.

In one plastic sack, I found bundled letters tied with ribbon or held
together by rubber bands. The distinctive style of my own handwriting
caught my attention. All my letters to my father from the time I ran
away from home until the present were in groups stacked in order. I
reached to the bottom and pulled out the earliest bunch. At random, I
selected one envelope only to find it was not one from me but one
from the Dean of Women at UBC. Filled with curiosity, I took out the
enclosed page. It read as follows:

February 13th 1959

Dear Mr. Lichman,

*Regrettably I must inform you of your daughter Caasi's
unacceptable behavior. The prefects in her dormitory have reported to me that she has been signing in well past the curfew
hour on more than one occasion. She was also caught smoking
cigarettes in the women's washroom. I am deeply concerned as
it may affect her eligibility to remain here as a student. I personally would regret any dismissal action as she is an excellent
student having achieved exemplary grades so far.*

*I am appealing to you to help resolve this issue quickly and
effectively.*

The signature and bottom part of the page was missing. Most likely, my father had taken that section with him to CPR Telegraphs to
send a Western Union telegram to the Dean of Women. I vividly recall
being summoned to her office and the telegram wordlessly handed to
me. My father had written, "Punish her to the nth degree," E.W. Lichman. His message was clear, and for a full week I daily scrubbed the

shared bathrooms, swept the hallways, and vacuumed the common room carpeting.

There was no avoiding laughing over this. From afar, my father had reined me in.

Still amused, I ventured into the next packet. The frayed elastic split off and the few letters cascaded to the floor. All were postmarked from Evanston, Illinois, at the time I was studying for my masters and then my doctorate degrees. The range of my interests was broad as I was exposed to Old Masters, Impressionist Art, Asian Art, Post-Impressionism, and Modern and Contemporary Art. My letters were filled with descriptive passages of works I had seen at The Art Institute of Chicago and artists who had captured my imagination. The letter I chose to scan was written about the photographer Manuel Alvarez Bravo and my favorite image, *The daughter of the dancers, 1933.* I detailed the geometric wall with the peeling paint, the lithesome playful girl, and the dance like position of her arm as she reached into the darkness of the building to her past.

Not easily forgotten was father's curt reply to my wordy description. "If you like old buildings battered by the sun and the cold, there are plenty in Montréal."

Not pleased, I located the letters from Normal, Illinois. I had been fortunate to attain a position at Illinois State University, Professor of Art Education. My work was enthralling, teaching art methods courses designed for elementary and early childhood art education majors. The city of Normal charmed me and I was thankful for having found a new and convivial place.

I noticed the postmarked date on one of my letters. It was 1967, the year I had made my first significant purchase.

Dear Dad,

Guess what! I am a homeowner. I found a Ranch style house in West Normal on a spacious lot surrounded by trees. It was built in 1953 so it is only fourteen years old and was kept in excellent condition. What I love best is the neighborhood, its proximity to ISU, the wooden flooring throughout, the living room bay window, the huge back yard and brick patio, and ce-

311

ramic tiling in the bathroom. The city of Bloomington is close by and the creative arts scene abounds in both communities. An art-deco design theater, very avant-garde, is located here. During semester breaks, I can see classic movies and independent films. My street is Primrose. The name seems to hold much promise.

   Sorry for the gushiness. I know I can be wordy. I hope you are well.

   Love, Caasi

There was a lapse in our communication for several years. We neglected each other and our lives went forward as if we were unrelated. My father ignored me in my house on Primrose and I was actively teaching and taking trips into Chicago to the newly established Museum of Contemporary Art. The museum enticed me with its exhibits of Surrealist, Minimalist, Pop and early Post-Modern Art. Discouraged by his lack of response to my news, I abstained from writing about all that fascinated me. The only message I received was one recorded on my answering machine. It was a harsh, prickly, and judgmental voice identified without difficulty. My Aunt Mildred, my father's sister, notified me of the passing of Grandmother Ada, my bubbe. Her shameful, unwarranted accusations of neglect of my father were like a slap in the face and the loss of my bubbe caused a thick, mute darkness to press on my chest.

   Back in the main room, I checked the closet. Hung within were my father's jackets. In the pockets were Métro tickets and pennies and other small change. A protective clothing bag contained my mother's muskrat coat smelling rancid. It was rammed in between his windbreaker, cardigans, and parkas. An old vacuum cleaner, several pairs of snow boots, and buckled galoshes were tucked under the clothes. Boxes of *Kleenex* and *Colgate* toothpaste were stored on the shelves. I merely stared at the contents of the closet sighing in surrender and frustration. I would tackle that problem the following day.

   One more chore awaited me, one that I had put off and wished to postpone forever. I opened the door to the bathroom for the first time since being in my father's place. The toilet was endlessly running but the flush was not working properly. The bowl was stained in colors resembling a bruise. Rolls of toilet paper were stacked on the lid of the tank. A pink shower curtain dangled pathetically from a few rings. Water dripped from the showerhead; the drip drop drip drop made a pinging sound into a rusty bucket. The tub was filthy and stained with lime and mold. On the counter above the sink were jars of *Vaseline*, bottles of tincture of iodine, and other medicinal solutions. No soap, washcloths, or hand towels were to be found.

I could no longer bear it, this room, this basement, this loathsome dungeon. It had become ghastly since my last visit. Held hostage here all these years, he paid the ultimate ransom, and was now set free to die elsewhere. This beset man was still my loved father; the only one I had or would ever have.

I grabbed my things, remembering my briefcase in the bedroom, and fled. Necessity this time drove me out.

Defer not off, to-morrow is too late

It was bitterly cold outdoors as the heavy cloud cover had lifted. The streets were plunged in shadows; silvery moonbeams glimmered on the darkly bald spots of sidewalk. Unthinkingly, I walked along Av Beaumont until hunger pangs prodded me out of my reverie. I found a small restaurant near Rue Hutchison that boasted original Montréal smoked meat sandwiches. Gratefully, I went inside and was greeted by a rather thickset, stocky built old man with an apron tied around his portly waist. His friendly eyes squinted inquisitively and then he winked at me in the seemly manner of a compliment.

"Don't stand shivering in the doorway; come in! Entrez!" he said, his voice a gruff growl. His wide grin let slip his teasing; he was evidently delighted.

"Voilà, today's specials; I hope you brought your appetite. Marcel will look after you."

Chortling, he then went back behind the counter to his task of slicing loaves of dark rye and pumpernickel bread. The one-page dog-eared handwritten menu had a few noodles stuck to the paper. Just before closing time, I seemed to be the only one there after the regular diners had left. Marcel, an airy, brisk young man with one earring and long strawberry blonde hair which had been pulled back, pony-tail style, directed me to a small beige *Formica* topped table perfect for one person. Tiredly, I sunk down on the provided lopsided chair as if the air had suddenly collapsed out of me. After placing my order, I leaned my elbows on the table resting my face in my hands. I took note of the fresh place setting, the copper-plated tin ashtray, plastic black finish napkin holder, and clear glass crystal salt and pepper shakers in a metal basket, all clean and nicely arranged.

Marcel reappeared balancing a tray. On it was a jar of *Maille Dijon* mustard, a bottle of *Heinz* ketchup, a small *Dixie* cup of coleslaw, a plate of sliced kosher dills, and a can of *Diet Coke*. He transferred the items to the table and then seemed to rethink his plans. He scurried off returning with a glass filled with crushed ice.

Smilingly, Marcel said, "Vous aimerez ceci."

The glass was illustrated with a red-haired little girl in a yellow frock and a scampering tree squirrel, and titled 'A Child's Fantasy'. As promised, I did like it. The scene reminded me of home. After the departure of winter, my back yard in West Normal would sprout red and yellow petal tulips; squirrels, flippant and full of play, would nimbly climb the branches of the old poplar. Revived, I lingered in the whimsy of balmy spring breezes.

Minutes later, Marcel served me a platter with a sandwich of smoked brisket on fresh homemade rye bread and a side of pommes frites. It was a mouthwatering feast. This was my first substantial meal in three days, other than the treats at Maria's and morning muffins and coffee at my hotel. I was sated after one quarter of my sandwich and all of the thin, crisp fries but ordered a second *Coke* sipping it slowly, biding my time.

Dabbing the mustard off my chin, I rose to go. I said a quick, "Merci beaucoup, délicieuse," to the proprietor, paid in cash, and left an excessive tip for the waiter. On the return trip, I made a stop at an all-night drugstore and bought two 100 watt bulbs, one to insert into the bedroom lamp and one for the entry way. I had diverted an idle hour, my cares thrown off, but I did not wish to waste the remnants of the evening.

Sweet downie thoughts, soft *lilly-shades, calm streams

The hour was late and I was reluctant to commence another arduous task. I chose instead to open more of my correspondence with my father that spanned the last twenty-four years. Appraising my own letters to my father was a way of reliving my life as he had distantly examined it. Each in turn was a footprint on the memory path to the past. The years were condensed to minutes but the details and the story unfolded acceptably. What I had experienced was alive again, warm and breathing on the pages.

> *March 27th 1978*
>
> *Dear Dad,*
>
> *I know I haven't been keeping you up to date on what's happening with me. But I do have some news to share. I have become seriously involved with Viktor Westen, a distinguished sculptor, painter, and conceptual artist. We met when I was attending a lecture series at the Field Museum in Chicago, literally bumping into one another amid the Egyptian mummies on display. He had been invited to talk about his large scale sculptured concrete and Italian glass mosaic murals. Viktor lives in Los Angeles most of the time and then goes back to Kivik for a month, the city of his birth in south-east Sweden. I really like him, more than anyone else I have previously dated. Will keep you posted.*
>
> *Love, Caasi*

My long-distance courtship with Viktor was exciting from the outset. Whenever he returned to Chicago, the novelty and randomness were renewed. His slender build, dark hair, glowing tan, and deep-set heavily lashed eyes reminded me of Claude, the little boy from the farm near Lac-Theodore. As we came to know one another, I marveled at his zest for life and his inventiveness. Early summer, he surprised me with a planned trip to Paris. I had never before traveled to Europe, and romantic Paris was a city I had only fantasized. Viktor booked our stay at *Hôtel des Grands Hommes*, a beautiful XVIIIth century building in the Latin Quarter within walking distance of the Luxembourg Garden. Each morning, petit-déjeuner, a sumptuous breakfast of freshly baked croissants, strawberry jam, whipped butter, and café au lait was brought to our room. We strolled on Blvd Champs-Elysées from the Arc de Triomphe to the Tuileries Garden past the stylish shops and grand cafés; buoyantly in love with Viktor and Paris, I floated along, my feet scarcely touching the ground. The Musée d'Orsay, Jeu de Paume, and Musée du Louvre kept us entranced for hours. Holding hands, we sat on a bench in front of Leonardo da Vinci's *Mona Lisa* pondering her enigmatic mood and smiling at one another. In our shared rapture, we had an attack of irrepressible giggles and the guard at the museum came by to shush us up.

Viktor listened assiduously to all that I said as if it were vital and perceptive. His expressive gray eyes with just a splash of blue seemed enraptured by every word engaging me as I spoke. At last I felt what I had not found before: someone who cared deeply about me, and I was gloriously alive in his world. Passionate yet tender, he held me in his arms and stroked my soft, long hair exacting a promise from me not to have it cut. I was elatedly intoxicated with Viktor, loving him with all my senses and bubbling over with happiness.

A gifted conversationalist, he described in detail his artwork and sculptures. He painted word pictures of his small village and the summer market stalls loaded with herring, apples, and flowers. I admired his photographs of the charming cottages made of red brick with red tile roofs, cobblestone pathways, and the spectacle of sweetly scented flowering plants bursting out in mid-spring.

We continued our dating; the visits became sporadic and his gallantry tapered off. I excused his inconstancy as he was hard at work sculpting large bronzes for an exhibit at the Los Angeles Pacific Design Center. Offering to accompany him on his next trip to Kivik, he artfully sidelined my request. His ardent gaze, which before had bored into my heart, now looked past me as if I had precipitously become gauzy or invisible.

In October, I discovered I was expecting a child and confided the news to Viktor. My joy was fleeting. It was then I learned that he was married, and his wife and eight-year old son were living in Kivik.

The next letter I opted to read included this worrisome disclosure. Perturbed, my father had marked the envelope with a black **X**. He delivered his riposte to me in his inimitable way. Even now I recalled his words.

You were led down the primrose path. I could have warned you when you chose to live on Primrose and go out with strangers. This deception now has deeper significance. If you intend to raise the child alone, you will pay a steep price. A child without a father is doomed.

Unconstrained heartbreak coupled with despondency conspired to sink me. I had an unnatural sense of moving through dark and deep waters unable to rise to the surface; the violent beatings of my heart were sounds of frenetic flailing like a cormorant trapped in a rocky cove. The anguish of being alone and forsaken called up past memories which had grievously shaped my destiny. I felt stranded as if on an uninhabited island with no one to share my sadness. Aching and stifled, I immersed myself in my teaching and took on extra classes returning home late in the evenings to tumble wearily into a disruptive sleep.

Months went by and I began to notice the subtle stirrings of new life. Sparks of pleasure and quenched dreams were rekindled. As I sought to protect what was mine, the promise of unimagined rewards gladdened me. I gave birth to a baby girl and named her Lilli. The rush of love for her was familiar after its long absence. As I cradled Lilli in my arms, a sensation of joy and tenderness crested like an ocean wave; in that instant, I too was in the warm gentle hold of the dearest of remembered hands.

Relying on stored images of my mother's graciousness and devotion, I nurtured and cherished Lilli. At times, the demands of my position at the university and caring for her seemed daunting. Her sweet face, framed by a mass of golden curls the color of poppies and sunbeams, lifted my spirits when they flagged. She intently watched me and lovingly wrapped her baby arms about my neck to smother me with kisses.

November 7th 1986

Dear Dad,

    Each day with Lilli can turn into an adventure. This will read like a children's story book and make you grin. Other than my Schmoo Oliver, you never permitted me to have a real pet, and I knew little about raising one. Lilli found a lost dog wandering in the nearby park. She brought him home, fed him, bathed him, and combed through his tangled coat. He had no collar about his neck and lacked identifying tags; Lilli implored to keep him. She named him Toto because his fluffy white tail, short ears, and long beige whiskers resembled Dorothy's dog from the movie Wizard of Oz. The dog is a steadier friend to her than Oliver was to me. He's willful and won't deflate. Lilli and Toto are inseparable. He showed up unannounced at her school to the amusement of her friends. Her teacher Miss McKee was less enthusiastic. I was called out of a tutorial at ISU to claim the dog. It was no easy feat as he was racing up and down corridors and darting into classrooms. Making my apologies to Miss McKee, while holding the squirming dog, was a challenge as I tried to be seriously repentant. The children were out of control and she was fuming. I ended up being the one scolded.

    Love, Caasi

Marginal memories of my father's influence on my early years intuitively guided me; deleted was his cruel and vicious method of delivery. An instance of a valued lesson took place on a Saturday afternoon. I was in the kitchen making a favorite dinner, chili relleno casserole. The Mexican cuisine containing roasted fresh poblano peppers, eggs, milk, and two kinds of cheeses was one that we had enjoyed in a Bloomington restaurant. Just as I placed the earthenware deep dish into the oven, I glanced at Lilli. She was scowling over her texts.

"Sweetie, what's wrong?" I asked.

"I'm struggling with the multiplication of fractions," she answered with a frustrated sigh. "The larger the bottom number, the smaller is the fraction."

"My father taught me fractions by visualizing apples and oranges."

"That's weird."

"Yes, but it worked."

From the fruit basket, I chose a fresh pineapple, an apple, and a pear. After I removed the spiny husk from the pineapple and washed the other fruit, I sectioned one at a time into two halves, then quarters, eighths, sixteenths, and finally sixty-fourths. As I patiently explained why the fraction with the larger number was a smaller piece of the whole, the tiled counter top became laden with chunks of fruit.

Lilli watched the progress, her green flecked hazel eyes alert and mischievous.

"Does this make sense?" I asked

"I figured it out right away," she answered teasingly.

"You didn't say so," I good-naturedly protested.

"I was having too much fun."

She skipped about, the curls and ringlets on her head playfully springing.

"And now we have fruit salad for dessert," she computed, "192 pieces."

Lilli's endearing qualities developed as if by magic. Our home re-sounded with exuberant youthful chatter. At Christmas time, her ballet class performed *The Nutcracker*; let down not to be cast as Clara, she gladly accepted a role as a dancing mouse. A few years later as Marion in her high school production she sang, ... *There were bells on the hill...But I never heard them ringing...No, I never heard them at all...Till there was you...* *

Her light-hearted tones made my eyes glisten with tears; like flick-ering stars in the night sky, they softly fell in a downy caress. Lilli's voice was reminiscent of my mother's; long ago, in rare moments of blitheness, she had been the first to enchant me with her singing.

I truthfully told Lilli about Viktor, her father, who she never met nor discussed thereafter. She indicated in her candid way that she was devoted to me and lacked nothing. With respect to my own past, I was

---

* *Till There was You*
Written by Meredith Wilson, 1957 Musical Play*, The Music man*

less forthright. I described my beloved mother, my sweet grandmother, my aunts and cousins tactfully omitting disturbing details, and portrayed my father discreetly. Discarding distorted impressions of culpability that had tormented me, I was capable of purely loving her. Serenely watching over her and sensitive to her needs, I helped her cope with life's challenges.

After my last trip to Montréal, my father congenially responded to my descriptions of Lilli's charm, wit, and intelligence. He took an avid interest in her well-being and her education, writing indulgent letters to her and enclosing cartoons and funny articles from magazines. Lilli reacted happily to his humor and his observations of the illogical and tacked the clippings to the little bulletin board in her room. I notified him of her acceptance into Trinity University in San Antonio, Texas. Departing from his severity which had impelled me to unreachable flawlessness, his lectures to Lilli were never harsh nor delivered jarringly. Wanting to safeguard her from all hazards, my father wrote a cautionary note.

Tell Lilli to be careful walking around campus alone at night. She must be able to sense what is going on behind or around her.

For so long, I desisted in confronting and accepting the obvious and what I suspected. As with a broken looking glass, each part showing only a shadow of the truth, I had to assemble what I refused to see. Misfortune and adversity might have softened my father's heart. He chose to let mischance bury him in an avalanche of pain. By creating obstacles, he clung to life in a perverse manner; it was more gratifying than empty bleak recesses through which hollow winds howled constant accusations. After decades of emptiness, I believed he yearned for a reconnection with pleasure, the sweet and precious kind that a grandchild provides. He opened one fortified door and affectionately admitted Lilli into his life. The dimension of his love for Lilli swept away the unfairness and the sadness harbored in my heart.

The clarity of this perception calmed me; the strife had streamed to an end.

An honourable conduct let him haue

The ICU at Le Centre hospitalier de St. Mary had become a friendly enemy. In the elevator, and walking the long hallways, and the short
distance past the curtained cubicles, I had too much time in which to
remember. These incessant musings and raking in the dust of old history anchored me. Unlike an essay that can be improved with editing,
deletions, or insertions, my conscience could not be re-written to serve
that aim.

My father was my first and most influential critic. His carefully
worded phrasing always expressed a measure of disfavor. Without his
censure and away from him, I was confident and contented in all that I
did and in my preferred career. What I had learned from my father's
nurse Emily invalidated my suspicions that I had frustrated his expectations of sounder choices. He spoke glowingly about me to others and
was proud of me. I found it impossible not to love him.

Warning me that he would not be receptive to a visit, I had too
readily accepted his assertions. In reflecting, I wondered if he would
have been pleased had I arrived unannounced with Lilli. Once there,
could I have forced him out of his seclusion? In his own words as he
had so often said in my childhood, *the answer was no*. I would never
have been able to change him or alter his chosen path. The tiny crack
in his outward veneer was his newly unfolding affection for Lilli.
Linked only by letters, his fancy for her was genuine; he and I remained at an impasse. My attempt to cross that divide indubitably
would have ended in failure. In this alone, my father and I had much
worthy blame to share.

All these thoughts at variance ran through my mind like two trains
wildly forging ahead on tracks destined for a collision. Having reached
the last cubicle, I pushed the loose drape aside and found my father's
bed empty and the linens freshly and efficiently arranged. Shocked, I
groped for the chair seizing the cool metal to keep from toppling. The
surface of the bed seemed to rise and fall in waves. Small dark par-
ticles flickered across my vision. The orderly arrived at that very mo-

ment to explain that my father had been moved to the cubicle closest to the nurses' station. I experienced instant relief only to be torn asunder once more in the understanding that this is done when a patient is close to death. I rushed to his new location. He was rasping in labored form with long pauses in between. Then he cried aloud in pain. The feeding tube and the oxygen prongs were missing. Only the I.V. remained dripping very slowly. The air was heavy with defeat.

I steadied myself and went close to the bed to look at his face, so waxen and drawn. Though believing he was already in a deep coma unable to hear, I spoke to him.

"Dad, how are you?" I asked.

The question was so crazy that I almost laughed at my inanity. I waited for his response but none came. Finding a more comfortable padded easy chair in the new location, I sat down and reached under the covers for his hand. It was a hand of ice. I clutched it for close to an hour and waited. Each time he struggled for breath or groaned, I faltered.

Fatigue gradually wore me down. Alone in Montréal since my arrival, accountable for my father's medical needs and personal effects, cleaning of his apartment, and a myriad of other details had enervated me. I dozed at his bedside, holding on to his hand. He woke me up.

"I told you not to bother with the bank," he griped.

I was so thrilled to hear his voice that I burst into tears.

"Don't cry," he said irritably.

Choking on the tears, I answered, "Dad, you made me strong to defy the world, but I could never be strong for you."

"You rode the Métro by yourself, that's something."

This rather simple accomplishment seemed important to him. Not getting lost reassured him that I could function on my own, his job as protector now coming to an end. When I had first arrived, he seemed to be clinging tenaciously to the tenuous thread of life left in him. He now accepted that his condition was terminal and had chosen his own course.

"Dad, is there anything more I can do for you?

"No, it's over."

A shadow of fear flitted across his eyes. Dying frightened him. I leaned over to kiss his cheek, but he turned his face so that my kiss landed on his mouth.

"I love you, Dad."

Untried words were voiced with an ease that only my father noted.

He frowned, thinking, working things out, and deciding.

"Caasi, remember... when you were young... I used to say I'd be late for my own funeral..."

"Yes...but..."

I never caught the joke of that as a child. The time for clarification had passed and only the absurdity of it remained.

"Are you late, Dad?"

"Let me go."

With these three simple words, my father regarded me with heart piercing tenderness. Then he closed his eyes, never to open them again. In the last moment of his life, his love for me was an absolute. Lingering, not wanting to part, I pressed his hand to my heart.

Graveside, at his funeral two days later, I placed the two small branches of fragrant lavender lilacs that I had found growing in the snow covered ground.

Acknowledgments of Sourced Chapter Titles

The eye-it cannot choose but see;
We cannot bid the ear be still;
Our bodies feel where'er they be,
Against or with our will.
William Wordsworth

Immortal? I feel it and know it,
Who doubts it of such as she?
But that is the pang's very secret-
Immortal away from me.
James Russell Lowell

Tumbling and jumping through a hoop…and dancing upon the
tight~rope.
Strutt, *Sports & Past. iii. iv. 188*

When the falsehood ceased to be credible the system which was based
upon it collapsed.
Froude, *Short Stud. IV. i. xi. 142.*

Affectation, a curious desire of a thing which nature has not given,
J. Rider, *Affectatio.*

From the imposter the entries pass to other hands.
1884 *Harper's Mag.* June 57/2 (*New York Custom Ho.*)

There is a Fault, which, tho' common, wants a Name.
Steele *Spect. No. 374*

I am too absent-spirited to count;
The loneliness includes me unawares.
Robert Frost

Laughter and grief join hands. Always the heart
Clumps in the breast with heavy stride;
Karl Shapiro

Let the world's sharpness like a clasping knife
Shut in upon itself and do no harm
In this close hand of Love, now soft and warm;
And let us hear no sound of human strife
After the click of the shutting.
Elizabeth Barrett Browning

Heh, heh, heh,
Who knows what evil lurks in the hearts of men?
The Shadow knows.
Le Roi Jones- *In Memory of Radio*

Even if it is a hard struggle
We will not be the ones who will fail
Winston Churchill

From goblins that deceive you, I'm unable to relieve you.
B. Taylor

And he said, "Do not raise your hand against the boy, or do anything
to him."
The Torah, *Genesis 22.12*

The merest flaw that dents the horizon's edge.
Longfellow, Sp. *Stud. iii. Vi*

Though I am young, and cannot tell
Either what Death or what Love is well
Yet I have heard they both bear darts,
And both do aim at human hearts,
Ben Johnson

Lilacs in the Snow

The siege will take a heavy toll, and few who live to the end of it will
survive the holocaust that must follow.
H. F. Rubinstein

I would think until I found
Something I can never find
Something lying on the ground
In the bottom of my mind.
James Stephens

The effect of comic books on the ideology of children.
Amer. Jrnl. Orthopsychiatry XI. 540

The popular notion that sleepwalkers never hurt themselves is far from
true.
G.H. Napheys *Prev. & Cure Dis*

A friend is he that loves, and he that is beloved.
Thomas Hobbes

Dear Mother, is any time left to us
In which to be happy?
Delmore Schwartz

One must have a mind of winter
To regard the frost and boughs
Of the pine- trees crusted with snow;
And have been cold a long time
Wallace Stevens

What price bananas?
Allen Ginsberg

A cold coming we had of it,
Just the worst time of year
For a journey, and such a long journey:
The ways deep and the weather sharp,
The very dead of winter
T.S. Elliot

Shuttles of trains going north, going south, drawing threads of blue,
The shining of the lines of trams like swords
Louis MacNeice

His Mind was so elevated into a flattered Conceit of himself.
1665 MANLEY *Grotius' Low C. Warres 165*

And yet my father sits and reads in silence,
My mother sheds a tear, the moon is still
And the dark wind
Is murmuring that nothing ever happens
Louis Simpson

Then, the sudden call for her
from upstairs, twice,
the way a girl's called in from play
Yehuda Amichai

The reproch of pride and cruelnesse.
Spenser *F.Q. 1596 vi. I. 41*

Lilacs in the Snow

A cold spring:
the violet was flawed on the lawn.
For two weeks or more the trees hesitate:
the little leaves waited,
Elizabeth Bishop

Like as, to make our appetites more keen,
With eager compounds our palate urge;
As to prevent our maladies unseen,
William Shakespeare

All but blind
In the evening sky,
The hooded Bat
Twirls softly by.
Walter De La Mare

And indeed there will be time
To wonder, "Do I dare?" and "Do I dare?"
T.S. Elliot

Now that the lilacs are in bloom
She has a bowl of lilacs in her room
And twists one in her fingers
T.S. Elliot

The beams, that thro' the Oriel shine,
Make prisms in every carven glass,
Alfred, Lord Tennyson

Since she must go, and I must mourn, come Night,
Environ me with darkness, whilst I write:
Shadow that hell unto me, which alone
I am to suffer when my Love is gone.
John Donne

We are such stuffe
As dreames are made on.
William Shakespeare

Thou'rt gone, the abyss of heaven
Hath swallowed up thy form; yet, on my heart
Deeply has sunk the lesson thou hast given,
And shall not soon depart.
William Cullen Bryant

Valediction: Forbidden Mourning
John Donne

Year, if you have no Mother's day present planned; reach back and
bring me the firmness of her hand.
Judith Wright

The apparition of these faces in the crowd
Petals on a wet, black bough.
Ezra Pound

Meanwhile.., Within the Gates of Hell sate Sin and Death.
John Milton

One would think, that every Letter was wrote with a Tear, every Word
was the Noise of a breaking Heart.
South, *Sermon IV. 31*

How easily our little world can go to pieces!
Conrad Aiken, *Gehenna*

Truth, we say, is not found exclusively in the possession of those with
a high 'intelligence quotient'.
H. Read, *Educ. Free Men iii. 1*

Children, leave the string alone!
For who dares undo the parcel
Finds himself at once inside it,
Robert Graves

No! Pay the dentist when he leaves A fracture in your jaw.
O. W. Holmes *Poems 149*

Scarce had she ceased, when out of heaven a bolt...struck
Alfred, Lord Tennyson

There are other circuitous erections of stone.
G. Chalmers, *Caledonia I. i. ii. 92*

Let us seek The forward path again.
Cary, *Dante, Par. xxix. 136*

The windows are small apertures...innocent of glass.
 J. Colborne, *Hicks Pasha* 60

The Deserted Village
Oliver Goldsmith

It mounts at sea, a concave wall
Down-ribbed with shine
And pushes forward, building tall
Its steep incline.
Thomas Gunn

I am a parcel of vain strivings tied
By a chance bond together
Henry David Thoreau

The terrible mournfulness..of the truth gnawed within her.
1880 G. Meredith *Tragic Com. (1881) 303*

My game was now quite the reverse from what it had been at starting.
1840 E. E. Napier *Scenes & Sports For. Lands I. i. 16*

The Pangs of Love
Marcel Proust, *Pleasures and Days*

The grossest errours, if they…be but new, may be perswaded to the
multitude.
 Ld. Falkland, etc., *Infallibility*

Ladies, like variegated tulips, show;
'Tis to their changes half their charms we owe;
Fine by defect, and delicately weak,
Their happy spots the nice admirer take,
Alexander Pope, *Epistle II. To a Lady*

What is our innocence,
What is our guilt? All
Are naked, none is safe.
Marianne Moore

We should all come home after the flare, and the noise, and the gayety.
Thackeray, *Van. Fair xix*

Fates That weave my thread of life in ruder patterns Than these
G. B. Shaw, *Admirable Bashville ii. i. 309*

Go in thy native innocence; relie
On what thou hast of vertue.
Milton *P.L. ix. 373*

How can she foresee the thick stranger,
Brother Antoninus, *The Stranger*

Am I then the sport, The Game of Fortune, and her laughing Fools?
Southerne, *Fatal Marr. 11*

Oh my love my darling I've hungered for your touch
A long lonely time
Unchained Melody, Al Hibbler hit song 1955
Music by Alex North; lyrics by Hy Zaret

I never knew any of these forward sluts come to good.
Fielding J. Andrews *ii. Iv.*

The most important formality connected with the graduation.
1858 Masson *Milton* (1859) I. 183

So spring has sprung, so what say I
So who's to care if birds can fly
And okay sure the grass has riz
So what else is new, so what else is?
There's no such thing as spring for me
There's no such thing and there won't be
Until we're walkin' hand in hand
That's how it is, you understand?
Hallmark, Inc., greeting card

Frenchmen, for us, ah! What outrage
Claude Joseph Rouget de Lisle, *La Marseillaise*

Of a solempne and greet fraternitee.
Chaucer, *Prol. 366*

Stamp we our vengeance deep, and ratify his doom.
Gray, *Bard 96*

Rain out the heavy mist of tears
Tennyson, *Love & Duty 43.*

Pain is the necessary contrast to pleasure.
Sir C. Bell, *Hand 190*

Time, place, and motion, taken in particular or concrete.
Berkeley *Princ. Hum. Knowl. §97*

I feel a weightless change, a moving forward
As of water quickening before a narrowing channel
When banks converge,
Theodore Roethke

The mind can weave itself warmly in the cocoon of its own thoughts.
Lowell *Study Wind. 56*

Want makes almost every man selfish.
Johnson *Advent. No. 62 35*

When everlasting Fate shall yield To fickle Chance.
Milton *P.L. ii. 232*

Then share thy pain, allow that sad relief;
Pope *Eloisa to Abelard 49-50*

A conscience thread-bare and ragged with perpetual turning.
1704 Swift *T. Tub* Introd. ¶25

And that deepe torture may be cal'd a Hell,
When more is felt than one hath power to tell.
Shakes. *Lucr. 1287*

Not willingly, but tangl'd in the fold Of dire necessity.
Milton *Samson 1665*

Defer not off, to-morrow is too late.
a1592 Greene & Lodge *Looking Glass* Wks. (Rtldg.) 129/1

Sweet downie thoughts, soft *lilly-shades, calm streams.
1650 H. Vaughan Silex Scint., Relapse 25

An honourable conduct let him haue.
Shakes. *John i. i. 29*

About the Author

A. K. Henderson, a Canadian born author, attended McGill University and the University of British Columbia. She received her medical degree as Arona Kagnoff from the University of California, Los Angeles. Her career spanned forty years; she was a highly respected and a much loved family practitioner in Southern California.

During the years in her medical practice, Arona's poetry was published in small presses: *Alura Quarterly* and *'up against the wall, mother'*. She authored articles and stories for *Medical Economics* and *Cortlandt Forum*. These publications received acclaim from fellow physicians worldwide and *Medical Economics* awarded her a certificate of merit for one of her stories. In spite of the demands on her time, she wrote a column titled *Woman to Woman Medicine* for *Orange County Media,* a monthly publication with a circulation of 120,000. Her style of professionalism and humor in the chosen topics was a favorable method of reaching a wide range of women who were otherwise reluctant to seek professional medical care.

Arona lectured on issues of adolescent medicine to women's groups to help improve relationships between mothers and daughters. She was dedicated to the physical and emotional health of young individuals and undertook a physician consultant position at an inpatient adolescent mental health facility. She served as a student health doctor at the University of California, Irvine and was a teacher of family practice techniques to the medical school students at the University of California, Irvine Medical School.

Arona currently resides with her husband James in Blaine, Washington, close to the Canadian border.

CPSIA information can be obtained at www.ICGtesting.com
Printed in the USA
268117BV00003B/1/P